Sweet TEMPEST

Veracity of The Gods
Book 2

K. D. MILLER

To all the Becks who never felt as if they fit anywhere quite right. You'll find your place. Keep going.

***

And to Shemar Moore. Thank you for being Poseidon in my head since day one. If you'd ever like to pose in leather pants and a trident, have your people call my people.
Or you can call my people.
Or...me. Just call me.

Please.

And much have I toiled in perils of waves and war. Let this be added to the tale of those.

— HOMER, THE ODYSSEY

CONTENTS

Dalton Pembroke slumped on the floor of his cell, vaguely registering the low voices from the hallway beyond the small concrete space. His tomb. They'd dropped him here yesterday after another round in the tank and he'd moved little since. He'd been submerged for days on end, drowning over and over, only to revive, his immortality keeping him in an endless cycle of torment. They'd take him out and give a day or so of rest for questioning or to change methods, but then it was right back to the torture. Sometimes it was the tank. Others it was the fire, burned nearly to the brink, the flames being pulled back at the last possible moment where he would regenerate once again. Vivisection was a favored pastime as well—being cut open and his insides removed while he was awake and fully aware.

He'd trained nearly all his life to withstand the torture he'd been enduring for the last...he had no idea how long, but his mind was beginning to break. He didn't know how much longer he could hold out.

For Skylar. You can hold out forever to keep her safe.

His lungs screamed in response as he took a shuddering breath, but he resolved to last as long as he had to. He *would* see his daughter again. Dalton couldn't leave her like this, thinking he was gone forever with no real explanation or a chance to say goodbye. He would find a way out of this and back to her. His captors had intended to capture her and use her to make him sing, but she'd thankfully been off the grid for some time. Perhaps she sensed danger and went dark? She was cunning and resourceful—and downright vicious when she needed to be. So, he had no doubts that was probably the case and that wherever she was, she was safe.

They were none too happy about not being able to find her though, and he'd taken the brunt of their frustrations. His lips curled upward, pride bowing his chest. His girl was a survivor in every sense of the word. They would never find her.

But if they did? Well, it was their funeral.

The voices drifted to him again and he tried to pay attention as best he could, though he faded in and out of consciousness.

"Trust me, you want to let me in there. I can get him to talk." Soft. Melodic. Female.

"But..." Male. One of the demon guards, because oh yeah, demons fucking *existed*. Dalton could still scarcely believe it, but he'd discovered a plethora of things he shouldn't have on a job recently. Gods and demons and realms and planes of existence and too much other shit to name. It was why he was here to begin with.

They had hired him to find someone, and he'd done it because he was damn good at his job, but the more he watched the girl, the more his gut told him she needed to be protected, especially from the people hunting her. Dalton always trusted his gut, no matter what. It had never steered him wrong, his Lupin instincts always directing him to the correct path. So, he'd kept her location hidden and done some more digging into the man who hired him instead. He'd hit pay dirt and though it had taken him a while to accept the truth of what he'd found, he eventually had. He'd been careful, but he'd finally let Lucas know he had information that he needed to share.

The next thing he knew, he was in his car as it exploded, ferried away at the last moment by the bastard himself, Elysium, and tossed in this prison. From what Dalton had gathered, Elysium wasn't actually the HMFIC, merely the henchman of someone far worse. Dalton had yet to figure out who in the hell had actually hired him and why they wanted the girl, and he supposed he never would.

The demon outside cut off as a pulse of power speared through the place, shaking the entire building. *Whoa.* The power was enough to make Dalton's battered body respond, instincts flaring. He forced himself to remain conscious, forced his senses to sharpen so he could pay attention properly, prepare for whatever was about to come through the door.

"What were you saying?" the female voice asked sweetly.

"Uhh, g-go on in. This better work though..."

"It will. And when it does, you give me the skinny on the enchantress, deal?" The demon muttered something in response, but the woman added in a stern voice, "I'll have your vow, demon." Sounding afraid, the demon croaked something in a strange language, but Dalton got the feeling it was something important. What kind of woman would this demon be so afraid of?

He heard footsteps and steeled himself, ready for questioning or to face whoever this new female was. He pushed himself upward into a seated position, resting his back against the back wall of his cell. His vision wavered, and he squeezed his eyes shut before opening them as wide as he could. He was weak from the torture and lack of food, and it was taking him longer and longer to recover. His lungs had yet to fully regenerate from the last burning and after the tank, every breath was sheer agony.

His heart thudded in his chest as the steps grew louder, but it stopped completely as she edged into the ring of light. No. *No, no, no.* He stumbled forward, pain forgotten, desperate to get to her.

"Skylar!? No. No, you can't be here!"

Had his mind finally broken? Was this a hallucination? He blinked rapidly, willing the scene before him to disappear, to float away like the dream it had to be. She waltzed forward and knelt by the bars. Her golden blonde hair was braided, a few strands lose around her face like always, her emerald green eyes shining with unshed tears.

"Daddy?"

"Rocket, no! What are you doing here?"

He slammed to his knees in front of her, wrapping his hands around the bars, ignoring the pain as the onyx burned his skin. He didn't care. He had to touch her, had to know this was real. She reached out and gripped his hands.

"I'm ok, dad. I promise. But you have to tell them what they want to know, ok? Tell them where she is."

He shook his head, confused. "But...she's just a girl, Rocket. She doesn't deserve whatever they have planned for her and trust me, they have plans. Big ones that could mean the end of *everything*."

She nodded, looking stressed, but sure.

"I know, but you have to trust *me*: everything will work out. I promise you. Do you trust me?" She searched his eyes, desperate and hopeful, the same gaze that had won him over in seconds when she was just eleven years old, and he nearly wept.

"Yes," he exhaled. "Yes, of course I trust you. With my life."

"Tell them where she is and let me take care of the rest. I'll come back for you soon, I just need you to stay put a tiny bit longer. All the players aren't on the board yet, so the game can't properly begin."

He didn't understand what she meant by that or what was really happening, but he didn't care. He just let himself have this moment with his daughter, this stolen moment of peace in a sea of unrest. She moved forward and kissed his cheek through the bars.

"Now, where is she? *Who* is she?"

Dalton...told her. He gave up the girl's name and location, feeling sick the entire time but trusting Skylar implicitly. She smiled and squeezed his cheek, but as she turned towards the door, his vision blurred again. Did her hair just flicker silver? His world tilted on its axis, dizziness and nausea hitting him like a wrecking ball. He yanked his hands from the bars, his skin ripping free where it was seared to the onyx, and doubled over.

He barely heard her speaking with the demon, something about an enchantress, an excited "oh goodie!" and then bright green light flared through the room, making him squint against the glare.

A woman flitted to the bars. Not Skylar. Light brown skin, silver hair and matching silver tattoos, purple eyes lit with excitement. *What the hell?*

"Sorry for that little bout of stolen identity, but good news, Skylar's dad! You don't have to stay put after all. A few things shifted, so the game has begun!" The door to his cell didn't just open, it *disappeared.* Dalton blinked several times, wondering if any of this was real. The woman looked at her wrist, studying a watch that didn't exist.

"Time's a-wastin'—let's hit the road!"

Confusion further muddled his already muddled mind. Who was this woman? Where was Skylar? Was she truly freeing him?

He got no answers before the darkness overtook him.

"That's it. I'm cutting it off."

Poseidon groaned, not even bothering to move from where he lay sprawled across his bed. He'd only just gotten home from a two-week bender with Dionysus that had culminated in an eight-some. *A ménage à huit?* He really wasn't sure what the right term was for the insanity he'd just committed. The females involved had been the seven wives of the Satyr king and he had *not* been thrilled to find Poseidon balls and fingers and tongue deep in his women.

Si had only survived because he was just about the smoothest talker in existence, and while he stalled for time, Dionysus had managed to get word out to Zeus. He'd sent Ares and Athena with a few heavy hitters (and a few dozen nymphs to grease the wheels), and Hyklon had eventually done the math and backed down, letting Poseidon go. It had been close though. Too close.

"Piss off," Si replied as he threw his arms over his eyes. He wasn't in the mood to deal with his brother.

"I mean it. Your cock is causing nothing but trouble. Time for it to go." Poseidon turned his head and cracked his eyes open. Zeus was standing a few feet away, twirling a blade between his fingers. Light sparked off of the golden symbols inlaid in the black metal. Poseidon shot upright.

"A godsblade?! Are you insane? Get out of here with that shit."

That knife was one of the few things in existence that *could* actually rid Si of his favorite appendage. Zeus got a wicked glint in his eye.

"It'll grow back…eventually." He lunged forward and Poseidon rolled off the bed just in time. Zeus had to be joking about this… right? Si thought back on all the trouble he'd caused lately. The fiasco with Hyklon was just the orgy-shaped straw that broke the camel's back. So, ok, maybe Zeus had a point, but still. Si backed away, eyes roving around the room, looking for something to use to fend off his lunatic brother.

"You're not serious."

"I'm like sixty-five percent serious. Maybe seventy." Between his hangover and his exhaustion, Poseidon was no match for the King of the Gods. Zeus had him in a headlock, blade poised between his legs in a matter of seconds.

"Zeus! Cut it out!" Si yelled.

"Gladly." The pressure increased ever so slightly, barely cutting through the fabric of his pants.

Si's voice rose an octave. "No! No! That isn't what I meant and you know it! Come on, man!" Zeus' laughter boomed as he released Poseidon. Si turned and shoved him in the shoulder, harder than he meant to, but he couldn't quite bring himself to care. "What in the fuck?"

"Oh come on, can't take a joke?" Zeus began to sit on the bed, looked at the tangled sheets, and seemed to think better of it. Si rolled his eyes. They were clean. He wasn't a *completely* disgusting slob.

Zeus instead settled into one of the oversized leather chairs that sat around the sunken firepit in the middle of the room. Poseidon went to the bar and seriously thought about making Zeus' a Seven and Seven and Spit, but decided to let it go. Zeus was right, after all. Si and his cock had been nothing but trouble lately.

Si handed Zeus his drink and sat heavily in the seat across the pit, propping his feet up on the stone edge. Zeus held his glass up to the light, studying the liquid and then his brother.

"I thought about it, but didn't actually do it," Poseidon assured him. Zeus nodded and took a long sip, letting out an appreciative *ahhh*.

"What the hell is going on with you, man?" Zeus asked after a few minutes of semi-comfortable silence. Poseidon sighed. He'd been asking himself that question for the last...gods, how long had it been now? Fifty years? A hundred? However long he'd been asking, he hadn't come up with an answer yet.

"I don't know," he said honestly.

"You've done some stupid shit in your ridiculously long life and trouble has always seemed to follow you around like a lost puppy, but now? It's like you're going out *looking* for it and the trouble you're courting isn't a puppy anymore. It's a fucking rabid hellhound. Do you know how close we came to all-out war with Hyklon?"

"We would have won," Si pointed out half-heartedly. He knew how stupid it had been and how badly things could have turned out.

"Eventually, yes," Zeus agreed, "but not without a lot of bloodshed and loss. Not to mention making enemies out of the Satyrs for centuries at least. What were you thinking, Si?"

"I wasn't," he admitted. "I just..."

Zeus leaned forward, elbows on his knees.

"What?"

Si drained his glass and rubbed his nearly shaved head.

"Do you ever just tire of everything? Tired of forever?" Zeus frowned and Si continued, realizing that he'd wanted to talk about this with someone for a while and had just never mustered up the balls. "There was a moment—only a small one, but it was there—where I almost...hoped that Ares didn't show up and save the day.

Where I hoped that Hyklon just...ended it." Zeus' golden brows shot upwards and Si quickly continued to assure him. "It was fleeting, and I wouldn't have actually let him kill me without a hell of a fight, but there was just this tiny part of me that thought *'finally.'*

"Si, don't say shit like that to me, come on."

Si held his hands up, waving his brother off.

"I don't actually want to die, not really. I'm just tired. Everything changes yet nothing really does. Nothing new to discover, nothing new to experience." He leaned his head back to stare at the ceiling. Through the skylight he could see the ocean churning above the enchanted dome that surrounded his castle and grounds. "I'm just...I don't know, feeling very immortal lately, I guess."

Zeus looked thoughtful. He could be a dick sometimes, throwing his "King of the Gods" arrogance around, but he never dismissed what anyone was feeling, always tried to understand. He eased upward and came to sit on the edge of the firepit next to Si's feet. He leaned his elbows on his knees again.

"I get it. I really do. I think we all hit these strides where immortality catches up to us sometimes. I've had a couple of them. Hades was practically a walking zombie for the past thousand years waiting for Persephone's reincarnate to finally show up—which, he's found her, by the way. That's going to be interesting as hell."

Si scowled as the memories of the day that the original Persephone tried to murder Hades rose to the forefront of his mind. Hades, chained and poisoned and bloody because of that back-stabbing bitch. They'd *barely* gotten there in time to save their brother. Persephone hadn't been so lucky and most days, Si wasn't the tiniest bit sorry for that. He wasn't sure what that said about him and he didn't really care.

"I'm not sure how to feel about that, honestly."

"None of us do. She doesn't have any idea of who she is—or was —as far as he can tell, so that helps a tiny bit I think, but it's still hard to think about Persephone being back and not wanting to end her all over again." Zeus shook himself. "But anyway, the point is that I get where you're coming from, but doing this reckless, ridiculous shit isn't going to help. It's one thing to screw your way through every realm in existence, but it's a whole other business when you put yourself and our friends in danger."

Si lowered his head, meeting Zeus' eyes, and sighed heavily.

"I know. I'm sorry. Really. The stunt with Hyklon's wives was stupid, I know. Insanely fun…" Zeus gave him a dry look and Si shot him a grin. "But stupid."

It had been fun. Sort of. Sex was *always* fun, but lately even that had just been…there. Something to pass the time. He enjoyed himself, too much usually, but it was like he was only giving it eighty percent effort at best. None of his companions complained, of course, but his heart was barely in it these days. He was in one hell of a funk and if the seven wives sexcapade hadn't gotten him out of it, he didn't know what would.

Zeus looked thoughtful.

"Maybe you need to stop being a manwhore and settle down. That's something different."

Si rolled his eyes with a laugh, playing his part of immortal bachelor. Everyone assumed that he'd never settled down because the last time he'd tried, his heart had been ripped into tiny pieces and tossed around like confetti. And sure, Calypso leaving had done a real number on him for a long time in the love department, but eventually he began to want more than meaningless sex with someone again. The problem was that he never felt even the tiniest shred of wanting more with anyone he came across. He'd begun to think that something was very wrong with him, like his ability to feel for anyone in that way had walked out the door with Calypso. Which he didn't understand.

Sure, he'd loved her and ok maybe he had fallen apart there for a while when she'd left him out of the blue, but he'd never felt that she was his one true match, that a piece of his own soul lived inside her, that they were destined to be together. Which meant his match *could* still be out there somewhere, waiting for him, right?

But he worried that if he truly was missing that essential part of him, that part that could feel anything more than physical attraction and a friendly type fondness for anyone, well…how would he find her? What if he already had, and he'd let her out of his bed without even knowing it? Or maybe he'd just been wrong all along and Calypso *had* been his, and without her, he really *couldn't* feel for anyone else? He rubbed his temples, the endless string of what-ifs making his head pound even worse.

"You're one to talk."

"Hey, I've had plenty of relationships over the years since Hera and I split, even though everyone likes to pretend I haven't. Granted, they rarely last very long, but at least I've had them. You've dated exactly zero people since Calypso."

He gave Si a pointed look and Si rolled his eyes, knowing he was about to get the *you've got to move on* talk. Si wasn't in the mood for it, so he hoisted himself out of the chair and made his way onto his balcony. He leaned his forearms on the stone railing, Zeus following suit, and they stared out over the silvery-white beach and the turquoise waters beyond. Outside of the dome, water surrounded them on all sides, churning a deep gray to match Poseidon's mood. He forced himself to settle, to push the thoughts aside and the water soon calmed, lightening to a pale midnight blue.

"Hell of a view, I'll give you that," Zeus said. "It's no Mount Olympus, mind you, but it'll do." Si laughed, feeling a little lighter than he had in quite a while. "Want to come crash the Underworld with me? I've got some things I need to talk to Hades about and if I'm not mistaken, he'll have Persephone two-point-oh by now."

As Si considered it, something on the beach caught his eye. A mermaid was emerging from the water, tail transforming into legs as she reached the sandy beach. Gloriously naked, with dark violet hair curling to her waist, she arched a lavender brow and gave the two brothers a wave and a smile. The kind of smile that means one thing and one thing only. Si sighed inwardly, really not in the mood to entertain, but...

He forced an affable grin. "I think I'll have to raincheck the Underworld visit. If you'll excuse me, I believe something has just been added to my To-Do List for the afternoon." A second mermaid emerged, joining the first. This one's fiery orange hair was braided into three thick plaits and when she smiled, the setting sun glinted off of her small fangs. *Oh the things they can do with those fangs...*

Si slapped Zeus on the back.

"I'm sorry—make that *two* somethings."

THREE

Someone was watching her.

Beck scanned the trees lining the parking lot of the small marina for the tenth time since arriving, and though she saw nothing, she had that feeling, the one that made the fine hairs on the back of her neck stand on end and a cold spot form in her belly. She'd had the same feeling of being watched months ago, but it had never felt threatening before it disappeared altogether. Now? It was back and her every instinct was on high alert, just screaming that she was in trouble. Her mother always claimed that someone might come after her one day if they learned who she was, but she hadn't really believed it.

Until now.

Strange men had followed Beck more than once in the past week, and she would bet large amounts of money she didn't have that someone had been in her house two nights ago. She didn't know who they were or what they wanted, but she knew it was nothing good. She was glad that her mother had gone off on one of her little trips. Of course, she hadn't given Beck any kind of warning, she'd just left a note on the counter one morning.

Back in a few weeks. – Mother

Beck rolled her eyes as she thought of it. The first time Beck had found a note like that, she'd been ten. The sad part was that she'd known how to take care of herself (and her mother) for a while by that point, so being left alone wasn't as terrifying as it should have been. Though Beck had no trouble being alone when her mother disappeared, she'd always been so damned *worried* when it happened, practically sick with it. What if someone figured out what her mother was? Or, the more likely scenario, what if someone heard one of her drunken rants damning the gods of old, assumed she was insane, and had her committed to a mortal mental hospital?

As worried as she would get, Beck had to admit that the trips were always a good thing in a way. When her mother returned from them, she was always better for a few weeks. Nowhere near what anyone would consider a good mother, but better than usual. She didn't drink as much, would actually attempt to take care of Beck, or at the very least, tolerate her existence more easily. It always went back to normal after a while, but for those few weeks, Beck was always thankful for the secretive rendezvous.

Now that she was older, and far sicker of her mom's shit, she welcomed the sporadic trips her mother would take, not even caring if she was better when she returned or not. Beck didn't care where her mother went or with whom anymore. All she cared about was having a few weeks of freedom away from the woman. What did that say about her? What kind of daughter thought that about her mother? *The kind with a mother like mine*, she thought bitterly.

Regardless of how annoyed with her mom she was ninety percent of the time, she was beyond relieved that her mom was gone at the moment, presumably somewhere safe. She just needed to stay put until Beck returned from this work trip, and then they would figure out what was going on.

"McQueen!"

Beck jumped, not realizing how lost in thought she'd gotten. Harlan was standing near the bed of his truck, hands full of equipment, red hair in its typical untamed mess and blowing in the wind. She jogged over to help him.

"Geeze, I was calling your name for five minutes, Beck. You ok?"

"Yeah, sorry," she murmured. "Just…thought I saw someone I knew." She glanced around the parking lot once more before forcing herself to focus. She hoisted one of the computer bags onto her shoulder with her own small duffle and grabbed an armful of binders and books. "Is this the last of it?"

"Yep, this is it. Oscar and the others already loaded the rest. We should be ready to push off soon." She followed Harlan towards the boat and wondered, not for the first time, if the thing would even survive the trip. Harlan seemed to read her thoughts. "She's far sturdier than she looks, I promise."

Beck arched a skeptical brow, but continued walking. Spending a week out at sea on this thing wasn't exactly her idea of a good time, but she had to admit that being well away from whoever was following her was worth it. The monstrosity masquerading as a seaworthy vessel was a cross between a yacht and a fishing boat, large enough that it had several cabins, a common room, and a kitchen below deck. It had seen better days, but it had actually probably been somewhat luxurious once upon a time.

The funny thing was that she was more worried about spending the night anywhere but her own home than the boat sinking. Nightmares had plagued Beck since her teenage years. They weren't exactly recurring, but they always started the same way: A sinister, shadowed figure stalked Beck as she ran down a dark, endless corridor. Gray doors with peeling paint lined the hallway, and she'd pound on them, screaming for help. Eventually, one of the doorways would open and the dream would transform into a whole new nightmare that she seldom understood. Though she'd trained herself to no longer wake from them screaming, she worried that she'd relapse and freak out the entire crew.

Oscar bounded up, meeting them halfway down the dock.

"Here, let me take those from you."

She gave him a half smile and he beamed back, all pearly whites and dimples that would make any girl look twice, mortal or otherwise. After a very lackluster history, Beck had all but sworn off men, but if she were going to try with anyone again, it would probably be Oscar. He was the most easy-going person she'd ever met. He got along with everybody, was always there to lend a hand, and he just seemed to be happy *all* the time. She sighed a bit, wondering what that might be like. She honestly wasn't sure if she'd ever really been happy in her life. Maybe when she was young, before her mother had gotten so bad into her bitterness and alcohol, but she hardly remembered it.

Mostly, all she could remember feeling throughout her life was stress and worry and resentment. *Gods, I sound awful.* She decided she was going to try to start being less of a...what had one of her coworkers at the bar called her? A hard-ass with no sense of fun. She'd wanted to be pissed at that jab, but she really couldn't: it was completely true. Beck had been so focused on keeping food on their table and the lights on, and making sure no one suspected anything "other" about them for as long as she could remember, that she hadn't had time for anything else, including fun. She wasn't an outright bitch per se, but she wasn't exactly inviting either.

Do I even know how *to have fun?* she wondered. She...wasn't sure. She'd been trying more with Oscar and the rest of the team, but she didn't think she was succeeding very often. Beck rubbed the back of her neck and re-adjusted the shoulder straps of the bags self-consciously. She'd never really cared too much about what people thought of her—at least that's what she told herself—but she truly liked this group and did actually want them to like her back. *I don't want to be a hard-ass with no sense of fun to them.* She promised herself, not for the first time, that she would try harder.

"Thanks, Oscar." His smile widened and the sunlight caught the golden flecks in his brown eyes before he hit her with an easy wink. Her stomach gave a small flutter at the sight. Maybe breaking her celibate streak with Oscar really wasn't such a terrible idea...

They made their way on board and, to her surprise, the entire thing didn't immediately sink with their added weight. Harlan shot her an *I told you so* look and gave the boat a loving pat. The rest of the team was already in the large meeting room that was being used as the primary work space. She waved to everyone as she entered, giving them the half tilt of her lips that passed as a smile for her. *See. I* can *do better.* They all smiled and waved or called in greetings in return.

Will was their oceanographer, quiet and reserved, but very sweet, with shaggy brown hair peeking out from underneath the faded blue ball cap that he wore at all times. Beck was pretty sure he even showered with the thing on.

Patrick was the tech guru and engineer. He was a total genius (literally) and sometimes seemed to be just as bad at peopling as she was, though for completely different reasons. At least he *was* a person. His long blond hair was typically in a man-bun that somehow worked for him.

Oscar was the dive expert and boat captain extraordinaire. Toned, tanned, and the life of the party...*and maybe future bed mate of one Beck McQueen?* She shouldn't...but maybe she would? Surely he wouldn't let her down in that department like the others had, right? A girl could dream.

And last but not least was Harlan. He was the historian, a bit older than the rest of the group, and the de facto "dad."

Together, they somehow formed a moderately successful team of treasurer hunters. After their discovery of the Lucia, a Spanish galleon that had been lost to a storm a century before with hundreds of chests of gold aboard, they had the means to hire an assistant. That's where Beck entered the picture.

She had no genuine interest in treasure hunting, but the job was at least more stimulating than pouring coffee and the pay was pretty damn good. Good enough, in fact, that she could quit the coffee shop all together *and* quit taking shifts at that disgusting bar she loathed. The bar itself was fine, if a bit divey. The real problem was the patrons. More specifically, the *male* patrons. If one more handsy mortal decided her ass was on the menu right beside the $4 Bloody Mary, she might try to contact her father just to smite them down. *Like he'd even answer.* She tried and failed to keep the familiar anger from rising within her chest any time she thought about her father. *More like sperm donor.*

So, she'd been more than happy to take the job organizing data and helping in the day-to-day running of the small company Harlan had formed. The group was strangely welcoming of her, despite her stand-offish nature, and she found herself actually enjoying coming to work—something she'd rarely experienced over the years. They coaxed half smiles from her more often than not and had even talked her into joining them for Trivia Tuesdays and Karaoke Thursdays at Captain Ronnie's a handful of times. *Maybe I'm making more progress on the being fun front than I originally gave myself credit for.*

After setting down the laptop and binders, Oscar directed her towards the private cabin she'd be using. The boys had graciously given her the Captain's quarters, so she had a room and small bathroom all to herself. The rest of them would bunk up two to a room. She smiled to herself as she tossed her bag on the bed. Had she finally found real friends? A group of people who might actually care about her? The thought made her heart leap, but she tried to tamp it down. She couldn't have genuine relationships with anyone, not when she constantly had to lie about who and what she was. Still, she was thankful that she had at least this much with them.

She made her way back on deck to watch as they pulled out of the marina. She leaned her forearms against the railing, enjoying the breeze on her skin and the salty smell of the sea. They were just beginning to pull away from the dock when that terrible feeling in her gut doubled. She cut her eyes to the parking lot, sweat breaking out on the back of her neck. *What the...?* She scanned the area, half hoping she would see nothing and that she could chock the bad feeling up to paranoia, when a man stepped out of the tree line.

Beck shot up, spine ramrod straight, fear sending cold tingles through her body. She gripped the railing so hard her knuckles turned white as their eyes locked. Despite being fifty yards off shore already, her senses were a thousand times better than a mortal's. As she watched, his eyes shifted from dark brown to blood red, and her own widened in shock. She'd never seen anything like it before. Whatever he was, he was no mortal, which meant she was in far more danger than she thought. As if he could read her mind, his lips curled up into a sinister grin.

"Soon," she heard him whisper, as if he were standing right beside her.

BECK TRIED and failed to keep the unease from roiling in her belly over the next two days. "Soon" the man had said. Would he be waiting for her when they arrived back at the marina? Maybe she could ride home with Oscar and buy herself enough time to sneak back to her own house, grab essentials, and bolt. What the hell did these people want?

She rubbed the pendant on the chain around her neck, as she always did when she was nervous or upset. It was a small, oval medallion with double crescent moons etched into the front, though you could barely make them out anymore. She'd had it for as long as she could remember and her mother told her it had protection magic woven into it by an extremely powerful enchantress. Beck often wondered if her mother was delusional, but she'd been lethally serious when she'd warned Beck of those that may wish to harm her or use her because of who her father was.

Beck had taken the threat seriously and she'd never taken the necklace off. She actually *couldn't*. Her mother explained that the magic only protected her while it was bound to her, which would continue until she willingly gifted it to another. Since she couldn't fathom why she would ever give her protection away to someone else, the necklace was stuck like Chuck. Would it be enough to fend off whatever was waiting for her on shore? She sure as hell hoped so.

Now, she helped Oscar get some equipment ready on the deck and was trying her best to focus. The boat lurched and she sucked in a quick breath. She didn't mind the water, and loved the beach to no end, but she watched enough Shark Week to know that she didn't want to go for a swim out here miles and miles from shore.

"Are we *positive* this hunk of junk will survive the trip?" she asked skeptically, eyeing the boat distrustfully.

Oscar smiled, rubbing the railing lovingly. He'd bought her from a retired banker who fancied himself a deep-sea angler, who'd bought it from the widow of a B-list movie star from the 80s, which explained the Hodge-Podge nature of the poor thing: the boat didn't know what she was supposed to be anymore. But Oscar loved the damn thing, had fixed it up himself with a little help from the rest of the team here and there, and it was obvious to everyone that she was his baby.

"Shh, you'll hurt her feelings. She may not look like much, but there's no way *Poseidon's Lady* could be anything but seaworthy." He had a faint Columbian accent that was all too pleasant. The odds of Beck exploring their small flirtations were increasing with every word he spoke, but she rolled her eyes at the ship's name.

"Poseidon can kiss my ass," she grumbled.

Oscar raised his brows. "What have you got against the God of the Sea?" He chuckled a bit, knowing how silly that sounded. She had to keep in mind that to everyone else on this boat, the gods were just old stories, but Beck knew the truth. She knew they were very real…and she was very much one of them.

Beck had been skeptical when her mother first told her who they were—*what* they were—and where they'd come from. Even as a child, she'd had the wherewithal to think that her mother had lost her damn marbles. But as time went on, she began to believe. She'd seen her mother's powers with her own eyes before they faded completely, and though her own powers weren't exactly prolific—or functioning most of the time—she felt *something* within her that she knew without a doubt no mortal felt.

So, she'd known that she was different, but she'd also learned that immortals existed, all manner of supernatural beings that weren't gods and goddess. She figured she was actually just one of them, like a vampire or a shifter, and her mom was delusional.

Determined to learn more about the supernatural world and to figure out the truth, Beck had gone to what amounted to a combination supernatural black market and nightclub when she was fifteen. Or she'd *tried* to go to the club. Just as she'd been working up the nerve to walk up to the front doors, a strange woman with even stranger silver tattoos, silver hair, and purple eyes had hooked her arm through Beck's, like they were old friends, and led her away.

"This way," she'd said in a sing-song voice.

"Hey! What are you doing?" Beck had stammered, trying to sound angry, but honestly, she'd mostly been relieved that the woman had stopped her. She'd been *terrified* to go into that place. Magic and power had pulsed from it, and though her mother claimed that Beck was a goddess, she felt like nothing more than a mortal. A tiny, completely-unable-to-defend-herself, runt of a mortal at that.

"Saving your scrawny butt," the woman said. "Fear not though my dear, it shan't be scrawny for long! You'll soon be a Four Alarm Hottie, with crazy junk in the trunk. Seriously, men will weep at the sight of it. Go to war for it. Write sonnets and rock operas in its honor." *What in the hell is wrong with this woman?* she'd thought. "Ok, maybe not any of those things *exactly*, but you will have an ass that won't quit, ok? Just trust me."

After they were several blocks away from the club, the woman had pulled her into a small alcove in front of an out-of-business repair shop. She'd spun Beck to face her, a smile on her face like she was seeing an old friend.

"You've gotten so big," she said, reaching out to brush Beck's hair from her temple.

"What do you mean?" Beck asked, enjoying the tender touch for a moment too long before she swatted the woman's hand away. "Do I know you?"

"Yes and no," the woman said vaguely. Before Beck could demand a better answer than that, the woman gripped Beck's shoulders and peered at her with those strange eyes, eyes that Beck somehow knew held a millennia's worth of knowledge and memories and power. Holy hell the *power* pulsing from the woman had been staggering. Beck had been utterly entranced, not even daring to blink or breathe.

The silvery tattoos on the woman's skin began to glow and her eyes shifted wholly silver. Beck's eyes had flared wide at the sight. Beck felt knowledge and certainty flow from those silver pools into her own soul. Complete and utter clarity that her mother spoke true rang through her mind. She was an actual *goddess* and therefore, so was Beck. The godly planes, different realms, the gods, the creatures —*all* of it was real.

Finally, the woman's eyes returned to their beautiful violet as Beck continued to stare unblinking. She nodded, as if she'd just confirmed something, or maybe congratulating herself on a job well done.

"See, your mother is not crazy. I mean she *is* crazy, like nuttier than squirrel shit kinda crazy, but you really are of the gods, my sweet. It is important that you know this truth." *Why?* Beck had wondered, but couldn't seem to make herself voice the question. The woman patted her on the head like a puppy and snapped her fingers. A taxi immediately pulled up the curb.

"Now, you get yourself home and don't come back here until you're old enough to know better." She began to saunter off but turned back. "Oh, I almost forgot: do not fear the nightmares. If you can learn from them, your power will be unlike anything we've ever seen." *Learn from them? Learn what? How to crap my pants in my sleep?* Beck wanted to quip. The woman's eyes had gone totally vacant for a moment and Beck frowned, wondering if she was alright. She shook herself and smiled brightly.

"I'll see you again soon!" she added with a wink. With that, she just disappeared into thin air.

Beck had reeled back, smacking her head into the cool bricks behind her. She'd never seen someone disappear like that. She knew some immortals could travel by portal from one place to another in an instant, but she'd never heard of someone being able to just *disappear*. Beck had stood there, dazed and confused and even a bit amused by the odd woman, feeling a strange kinship with her, before hopping in the still-waiting taxi. If the driver had seen the woman disappear, he gave no indication, only asked Beck where she wanted to go and started chatting about the weather. Beck thought hard on the drive home. Her overall takeaway from the strange encounter? Her mother wasn't crazy. Beck was an actual *goddess*, the daughter of the most powerful god ever to exist.

So, yes, Beck knew the gods were real. She also knew that they were a bunch of assholes with no regard for anyone but themselves. At least that's what she grew up hearing from her mother. As she'd gotten older, she thought that maybe some of her mother's stories weren't *entirely* true and maybe not everyone in the godly planes could be so bad (she'd quite liked the silver-tattooed lady after all), but she still believed that the gods themselves were nothing but trouble and had a deep-seated hatred that would forever be a part of her.

They had banished her mother to the Mortal Plane to begin with, so they were the reason that Beck's life was the shitshow that it was. They were the reason she had to grow up far too quickly, living like a mortal, *suffering* like a mortal. Beck didn't particularly mind mortals, didn't disdain them the way her mother did at least, but she couldn't deny that she felt jilted being forced to live among them. She was a goddess for fuck's sake, and here she was, pouring coffee and scrubbing toilets for most of her life. Talk about being dealt a shitty hand from the fates.

So, yeah. The gods could all fuck right the hell off, please and thank you.

Beck pulled herself from her stewing and forced a small half smile back at Oscar.

"I just always got the vibe that the gods were a bunch of power-hungry jerks. I'm sure he's no different." She jutted her chin towards the open sea, as if Poseidon himself were out there listening. Oscar laughed and scanned the horizon.

"Well, let's hope that Poseidon doesn't mind your opinion of him too much. I'd hate for him to bring a storm down on us out here in retribution." She laughed, but gasped when the boat lurched again, more violently this time. She heard a scream from within the hull, but it was cut off so abruptly that she thought she must have imagined it. It must have just been equipment malfunctioning or something. She stumbled into Oscar, clutching at his arms to steady herself. He held her until the rocking subsided and she could stand on her own.

"What's going on?" she asked, worriedly. *Shit, could he really have heard me? Was he making a point? No way…*

"I don't know, maybe engine trouble. I better go check. You stay here—what the hell?" Oscar's usual smile disappeared as he looked across the deck. A man stood there, a man who was not a member of this crew and had not been on this boat moments ago. Beck's body went cold, icy fingers of dread tickling up her spine and locking her in place.

It was the man-that-wasn't-a-man from the parking lot.

"Who are you? What the hell are you doing on my boat?" Oscar demanded. She was sure he envisioned some sort of pirate scenario, but this was so, *so* much worse.

"Give me the girl," the man said, his voice low and gruff, the sound making her ears prick uncomfortably. It was like nails in a blender, the kind of sound that just made you shudder. Oscar cut his eyes to Beck.

"You know this guy?" She shook her head, unable to speak. He nodded and shifted so that he was in front of her, blocking her body with his protectively. She begged her power to respond. It was sporadic at best, but if there was ever a time that she needed it, it was now. She had inherited some of her mother's ability to manipulate people's perceptions, to make them see what she wanted them to, but any power she'd inherited from her father had been lost...or maybe taken from her when he abandoned her. *Which really sucks because some lightning bolts from my eyes or something would come in handy right about now.*

She was desperate, pleading with herself, begging what little spark of power she did have to cooperate. *Come on, come on, come on. Please...*

Nothing.

At.

All.

Beck gritted her teeth, fuming. She wanted to scream in sheer frustration. She was a goddess, the daughter of arguably the most powerful of all the gods, and yet her mother's banishment had somehow hindered her own powers from manifesting correctly. *This is horseshit!* She cursed the gods once more. Every single one of them could spend an eternity stepping on Legos barefoot if she had it her way.

"Your other friends are already dead," the man grated. Beck's heart lurched. *No. Please no. He has to be lying.* "Give me the girl and I will spare you, mortal. Make your choice quickly. I will not ask again."

His eyes shifted to that blood red again, and *fangs* extended from his upper teeth. Long and thick, with what looked like serrated edges. Nothing like the sleek vampire fangs she'd seen in the past. Where vampire fangs had always been kind of hot to her—it was well known that vampire fangs could equal great pleasure (not that she knew from experience unfortunately)—this thing's were *terrifying.*

"Dios mio," Oscar breathed. The thing raised his hand and before either of them could comprehend what was happening, a ball of fire shot towards them. Beck screamed and Oscar yelled out, ducking down and covering her body with his own. The ball hit just to their left, taking out the railing beside them. Flames licked along the splintered wood and debris, the heat singeing the hairs on her arm. They both straightened, wide-eyed and hearts beating wildly.

"That was a warning. Next time I will not miss."

"Oh god…" Beck tried desperately to bring up any of her powers. She felt a tiny flicker of heat in her chest and hope rose up. *Come on…*

A look of confusion passed over the thing's face. He glanced left and right quickly, as if…looking for someone! It had worked! She'd made him think they'd disappeared! Her mother had told her that some gods and goddesses could "phase," or teleport from one place to another in the blink of an eye, like the silver-tattooed woman had. Maybe this thing would believe that she'd done it now. Yes, this could work. If she could just…

No! She felt the heat retreat, as if sucked back into itself. The thing's eyes narrowed back on her, and he tilted his head to the side.

"Hmm, clever…but weak. Perhaps they lied about who your father is. I would have expected more from the daughter of one such as him." *Ouch. Ok, low blow.* Without warning, he raised his hand once more and fire shot forward, directly towards Oscar who was still shielding her. He yelled out and shoved her to the side seconds before the ball reached them.

"Oscar, no!" she screamed, but it was too late. The fire hit him square in the chest. He flew backwards, slamming against the railing. She stared in horror as Oscar's body crumpled to the ground, bloody and broken and burning. The thing was suddenly there, grabbing her arm hard enough to make the bones creak. She bit down, trying desperately not to cry out, and tasted blood in her mouth.

"They've been searching for you for a long time," he rasped, smiling that wicked smile again. *They?* She shuddered at the sight of his fangs. Beck struggled against his hold, trying desperately to pull away, but it was no use, he was far too strong. He knew it too and laughed at her feeble attempts. Anger rose swiftly, taking her by surprise and replacing her fear long enough for her to meet his gaze head on.

She saw shadows out of the corner of her eye, but didn't bother to see what they were. All she cared about was the prick who had hurt Oscar and was planning to do gods knew what to her. He looked just past her shoulder and his jaw slackened for a moment, confusion clear in his eyes.

"Fuck you," Beck bit out before spitting blood in his face. His eyes focused back on her, filling with rage. He growled, the sound so menacing that her heart skipped a beat. A cruel, unearthly smile curled his lips upward...lips that were now black and cracking? She gasped as his entire face changed, skin becoming gray and scaled, almost like a snake, but the texture looked far rougher. *What in the actual fuck?!*

His original face flickered back over his hellish one, but she couldn't linger on the thoughts of it for long. He tightened his grip and snapped her forearm like a twig. She screamed in agony, her knees almost buckling. White hot pain laced through her arm, a burning so intense she thought she might vomit.

She was gasping for breath and the thing was laughing, low and rumbling, when something slammed into him. *What the...? Oscar!* How he'd gotten up after that hit, she didn't know, but her heart ached as he used the last of his strength, the last moments of his life, to try to fight for her. Oscar's attack startled the thing enough that he lost his grip on Beck's arm. She stumbled backwards, cradling her broken arm against her chest, and knocked into the aquatic drone that was barely hanging on to the edge of the deck amidst the fire and wreckage of the railing. It tipped, plummeting into the water. It was a moment too late that she realized her feet were tangled in the ropes that had been holding it in place. They snared her ankle, tightening painfully.

Her wide eyes met Oscar's now vacant ones for a split second before she was yanked backwards, her knees and elbows cracking against the deck sending an explosion of pain through her, before she tumbled over the edge and was free falling towards the waves. She barely had time to suck in a lungful of air before she went under. The shock of the cold water nearly stole that precious bit of breath from her. The drone sank like a stone and she was being pulled along with it.

She tried to fight against the pull and make her way upward, but the drone outweighed her by at least a hundred pounds. She quickly abandoned the idea and instead tried to claw the ropes off of her ankles. Her broken arm was useless, but she tried as hard as she could with the other. Nails bent and broke, skin ripping off the edges of her fingertips as she fought desperately to free herself. Blood joined the surrounding water, bright red against the dark gray.

It was no use.

The weight of the drone was only tightening the ropes with every second that passed and her fingers we becoming numb. *Oh gods. I'm going to die.* Though she knew that it wouldn't be a permanent death, she began to panic. She would "die" for a time, though it was more like passing out she supposed, but her immortality would revive her and she would relive the ordeal over and over until someone found her...*if* they ever did. And it wouldn't be without pain. Already, her chest was burning and her head began to pound.

Fear spiked as she realized that all of that was just conjecture. Drowning *shouldn't* be able to kill a god permanently, but her mother's banishment had affected other aspects of her in odd ways, like her powers malfunctioning. So, she really might be dying here and now. For real.

Beck was just about out of air. These might be her last moments of life and panic set in like a lead weight. Panic and disappointment so strong it startled her. She realized in that moment how much she hadn't done, how she'd barely really *lived*. She'd been so focused on survival and keeping her mother and her antics hidden away from mortals, that Beck had done little else. She was having a full on *It's a Wonderful Life* moment...except hers wasn't wonderful at all.

Looking back, she realized that she'd never really had friends before she joined Harlan and his team, barely even ever had *fun* that she could recall. A handful of times maybe, but even in those moments, worry had always been heavy on her mind and she hadn't fully enjoyed herself. Don't even get her started about her lack of a love life. She was so damned disappointed in herself, in her life—or lack thereof.

I'm not ready to be done. Not yet. She wanted more. She wanted to see things, do things...and, as ridiculous as it sounded—and as much as she *shouldn't* want it based on the disaster that was her mother's experience—she wanted to know what it was like to love someone. Beck wanted to have someone in her life who actually knew her, understood her, and put her well-being as a priority.

So, actually what she really wanted was someone to love *her*, not the other way around. She thought that her mother cared for her in a way, but Beck knew that she'd never truly loved her. Her mother blamed her for their circumstances and reminded Beck of that fact often. And, she supposed, it *was* her fault in a round-about way, but it didn't warrant her mother being so damned...*un*motherly with her.

She gritted her teeth, the pressure in her chest bringing dark spots floating across her vision. Now was not the time to throw a pity party. Now was the time to fight. She'd never given up before. Beck saw challenges and found solutions, simple as that. *But how the hell am I supposed to fight now? What solution could there possibly be here?*

An idea sprang to mind. A stupid, terrible idea that she immediately hated, but when her lungs burned so badly she thought they might burst, she decided it was her only choice. With her last precious seconds of air, Beck opened her mouth and screamed his name into the abyss:

"Poseidon!"

FOUR

Poseidon shot upright in his bed. Someone had just called out to him from the sea within the Mortal Plane. His kingdom, Aqueous, was a separate plane of existence, but Poseidon was connected to the seas on all other planes as well. He could sense when those in the Mortal Plane were in distress on the water, but this was different: someone had literally called out to him. *By name.* That hadn't happened in thousands of years. *What the…?*

His heart thudded against his chest, a strange sense of panic rising. He reached out within his mind, searching the waters, letting them speak to him and show him where the cry had come from. He didn't even take the time to think about it. As soon as he'd found the location, he phased there directly.

A girl was being dragged downward, ropes wrapped tightly around her ankle and anchored to something plummeting down to the depths. Dark brown hair floated around her ethereally, and the blue light that emanated from him highlighted high cheek bones and what he would bet his left nut were achingly adorable dimples. She was a slip of a thing, floating there looking so incredibly helpless and vulnerable. His chest tightened uncomfortably. He scented blood and out of the corner of his eye he saw sharks beginning to investigate.

"Back off, boys. *Now,*" he added, lacing power and authority into the final word. The creatures cowered, immediately swimming any direction that was away from him and this girl as fast as their fins would take them. He looked her over, not seeing any obvious wounds, at least not at first. Then he caught sight of her fingers. The girl had fought to get free, he realized, clawing at the ropes until her fingertips were raw and bloody, nails torn or gone.

She was a fighter. Strong. Beautiful. *And she called out for me.* Extremely odd since most mortals thought the gods nothing but myths nowadays.

The powers that be often got huffy when the gods intervened in mortal lives too often, but something was telling him that he needed to save this girl. He had done little to intervene in a hot minute, so he figured he'd get a pass this time around. Decision made, he severed the ropes around her legs and phased them back to his throne room. He laid her down and pressed a hand to her chest, searching for a heartbeat. He felt nothing and that tightening in his own chest intensified. *No...Wrong...Save her...*

He didn't understand the tiny voice whispering within his mind, barely even heard it. *Had* he actually heard it? Was he imagining things? Going crazy? What could possibly be so important about this girl? Was it just that he'd been doing nothing important with his power and immortality lately, and this was a chance to change that? To be of use for something other than wringing orgasms out of his partners every night? To be worthy of the title of God of the Sea?

He knew that mortals did something called "CPR" when someone wasn't breathing, but he was afraid to try it himself. He was so strong, he could shove his hands straight through her chest cavity *and* the floor beneath without meaning to. Too risky. Instead, he closed his eyes and drew the sea water from her lungs, hoping it would be enough.

"Come on, beauty. Come on..."

The water was gone, but she still wasn't rising. His own heart began beating frantically within his chest. What was that about? Sure, it would be tragic if the poor girl didn't wake, but that was just the way of it. Mortals were fragile. They perished all the time. *And yet...*

No, he wasn't done yet. With no other options left, he forced himself to be as gentle as possible, using only his fingertips and the barest of pressure as he pressed against her chest. Sweat dotted his brow as he concentrated on not pulverizing the heart he was trying to coax into beating once more.

"Come on..."

Finally, she coughed and sputtered, her back arching off of the floor. *Yes!* He quickly helped to turn her to the side, and she clawed at the floor, gagging and gasping for air. The pressure in his chest eased slightly. The coughing subsided after a few moments, but she was still gasping for breath, sounding like she'd just run a marathon. He summoned a glass of water and held it out to her.

He smiled at her and she...*glared* back, knocking his hand away. The water sloshed over the edge and the entire glass nearly went flying across the room. He set it aside and held his hands up, showing her he meant no harm.

"Hey, you're ok. You're safe. I won't hurt you." She must just be scared and confused—she'd nearly died and then woke to a strange man hovering over her after all. Soon, the fear would shift into awe and wonder and a whole lot of arousal. He grinned inwardly, waiting for the moment. He'd be lying if he said he didn't enjoy it every single damn time. *Any second now...*

But as she scooted away and pushed herself up onto unsteady legs, tucking her left arm against her chest—*was she injured?*—the awe and wonder and arousal never came. No, the only thing radiating out of this girl so strongly he thought it might burn him, was *hatred*. Pure, unadulterated hatred.

"Get away from me," she spit, her voice a little raspy from coughing up half of the Atlantic.

His brows drew down. "Ok, am I drunk or—actually wait, let me rephrase because I am, in fact, a little drunk. Am I completely plastered, or did I not just save your life?"

She jutted her chin. "One good deed in a sordid history of despicable ones. Congratulations," she said, sarcasm thick in her voice. *Whoa, what in the hell?* He'd never encountered animosity like this. Everybody loved him. *I'm a fucking delight.*

"And what, pray tell, could you possibly know of my 'sordid history'?" He asked, half way between irritated and curious. Poseidon wasn't often met with this kind of hostility unless it was in battle. Hell, not just not often. *Never.* He was *always* met with lustful glances and panties being thrown across the room. Sure, he'd wanted different, but come on! This wasn't cool. He shot a quick annoyed glance upward. The fates were fickle, and he had a feeling now they were just screwing with him.

She curled her lip in disgust. Actually *curled her fucking lip*!

"I know all about you. You're Poseidon." He inclined his head, though he wondered *how* she knew who he was. Even most of the supernatural beings in the Mortal Plane didn't know the gods actually existed. "I know that the gods are all loathsome creatures who prey on those weaker than them." His brows shot upwards, surprised by the venom and conviction in her voice. Sure, Zeus had a temper and Hades got a bad rap because of the whole King of the Underworld thing, but loathsome? Really?

"And why, exactly, do you believe we're so loathsome?" he grated, though he was trying to keep his temper in check. He rarely let anything rile him enough to let it loose, but when he did...Well, he'd wiped entire cities off of the map in the past when his temper had gotten the better of him. *Like when Callie left me...*He forced the memory away. It wasn't his proudest moment, and he'd had to create an entirely new realm for the peaceful Treyholds when his storm had decimated their home island. He still felt like an ass over that one.

"Please," she said, laughing without humor. "Hades kidnapped and imprisoned Persephone, probably forcing himself upon her at every opportunity like an animal. He tortures souls for eternity for pure enjoyment. You control the sea, unleashing your wrath on unsuspecting mortals whenever the mood strikes you, probably laughing about it all the while. Zeus is a vengeful, womanizing tyrant who tosses people aside like rubbish when he gets what he wants from them. Hera, Demeter, Ares—all of them irredeemable pathetic excuses for deities. I could go on and on with the sins of your ilk."

"My *ilk*?" he asked incredulously. Though he didn't raise his voice, the sea around them churned with his rising anger. He leaned forward and said in a low voice laced with power, "I would advise you to be careful, girl. I'm generally known to be fairly laid back, but even I have my limits—one of which is being insulted in my own home."

She glanced around, as if just realizing where she was. She eyed the angry-looking water warily, and he thought for a moment logic would prevail and she would back down, but instead, she shoved her shoulders back and returned her gaze to him, ice blue eyes burning him with their intensity. Normally, those eyes could have taken him to his knees, but this female was slowly making her way onto his shit list and he'd only known her for three minutes. So, at the moment he didn't give a flying fuck how striking her eyes were.

"You have quite the strange way of saying thank you by the way. For saving your life," he clarified in a scathing tone. Her nostrils flared and she clenched her jaw. Would she thank him? He almost smirked. *No, she would rather eat fire than ever thank me.*

"I would like to leave this place. Immediately."

"Wish fucking granted." Si moved forward and she hastily stepped backwards. He exhaled roughly through his nose, grappling for patience. Had anyone ever ruffled his feathers this much in such a short amount of time? No. The answer was absolutely fucking not.

"I have to actually touch you in order to phase. Fear not, you can burn your clothing when you return home to get my *ilk* stains off of you." She swallowed hard, looking the tiniest bit sorry for half a second before she hardened her features once more.

"Do what you must." She stood her ground this time as he made his way to her in two long strides. The sooner he got her out of his palace and back to her own damn plane, the better. *This is what I get for trying to help people, for wanting something different out of life.* He didn't know who she was or why she wasn't the least bit surprised to be in the presence of a god—insulting said god for that matter!—but he did know that he wanted her gone. ASAP.

That tiny voice attempted to provide a rebuttal but he growled inwardly, silencing it. He gripped her right bicep gently, careful not to jostle her injured arm. He was pissed, but he wasn't an asshole despite what this girl apparently thought.

"Where would you like to go?" he grated. She seemed to debate where to tell him, but finally rattled off the location of a marina. He phased them to the edge of the water, landing under a large dock. He kept them cloaked, unable to be seen, heard, or sensed by anyone. Si *used* to visit the Mortal Plane often, freely moving about without issue, but then he'd discovered a mortal who bore a slight...ok, an *uncanny* resemblance to him. So much so that they'd *triple* checked to be sure he wasn't some long-lost son Poseidon knew nothing about.

Normally, not a problem—it had happened a few thousand times over the history of the world, a cosmic joke from the powers that be to show the gods that they weren't *that* special, he supposed —but this particular mortal decided to be an actor, gaining popularity playing an FBI behavioral profiler on a popular television show.

Si had seen the show, enjoyed it even, but because of it, he couldn't freely roam around without being plagued by paparazzi. *Paparazzi* for fuck's sake. He sighed. He missed the olden days of the Mortal Plane, before technology had gotten quite so revolutionary. Don't get him wrong, he enjoyed plenty of things that mortal advancement provided—movies, television, video games...lingerie— but he missed the simplicity sometimes. And he sure as shit missed being able to mingle (*aka fuck*) his way through the plane without hassle. So, now on the rare occasions he came to this plane, he remained cloaked out of habit.

He immediately let go and stepped away from the girl. It had been a while since he'd wanted to *stop* touching a female, but this one irritated him like no other. She peeked out from under the dock, looking towards the parking lot. She was shot through with tension, even more so than when she was in another plane of existence. *What is that about? Actually, whatever, not my problem.*

"Well, I would say it was nice meeting you, but I'm not a liar so..." He shrugged and prepared to phase back to his castle. He needed to find somebody to get him out of the foul mood this female had put him in. *A few somebodies maybe.* She gasped and ducked back quickly, not realizing they were hidden. He paused, sensing genuine fear from her, and curiosity got the better of him.

He glanced where she'd just been looking and saw several men gathered in the gravel lot. His eyes narrowed, looking past the false faces they'd placed over their true forms. No, not men—demons. What the hell were demons doing here?

The largest of the demons spoke to the others.

"How did you lose her?" he demanded.

"I told you, she went over and by the time I took care of that damned mortal and looked over the edge, there was no sign of her."

"Oh gods, no. Oscar," she whispered, her hand flying to her mouth and her eyes glinting with tears. He shifted his focus back to the demons.

"You didn't follow her down?" the leader asked, anger radiating off of him.

"I have wings, Zelishian, not fucking *gills*," the other shot back. "The current was strong as hell out there, it could have dragged her anywhere."

"Well, you better become a skilled diver in a fucking hurry, Rashum. You're going to scour every inch of that water if you have to." Rashum ground his teeth but didn't respond. "You two, go to her house. She's either still out in the water, or she made it back and will come home soon enough. Either way, we *will* find her."

"Be on alert," Rashum added. "She has *some* power, though it doesn't appear to be very strong. Still, be prepared."

Poseidon glanced sidelong at her, wondering what they meant by that. She didn't seem like anything extraordinary to him. She was attractive, sure—startlingly so if he were being honest—but still, just an ordinary girl. Was she a witch or enchantress perhaps? But if she was, why didn't she use her own power to save herself from the depths?

"We aren't sure what she might be capable of, but we *have* to find her. We've never been this close. You cannot imagine the punishment in store for us if she's lost."

They all paled. Most of the group were Lackromite Demons, or *Lackey Demons* as they were more commonly called. They were decent fighters and could follow simple orders, but weren't particularly smart, so you never hired them for complicated or delicate jobs —more for things like kidnappings, the front lines of an army, low-level security, that type of thing. The good thing about them was that they bred like rabbits and were fully grown within two years of birth, so there were always more to be found.

Basically: they were disposable.

However, Zelishian was a Rathos Demon. They were renowned for their skill in battle, cunning minds, and overall badassery. One of Hades' most trusted guards was a Rathos Demon named Jeff. So, if even Zelishian was afraid, then whoever they were working for was bad news.

"Shit, shit, shit," the girl whispered, sounding panicked and stepping further back under the safety of the dock. *This is all very interesting but...again, not my problem.*

"Ok, well...bye then."

"Wait!" Her ice blue eyes were wild with fear. Poseidon could practically see the wheels turning in her head, frantic to make a decision. After the briefest hesitation she said, "Take me with you."

He barked out a laugh.

"And why, in the name of all the despicable gods, would I do that?"

"Please, I...I can't stay here. They're after me."

He narrowed his eyes, slight intrigue fighting its way past irritation and annoyance. He crossed his arms over his chest. "Why?"

"I don't know," she said, sounding sincere. "Maybe..." She licked her lips, eyes darting around like a scared animal. "Maybe to use me to get to my father, I'm not sure though."

"Who's your father?"

She shook her head. "It doesn't matter. Look, I may not know what they want, but I do know that they won't stop until they have me." He considered her for a long moment.

"And why would I allow someone who clearly despises me and my brethren to stay in my palace?"

"I didn't say I intended to stay *with* you," she said, narrowing her eyes. Clearly trying to stem her annoyance, she added in a somewhat more neutral tone, "I'll find somewhere else to stay. Surely there are like...hotels? Inns? Hostels? Something for travelers."

Si tilted his head in the direction of the parking lot. "*He* doesn't have gills—do you?"

Her dark brows drew down in confusion. "Huh?"

"Aside from my castle and the grounds surrounding it, all of Aqueous is underwater." Her eyes widened. She knew of the gods—though it seemed someone had sorely misinformed her on several things—but she apparently didn't know *that* much. She opened her mouth to speak but he interrupted her, holding up a hand. "And I have no plans to allow a freeloading mortal to stay in my home. No offense." He pursed his lips. "Or maybe offense, actually. You've been pretty fucking rude. So, yeah, on second thought: *all* the offense."

She narrowed her eyes and flared her nostrils in anger. "I am *not* a mortal." Her ice blue eyes darkened slightly, a flash of deep cobalt, and Poseidon arched a brow. *Interesting.* She inhaled deeply, as if searching for calm. "But what if..." Wheels turning again, ideas being presented and tossed aside until finally, one landed. "What if I work to earn my keep? You have to have staff or...or servants, right?"

He gave her a skeptical look. "You would work for me? Literally *serve* me?" She clenched her jaw and glanced towards the parking lot again.

"Not as a concubine or a whore or anything like that—" Si rolled his eyes. As if he'd allow such things in his kingdom. "—but yes, if that's what it takes," she said, shoulders square, voice resolute. She must be really desperate to escape if she would swallow her pride and willingly work for someone she hated so much—for reasons he would love to understand.

That tiny whisper fluttered through his mind again, as soft as the wind rustling through the trees. *Help her.* He scowled at the voice, but he supposed that despite her insults and obvious disdain for all things god-related, he didn't want her harmed. Unlike her assumption of him, he didn't actually enjoy when others were hurt needlessly. He sighed, defeated, and stepped forward to grip her arm once more before he could change his mind. He phased them back to the throne room and promptly released her, putting space between them as quickly as possible.

She looked around, seeming to really take in the room for the first time. He followed her gaze, trying to see it from her perspective. One entire wall was nothing but glass, ocean just beyond it. Parts of the castle abutted the edge of the enchanted dome, giving some rooms the feel of being completely submerged and surrounded by water. The floors and remaining walls were white marble with the faintest of gold and blue striations running throughout. His throne sat on a small raised platform just in front of the sea wall. It was made of blue sea-glass, the high back carved to look like crashing waves. His trident stood beside it, magnificent and glowing faintly.

He couldn't help but smile. His trident was a part of him, basically another appendage, and he loved it *almost* as much as his more infamous one. She gasped when her eyes landed on the opposite wall where a giant skull hung.

"What in the hell is that?"

More than fear, he saw fascination on her face as she moved towards the wall, her hatred seemingly forgotten for the moment. *Surprising female.*

"That is a leviathan." She tore her gaze away from the skull and back to him, shrugging her shoulders and shaking her head, the universal sign for *I have no idea what you're talking about.* "It's like a sea dragon of sorts," Si explained. Her brows shot upward before she turned back to stare at the bones.

"My father gave me this kingdom, but some of the inhabitants weren't ready to call me king in the beginning. I had to battle for the right to lead them. I had to earn it." He nodded to the skull. "That was the mightiest of the creatures and once I bested him, the others revered my strength and cunning and honor. They came to obey me. To respect me."

"So you keep that there as a trophy?" she asked, disapproval thick in her voice.

Si shook his head. "Not a trophy. A reminder."

She turned back to him once more, arching a brow in question, again the contempt gone for the moment. *Gods, she really is beautiful... when she isn't looking at me like something a chimera shat out.*

"A reminder of what?"

"That things are rarely actually *given* to you. You must work for what you want, and be willing to do what has to be done to get it." *Why am I telling her this?* She tilted her head as she stared at him, seeming to see much more than anyone else. It made him uncomfortable. He cleared his throat and made his way to the bar. He needed a drink in the worst way.

"Can those...things come here? The ones from the marina?" She wrapped her arms around herself, hissing in pain as if she'd momentarily forgotten her injury. She was shivering and he didn't know if it was from cold or fear. Maybe both. He sighed, his good nature getting the better of him, and he stalked to one of the alcoves built into the walls. Most had small seating areas and several had—*bingo!*

Blankets. He offered it to her without a word. She took it with her uninjured arm, clearly trying to work out how to wrap it around herself without the use of two hands. He pursed his lips. He didn't have a great deal of healing power, but he had enough for minor jobs. Enough to mend a broken bone, surely. Maybe. He met her gaze.

"I can fix that if you'd like." He nodded toward her arm.

She debated, but finally seemed to realize that being healed by an enemy was better than walking around with a useless arm. The girl finally nodded but watched him warily as he slowly extended his hand towards her. She tensed when he placed his hand atop her arm, though she didn't cry out. Heat flooded to his palms, a faint blue light emanating from it over her skin. She gasped in surprise, and then hissed in pain as the bone snapped back into place. She sucked in shallow breaths through gritted teeth, refusing to make any other noise. The girl was tough, Poseidon would give her that.

"Ah, sorry. It's been a while," he said. Her breaths slowed as the pain began to fade. She moved it gingerly, turning it this way and that, and raised her brows in surprise. A soft 'whoa' slipped from her lips. She nodded and he assumed that was all the thanks he was going to get. She wrapped the blanket around herself and he moved away, flopping down onto his throne.

"To answer your question: those things are demons, and no, they cannot. Not just anyone can enter godly planes without permission or assistance. If they attempt to breach my barriers, they will pay dearly." After a moment's hesitation he added, "You're safe here."

The girl huffed out a humorless laugh. "What that must be like," she whispered to herself. Was feeling safe something she wasn't used to? The thought bothered him though he couldn't explain why. She began to stroll around the room, and he watched her in silence, a bit entranced with her sensual grace as she moved. She was petite—practically tiny compared to his six-and-a-half-foot tall frame—but she had curves that would make any male take notice. He scowled to himself. He shouldn't be having lusty thoughts about this girl, especially given the fact that she had made it very clear that she wanted nothing to do with him, despised him even.

"So, uh...you look different than I thought you would," she said, attempting to make conversation he supposed. He huffed out a laugh and shook his head. He knew where this was headed, but since she was taking a break from the animosity for a moment, he figured he'd play along. She made her way towards the throne and he sat up straighter. She quirked a brow in question as she reached a hand out towards his trident, and he nodded, letting her know that it was ok to touch it. She ran a finger along the tip of one prong, and for some reason, the action sent a direct wake up call to his cock. *Don't ask me to explain that one.*

"And what were you expecting?"

She hiked one shoulder. "Aquaman?" She *almost* smirked. "Do you even know who that is?"

He inclined his head. "My brother's oracle has seen to it that we are all well-versed in mortal movies and television." She seemed intrigued and somewhat amused by that. Her change from hating him with every fiber of her being to engaging in civil conversation like normal acquaintances was a bit confusing, but he was willing to go with it.

"So, yeah, I was expecting more Jason Momoa, but you actually look almost exactly like—"

He leaned forward with a grin, showing off what he knew to be a panty-eviscerating smile.

"Oh I know exactly who I look like, *Baby Girl.*"

Her eyes widened, pupils dilating slightly, and her breath seemed to catch in her throat. She swallowed hard, eyes dipping to his lips before darting back up. His smile shifted to a self-satisfied smirk, and she scowled in response. She may hate him, but she wasn't completely immune to his charms. Would anything happen between them? Absolutely not. But he was who he was—flirting was fun even when nothing was going to come of it.

She took a step back, that bitter hatred settling back over every inch of her body. She looked angry at herself, as if she were pissed that she'd let herself slip for even the briefest moment.

"I'm tired," she said flatly.

"Yes, I supposed drowning can have that effect. We have much to discuss, but for now, let's get you settled in." Hellbent on antagonizing her, he added with a grin, "You start work in the morning after all."

FIVE

Beck couldn't believe she'd just been lusting after Poseidon. Granted, he was the most attractive man she'd ever seen, *absolutely* the most attractive she'd ever been in the presence of, with his golden amber eyes, light brown skin, perfectly perfect smile, muscled chest clearly visible through the tight t-shirt he wore...*Ok that's enough, Beck.* But not only did she hate every cell in his perfect body, he was her uncle for fuck's sake.

Utter disgust roiled through her right on the heels of just about the strongest flare of lust she'd ever experienced. *There is something seriously wrong with me.* She mentally shook herself as a stunning woman entered through the towering wooden doors. She was every bit of six feet tall, dwarfing Beck's five-foot-three, and just oozed otherworldly allure.

"Nerina, this is...oh, I guess I never caught your name. Too busy with the whole saving your life and being called nasty names in the process thing, I suppose," he said sarcastically.

"Beck," she snapped before pressing her lips into a thin line. She knew she needed to rein in her temper and bite her tongue. The person she was hurling insults and a bad attitude at was a vengeful god with a history of using his power to wipe out anyone in his path...*or was he?*

She was possibly questioning quite a few things her mother had told her right about now. If the gods were all so terrible, why had this one wasted his time saving her at all? Why even answer her plea for help to begin with? *Unless he plans to toy with me? Play games with me or...worse?* Despite everything she'd been raised to believe about him and everyone in this world, her gut was telling her that he wasn't some ruthless, evil being hell bent on causing harm to others. Her gut was also telling her...things she didn't understand and would be ignoring completely. Bottom line was that she didn't know if he was a saint, but she didn't think that he would do anything to hurt her as her mother had always promised anyone in this world would.

"Beck," he repeated, and she forced herself not to enjoy the way it rolled off of his tongue. She ground her teeth, hating herself for even feeling the tiniest bit of attraction to someone she hated so viscerally. *Plus—ew! Uncle!*

"Anyway, Beck here will be working here for the time being. Get her set up in a room please. Work wise, have her do whatever you need and let me know if she gives you trouble." With that, he waved them away and disappeared. Just *poof!* Gone in the blink of an eye. She wondered if that was a skill that she could learn.

Nerina held out her arm, ushering Beck out of the throne room. Beck took one more lingering look over the space before she followed the woman out. She'd never been in a throne room before, but she believed whole heartedly that this one had to be the most breath-taking of any in history. An entire wall was glass, looking out into endless water. She supposed that could be a bit intimidating to some, terrifying even, but she found it brilliant and calming. The floors and walls had just enough accents of subtle gold to give off an air of luxury without being gaudy. Even the skull of that giant beast —what had he called it? A leviathan?—had intrigued her and gave the space a bit of rugged charm.

Part of her hated that her anger towards him had ebbed so quickly, even for a few moments. Her mother would be so disappointed in her, but it was like something inside of her was drawn to him. Maybe not him, exactly, but to this world in general? She'd felt so alone her entire life, stuck in a world where she didn't really belong, impossibly different from everyone around her. So, being here, even around someone she was meant to despise, she couldn't stop herself from being *excited*. Excited to just be somewhere where she didn't have to hide, where others were just like her, where she felt like she could actually belong. It felt like finally coming home. *Sorry mom.*

Thinking of her mother sent a swift jolt of worry through her. Beck squeezed her eyes shut, hoping that her mother was still safely away and didn't come home to those things waiting on their doorstep. She had little in the way of warm and fuzzies towards her mother, but she didn't want her attacked by those monsters. She would have to find a way to get in touch with her and warn her, but that was something to tackle tomorrow.

Beck focused back on the woman beside her. Nerina's cerulean hair seemed to float down her back as she walked with an easy, gliding grace, as if she were swimming. Small white shells and shark's teeth were woven within the strands at random intervals. Her eyes were a startling yellow-orange, the pupils slitted like a cat's.

"I'm assuming this is your first time in Aqueous?" she said with a smile that revealed several tiny fangs. *Whoa.*

"I've never even left Florida," Beck answered.

"And why are you here, exactly?"

"Umm…" She wasn't sure how much to reveal about her circumstances. Nerina cut those odd eyes her way and gave her a reassuring smile.

"It's ok to have secrets. Whatever your reasons, know that you are safe here. Poseidon is a much-loved king and he takes the protection of his people seriously."

"But I'm not his people."

"You are so long as you reside in this castle," she said with a shrug. That warmed Beck's chest for some stupid reason. "Now, we just came from the throne room, obviously. Poseidon's personal chambers take up the entire northern tower. Kitchens, dining rooms, ballrooms—all of that is in the western wing." She waved her hands in vague directions, the light glinting off of small black claws on the tips of her fingers. "Training rooms, libraries, and guest quarters in the eastern wing. I'll give you the full tour tomorrow, but for now I'll show you to your room which is in the southern wing, this way." She looked Beck up and down. "You look like you could use a warm bath and some rest."

A warm bath sounded like heaven, and though she was exhausted, Beck wasn't sure rest would come. She'd settle for the bath part though.

"Thank you," Beck said quietly, forcing herself not to take out her anger out on Nerina. She was going to be here for the foreseeable future until she worked out a better plan, so she needed to play nice.

Nerina inclined her head and they walked the rest of the way in silence. Beck was too keyed up, her mind spinning far too quickly in too many directions for her to even notice much about the castle as they walked other than the fact that it was huge and opulent. Finally, Nerina stopped in front of an oversized doorway down a wide hallway filled with many almost identical doors.

"This is you. Most of the rooms in this wing are empty as most of the other servants and staff do not live in the castle full time. If you dislike this one, feel free to change to any vacant room, just let me know which. If the door is gold, it is occupied." She slid a small dial beside the door, changing the color from silver-blue to gold. "See? We'll go over your duties tomorrow morning and I'll introduce you to the rest of the staff. For now, bathe and rest. I'll have food sent up as well."

Beck nodded, surprised—and suspicious—of the hospitality. Again, the stories she'd been told weren't meshing with what she was experiencing firsthand. She shook herself, her head pounding as she tried to sort through everything. She began to step forward into the room when Nerina grasped her arm. Easy enough not to bruise or be painful, but hard enough to show that she was far stronger than she looked and to garner Beck's full attention. Her small claws pressed into Beck's arm, but didn't break the skin.

"I don't know why you're here or who you are to Poseidon, and it isn't any of my business, but just know that if you do *anything* to hurt him or this kingdom, you will have to answer to me." Her eyes flooded black and her fangs lengthened as she peeled her lip back. Beck's eyes widened, heart thudding in her chest.

"I...I don't plan to harm anyone, I promise. He..." She exhaled roughly before continuing, somewhat begrudgingly, "He saved my life and I'm in his debt. I just want to earn my keep until I can figure out what to do next. I swear." Nerina's eyes shifted back to normal, her fangs retracting. She smiled and nodded.

"Good. Then we'll get along just fine, Beck." With that, she'd turned and sauntered off in that strange swim-glide-walk way she had.

Hours later, Beck lounged in bed with dry clothes, a full belly of strange, but delicious food, and stared at the ceiling. She didn't even know where to begin unpacking everything that had happened. She supposed the biggest thing was the fact that demons were after her. *Demons* for fuck's sake! She had no idea why, other than something to do with her father, as she told Poseidon earlier. Should she tell him about Zeus? She'd chosen not to divulge that information before, worried that there was some godly version of *bros before hoes* that would extend to any unwanted offspring. But if this really was about her father, maybe he could step in, or hell, he may even know who was sending those goons after her in the first place.

If not, that led her to her next issue: what the hell was she supposed to do? She couldn't stay here working for Poseidon forever, but she obviously couldn't go home either. Not yet anyway. Should she try to find her mother and they could go into hiding somewhere? Maybe they could go wherever she went on these little trips of hers.

Beck rubbed her temples, not liking the feeling of not being in control. She'd always been the one to see a problem and find a solution. When her mother became basically useless as the years went on, her power to make mortals believe whatever she wanted them to becoming nonexistent? Beck found a way to put food on their table. When she felt too guilty about stealing food? She found a way to earn money instead. Not earning *enough* money? She worked more than one job at once. Providing plausible excuses and explanations when warranted, keeping her mother (mostly) contained and hidden, keeping them both alive and marginally content—Beck handled it all. No matter what it was, she *always* figured out a way. But with this? She had no idea. She couldn't fight off demons for gods' sake.

"Obviously. Look how the boat turned out," she grumbled to herself, pain and guilt clawing at her chest. She threw her arms over her face, not wanting to think anymore but not being able to turn her brain off. She was pretty sure being here in a godly plane was doing something to her, like it was awakening things in her that had been dormant on the Mortal Plane. Everything was new and exciting, yet familiar and comforting somehow. And the fact that she was immediately drawn to Poseidon, something deep within her chest demanding that she be near him? She couldn't even begin to work that out and refused to try. She hated him, plain and simple. Whatever instinct was trying to tell her otherwise needed to shut the hell up.

Eventually her mind calmed enough that sleep found her. Even the nightmares stayed away that night, her exhaustion too strong for them to fight their way through. Even all these years later, she'd yet to figure out what the hell the silver-tattooed woman had meant about those, telling her not to fear them. Her nightmares were *terrifying*. Of course she feared them—wasn't that the entire point of a nightmare?

All too soon, a knock on the door woke her. Beck groaned and pushed herself up, glaring at the door as the knocking continued.

She squinted towards the window and saw muted sunlight peeking below the curtains. She sucked in a deep lungful of air, held it for a few seconds, and let it out in a woosh. *Here we go.*

She had no idea what was in store for her today. Would Poseidon make sure she was scrubbing toilets all day as a way to punish her for yesterday? Or just for his amusement?

"Jokes on him, I've scrubbed more toilets than I can count," she muttered to herself as she padded to the door. She opened it to find a very wide-awake Nerina.

"Good morning," Nerina greeted her, far too cheery for Beck's taste. She wore a light, flowy gown in a deep berry-pink shade that looked simply beautiful against her pale skin and blue hair. It tied on the tops of each shoulder with golden string, tiny shells hanging along the strands.

"I don't consider any morning good until I've had coffee." Beck sucked in a quick breath, her eyes going wide. "Oh gods, please tell me you have coffee here." If the answer was no...well, she would seriously consider just taking her chances with the demons.

Nerina laughed, the sound like music. Melodic. Alluring. Hypnotic. *What* is *she?* "We have something akin to coffee on the Mortal Plane, yes. I believe you'll find it far superior to anything you've tasted there. Most mortals find the food and drink in any of the godly planes simply divine."

Beck gritted her teeth. "I'm not a mortal," she grated.

Nerina raised a navy brow, gaze roaming over Beck as if searching for proof of her claim. She shrugged. "Whatever you say. Now, get dressed—you're late."

"Umm, dressed in what? You took my clothes from yesterday and all I have is pajamas" Beck said, pulling at the fabric of the incomparably soft tank top she'd been given to sleep in along with matching pants. Nerina flashed a sly smile.

"Check the closet. I think you'll be pleased." Excitement shot through Beck, but she tried to hide it, giving a simple nod and telling Nerina she'd be out shortly. As soon as she closed the door, she raced across the room to the large walk-in closet. She knew that whatever clothes were inside weren't *really* hers, but that didn't dim her excitement. Beck rarely got to splurge on things like new clothes, and even when she did, they were usually only new *to her*. She had become a thrift-shop shopping aficionado over the years, a yard sale shark.

She threw open the doors, excited to see whatever may lie within, only to be sorely disappointed.

The closet was completely empty.

"What the hell? Is this some kind of joke?" She shoved hair out of her face, irritated at being tricked. "I should have known anyone in this gods' forsaken place would be an asshole, just like the gods themselves." She walked inside the space, just to be sure it was truly empty. "Seriously!? Not even a pair of clean underwear?" A slight tingling filled the air, a bit like static, and Beck jumped back with a yelp.

There on one of the low shelves, was a pair of black lacy briefs. Her favorite style. She eyed them for a moment, wondering if this was somehow another trick. She glanced around with narrowed eyes, but eventually her curiosity was too much. She snatched them up: completely real. "Holy shit..." Beck's brows furrowed as she thought it through, and then she blinked as an idea struck: did the closet give her whatever she asked for? *No freaking way...*Only one way to find out.

She took a deep breath and quietly said, "Umm, jeans? And a white v-neck t-shirt?"

Beck huffed out an incredulous laugh when the items appeared on the shelves, in the exact cuts and styles she preferred, and she knew they'd be the perfect sizes. She ran her hands along the jeans and gave a little moan of delight. They were ten times nicer than any she'd ever owned, so soft they felt like butter. The t-shirt was the same, the material like simple cotton, but softer than any cotton you'd find in the Mortal Plane. She asked for a bra to match the panties, and some Chucks, combed out her hair, and headed out into the hallway.

"I see you figured out how the closet worked all on your own. Quite quickly as well. I'm impressed." Nerina smiled, then tilted her head, her gaze roaming over Beck's body. "*That* is what you requested? Out of literally any items of clothing in the entire universe?" Beck hiked a shoulder, feeling slightly uncomfortable. She did feel a little underdressed next to Nerina's beautiful toga-like gown now that she thought about it. Maybe that's the type of thing everyone here wore? Should she change? "Well, you are most definitely one of those females who can pull off any look, that is for sure."

Beck thought for a moment Nerina had to be mocking her but... no. She sensed nothing but sincerity from the woman. *How refreshing.* Though Beck didn't socialize much and hadn't been in real school since second grade, she'd encountered too many girls to count over the years who pretended to be nice, but were actually horrible. She gave Nerina a tentative twitch of her lips, her approximation of a smile.

They walked in the opposite direction that they'd come from the previous night. Nerina pointed out rooms and spouted out directions as they went, making quick introductions when they passed others. Beck had a feeling she would need a map, and voiced the concern to Nerina. The beauty chuckled and told her if she were ever lost, she needed only to ask the castle and it would lead her in the right direction. *How freaking cool was that? Ugh.* She mentally smacked herself. It didn't matter how cool their toys were, they were still the gods that had made her life a living hell. Maybe not directly, but they were involved, and therefore guilty nonetheless.

Beck pulled up her familiar hate and clung to it with an iron grip. It was her new security blanket. She needed to remember what her mother had always told her: *the gods are deceiving.*

"How many people live here?" Beck asked, awed by the variety of beings she was seeing. Some looked completely human, others like creatures out of a mortal science fiction movie. They all seemed friendly—yet another thing that just didn't jive with the awful picture her mother had painted of this world. *Deceiving, remember? Keep your head on a swivel.*

"Poseidon is the only one who actually *lives* here really, but many others come and go, staying a few days or weeks if the mood strikes. As I said, most of the other staff members don't live here, but rooms are always available should we wish to, and more rooms will appear as necessary. The castle is ever changing and Poseidon can manipulate any aspect of the Plane that he wishes."

Beck could hardly believe the sheer size of the palace, let alone how gorgeous it was and the magical properties it possessed. Her mother had secured them a lovely home on the beach in the Mortal Plane before her powers had waned, but it was *nothing* like this. Spiraling staircases, ornately carved statutes in small alcoves along the corridors, breathtakingly beautiful paintings of gods, goddesses, seascapes, battles, and other worlds Beck could scarcely imagine but longed to see.

At what she assumed was the main entrance, a huge, open foyer left her speechless. The floor was a mixture of different colored tiles and as she tilted her head, she believed from above they must create a symbol or picture. The front doors were easily forty feet tall and the ceiling towered even higher than that. She looked upward and spun in a slow circle as she took in the sight. A huge chandelier dominated the middle, sea glass in different shades of blues, teals, and greens hanging from the various sconces like dripping icicles. Beyond it, the ceiling was painted like the sea, so realistic she was surprised she couldn't feel the spray of the waves on her face.

"Whoa," she whispered, awed beyond measure.

"I'm quite biased, but I believe Poseidon's castle is by far the most beautiful," Nerina said, a smile in her voice. Beck snapped out of her daze and cleared her throat, slightly embarrassed how entranced she'd been.

"So, uh...you didn't find it odd that the God of the Sea told you to give a random girl a job with no explanation?" Nerina huffed out another of those musical laughs.

"I've been with Poseidon for many centuries now. Him asking me to find a girl a job is *far* from the strangest request he's made." Beck's curiosity was immediately piqued. What other kinds of things had he asked Nerina to do? And just how many females did he have hanging around? *And why in the hell is that thought...bothersome to me?* She mentally shook herself. *Uncle. Uncle. UNCLE. Oh and evil. That too.*

"Besides, it's not my place to find his requests odd or not. He asks. I do. Simple as that."

Nerina led her to the kitchens and offered her a large mug of something dark and swirling that smelled like heaven in a cup. Beck moaned at the first sip, literally *moaned* like she was on the verge of orgasm. *Maybe I am. It's* that *good.* It was the most amazing thing she'd ever tasted, the most amazing thing she could even imagine tasting. She knew beyond any doubt that this had ruined her for all other pathetic excuses for coffee in the world.

After finishing her cup in record time, Nerina got down to business. Since Beck wasn't familiar with any of the dishes typically served in this plane, she wouldn't be on kitchen assistance quite yet. Instead, she was designated to cleaning duty. She didn't really mind honestly—cleaning had always been oddly satisfying to her—and she figured it could be much, much worse. If Poseidon had wanted, she could be biding her time in his kingdom locked in a dungeon.

Nerina was showing Beck the laundry facilities when the sea-glass bracelet on her wrist began to glow. She tilted her head, as if listening to something, and then put down the basket she was holding.

"Poseidon would like to meet with you. Come."

"How do you know that?" Beck asked, puzzled.

Nerina held up her wrist. "This allows us to communicate tele-pathically. It comes in handy in such an enormous castle." Nerina led her back to one of the smaller dining rooms. "When you're done, you can start cleaning the rooms down the south corridor in the east tower." She pointed in the direction Beck had thought was the right way. "I'll meet you there later."

With that, she sauntered off, snapping her fingers and yelling at a male at the other end of the hallway about the gardens. Beck reached out to grip the handle, closed her eyes, and took a deep breath. After much deliberation, she'd decided she was going to tell Poseidon about her father. She wondered how he would react to learning that they were actually related.

"Guess it's time to find out," she whispered and pushed open the door.

SIX

Poseidon heard the door to the dining room ease open. She was here. The girl—Beck—had been on his mind all night. Not in *that* way (or, ok, maybe a little bit in that way), but the more he thought of her, the more questions rose in his mind, keeping him from sleep despite the rigorous activities he'd taken part in prior to bed time with a handful of nymphites, the water-dwelling cousins of the nymphs found in the Mortal Plane.

He needed to know more about her. Or *anything* really. Si was slightly embarrassed that he knew her name, that she had a strange hatred for the gods, and literally nothing else. He may have been a bit hasty in allowing her to stay in his home without knowing jack shit. His brothers were typically the targets of spies, assassins, and general beings-wanting-to-do-you-harm types, but still, he was one of the most powerful gods in existence and there were plenty who would try to take this kingdom from him, or use him to harm his brothers.

So, he and the girl needed to have a little chat. It had nothing to do with the fact that he was nearly desperate to see her again. Not at all. Although, that in and of itself was strange. He had felt nothing like that in almost too long to recall.

He wondered which version of her he would get this morning: the one who seemed keen on slitting his throat in his sleep, or the one who seemed fascinated by him and his home. He finished reading the last few lines of the report in his hands before setting them aside and finally glancing up. His "good morning" got stuck in his throat. She was in a simple outfit of jeans and white t-shirt, but she wore it as if it were the most magnificent evening gown. She was only slightly over five feet tall, and though she was thin, she was shapely, her hips flaring out alluringly. She truly was a stunning little creature. His cock agreed. *No, down boy...*

He studied her as she made her way slowly forward. Though she moved with a subtle, sensual grace, her body was shot through with tension. *Nervous about being here with me? Or just hating me so much that she's on edge?* Now that it was dry, he noted that her hair was a lighter shade of brown than he'd originally thought, with streaks of honey blonde woven within. The strands fell in a glossy waterfall of waves past her shoulders. A few wayward strands swept across her chest, drawing his eyes down, past the small, oval medallion around her neck, to the V of her shirt. They riveted to the tiny strip of black lace that he could see when she shifted slightly, to the gentle curve of her plump breast...*Snap out of it*!

He forced his gaze back up, annoyed that he had a semi just from seeing her for two damned seconds. What was going on with him? She was here so that he could determine that she wasn't, in fact, trying to kill him (or working for someone who wished to), and then to work to earn her keep, as they'd agreed. She was not here so that he could eye fuck her. Eye fucking led to actual fucking, which could lead to awkwardness around the castle when he wanted nothing more afterwards if she wasn't clear on the rules. *Would love something more with* somebody *though...*

His eyes met hers and the hatred wasn't burning there quite as brightly as it had been before. No, something *else* was burning there for a moment, blazing hot enough to make him shift in his seat. She quickly shook herself and the cold animosity settled back into place, like water dousing a campfire.

"Good morning, Beck," he said in a bored tone, refusing to acknowledge that he enjoyed how her name rolled off of his tongue.

"Morning," she said in a stiff, slightly raspy voice. He wasn't sure if it was always this way or if was from the near-drowning, but he... liked it. He nodded toward the seat to his right. She sauntered forward and sat in the chair to his left instead. His lips twitched. *Is she going to fight me every step of the way?* He thought he might enjoy it, actually. He'd wanted different hadn't he?

She inhaled and her pupils dilated, her body somehow going languid and rigid at once. Did his scent affect her? She closed her eyes and shook her head slowly—not at him, but as if she were having a silent conversation with herself. When she opened them again, the hard edge was back once more. She seemed to be fighting some strange, internal battle he couldn't begin to understand. *Confusing woman.*

"I have questions," he said, diving in without preamble. He was the God of the Sea, the ruler of this plane. He would demand answers and she would give them. Simple as that.

She seemed to steel herself before answering, "I'm sure you do and I'll answer them to the best of my ability, but...I need a favor first."

He arched a brow. "We're kind of in the middle of the last favor you asked for if I do recall..." he said as he motioned to her and then the room around them, silently saying *you're here aren't you?*

She ground her teeth. "Yes, I'm well aware, but you can add this favor to my tab. Call in whatever payment you'd like—within reason," she added quickly. He studied her and she tried and failed not to squirm under his gaze. He liked that.

"A boon then. You'll owe me whatever I ask—within reason— whenever I ask of it. What is this favor?"

"I need to know if anyone from the boat I was on survived. They were my friends...or well, the closest thing I had to friends anyway," she added quietly. "I just need to know." After a long moment she added a soft, "please." Her eyes softened, that hard glint melting the *tiniest* bit.

Fuck. Why did her simple plea hit him right in the chest? Maybe the fact that even without knowing a thing about her, he knew without a doubt that she was strong, yet great vulnerability lurked beneath that. He didn't think most people would ever know it was there, would never even think to look for it, but he could see it. He wanted to do this for her, and since he was a god and could do whatever the hell he wanted...

"Wait here," he said, forcing himself to sound exasperated, and phased to the spot where he'd found her the day before. He closed his eyes and reached out around him, speaking to the water, letting it speak to him. Water held memories. *Show me,* he commanded. Before him, like a movie screen with slightly fuzzy reception, he saw himself appear before an unconscious Beck being pulled lower by the rope wrapped around her ankle. "Already know this part..." He began searching other memories, asking the water what he needed to know. Soon the scene transformed to a boat floating along the surface...or what was left of a boat.

He phased there and saw smoke rising from the wreckage. The scent of charred wood and...flesh flooded his senses. He made his way onto the vessel and immediately saw a body on the deck, a gaping hole in his chest and his body badly burned on one side. Was this the man she'd worried for? The Oscar that the demon had spoken about? He felt a pang in his chest, knowing that this would upset the girl. *Odd.*

Si continued his search through the small ship, looking for any survivors. He found none, just more bodies. He sighed and left, commanding the water to guide the vessel home again. It would be found soon and the bodies—her friends—could be laid to rest properly. He phased back to the dining room and her eyes lit up with hope when he appeared. He didn't want to be the one to cause it to fade, but he wouldn't lie to her. The light dimmed as she read his face and realization struck. Her shoulders slumped, curling inward. Tears welled but didn't spill. She clenched her teeth and her fists.

"I'm sorry," he said, sincerely.

She sniffed hard once and seemed to force the tears away. She said in a deadened voice, "It's my fault. Those...demons killed them coming after me."

"And why were they coming after you?" he asked, as gently as he could. He hated that she was upset, but he needed answers. Alarm bells were ringing in his head. Demons after a seemingly mortal but beyond beautiful girl who just *happened* to call out to a god she clearly hated for rescue, who then maneuvered herself into his home? When it was widely known that Si typically thought with his dick first and his brain second? It screamed "trap!" like that strange-looking creature in that space movie Emmie had forced him to watch. He told himself to calm and not jump to any conclusions yet. *Give her the benefit of the doubt here.*

She took a deep breath and let it out slowly. "I told you, I don't know." He gave her a look that was half skeptical, half annoyed and she continued hastily. "Seriously, I don't. They've been following me for weeks...well, longer actually." She frowned, as if just remembering something. "I *felt* like someone was watching me months ago, but I never felt threatened by it and they never showed themselves. Then the feeling disappeared completely until a couple of weeks ago. It came back but this time it felt...dangerous, and then I started being followed. I managed to lose my tails every time, but then the night before the trip, someone had been inside my house. I...I was going to use the trip to figure out what to do about it and then that *thing* appeared on the boat. Oscar..." She swallowed hard as tears pooled once more.

Was Oscar *more* than a friend? Why in the hell did that thought bother him? Make him...jealous? No, absolutely not. Poseidon didn't *do* jealousy. With his lifestyle, it was pointless and would hardly be fair for *him* to become jealous of someone when everyone that entered his bed…or shower…or swing…knew what to expect and that jealousy wasn't something that would enter into the equation before, during, or after. Not to mention—he was the God of the Sea. He simply would not be jealous of some dead mortal. *Rest his soul*. Si forced the ridiculous feeling away.

"He saved my life," she finished, voice thick with emotion and becoming even raspier, but still, the tears didn't fall. *Tough female*.

"I am sorry about your friend," he said, putting a weird emphasis on the word *friend*. He shifted his thoughts to his next question. "What did the demon mean when he said you had "some power"? You said you weren't a mortal, so what are you exactly?"

She began toying with the medallion around her neck, rubbing it between her thumb and forefinger. The design was worn away almost completely, so it was obviously something she did often.

"I…don't see how that's any of your business." She jutted her chin stubbornly. He didn't deign to respond to such nonsense. Of course it was his business. Not only was he a *god*, so pretty much anything and everything was his business if he desired it to be, but she was a guest in his home. He leaned back and crossed his arms over his chest, staring her down. She got the message and for a moment, her eyes darkened in irritation, the ice blue shifting to that deep cobalt again. Her irritation didn't annoy him this time. No, he was…amused. *This is kind of fun*. Gods, was he that desperate for something different that going toe-to-toe with a maybe-not-mortal was this entertaining for him? *Pathetic, party of one…*

"What difference could it possibly make to you what I am? I'm holding up my end of the bargain." Her irritation was growing, and his amusement grew with it. He stretched his arms over his head, bringing his palms to rest against the back of his neck. He tilted his chair back to balance on two legs as he propped his feet up on the table. The picture of ease. Her annoyance skyrocketed and he smirked.

"My house. My rules," he said simply with a shrug. Her eyes narrowed, and he knew that she would have gladly castrated him in that moment. The thought made his smirk grow. Why did he enjoy pressing her buttons so much? *Something new after centuries of monotony.*

She stood quickly, her chair scraping across the stone floor. She slammed her palms down on the table.

"Fine, you want to know what I am?" She leaned forward, fire in her eyes. "I am your fucking *niece.*"

SEVEN

Record scratch.

WHAT?

The front legs of Poseidon's chair slammed down as he shifted forward in his seat, eyes narrowed and brows drawn.

"Come again?" he said, unsure he'd heard her properly. She straightened and threw her shoulders back.

"I am the daughter of Zeus," she declared with absolute conviction. "Whether or not he wants to admit it," she added in a low grumble. Zeus' daughter? Is that why Si felt the tiniest flicker of connection with her? They were *family*? Tiny as it was, that flicker of connection, of interest beyond the carnal was the most he'd had in almost a thousand years. *How pathetic am I? Wait a second...*

Poseidon frowned. Despite his reputation, Zeus was not the bastard that he'd been made out to be in the mortal stories. Part of that *may* have been Poseidon's fault. He *might* have made sure that Hermes spread the rumor that Zeus and Hera had wed one night when Zeus was blackout drunk. Allegedly.

Ok, he did it, one thousand percent, but in his defense, it was Hades' idea to begin with and they'd only meant it as a joke to freak

Zeus out. You know, coming to the next morning all *oh gods, what have I done?* and all of them laughing hysterically as he had a panic attack. They never imagined it would paint him as an adulterous douchebag for all of eternity when he repeatedly "cheated" on his "wife." He and Hera had never been married, though they did date off and on for a few centuries, and Zeus never cheated. *So...My bad, bro.*

So, though the mortal version of Zeus may have gladly abandoned one of his children and not thought twice about it, the *real* Zeus would never do such a thing. He had many children and was a good father to all of them. He had monthly fishing dates with Hercules for fuck's sake. If this girl really was his daughter, Zeus must not have any idea that she exists. *That's only if she's actually his.*

Si shifted his gaze to her neck. He rose and slowly moved around the edge of the table to where she stood, still fuming. He reached out towards her and she drew back, actually smacking his hand out of the way. *Well, that's a first.* Normally females—and males, for that matter—were begging him to touch them, practically forcing his hands upon them.

"What the hell are you doing?" she snapped.

He held his palms up in surrender. "I'm checking something. May I?" She eyed him warily, but slowly nodded. He reached out again and pulled her silken hair away from her neck. She inhaled quietly but remained still as a statue. His eyes roamed over the skin there, skin that looked as soft and supple as cream...*Snap out of it! She might be your...*

An unexpected surge of relief rushed through him when he didn't find what he was looking for. *Thank all the fucking gods.* He shifted his gaze back to hers.

"No, you aren't."

"Aren't...what?" she asked, slightly breathless and looking a bit dazed.

"Aren't Zeus' daughter." The dazed look evaporated in an instant, indignation taking its place.

"Yes, I am damn it!" She actually stomped her foot, and it was just about the cutest thing he'd ever seen. "Just because he…abandoned my mother and chose to pretend that I didn't exist doesn't make me any less of his daughter."

"I don't know who your mother is, but I can tell you without a doubt that your father is *not* Zeus." Her lips thinned and he stopped her before she could go into another tirade. "Look, all of Zeus' children have a small birthmark in the shape of a lightning bolt just there." He pointed to the spot on her neck, just below her ear. "Every single one of them. Zeus' own ego-stroking calling card so to speak."

A flurry of emotions crossed her face: disbelief, anger, hurt, confusion, then more hurt. As much as the fact that they were *not* related floored him, he didn't like that she seemed upset by this news.

"I'm sorry if this upsets you, but isn't it better to know the truth?"

Was it better to know the truth? Beck wasn't sure. The sick feeling churning in her stomach said no the hell it wasn't. She grappled for something to hold on to as her thoughts became a swirling vortex of *what the fuck.* Finally, she grasped onto something: why should she even trust that he was telling her the truth? *The gods are deceiving.*

"How do I know that you're not lying?" He rolled his eyes but held up a finger, asking for a minute. She crossed her arms, clutching onto that hatred and annoyance, clinging to the idea that Poseidon was just a lying sack of shit like all the others. *But why?* Why *would he lie about this?…*

A few moments later, a man appeared in the middle of the room.

"You rang?" the newcomer asked with a smirk. He was gorgeous. Drop dead gorgeous, in fact. Golden curls framed an angelic face that would make you do devilish things. His eyes were a strange mix of purple and blue and though he was shorter than Poseidon, he was just as muscular. He wore leather pants and no shirt, his chiseled chest and abs glistening with sweat. *Wow. Wowwowwow.* Poseidon caught her staring and clenched his jaw.

"Couldn't have put a shirt on first?" Poseidon asked sarcastically.

"You said ASAP. I came ASAP." He shifted his gaze to Beck. "Don't worry, that is the first time I've *ever* said those words." He winked and she didn't know what to do. She wanted to laugh and also fan herself. Instead, her lips parted and she stared a bit dumbfounded, her anger forgotten for the moment.

"Hermes," Poseidon growled.

"Oh, right. What's up, Si?" *Si?* Was that what his friends called him?

"Please explain to our guest the markings on Zeus' children." Turning to Beck he added. "This is Hermes. He's the messenger of the Gods, but also the archivist of all knowledge and the one responsible for providing mortals with versions of our history for their legends. It's why many of the stories are only half truths. Hermes likes to take liberties with some tales."

Hermes smiled and bowed, tossing wayward curls off of his brow as he straightened. "I do so like my liberties. It makes things so much more *fun*. You'd be surprised how utterly boring some of us are," he added with an exaggerated roll of his eyes. Was he flirting with her? And did she...like it? *No, no, no...Maybe?*

"But, back to the topic at hand: Zeus' children all bare a mark on their neck, just below their ear." He reached forward as he said in a sultry voice, "Just here..." She inhaled sharply but didn't flinch away. She felt her cheeks heat but just before he made contact with the same spot Poseidon had inspected earlier, the God of the Sea growled.

"Knock it off, Hermes." A pulse of power shot through the space and she blinked rapidly, pulling herself from the strange haze she'd been in. She cleared her throat quietly and Hermes smirked, giving her another wink. He did step away from her though, arching a questioning brow at Si who merely scowled in response.

"Hmm," the messenger god said, amused. "Anyway, the marks are in the shape of a lightning bolt, which is a bit on the nose if you ask me," he said with another dramatic eye roll, "but he's the King of the Gods, so who am I to judge, right?"

"And all of his children have this mark? There isn't an instance where one wouldn't?" she asked.

"Yes, every single child. It's impossible for any offspring of his to *not* bear the mark."

Her shoulders sagged slightly. She...believed him. What reason would he have to lie about this? But if that was the case, then that would mean that her *mother* had lied to her for her *entire life*. Why would she do such a thing?? All the rants she'd been forced to listen to, her mother going on and on about how she should be the queen and that Zeus would regret what he'd lost and blah blah blah. She'd heard it a thousand times over the years. Her mother had even made their last name *McQueen* as a not-so-subtle nod to the title she believed she should hold for crying out loud. Beck clenched her fists, her nails biting into the skin of her palms.

"Uhh, this is apparently not the news you wished to hear?" Hermes glanced between her and Poseidon. She couldn't form words just yet so she simply gave him a hard shake of her head. "Ah, well... I'll just go then, shall I? Si, you can fill me in later." With that Hermes disappeared and she continued with her confused fuming.

She really shouldn't be surprised that her mother had lied. With everything else she'd done to Beck over the years, this shouldn't shock her at all, but damn it, it did *hurt*. Her mom would never win any Mother of the Year Awards, but lying to her daughter about something so important? She wouldn't have thought her mother capable of that.

Wait a minute. Maybe she had *thought* Zeus was the father? Maybe her mom had been sowing oats with multiple gods, so paternity might be up in the air. For whatever reason, she'd locked on Zeus being the father in her mind. Yes, that makes perfect sense! So, she hadn't *actually* lied to Beck all these years, she just hadn't known the one hundred percent truth, and needed a full-on *Maury* moment to clarify. Beck wasn't ready to believe that her mother had deceived her repeatedly on purpose...though her mother's own words echoed in her mind now: *the gods are deceiving.*

She squeezed her eyes shut for a moment. She was going to roll with the idea that her mother had just been mistaken. Either way, Zeus had still banished her and taken away her immortality because he *assumed* he'd knocked her up. So, the fact that Beck wasn't actually his didn't absolve him from his douche-baggery. *Yes, the gods still suck.* Beck felt steadier with that knowledge back in place. She wasn't quite sure what would happen if it were proven wrong. She couldn't even think of it.

Poseidon's voice broke through the storm of thoughts in her mind.

"Who is your mother? Why were you living in the Mortal Plane to begin with?" She didn't want to tell him who her mother was. For all she knew, there was a guilty-by-association rule among the gods, and if he found out that Beck's mother had been banished, maybe he'd be required to kick *her* to the curb too, right into the hands of the waiting demons. So, she ignored the first part of his question and focused on the second.

"My mother...fled to the Mortal Plane when she became pregnant with me. She *thought* Zeus was my father and that he'd be angered by the pregnancy, so she hid me away." It was sort of, kind of close to the truth. Truth-adjacent maybe. She *had* fled to the Mortal Plane—upon threat of death if she didn't leave. And she *had* thought Zeus was Beck's father, whether or not truthfully, Beck didn't know yet. And she *had* hidden Beck away—not from Zeus exactly, but from everything having to do with the godly world. *See. Truth-adjacent.*

Poseidon studied her, those golden amber eyes seeming to stare to the core of her. Whatever he saw there seemed to convince him of something, though she didn't know what. He nodded to himself and she realized how close they were standing to one another. He'd evidently moved closer after Hermes left while she'd been lost in her thoughts. Her mind went back to that moment when he'd gently moved her hair aside. Her entire body had reacted to his nearness, goosebumps and shivers erupting over every square inch. She'd had to force herself to remain still and not lean into his touch. And that scent again. *My. Gods.* It was intoxicating. Salty air and sunshine mixed together, though she couldn't begin to explain what sunshine even smelled like.

What the hell is wrong with me? Beck had never had such strong reactions to a man before. It had to just be because he was a god. Surely that came with god-level mojo, right? But her physical attraction to him only fueled her anger. Of course he would have some kind of mystical ability to force her to want him!

Against her will, her eyes roamed over him again. Desire rose within her, startling her in its intensity. Again, she cursed herself and him for this strange attraction. Part of it had to just be the fact that she was…pent up, to put it mildly. Beck had given up on dating or even "hooking up" with anyone in the Mortal Plane years ago and hadn't gotten any action that didn't come from her trusty rabbit in just as long. She'd been too freaked out about her stalkers over the past few weeks to have any dates with herself, so her libido was on overdrive. As Poseidon's eyes dipped to her lips, it hit her just how badly she needed a little release. *Oh gods, he can't look at my lips like that…*She squeezed her thighs together and swallowed hard.

"I…I should get back to work," she said, embarrassed by how husky her voice had gotten. She cleared her throat. *You hate him, you hate him, you hate him.*

"We are done…for now," he said, dark promises lacing the words. No. That was her imagination. She just needed to get away from him and his drugging scent. She needed air and time to think through this whole *Zeus isn't actually my father* thing. She hastened from the room, refusing to look back over her shoulder as she left, though she could swear she felt his eyes on her, burning her skin like a brand.

EIGHT

Poseidon tried and failed to stay away from Beck over the next two weeks. He watched her from a distance, trying to learn more about her. So far, he'd determined that she worked harder than anyone else in the entire castle except for Nerina, she had an addiction to ambrosian brew, and she never smiled. Never. He hadn't seen it a single time. The closest he'd seen was a small curl of her lips and even that had only happened a few times at best. A ridiculous need to be the one to pull a true smile from her dogged him constantly. It was just a new challenge, that was all. A game to play where he could be the victor. Nothing more.

At times he thought she was thawing from her icy hatred of him and all the gods. She would light up at some new discovery, or close her eyes in what appeared to be contentment, but then she would shake herself and the armor would be back in place, that burning anger radiating from her in waves. He still didn't know what power she possessed, but he had surmised that she was indeed a demigoddess of some sort. Her father may not be Zeus, but he was fairly positive that her mother was, in fact, a deity. He assumed a minor one, or perhaps she herself was a demigoddess. Now to just figure out who.

If she'd seemed to think Zeus was the father of her unborn child, then Zeus had to have been boning her at some point.

That would be quite a list to wade through, almost as long as his own, but Poseidon had faith that they could figure it out. All he had to do was leave his plane and go check. And he would. Soon. He had a lot to deal with and he was busy, alright? It had nothing to do with the strange urge to get closer to the girl and the odd feeling he got when he thought about being away from the plane without her. Definitely not. Although, he had to admit that he *did* dare to let himself hope: if the tiny bit of connection he'd felt towards her hadn't been because of a familial bond, it had to be something else. So, that meant he was feeling the beginnings of *something* for the first time in centuries upon centuries. Not love, or even longing of course, but some emotion beyond lust. It wasn't much, but it was something! *Maybe I'm not completely broken after all.*

"How is our newest guest acclimating?" Poseidon asked Nerina one afternoon as they went through the never-ending list of requests and complaints from the various realms and residents within his kingdom. She quirked her blue brow at him, telling him that she knew damn well that he'd been spying on the girl. It wasn't spying. It was research. *Reconnaissance, if you will.* Big difference! He was still wary of her and still needed to be sure she hadn't been sent there for some nefarious purpose. He was being a good king and smart (for once in his life). That was all.

Choosing to let him let him keep up his ruse, Nerina smiled and answered.

"She is fantastic, truth be told. A little cold with others perhaps, and hyper focused when given a task to complete, but she is by far the best staff member you've ever had."

"Present company excluded, of course," he said with a grin.

"Of course." She gave him a wink and then a studying look. "Why is she here?"

Why *was* she here? Sure, she had needed help and he liked to play hero sometimes, but he still hadn't completely figured out why he'd answered her call in the first place or agreed to let her take refuge in his home. He could have saved her from the water and deposited her on the shore for some mortal to assist her without ever even showing himself. He had no real answers, so he gave Nerina a version of the truth.

"She was in trouble and we made a bargain for her safety within my kingdom."

Nerina *hmm*-ed, looking thoughtful. "But she seems to..." She pursed her lips. "Well, it appears that she..." She frowned, obviously trying to find the right words and coming up short.

"Hates all of the gods with a fiery passion that rivals the suns of the Inferno Realm?"

"Yes, that!"

"I haven't gotten to the bottom of it yet, but I plan to."

She shrugged. Nerina wasn't one to be bothered by much.

"Well, don't run her off. She's actually warming up to me a bit and I like her. Plus, she's amazingly helpful." She stared out over the table. "You know, she can do much more than she's doing now. She's smart. Her mind is exceptionally sharp and she's resourceful, always coming up with a way to fix a situation. She may not be the most "people person" of people, but she would be a great aid to you in things like this." She gestured to the mess. Si rolled that around in his mind. He knew she spoke true. Beck *was* smart, a resolute determination emanating from her at all times, and could do far more than simple cooking and cleaning.

And if she took on duties like this, she would need to spend a far greater amount of time with him. A thrill shot through his body at the idea. He thought about her accompanying him to the realms, walking, talking, perhaps even laughing? Discussing the needs of the kingdom over dinner or by the crackling fire. The images in his mind quickly transformed into doing *other* things in front of the fire and he nearly moaned. *Nope. Bad idea.*

"I'll take that under advisement," he hedged. Nerina smirked as if she could track the direction of his thoughts. She probably could. She knew him almost as well as his brothers did.

He let out an annoyed sigh. He couldn't concentrate anymore. The words on the pages were blurring into nonsense. He was strung tight, needing a release of this energy. Except...ever since Beck had arrived, he never relaxed, no matter how many *releases* of any kind he'd had. Maybe she was part enchantress after all and she'd cursed him to be in a constant state of wanting. But not just wanting. Wanting *her*, specifically. He'd entertained bedmates all week and his thoughts repeatedly flitted back to the delicate column of her throat, the way her pulse had jumped when he'd shifted her hair to check for Zeus' mark; the icy blue of her eyes and the way they seemed to melt for him at times; the way her ass looked in the jeans she favored wearing.

He scrubbed a hand down his face, irritation simmering. He shoved his chair backwards and rose.

"I'm going to train."

"As you wish," she said with an incline of her head and a smile playing on her lips.

He called to Dante and the rest of the Elite, asking them to meet him in the courtyard. They were Zeus' personal guard and the fiercest warriors in existence. Meaning they were some of the few beings other than his brothers who could give him a real training session. He was in the mood to fight. He needed to burn off some of this pent-up energy and fast. He phased to the courtyard, summoning his trident, and began pacing as he waited. Thankfully, the silver-winged soldiers arrived within a few minutes, grinning.

"In the mood for a good ass-kicking today, Poseidon?"

Si yanked his shirt over his head and tossed it in the sand.

"Bring it on, Feathers."

Dante grinned at the nickname and discarded his own shirt. The others followed suit, their wings flaring behind them. They were, in fact, feathered, but the feathers could turn solid and sharp as razors at will. Delicate one second, deadly the next. Si strode to the middle of the space and bent his head to one side, then the other, neck muscles stretching. He twirled his trident effortlessly and smiled at the group surrounding him.

"Begin."

BECK WAS MAKING HER ROUNDS, delivering clean towels to the many bathrooms, when she heard a commotion coming from somewhere nearby. Cheers and jeers and the clash of metal. A fight? Her curiosity forced her towards the sounds. She entered a long, open-air corridor that looked out over a large courtyard. Stone railings and arches surrounded the space, beautifully crafted with silvery ivy-like vines and some kind of blue-green flowers she'd never seen before covering the surfaces, lazily climbing up the columns. She realized that there were three other similar corridors, forming a rectangle above the courtyard. She made her way to the railing and nearly gasped.

Poseidon was below, fighting a hulking warrior with huge silvery wings while several other equally hulking warriors with equally huge silvery wings surrounded them. The angel-man swung a golden sword and Poseidon wielded his trident. Her heart leapt, worried for his safety for a moment before she realized that this wasn't some kind of attack, it was a play fight. Well, not so much *play* as they were all covered in blood and dirt, but they weren't actually trying to kill each other. She hoped. *Why do I hope?*

The largest of the angel-men smiled at Poseidon while wiping blood from his lip. Despite the gory sight, he was flawless, glorious even. Sculpted muscle, perfect, proud features, sun-kissed golden skin and sandy-blonde hair. Was every being in this place practically perfect? It sure as hell seemed so.

"You are in a mood today," the angel-man said, tossing his sword from hand to hand easily, a mocking smirk forming.

"Scared, Dante?" Poseidon responded with an arch of his dark brow. They attacked each other at the same time and their speed was utterly amazing. Also amazing? Poseidon. He was shirtless and dear gods the sight was enough to make her knees tremble. His back was to her, but that was enough.

His shoulders were broad and sculpted, the muscles in his lower back tapering to a small 'V' shape at the base of his spine. His brown skin was damp with sweat, the drops sparkling in the sun. The muscles in his arms bulged and flexed as he moved and she couldn't stop staring. *Perfect.* Every inch of him was perfect. He was fluid as he spun and lunged, moving as gracefully as the water that surrounded the castle. He was also brutal with his attacks, skilled beyond comprehension.

Beautiful.

Deadly.

Mine.

Beck scowled at herself, pissed that she'd let that stupid whisper become louder in her mind. She didn't understand why it kept insisting that he...belonged to her. Or she belonged to him. Or whatever! *No. No, this isn't real. It's just...*Ah, yes. Her dry spell! That had to be the culprit, making her have these ridiculous feelings. She'd been thinking of him almost non-stop, forgetting that she despised him and feeling a nearly irresistible urge to be near him. She often wandered towards his chambers before catching herself and turning tail the other way. It had to be the dry spell. It just...*had* to be. Beck refused to believe any alternative.

You hate him! she reminded herself. *Hate them all!* But...did she, really? She'd been wavering in her conviction the past few days. She'd heard the others in the castle speaking of him and, to her irritation—*pleasure?*—it was all good. Great even. He was a fair and just ruler who cared about his people, brutal to those who threatened his kingdom or those within it. The creatures under his command revered him as a leader, obeying out of love and adoration, not mere duty or compulsion. He was kind and funny and loved his brothers fiercely.

She'd heard talk of the other gods as well and the overall take-away: they were mostly pretty great. None of it jived with the picture her mother had painted and forced her to stare at every day of her life. Beck couldn't understand. Or, maybe she could, but she didn't *want* to. If she let herself accept what was in front of her, it proved that her mother had lied to her about nearly everything. But why? What did she have to gain by Beck hating the gods? Neither one of them had any reason to believe she'd ever actually meet them, so what did it matter what Beck thought? Had her mother just been so angry at Zeus that she decided that every god was damned in her eyes as well? Was her mother just plain delusional? Beck's head throbbed every time she began down this road.

Thankfully, a deep, sensual laugh drew her from her thoughts. Her gaze landed back on Poseidon. Again, she studied every inch without meaning to. The more she studied, the more she *craved*. She curled her fingers tightly against the towels in her arms. She wanted to sink them into his shoulders and pull him to her, run them through his shorn hair, scratch them down the smooth skin of his back...

"Magnificent, isn't he?" Nerina whispered at her ear.

Beck yelped and Poseidon stiffened. He turned, eyes immediately locking with her own. His lips curled into the most devastating smile, a mix of cocky and sexy and *dear gods* she couldn't breathe. Her eyes drifted downward, and she was done for. Blood and sweat trickled over the hardened planes of his body, the muscled chest and six-pack abs. *Eight pack? Twelve? The whole damn case?* The sight made her pulse race.

He had a tattoo on his chest, just to the right of his heart. Circular with waves, flames, and lightning bolts? She couldn't force herself to study it long enough to pick up on all of the details. Her eyes were desperate to take in more of him, all of him. They trailed lower still, zeroing in on the indentions beside his hips, just above his low-hung leather pants. A mortal she'd worked with at a small cafe had called them "Make Girls Stupid Buttons." Oh yes. Those buttons wiped out every last brain cell in Beck's head, leaving her as nothing but a lust-fueled shell who could think of nothing but running her tongue over those indentions. She was like those cartoon dogs with their mouths gaping and their eyes turning to giant throbbing hearts, except Beck's would be giant throbbing...

She swallowed hard. She tried and failed to shepherd her waylaid thoughts. Beck tried to remember her hatred but her mind wouldn't obey. Hatred? What hatred? She needed and oh boy she needed *now*. She'd never been as attracted to anyone as she was to Poseidon. Not even close. Her breaths became shallow as she pulled her gaze back to his. That smile wasn't melting her panties, it was *disintegrating* them, erasing them from existence. They didn't stand a chance. Her nipples hardened, aching for his hands, his mouth. Heat pooled in her belly and lower. His chest rose as he inhaled and he went rigid. His eyes flickered, near black with whiskey striations replacing the golden amber. Beck's lips parted on a soft gasp.

They stayed locked in the weird trance until one of those winged men tackled him to the ground. Poseidon let out a muffled "oomph" and the angel-man—Dante—grinned triumphantly as he pinned Poseidon's shoulders to the ground with his knees, the tip of his golden sword poised just below Poseidon's chin.

"Rule Number One: No distractions." Dante looked to Beck and winked. Poseidon followed his gaze and she allowed herself one more heartbeat to stare at him. *Just one more. Maybe two. Ok, that's enough.* She shook herself, coming back to reality. *What in the hell?* She felt her cheeks flush, and she hustled away from the corridor without a backwards glance.

Beck needed to breathe. She needed to think. She needed to be as far from Poseidon and his stupid intoxicating scent that she could somehow smell from above the courtyard, even over the blood and sweat and dirt, away from his stupid perfectly-sculpted body that shouldn't be allowed to exist, away from his sexy grin that made her want to smile in return. She didn't know how to deal with any of this.

Eventually, Beck stopped fleeing, and leaned heavily against a wall in an empty corridor. She banged her head several times against the stone, unbelieving that she'd just reacted that way. Nerina caught up to her soon enough and gave her a kind—and knowing—smile.

"I didn't mean to startle you."

"It's fine. I shouldn't have been..." Staring at Poseidon like she wanted to ravage him right there in front of everyone? Imagining his touch, his lips, his tongue on every inch of her body? Thinking that she would throw her whole life away if it meant getting to spend one single night with him? She shook herself, grinding her teeth. "Slacking off from work," she finished lamely.

Nerina waved her off. "You've been working harder than anyone else here. You deserve a break. Care to accompany me to the beach?" Beck blinked, surprised by the invitation. She chewed her lip, unused to being invited to hang with people other than the team. A pang hit her chest hard enough to make her breath catch. She blinked the sudden tears away.

"I...yes, I would like that."

IT WAS the most beautiful beach Beck had ever seen. It put every tropical paradise she'd ever seen a picture of on the Mortal Plane to complete shame. The water was a light turquoise, the sand a mix of silver and white and so soft she wanted to dig her toes in and never leave. It was warm, but not too hot, and a soft breeze blew in off of the waves. Creatures unlike anything Beck had ever seen leapt within the waves, similar to dolphins but with small wings of every color of the rainbow, and new colors she had no names for, upon their backs.

Palm-like trees dotted the shoreline, their fronds sparkling silver and when the wind rustled them, it sounded like tinkling bells. Bright purple and yellow flowers grew from vines wrapped around their trunks and they smelled like sheer bliss, a spicy-sweet scent that reminded her of those fruity rum concoctions everyone loved to drink while they lounged on mortal beaches. She hummed Jimmy Buffett's *Boat Drinks* quietly as she settled onto her towel.

Nerina lounged beside her—topless. Beck had been a little taken aback at first by all the chesticles on display. Ok, a lot taken aback. She wasn't a prude or anything, but, well, she wasn't used to hanging around with topless women either. It didn't *bother* her, but she couldn't stop herself from blushing a bit...and staring. Often. Nerina's boobs had her own beat by at least two cup sizes, and though full, they were so...*perky*. They were like those perfect racks you saw in high-end mortal adult films. Not that she'd watched those or anything...Ok, maybe once or twice. Bottom line was that Nerina's body was what the mortal men at the bar had called "bangin'." She thankfully did wear small bikini bottoms, the cerulean matching her hair perfectly.

When the sunlight caught Nerina's skin, Beck realized it had a faint iridescent sheen to it, almost like scales. Curiosity finally got the better of her.

"Are you a mermaid?" she blurted.

Nerina laughed. "No, though their kind and mine are distant cousins so to speak. There are plenty of mermaids in this plane though. I'll introduce you to some." Beck's brows rose in astonishment. "I'm a siren." *Holy shit.*

Mermaids. Sirens. Winged warriors. Gods.

Everything was so new and exciting, but each new discovery also left her frustrated. These were all things she *should* have known about and experienced her entire life. If not for the gods. If not for her mother. If not for fate deciding to dick her over big time. She ground her teeth but tried not to let her mood plumet. She was enjoying this hang-out with Nerina more than she cared to admit. It was nice. *Beyond* nice. Beck finally felt...normal for the first time in her life. Just a normal girl hanging out with a friend on the beach. She wanted to soak up every second of this.

"My turn: what are you?"

"I'm..." What was she? *Who* was she? She'd never fit in anywhere before and that hadn't changed. In fact, she was even farther out of any box now that she didn't even know who her father really was. Was he even a god? Maybe another kind of immortal? The mailman?

So, yes, what a question: who the hell was Beck McQueen? She was a girl who had a barely-there mother who tolerated her on good days and despised her on bad ones; a girl who had scraped and fought every day of her life just to survive; a girl who felt so alone sometimes that it nearly crushed her; a girl who had kept herself closed off from everyone around her for her entire life.

A girl who had no fucking clue who she was.

Beck let out a long sigh. "I don't really know anymore."

"It's ok to not know yourself. It will come in time and then it might change again," Nerina said, understanding the true meaning of Beck's words. Beck decided then and there that even if all the gods did turn out to be vile assholes, she liked Nerina very much.

They laid in peaceful silence for a while, soaking up the sun that mystically rested in the sky *within* the dome. Beck had always loved the beach and the one thing her mother had done right in their banishment was her choice of location. Beck had spent most nights sitting in the sand near the pier by their house, letting the lull of the waves calm her and distract her from, well, just about everything. Granted, she'd spent a lot of her time staring at the waves cursing the God of the Sea and everyone else from her mother's world. Maybe she...shouldn't have? *Ugh.* She knew nothing anymore. *I have gone full Jon Snow.*

She was *trying* to let go of some of her anger and ingrained hatred, trying to have a somewhat open mind about everything because she was convinced her mother had exaggerated the extent of the gods' crimes, but every time she felt herself releasing a bit of it, she'd immediately grab it again, holding to it in a suffocating grip. It was like a safety harness and she was hanging on the edge of a cliff. Could she ever let it go and just free fall into the unknown? Could she possibly believe what her gut was admittedly telling her? That the gods were not what her mother had made them out to be. Not only that, but that Poseidon was...meant to be in her life? She felt ridiculous even letting the thought form.

Beck kept shifting in her frustration, her thoughts refusing to calm. She put both arms at her sides, only to shift one behind her head a moment later. She bent one knee up, then dropped it again, then flopped to her stomach and back again.

"Ok, enough lying around," Nerina decreed, clearly seeing that Beck was incapable of being still and probably tired of hearing her move every two seconds. Nerina stood and looked around, clearly trying to find something to distract Beck with. "Come, I'll show you the sapphire caves."

Beck perked up at that, her frustration nearly forgotten. Sapphire caves? *Yes please.* Beck smiled and rose, brushing sand from her hands and legs. She bent at the waist to toss her hair up into a messy bun and yelped when blue lighting flashed through the cloudless sky, striking directly into the sea. Nerina tilted her head, a curious expression on her face. She shifted her gaze over Beck's shoulder, towards the castle.

"So very interesting..." Nerina muttered, a smirk lifting her lips, her tiny fangs glinting in the sun.

Beck turned, following Nerina's gaze and sucked in a breath. Poseidon stood on the wide balcony jutting from the top of the largest tower of the castle, overlooking the beach. He was still shirtless and still bloody and dirty from the fight, and he was gripping the railing so hard that the stone cracked beneath his fingers.

"Are there usually storms within the dome? Storms without, um, clouds or rain?" Beck asked without looking away from the god. His eyes were locked on her and though he was way up on the balcony, she could see that they were burning with something she dared not let herself name. Could he possibly want her as much as she wanted him? No, there was no way. He was basically a sex god, and she was... well, *her.* Even so, he continued to stare with that look, the one that seemed to say *I want you naked and writhing beneath me this instant.* Her stomach fluttered and she couldn't pull her gaze away.

"Only when our great king is...in a mood," Nerina said a bit cryptically. Oh. Had she misread that look? Was he angry with her? Mad that she was out here relaxing instead of working? His eyes pulled away from hers, slowly trailing down her body. She could almost feel it, like a feathery soft caress against her skin, as they roamed over her chest and stomach, down to her hips and legs before slowly working their way back up again. His tongue traced his bottom lip, and she shivered, goosebumps erupting across her skin and her nipples hardening.

Nope, he definitely wasn't angry. He was something else entirely. Something that made her melt, something that made her forget everything else in the world except the way he was looking at her. Something that was dangerous on so many levels.

Her lips parted, her chest rising and falling quickly. His gaze continued to burn into hers before he suddenly broke off, surprise lighting his features as he turned to look over his shoulder. A gorgeous woman approached and joined him near the railing, wearing a gown that seemed to be made of clouds, thin wisps of soft white covering her *wowza* curves. All that heat that had been building within Beck turned to ice in an instant. Beck balled her hands into fists as something ugly and clawed tore through her chest. She wasn't jealous. Not at all. How ridiculous!

Then it hit her: he may have been ogling her, but he was about to be balls deep in someone else. The jealousy that wasn't jealousy quickly turned to annoyance. Beck's cheeks heated in embarrassment. She felt so incredibly stupid. Sure, she might have caught his attention for a moment, but it wasn't like every other female in the universe didn't do the same. She'd heard the rumors. He was a great king, loved his brothers, blah blah blah. Sure, that was all well and good, but he was also a notorious player, a different person—or *persons*—in his bed every night. He never settled down, never dated. He had his fun and then moved on to the next target. Did he think to make her another notch on his endless bedpost? No way. Not happening.

But apparently her body didn't get the memo. It was still screaming for his touch, demanding that she go to him and slam her mouth to his, wrap her arms around his neck and her legs around his waist. Hell, a part of her was even screaming to toss the other woman over the balcony by the hair, a fierce and strange possessiveness scorching through her and making her chest heat—her power? She scowled inwardly. *You don't help when I'm literally fighting for my life but you show up now to help me have a catfight over a guy?!*

Beck shook herself, forcing her body and mind to chill the fuck out for a second. It was just the damn dry spell! She just needed to get laid. That would stop her body's ridiculous reactions to him. It wasn't *him*, necessarily, it was just that she was in desperate need of a few big Os and he was exceptionally good looking. That little voice tried to argue but she silenced it.

So, she just needed to find someone else to slake these desires and that would stop thoughts of Poseidon from invading her mind at all hours of the day and night. *Yes, this is sound logic.*

Maybe Nerina could set her up with someone. There seemed to be a plethora of good-looking males in this plane. Why *shouldn't* she give one of them a try? She'd sworn off men on the Mortal Plane, but that was then, this was now.

And maybe she could do more than just scratch an itch.

She thought back to when she'd been certain she was going to die beneath the water. She'd finally admitted to herself that she'd wanted to be loved. And she deserved to be, didn't she? She'd never really thought of herself as worthy of much. Her mother didn't love her, her father wanted nothing to do with her. The first guy she'd dated had nailed and bailed her when she'd finally given it up. The second had merely slept with her as a one-night fling to make an ex-girlfriend jealous. The third and final attempt had been a decent guy, but neither one of them seemed able to let their guard down, so it had amounted to little in the end. The one time they'd tried to have sex, neither one of them could make themselves very...interested.

After all that, Beck figured that there was something wrong with *her* and she'd stopped trying to connect with anyone. She'd focused solely on keeping her and her mother alive and off the radar, which was a full-time job in addition to her *actual* jobs anyway. She'd existed but not *lived*.

But, you know what? Screw that. She was tired of feeling that way. She *was* worthy of love and adoration and respect, damn it. Beck jutted her chin, feeling some of the walls she'd spent so much time building within herself begin to crack and crumble as she let herself believe it for the first time in her life. She could let people in. Probably. No, she could if she tried, she was sure of it. It might take some time but, she...wanted to? A metaphorical lightbulb flared to life over her head. Here within this plane she wouldn't have to hide what she was. She *could* let someone get to know the real her, whoever that was, and have a *real* conversation with someone for the first time in... ever.

So, yes. She deserved a shot at something and being an easy lay for the playboy of the gods was *not* it, no matter how sexy he was. Beck shook herself and turned around, stomping towards Nerina. She kept her tone level and easy as she said, "So, about those sapphire caves."

Beck was avoiding him. Or he was avoiding her. They were avoiding each other. Poseidon didn't know what the hell had passed between them when she'd spied him during his training session with the Elite days ago. Her eyes had flickered cobalt and he could smell how...*appreciative* she was of the view. He'd nearly gone to his knees when her scent had hit him. Sweeter than any poppy wine, any honey. He craved a taste so badly he could barely stand it. *No. No, no, no.*

He would not be tasting anything! For...reasons that he'd told himself a thousand times but couldn't quite remember at the moment because his treacherous mind was only recalling the way she'd looked on the beach that same day. She'd been lying on a towel next to Nerina, a barely-there black bikini covering her flawless, creamy skin. The sun had darkened it a shade and he would bet that he could have tasted it on her skin. Would she have tan lines from the small strings? Why was that so ridiculously enticing to him? Two small triangles of material had covered plump breasts, a perfect handful. *Perfect for* my *hands.*

He thought he might burn down entire realms to see what the material hid. He imagined what they might look like. Would dusty pink nipples top those beautiful creamy mounds? Would they beg for his mouth? Would she like that? Being licked and teased? Would she moan his name? Hold him to her and dig her nails into his shoulders? He shuddered at the thought.

Her waist was lean, her hips flaring subtly. Her legs were shapely and toned, same with her arms. She was delicate but not fragile. He'd been entranced—and then she'd stood, her back to him. He'd lost his breath and nearly pulverized the stone railing beneath his hands. He'd never seen such a perfect ass in all his existence. He'd thought it looked divine in jeans? In that bikini bottom, the cut showing off the bottoms of her cheeks…well, he finally understood what mortals meant by "an ass that don't quit." When she'd bent over, giving him the most glorious view in all of the kingdom, he'd lost control of his power for a moment. Blue lightning had streaked the sky, a bolt slamming into the water.

What the hell had that been about? Sure, the sea often matched his moods, churning and dangerous when he was pissy, clear and soft when he was happy. But lightning within the dome? That was rare. Even stranger was that with the lightning, he'd felt *something* leap within his chest. A feeling that seared him to his soul. But it was there one heartbeat and gone the next, so perhaps he'd imagined it completely. And the way she'd been looking at him in return? He was seconds away from phasing directly to her, kissing her full lips and tunneling his hands through her hair. Her nipples had puckered beneath the fabric of her bikini, her breaths growing quick and shallow and the sight had driven him mad. She wanted him as much as he wanted her, he was sure of it in that moment.

Until Helena had joined him on the balcony. It was like someone had dumped a bucket of cold water on Beck. All the lust he'd seen immediately disappeared, her body coiling with tension. Her eyes turned as cold and hard as the ice they resembled. He understood what she must have thought about Helena, but for once, she had the wrong idea. Helena was merely there to speak with him about an upcoming ball she was hosting up in Empyrean and wanted his help. One of his many hidden talents was party planning. Sure she'd been scantily clad, but that was just how she always dressed. Many who resided in Zeus' kingdom dressed in such a manner, their dresses made to resemble the clouds that surrounded the plane. Poseidon felt the need to explain the situation to Beck, but had stopped himself time and time again. Why should he explain himself to her? *Because there was the fleeting flash of hurt in her eyes that day and that made your chest ache, you idiot.*

He groaned now, rubbing his hand over his scalp. This woman was driving him mad. Needing a distraction, he reached out to his brothers. No answer from Zeus, which wasn't completely unheard of. He was the King of the Gods with lots of kingly business to attend to —which was usually tantamount to letting his cock lead him somewhere to play. *And he gives* me *shit.* Si rolled his eyes and gave Hades a try.

-So, uh, how's the wife?- he asked. Hades had indeed brought Persephone's reincarnate to his kingdom and Poseidon wasn't sure how to feel about it. He knew it was necessary to finally end the war with their disowned brother, Maynard, but he still didn't like having that bitch back in their midst. Definitely didn't like that Hades was going to marry her all over again.

Stupid prophecies. Si *hated* them. They were almost always convoluted nonsense and left you with more questions than answers. But there was a prophecy that involved the Queen of the Underworld returning in order to end their brother once and for all. Maynard was the black sheep with an even blacker heart, and though all of them had seen the darkness within him, Hades had been the most outspoken about it. So, Maynard had made it the mission of his eternal life to take Hades out. He'd almost done it once, too, with the help of Persephone. And now she was back, destined to be queen once more, but this time in the form of a saucy little number named Skylar Pembroke.

-Former wife. And currently scouring the castle looking for weapons- He could hear a smile in Hades' mental voice. *A smile??* Was he *not* burning with hatred towards her anymore? It actually gave Si a bit of hope. If Hades could get over his hatred for Persephone, surely Beck could get over her hatred of him and the rest of the gods... right?

-Weapons? Really?- Persephone had been very anti-weapon. Well, until she'd driven the godsblade into Hades' spine. Si's mood soured instantly.

-Apparently Skylar differs greatly from her former self. She's absolutely savage.- Another smile in his voice, laced with something else entirely.

-Dude, I can practically see your hardon from here-

-Oh fuck off- Hades spit. *-It's...complicated.-* Wasn't everything lately? Though Si was happy that maybe this version of Persephone wasn't a murderous bitch, he was still wary and needed Hades to be careful.

-Speaking of hardons, I hear you've got a new tasty morsel working in your digs-

Si gritted his teeth. Hermes was such a fucking gossip.

-She's just a girl. What of it?-

-Is she a single girl? Maybe I can set her up with Charon. If I have to hear about him and Emmie roleplaying one more time...-

Rage flared in Poseidon's chest at that suggestion. The idea of the ferryman and Beck sent fire through his veins, a possessiveness he'd never felt before rearing forcefully like a beast inside him. The beast quieted again, gone as quickly as it had come, and Si rubbed his temples. *What the hell is happening to me?*

Why should he care who Beck fucked? Especially since he was still entertaining himself with anyone who would have him. He wasn't particularly *enjoying* it per se, but it was something to pass the time and he thought that if he just kept at it, eventually the joy would return and he'd finally feel satisfied. So, no. He didn't care if she dated Charon or anyone else for that matter. Jealousy wasn't allowed in his kingdom. End of story. She could screw whomever she wanted.

He ground his teeth, but kept his mental tone light when he responded.

-She's seen me shirtless, so I've already ruined her for any other male in the world-

Hades let a deep laugh rumble through their connection. They caught up a bit more before saying their goodbyes. Poseidon worked the rest of the day, keeping busy and forcing his mind to leave thoughts of Beck behind. He laid in bed later that night, staring at the sea above him. A mermaid swam by and slowed, giving him a wave and a wink. She arched her brows in question: did he want her to come inside. He sighed. Did he? He should. The old Si wouldn't have thought twice but he wasn't in the mood. He smiled at her, told her maybe another time, and waved a hand to turn the glass opaque, a sky of false stars now shimmering above him. He tossed and turned, unable to settle. No matter how much he willed them not to, his thoughts kept circling back to Beck.

"Damn. It," he growled as he slipped his hand beneath the sheet. He gave in, letting her invade his mind as he began to stroke.

Nerina had set Beck up with three different guys so far—an Eau Demon with a very intriguing tail, a merman, and a demigod—but she had made little progress on her whole connecting with someone thing. They'd been nice enough, but conversation hadn't flowed easily and as much as she was trying, she was still closed off. To make matters worse, she hadn't even been able to get a good hook up out of the deal. She'd made out a little, which was fun and a relief after so long without that kind of contact, but the thought of doing more than kissing any of them left her cold. And that had *nothing* to do with the fact that she couldn't get Poseidon out of her head. Nothing! *He's a player, he's a player, he's a player. Oh and you hate him, remember?*

Yes. Hate. It was still there...sort of. She was trying to hold on to it, she really was, but it was becoming harder and harder. The more time she spent here, the more she felt like she *belonged*. She figured it did make some sense. Beck was a goddess, at least partly, so she *should* feel like she belonged in a godly plane among other mythical beings. She didn't have to hide here, didn't have to pretend to be someone she wasn't, on edge every moment of every day. She felt like she could breathe for the first time in her life.

And, as much as it pained part of her to admit it, as irritated as she was with Poseidon, she found that she *couldn't* hate him, not in the way she had originally. It was like some fundamental part of her refused to *let* her hate him in that way now that she'd actually met him, stopping her every time she tried. She didn't understand it but trying to fight against it was exhausting. Maybe she should...stop? *Could* she stop?

She thought maybe she could at least try. Beck hadn't seen him in a few days and she was fairly convinced that he was avoiding her. But she had been avoiding him too, so it was fine. Now her heart sped as she walked the halls of his wing. Would she bump into him? Did she want to? She...did. Beck didn't want to admit it, but she had actually missed seeing him.

"Stop being ridiculous," she scolded herself. She tossed her shoulders back and turned down the wide corridor that would lead to his chambers. If she saw him, so be it. It was fine. Everything was fine.

As she neared his large, elegantly carved door, she slowed, tilting her head. She heard...noises. Lots and lots of noises. She sidled quietly up to the door, pressing her ear against the cool wood. Her eyes flew wide. What in the world could be happening in there to produce sounds like that? And what would someone need to do to make *her* make those sounds? Images rose, her cheeks flushing. She should back away. And she would. Any second, really.

Moans, throaty pleas for more, gasps of pleasure or pain or both. How many people were in that room? Definitely more than two. How did that even work? Did they take turns? All go at once like a big dog pile? With each new question, more heat flooded her system. She thought she heard Poseidon, and she shivered. Hearing him in the throes made her maddened with lust, wanting to witness it herself... and also nearly overwhelmed with white hot jealousy. *Again.*

Stupid, stupid, stupid.

"Looking for something?" a voice whispered low at her ear.

She gasped and turned, hand flying to her heart. Nerina smiled wide, not even trying to hide her amusement.

"Would you stop that!?" Beck whisper-hissed. "You're like a ninja. I'm going to get you a bell."

Nerina tilted her head as a scream of pleasure sounded from behind the door. Beck's eyes went wide and her cheeks heated again, and to her dismay, Nerina didn't miss the reaction.

"Have you never had sex before, Beck?" Nerina asked, honest curiosity in her tone.

"Not that it's any of your business, but of course I have," she snapped back in a whisper. She'd had sex...just not *good* sex. The nailer-and-bailer had been what the mortals called a Two Pump Chump. He was in and out in less than ninety seconds. She tried not to let that miserable experience taint sex for her in general—everyone's first time was supposed to be less than spectacular, wasn't it? The second guy hadn't been much better and had *cried* afterwards, lamenting how much he missed his ex and inadvertently convincing Beck that she must be the worst lay in history.

So, in her experience, sex most definitely did *not* equate to the sounds she was hearing in Poseidon's bedroom. Not even close, which was one of the main reasons she'd sworn off it over two years ago. The lack normally didn't bother her that much honestly. She was too busy to worry about dating and screwing anyway, and she was perfectly capable of helping herself out when the mood did strike. But since she'd come here, she'd had *urges*. Intense ones. And they were quickly spinning out of control.

Beck tried to blame it on being on a godly Plane. It was awakening all sorts of things within her, even her power seemed to be a bit stronger here (though she still couldn't manage to access it properly), so maybe this over-active sex drive was just a goddess thing that had been blocked while on the Mortal Plane. That could account for some of it, but if she were being honest, she knew that it was mostly due to the sexy beyond reason God of the Sea.

Nerina held her hands up in surrender. "Ok, ok, I'm sorry. You're right, it is none of my business. I'll leave you to your...work," she said with a wiggle of her brows. She glided off and Beck did the super mature thing and flipped her off behind her back. She took a deep breath and turned on her heel. She would tend to the other rooms in this wing and then check back on Poseidon's chambers later.

Beck went about her work but her mind kept returning to the things she'd heard and the images they conjured. She rubbed the back of her neck as she imagined different scenarios, sometimes as if she were watching Poseidon doing things with others, sometimes as if she were the one doing them with him. Her skin heated, and she practically throbbed with desire. *Get a freaking grip.*

She blew out a harsh breath and continued on to the next room. Her steps faltered as she passed a door—a door that was always locked. Now, it stood slightly ajar. She glanced left and right down the hallway, but saw nobody. She really should just close it and move on, but before she could even think, she was slipping inside and quietly closing the door behind her.

The space was dim, only a bit of light streaming in from behind a curtain to her left. The right side of the room was mostly in shadow, but she thought she spied the outline of a large, wing-backed chair, a side table, and bookshelves lining the walls. She moved forward towards the shelves on this side of the room and began poking around. What kinds of things did Poseidon keep here, hidden away? What things did he like and treasure?

She skimmed her fingers along the spines of the leather bound books, across the shark's tooth larger than her hand, and over the other assorted knickknacks. She sucked in a sharp breath when her fingers skimmed over a glass sphere, about the size of a softball. The glass felt hot beneath her fingers and some strange sense of...something rippled through her. Almost like some kind of recognition, like that nagging feeling you get when you see someone and just *know* you've seen them somewhere before but can't for the life of you remember where.

She picked up the sphere and frowned—it was far heavier than it looked, feeling like it was made of lead. She squinted at it, turning it this way and that. Some kind of swirling black smoke filled the glass, spinning faster as she stared.

"Snooping is a nasty habit," a voice purred from the other side of the room. A lamp flared to life, flooding the room in bright light, though it flickered ominously as a green mist curled around the space. A woman unfolded herself from the chair that had been in shadow. Ebony hair whipped around her as if wind blew within the room, though Beck felt nothing but intense and terrifying power. The woman's eyes were wholly white and what looked like black blood leaked from the corners. She opened her mouth and red fangs dripped with more of that black, viscous liquid. She was the most fearsome creature Beck had ever seen.

Beck squeaked, not even able to scream properly. She jumped backwards and dropped the sphere, but instead of shattering glass, she only heard was a soft thud. She glanced down to see that the ball had fallen in the middle of a big, fluffy pillow. Well, that was a fortunate accident. Beck flicked her gaze back to the woman, fear making her heart leap into her throat and her own power stir in reaction. Not enough to actually be helpful of course and she cursed her stupid malfunctioning gifts for the millionth time.

"I-I'm sorry, I was just...I..."

"Ha! Totally kidding," the woman said as the mist disappeared and the lights remained steady. Her eyes turned violet with a ring of lavender around the iris, her hair silver. The black blood disappeared along with the fangs, smooth brown skin and a brilliant white smile now in their place. She looked familiar...

"Snooping is actually one of my favorite pastimes. Top three for sure. It's how I learned that Ares is a boxer-brief kind of guy, while Zeus prefers to go commando. Hercules likes these little bikini types..." She frowned. "Not *all* of my snooping is underwear related, though it does kind of sound that way right now. So, anywho, what are we snooping for?" she asked, rubbing her hands together eagerly.

"Uhhh..." Beck stood there, dumbfounded, trying to figure out what was happening.

"Oh, right. Sorry. Let me be kind and rewind here. I saw you a few months back, at that supernatural club, remember?" *Lightbulb.* She *was* familiar! But...

"That was *years* ago."

The woman frowned and tilted her head. "Was it?" She pursed her lips and then shrugged. "I lose track sometimes, you'll get used to it. It seems like yesterday but also like I've been waiting for you for eons. The curse of an oracle I suppose."

"Oracle? Like you can see the future?"

She smacked her forehead. "Ah, yes. I suppose I didn't properly introduce myself the most recent time we met." Most recent? As in, there had been others before that? "I'm Emmeralda—Emmie. Seer extraordinaire." She gave a flourish of a wave and dipped her head. "You may tremble in awe if you wish." Emmie glanced up at her. "No, seriously. Go on. Tremble in awe."

"Uhh...ok...hi?" Beck bent to pick up the glass sphere and return it to its proper place.

"You're welcome for that by the way." Emmie nodded to the pillow. "It would have been a real mess if that had broken. It's not time for him to come out and play yet," she said in a tone that reminded Beck of someone scolding a puppy. "That's the king of the wraiths in there, all shrunk down and adorable, but he will be royally pissed and unleash hell once he's released from his imprisonment. He and his kind used to serve a real nasty bit of work named Balthazar."

Beck eyed the smoke again and a pair of crimson eyes appeared within the swirling wisps. It—he?—indeed looked pissed but also… curious, and that sense of recognition came back again. *My nightmares. I've seen things like him in my nightmares.* She swallowed hard, sat the sphere down, and hastily backed away.

"So, you said you'd been waiting for me. You *knew* I would end up here?"

"I know *lots* of things," Emmie beamed. Her eyes shifted to the medallion around Beck's neck and her smile faltered a bit, her expression darkening. "Not all of them fun, unfortunately." She pulled her gaze back up, smile returning. "But you being here is definitely a fun one. I can't wait for girl's night! It's going to be epic. Maybe the best one in the history of all girl's nights."

"Girl's night? With whom?" Beck asked. She'd never participated in such a thing…mostly because she'd never been invited to one.

"With the girls. Duh. I know you don't know it yet, but we're all besties and one day, even sisters in arms! Trust me," she said, tapping her temple knowingly.

"Um, ok then I guess…" Beck thought she might be…eager for girl's night. Maybe she would test out the whole opening herself up to people thing on girlfriends first, then move onto boys. Yes. Good plan. Take the penis out of the equation, it only complicated matters anyway.

"Oh, your mother is fine, bee-tee-dubs." Relief surged, followed promptly by guilt. Beck had nearly forgotten her mother completely in her weeks here, but she was glad to know that she was safe. But also—

"You know my mother?" Beck asked, brows drawn. Emmie nodded. "Where is she?"

"Somewhere special," Emmie said vaguely. "The important thing is that your daddy doesn't know where either of you are for now."

"My...wait, you know who my father is too?"

"Yup. I'm like a paternity test factory over here. I got some juicy results for my friend, Skylar, to spill soon too. Or I mean, spill 'on accident' of course," she added with an exaggerated wink, doing air quotes. She gestured in the air with a roll of her eyes. "*They* get mad when I meddle too much, but I'm a pro at toeing that line perfectly. The word "oops" goes a long way with these things you see, especially for me. I have an unlimited number of free passes, really." She leaned into add in a conspiratorial whisper, "They don't like to admit that though."

Though she had no idea what Emmie was talking about for the most part, Beck's heart was racing. She could finally know the truth about her father! Her excitement faded, something telling her it wouldn't be that simple. She narrowed her eyes at the Seer.

"You aren't going to tell me who he is, are you?"

"Negative, Ghostrider." Beck ground her teeth, her mood immediately plummeting. She was going to get whiplash from all these different emotions. "All in good time, my dear. I promise. Now," Emmie tilted her head as if listening to something far away. "Ah, yes. You should go finish your work. Poseidon's...erm...*gathering* is ending now. I'll send you the e-vite for girl's night soon. Toodles!" With that, she disappeared, but then immediately appeared again. "Oh, and I understand that you did not take my previous advice," she said in a scolding tone. "Work on the nightmares. I rarely give advice that isn't important." She gave Beck a stern look. "They will be his salvation one day."

Whose salvation? Work on the nightmares how, exactly? What did that even mean?

"Umm, I'll...try?"

"That's my girl. Ok, byyyeeee! Muah!"

Emmie disappeared again, for good this time. With a shake of her head, Beck made her way back to Poseidon's room. She would try to dissect the strange encounter with Emmie later. As she came around the corner, a group of females *and* males were leaving Poseidon's chambers. More images. More curiosity. More heat. *Stop it!* One female caught her eye and smiled. She looked familiar...oh. She was one of the mermaids that Nerina had introduced her to. *Cora, I think?* She waved goodbye to the others who all looked exhausted and orgasm-drunk—*what that must be like!*—and leaned against the wall languidly as Beck approached.

"You've got judgey face," she said without preamble.

"I—what?" Beck asked, blinking.

"You look like you're judging the hell out of what just happened in that room." She didn't look mad about the judgment which was good because Beck wasn't *trying* to judge. And she wasn't actually judging, at least not for the reasons Cora was probably thinking. Though Beck was extremely inexperienced, she wasn't a prude by any means. She was so damned curious about too many things in the bedroom department, things she longed to try and experience. So, she wasn't judging whatever had happened in that room—she was judging what happened *afterwards*.

"No, I'm not, I promise. What happened in that room sounded..." Hot? Sexy? Utterly intriguing? She swallowed hard and refocused. "I just don't see how you can be ok just being used and kicked the curb like that."

Cora shook her head and let out a soft laugh. "It isn't like that at all. Everyone knows exactly what is and isn't expected in Poseidon's bedroom. He doesn't make promises of more to lure unsuspecting partners into his bed, just to disappoint them later, I promise you. He isn't cruel. Not in the slightest. He makes it very clear that everything that happens there is for fun and pleasure with no strings attached, no expectations. Although..." She looked contemplative.

"Although what?"

"Well, there is always a moment, usually afterwards, when it's like he's holding his breath, waiting for...something. *Desperately* waiting. Like he wants more, but something always holds him back.

Most people wouldn't notice it, but I've been with him enough that I've finally started catching it. His shoulders slump ever so slightly though he keeps that easy smile on his face. He's waiting for something to happen, like a connection to shift into place. Maybe *the* connection." *The* connection? What did that mean? "But it never happens."

Cora pushed herself off of the wall and brushed the skirt of her flowing gown. "I hope he finds whatever he's looking for. He deserves it more than just about anyone I know. But bottom line: he is *not* the use 'em and lose 'em type." With a smile, she turned and glided off, her steps like Nerina's: fluid and graceful. She called over her shoulder, "He phased off somewhere, so you can go ahead in if you want."

Beck didn't know how to feel about what Cora had just told her. Poseidon wasn't just a jerk playboy? Sure, he had his fun between the sheets more than any other being in the universe it seemed, but if he wasn't using people or hurting them...She sighed. *Then I have no reason to keep that on my list of reasons to hate him.* Her list was growing shorter and shorter by the day and soon, there would be nothing left. The thought terrified her.

If there was nothing left for her to hate, then she might...do the opposite. That stupid voice in her head sure as hell seemed to think that was a good idea. She squeezed her eyes shut. *No. Just, no. I will not be falling for someone who only has casual sex with no lasting relationships.* It didn't matter that it wasn't done cruelly and no one was hurt in the process. She needed more than that, and she doubted he would break his rules for her.

Beck entered the room, not quite knowing what she expected to see: sex toys all over? Used condoms?...Stains? Her eyes widened in surprise. Apart from rumpled sheets, empty glasses and bottles, and an array of blankets and pillows strewn across the floor, the room looked fairly normal. She expected it to smell...well, she didn't know how a room should smell after an orgy, truth be told. Sweaty, maybe? But the only thing she could smell was something crisp and somewhat citrusy, almost like someone had already cleaned up, and beneath that, Poseidon's luxurious scent. She inhaled deeply which was a huge mistake. The scent surrounded her, cocooned her, fogged her brain.

She began picking up the bottles and spied one hiding under the bed. She ducked beneath to grab it and when she straightened, she dropped every single one, glass shattering all around her feet.

Poseidon stood across the room, his back to her.

Completely naked.

TEN

Poseidon whirled when he heard glass shattering. He'd known someone was in the room when he'd returned from his swim, but he'd assumed it was one of the group who'd forgotten something or was going to negotiate for thirds...or was it fourths? To his immense surprise, he turned to find Beck, staring right at him, mouth agape. He wasn't bashful by any stretch of the imagination, but he *should* cover himself in front of her. And he would...any minute...as soon as her eyes stopped roaming over his body in that greedy manner.

His skin heated every place that her gaze fell. His chest, his stomach...She hesitated for the briefest second before her eyes lowered. They went wide and flashed cobalt and his shaft hardened under her gaze. *Gods, I can almost feel her eyes on me.* She gasped and clenched her hands into fists at her sides, but didn't look away. No, she stared raptly. Her cheeks and chest flushed, the faintest rose coloring her creamy complexion. Did she like what she saw? Did she want to touch him? Taste him? The mere thought of her hands or mouth upon him made his cock pulse and a low groan rumble in his chest.

The sound seemed to break her trance, and she yanked her eyes upward to meet his.

"I...Ah gods. I'm sorry. I was cleaning. I thought you were gone. But you obviously aren't gone. You're very here and very, *very* naked and I...wow, my gods...I mean, I..." She squeezed her eyes shut and he pulled his lips in to keep from laughing. Beck was flustered and boy oh boy did he like it. She opened her eyes once more but when her gaze immediately darted downward, she shut them again, cursing under her breath. Shaking her head, she said in a raspy voice, "I have to go."

She sprinted for the door, keeping her eyes half shut, only slitting her lids enough that she could see where she was going. He was torn between amusement, pride, and disappointment. He *wanted* her eyes on him. He wanted a hell of a lot more than that on him, but mostly, he didn't want her to go. *Interesting*.

"Wait!" he called. She froze but kept her back to him. She was trying to hide it, but her breaths were quick and shallow. Aroused? Nervous? Both? He donned leather pants, groaning and grinding his teeth as he laced the ties over his straining erection. *Down boy, fuck.* He'd just gone several rounds with several individuals, but two seconds with Beck staring at him like that had him harder than he'd been all day. "I'm clothed. You can turn around."

She turned and swallowed hard when her gaze landed on his still-bare chest. She followed a droplet of water with her eyes as it slowly made its way downward. Did she just lick her lips? *Gods help me.* She yanked her gaze up once more and scowled.

"Shirt too," she demanded. He rolled his eyes and tried to hide a smile, but pulled a black t-shirt on as well.

"Happy now?" She gave him a clipped nod. "Would you...um, like a drink?" Was *he* nervous now? What the hell?

"I...shouldn't. No, I'm fine. If that's all, I have work to do."

"That's what I want to talk to you about," he blurted, an idea rising up as Emmie's words from this morning finally made sense. They always did—eventually. Sometimes eventually was decades or centuries later, but at some point, they would always finally click.

He'd woken and gone to train only to halt just past the door to his throne room. Backing up, he found Emmie lounging on his throne, using a tip of his trident to clean her nails. He'd stopped being surprised by her random visits long ago, so he merely strolled in and plucked the weapon from her grasp.

"Good morning, Emmie. To what do I owe the pleasure of your company today?"

"I just wanted to say hi and tell you not to worry about Hades—he's driving Skylar mad in the best ways but she has no plans to go all stabby stab on him or anything. Well, not mortally anyway. Ha! Mortally. That's funny, because, ya know, *immortal*…laugh at my joke, Si," she said with narrowed eyes. He chuckled and she grinned. "Also, double check your defenses as a little birdie told me that you'll soon be having unwanted company attempting to enter your kingdom. Also also, I think someone needs a promotion."

He let all of that information settle in his mind. He would love to know more details about Skylar driving Hades nuts. As long as she wasn't planning to off him, Poseidon thought his brother could use a little ass kicking to be honest. Her warning about unwanted guests had his hackles raising. No one fucked with his kingdom. He would tell his guards to be on high alert and increase patrols. The last bit… he didn't have a clue.

"A promotion?"

She smiled brightly. "Yep! Big corner office, company car, 401(k) plan—the works."

"Umm do you want to give me a little more direction here?" She morphed momentarily into Moira Rose.

"David, I cannot show you everything."

Not missing a beat, Si replied, "Ok, well can you show me *one* thing?" She shifted back to herself, jumping up and down and clapping her hands.

"I told you it was a great show! You binged it didn't you? I knew you would. I mean I *knew* you would because: oracle," she said with a *duh* expression. "But I also knew you would just because I am a genius and I know my boys so well."

She resided mostly with Hades in the Underworld and he considered her "his" Seer, but she had a habit of flitting between the three brothers like a loving, frustrating, sometimes lucid sister who they wanted to both hug and stab depending on her mood. She liked to refer to them as *her boys* and Si couldn't deny that it always made him smile.

She'd pinched his cheek before giving it a quick kiss, phased away, and he'd tucked away her strange message to think about later, knowing well enough to trust that it would make sense at some point. Now was some point.

Beck tensed. "I've kept up my side of the bargain, I swear. I haven't been slacking. I'm sure Nerina would back me up here. I only venture to the beach when I've finished my duties for the day. I—"

"Easy, killer. That's not what I meant. Would you join me out on the balcony? Please?" he added when it looked like she wanted to run again. She sighed but gave him a sharp nod and made her way towards the towering doors. He let her pass in front of him, telling himself not to inhale her exquisite scent or check out her ass in those gods damned jeans. He failed in both tasks. Si's eyes slid closed as her natural perfume hit his blood stream like a drug. It was a subtle mix of driftwood fire and honey. Sweet. Smoky. Addicting.

He followed her out and gestured to a table and chairs. She sat, rigid at first but she slowly relaxed as she took in the view. He summoned two drinks, sliding one towards her with an arched brow. She took it and sipped as she studied him over the rim.

"So, as I said, I wanted to talk to you about your duties. I'd like you to take on new ones."

"Like what, exactly?" Another appreciative sip. She relaxed further and he did as well. He felt at ease just being near her, a tension in his chest he hadn't really noticed releasing its grasp on him.

"I need an...assistant? Advisor. Advising Assistant? Assistant Advisor?" She arched a brow and her lips curled upwards the tiniest bit at the corners. "Shut up. Look, I don't know what the right title is, but I have many things that need my attention throughout the kingdom. Concerns and complaints and requests from my people. Repairs to be made, visits to check in on the different realms, kissing babies and signing autographs," he said with a grin. Her lips tilted up another fraction of an inch. *Getting there!* "Things like that. I would like for you to assist me."

"And advise you," she added, amused mocking in her tone. He eased back in his chair, spreading his long legs out before him. He caught her checking him out appreciatively before she caught herself and shifted her gaze out to the ocean instead. Male satisfaction pounded in his chest. She might still hate him sometimes, but she wasn't immune to him physically, not even a little bit. *Maybe there's something here...*

"Yes, exactly," he confirmed with a chuckle. She swirled her drink in her glass, pulling her gaze away from the beach to study him. He forced himself not to move under her scrutiny as her icy blue eyes bore into him, stripping him bare. What did she see? The cocky, laid-back, lust-fueled God of the Sea? Or the real self he kept hidden beneath the façade, the one who felt broken and unworthy and wanted so desperately to connect with someone that he would give almost anything for it?

"Would this be in addition to my other duties? Or replacing them?"

"Replacing them."

She kept studying him, her cool demeanor in place, but she rubbed her fingers across that medallion.

"So...I would work alongside you. All day, every day?" The pulse point on her throat beat quicker. Did she like the idea or was she repulsed by it? He couldn't tell.

"Not all day and every day. Working directly for the boss has it perks—you'll have ample time off to do what you please. But yes, whenever I need assistance, you would be with me." She kept rubbing that medallion, rolling the idea through her mind. Would she agree? He realized he wanted her to. *Badly*. "Come on. You'd get to explore the entirety of Aqueous, see things you've never even dreamed of, even venture to the other godly planes as well. It's got to be better than cleaning kitchens and doing laundry. What do you say?" *Please say yes.*

His heart thudded as he realized what was happening. He wanted to spend time with her and not just because he wanted her in his bed. Which, of course he did, he would be a fool not to. She was beyond gorgeous and oozed an innocent sensuality that he longed to explore. But beyond the physical, he had the desire to actually *get to know her* and the desire grew stronger every day. It wasn't much, but it was something! Perhaps he wasn't a lost cause after all. He *could* feel things. The fact that he was so excited to simply want the *beginnings* of a friendship with someone was just plain sad, but he would take what he could get.

Her eyes had lit with excitement at the mention of exploring the kingdom and venturing off-plane, though she tried to keep her features schooled into that cool indifference she often wore. *Come on...*

"I...yes, I'll do it," she finally said, and he fought to keep his excitement contained. "But you remain clothed at all times," she added, sternly. He barked out a laugh and her lips twitched again. *I will coax a smile one of these days*. It was his new eternal life's mission. They sat in silence for a bit after that, not comfortable but not completely *uncomfortable* either. It was better than the seething hatred she'd radiated when she'd first arrived. He was still dying to know what that was all about, but he didn't want to push. Maybe after spending more time with him, he could uncover all of her secrets.

Because Beck was most definitely keeping secrets.

POSEIDON WOKE the next morning early, eager to start the day. Which had nothing to do with his new Assistant Advisor. Or Advising Assistant. Or whatever. He'd debated on what to do first, but had finally settled on a rousing day of...paperwork. He didn't want to overwhelm her from the start, so they would simply start by going through and answering correspondence. *Super sexy, Si.* As he pulled on a shirt, he frowned. Would she be bored? Did it matter?

He second guessed his choice a thousand times as he waited. Finally, she arrived in his oversized study, looking around the space appreciatively. He had another, smaller one that he also used but that felt a bit too intimate, so he'd opted for this instead. She wore those jeans that were slowly becoming his new favorite fashion trend and a midnight blue tank top. He absolutely did *not* notice how the material hugged her slight body or the way it dipped, showing the soft curves of her breasts. Not at all. That would be inappropriate.

She carried a cup of steaming ambrosian brew and his lips curled upwards. *Addicted.* Her body was tense and he wasn't sure if it was from the mysterious hatred emerging again or if she was nervous. For the new job duties? Or just being around him?

She eyed the large table which was absolutely covered in correspondence. Letters, scrolls, books, shells, all scattered, lying wherever he had haphazardly tossed them when they'd arrived. He rubbed the stubble on his jaw. Ok, so maybe he'd been slacking on this part of his kingly duties for a while. *Oops.*

To his surprise, her strain seemed to ease as she studied the mess, an eagerness lighting her eyes.

"So, this monstrosity is our first task," he said, waving his hand at the table and grinning. Her lips quirked the tiniest bit.

"I was going to go with clusterfuck, but monstrosity works." He chuckled at that and ignored the way her saying *fuck* made his cock jump. She slid into a seat to his left and surveyed the chaos.

She took a long sip and asked over the rim of her mug, "Ok, so do you have a system in place or am I at liberty to do my thing and fix this?"

"No system," he confirmed. "You have free rein."

She nodded and started to go through the documents. She read so quickly that he didn't understand how she was actually seeing the words. She made different piles based on the type of correspondence or type of response necessary, urgency level of response, and of course a pile for what she deemed *junk mail*: invitations to parties that had long since passed and requests that had already been fulfilled by someone who wasn't him since he was a slacker. He hadn't realized how much he'd been neglecting since he'd been in his funk, and embarrassment and disappointment roiled. He'd always been revered as a truly good king, his subjects loving him. And he'd let them down. *Need to do better.* With Beck's help, he vowed he would.

He tried to concentrate on the pile she'd pushed his way—the most pressing things she'd found so far—but he kept watching her out of the corner of his eye. She sat perched in her chair, legs folded beneath her, seemingly growing more at ease with every hour that passed. He grinned when he realized she was barefoot, her shoes abandoned under the table somewhere. She'd tossed her hair up into a loose knot on top of her head and a few tendrils fell lazily across her forehead and temples. He had no desire to brush them away, to feel the silken strands against his skin. None whatsoever. *Gods, maybe this was a terrible idea.* The sunlight from the oversized window highlighted the blonde streaks, turning them golden honey. She chewed on her full bottom lip absently as she read, rubbing that medallion. He wondered where she'd gotten it, why it was so impor-tant. The fact that he even cared thrilled him. *Progress!*

It wasn't that he was callous to his partners or acquaintances up until now, it was just that he didn't have the urge to dive deeper than *what's your name, what's your drink,* and, depending on how the evening went, *what's your favorite position.* If they shared, he listened attentively, he never ignored them. It was just that he had never been the one to ask in the first place or any additional follow up questions. No one seemed to mind since his expectations when it came to anyone wanting more with him were very clear, but he still worried that he came across as uncaring. He wasn't. Or he didn't mean to be. He cared, he just didn't *care*. It was complicated.

Her eyes flared wide and she cleared her throat delicately, seemingly torn between embarrassment and amusement.

"Uh, I think this one would be considered, um...fan mail." She passed the parchment over and he scanned the sprawling writing. *Oh my*. He rubbed the back of his neck. Whomever had sent this had gone into great detail of the things he or she wished to do to Poseidon, many of which he was fairly sure were physical impossibilities... and he'd *never* used his trident for that purpose before in his life! He cleared his throat and crumbled the parchment into a ball, tossing it over his shoulder.

"Yes, well, that was...educational," he said, trying to keep his tone light. Her lips quirked up on one side, revealing the barest hint of a dimple. *Gods help me.*

"Educational, yes. That's one way to put it." They both went on with their piles, an easy silence settling over them. Her eyes never left the paper she was scanning as she said, "So...strawberry syrup...?"

"It makes a big mess, is quite sticky, and I don't recommend it," he replied, not pulling his eyes from his own missive either. She huffed out a soft laugh and they spent the rest of the day getting work done.

Beck had been a little apprehensive at first to take on the new role, working one-on-one with Poseidon. She had to have multiple pep talks with herself beforehand to prepare for being assaulted by that glorious scent and his killer smile so often. She was managing. Mostly. She was keeping her hands to herself at least, so there was that. Her physical attraction to him was ratcheting up to extraordinary new heights and more than once she'd caught herself leaning towards him or reaching out a hand.

But on top of the physical, she thought she might be starting to... *like* him. Like, *like* him, like him. Not tolerate him, not feel indifferent towards him, but actually fucking enjoy his company and want more of it.

She'd tried to hold on to the last dregs of her hated, but it had all but disintegrated in her grasp. It was an unfounded hate and one she didn't truly feel, not anymore. It was one that had been bred into her, and, with nothing to discredit it, it had become a part of her. Now, she saw it being proven wrong again and again before her eyes. She couldn't speak for *all* the gods, of course, but everyone and everything she'd encountered in this plane so far were nothing like the vile creatures her mother had described, not even close. They'd been kind to her when they didn't have to be, offered her help or to show her around.

So, yes, she didn't hate Poseidon any longer and maybe she *was* starting to like him. Not like anything would come of it. He'd made mostly casual conversation over the first few days as they began to feel each other out, but he'd dug a little deeper every day. He seemed both confused and intrigued by his quest for information, which only confused and intrigued her in return. Did he not typically try to get to know his staff? Or anyone in general? But he was trying with her. She figured at least part of it had to just be out of suspicion. She was a stranger who had called out to him while being hunted by demons for unknown reasons, who then wormed her way into the heart of his kingdom. Even she could see how that looked a little sketchy.

So, maybe he was just working his charms to glean more information on her and her situation, to determine whether she meant him ill...but her gut was telling her that it was more than that. Her stupid gut was telling her all kinds of things and she was getting tired of it. It was ridiculous! But the pull was growing stronger and stronger each day and fighting it was getting harder and harder. She felt like a magnet, pushing so hard against the force trying to guide her towards Poseidon. All she needed to do was flip over and she would fly to him, stuck forever. *As you should be*, that damned voice whispered.

She'd been surprised by how much she enjoyed her new duties. She truly liked the work, enjoyed organizing his messes and bringing order to the administrative side of running a kingdom. A side she'd never really thought existed for gods, but she supposed a king was still a king, no matter what kind of land he reigned over.

This morning he'd asked her to meet him in his chambers instead of the study, and now she knocked tentatively on his door.

"Come on in," he called from within. She entered and her stomach rumbled when she saw the huge breakfast spread laid out atop an equally huge carved table. He waved at her to help herself while he spoke to someone who looked to be a soldier of some sort. The man wore leathers and armor, a sword strapped to his hip and a trident etched into the middle of his breastplate.

Beck headed to the table, piling down a plate with the most delicious array of some kind of meat that reminded her of bacon, and fruits unlike anything she'd ever tasted on the Mortal Plane. The juices were sweet and sour, electrifying her taste buds in ways no food ever had.

She studied the room as she ate. She'd been here before, of course, but she had been distracted by...things and hadn't taken the time to really look around. She forced the memory away immediately, not needing to recall a naked Poseidon in all his glory standing just feet away from where she now sat. *No, no, no.* How many times had she pulled that memory up in her mind as she lie alone in her bed? Of course, when she did that it transformed from a memory into a fantasy.

In it, instead of her trying to run, she sauntered towards him with a confidence she'd never known in real life. She ran her hands over his damp chest, flicking her tongue against a dark nipple to catch a bead of water before sinking to her knees before him. He tangled his hands in her hair, guiding her mouth forward...

She snapped out of the fantasy, shaking herself and refocusing on the room. A sunken seating area occupied the middle of the space, a fire pit in its center that she assumed created some kind of cool smokeless flames. Low couches and sleek, but comfortable looking, chairs were arranged around it. A fully stocked bar occupied one wall and his bed sat on the opposite side. It was twice the size of any bed she'd ever seen before, the headboard made of a deep, rich wood. She tilted her head to the side as she studied it, but her eyes were soon drawn upward.

Much of the ceiling was glass, the ocean churning just beyond it. Sunlight filtered down through the depths and all manner of sea life swam by. Mermaids and sirens waved or inclined their heads to her.

She gave small, somewhat awkward waves in return. Some flashed Poseidon sultry looks—or just plain flashed him, their breasts exposed. *Does everyone here have perfect friggin tits?* She glanced down at her own chest a little self-consciously. She had a decent handful on a good day, but underwire was definitely her best friend. Then she forced the doubt away and inwardly shrugged. *Oh well.* She was happy with her body so anyone who wasn't could screw off. *And I've caught Poseidon eyeing my assets more than once,* she thought with an inner smirk. She'd always told herself it didn't matter—from what she heard, basically anything with a pulse could turn him on—but she still let it boost her ego a bit.

Poseidon finished speaking with the solider. He gave the God of the Sea a deep incline of his head before striding out of the room. Poseidon slumped in a chair next to her, looking tense. Was something wrong? He reached over and picked a purple berry off of the platter and popped it in his mouth.

"Everything alright?" she asked, momentarily distracted by the way he licked the juice from his finger. *Dear gods. Why is that so damn...sensual?* She swallowed hard and tried to pull her eyes away from his lips. She failed.

"Hmm?" he responded, a bit distracted before he shook himself. "Oh yes, everything is fine. Someone has been trying to gain entry into my kingdom—someone who has *not* been invited. That was Cyril, the head of my army. We were just discussing defenses and protocols." Unease unfurled in her stomach.

"You don't think it's those demons, do you? The ones after me?" Beck asked, voice shaking ever so slightly as fear skittered up her spine.

"I don't think so, though I would still love to know why they're looking for you," he said pointedly. She hiked her shoulders, telling him that she really didn't know. "I actually just think it's my asshole brother trying to make trouble."

She frowned, confused. He usually spoke of his brothers with fondness, though sometimes edged with amused annoyance. But this time he spit the word *brother* with genuine hatred, his eyes flashing dark for a moment.

"Um, Zeus or Hades?"

"Oh...um, well neither actually."

He explained about their fourth brother who had been written out of any mortal histories and records, how he was constantly fighting to overthrow Hades and take the Underworld from him.

"He rarely messes with me or Zeus, but sometimes he gets bored and sends his little cronies to cause trouble just because he can. So, I'm sure that's all it is. Perhaps he's learned of the prophecy and is lashing out anywhere he can," he added, mostly to himself. Prophecy? There was so much she didn't know. About Poseidon. About the gods. About this world. She *was* dying to learn it all though. Despite being unsure of the gods as a whole, she felt more like herself here than she ever had in the Mortal Plane. She felt as if she belonged here, so she wanted to know everything she possibly could.

He shifted his gaze to her and smiled that easy, sexy smile. "No need to worry. I protect what's mine." The words sent shivers down her spine. *His.* He meant his kingdom, obviously, but her mind had latched onto that 'mine' and run a marathon away from rational thought. Their gazes held and something began to stir around them, heavy and foreign and delicious. She cleared her throat and changed the subject abruptly.

"So, you don't mind being watched twenty-four-seven?" she asked, pointing to the ceiling.

"No, I don't mind being watched," he said, a sensual undertone to the words. Would she like to watch him? She thought she...might. Again, her mind flashed back to when she'd seen him. *All of him.* She shouldn't have looked but *oh my* did she look her fill. She'd eaten up every inch of the view and admittedly didn't try very hard to keep her eyes from roaming downward.

Huge. Hardening before her eyes. *Mouthwatering.*

Just the memory made her squirm in her seat. Would she have

liked to watch him stroke himself as she stood across the room? Eyes locked on her as he moved his fist up and down his thick shaft, watching her watch him? Instant rush of heat. *Oh yes*. She would like that very fucking much.

He pulled her from her wayward thoughts, continuing the conversation. "But not constantly. I do need privacy occasionally." He waved his hand and the glass fogged, going from crystal clear to cloudy gray to completely black, tiny pinpricks of light glowing to mimic the night sky and lamps flared to life all around the room.

"Whoa," Beck breathed. It was mesmerizing. She couldn't decide which view she liked best: the sprawling ocean or the faux constellations. Her eyes wandered back to the bed. Again, she squinted at the headboard, confused.

"Do you sleep walk or something?"

Now it was his turn to look confused.

"Umm, not to my knowledge. Why?"

"You've got straps attached to your headboard. I thought maybe it was to keep you in bed."

He arched a brow, his confusion melting into a mix of pure carnality and amusement, those sensual lips curling upward.

"Well, yes, they *are* used to keep a person in bed..." He let the sentence hang in the air between them. *What is he trying to—*

"Oh." Her eyes flew wider as it really hit her. "Ooohhhhhhh." She blushed with embarrassment...and arousal. *What the hell?* She'd never even thought about being tied up before, but the second Poseidon uttered the words, the second she pictured her—or him— tied there on his massive bed, she was instantly curious and...ok, yes fine. Wet. She was curious and wet. Happy now? *What the fuck is happening to me?*

When she glanced back to him, his pupils were dilated and he was clenching his jaw so tight she thought the bones must be ready to splinter. Was he having similar thoughts? Or...could he tell that she was aroused? *Oh gods*. Her flush deepened, and she swallowed hard, averting her eyes to study her plate. She peeked up at him through her lashes and when their gazes locked, that weird tension began to build again, stronger than before. Her embarrassment disappeared and in its place was hot, carnal lust. His eyes darkened and he started to lean forward across the table. Oh gods, was she leaning forward too? *Shit. Ok, time to change the subject and get the hell out of his bedroom.*

Somehow she managed to lock her muscles in place. She cleared her thought quietly and said, "So, um, what's on the agenda today?" He blinked and eased back in his chair, frowning slightly as if he didn't realize he'd moved.

"I thought you could accompany me to some of the settlements outside of the castle grounds. Maybe journey to a few of the other realms." Was his voice a bit gruffer than usual? Dear gods, talk about a bedroom voice. Beck clenched her hands into fists in her lap. *Need. Out. Of. Here.*

Then a thought occurred to her and she pursed her lips.

"But you said everything was underwater. Do you have scuba gear?" She'd wondered about this before when he'd mentioned traveling outside of the dome. Guess she was going to find out today.

He smirked and wiggled his fingers at her. "Even better than scuba gear." He stood and crooked his finger at her. *That's all it would take, isn't it? A crook of his finger and I'd be his.* No! Maybe? Ugh! Her mind was becoming too jumbled, her emotions a confused mess that was changing far too quickly for her liking. A couple of weeks ago, she would have gladly burned his entire kingdom to the ground with him inside it. Probably laughed while she did it. Now she was trying to get to know him, enjoying spending time with him, and constantly fantasizing about him. Hell, thirty seconds ago she was ready to leap across the table and into his lap.

She moved towards him cautiously. When she neared, blueish light flared in his palms, traveling up his fingers. She gasped and stilled. She wasn't afraid, but *mesmerized.* She'd never seen power like this before. She could feel it charging the surrounding air, like static but thicker. All gods and goddess had power, but the brothers were something else entirely. It was heady and terrifying and, alright, maybe a little sexy too. A lot sexy. Whatever.

"What are you going to do? Give me gills and flippers?" she joked, though she wouldn't mind having a mermaid tail for a day. She'd loved the mortal stories of princess Ariel as a child. Beck had related to the mermaid with the whole not-belonging-in-the-human-world thing. Of course, Ariel had *chosen* to be there and Beck hadn't, but still. Now that she'd met real life mermaids and seen how magnificent they were in the water, she absolutely wouldn't mind splashing around for a day.

"Even better. It's difficult to explain, but I'm going to mark you, sharing a bit of my power with you. The rune will allow you to move freely through the water just as the inhabitants and I do." She thought that over and he gave her all the time she needed, letting her decide. She appreciated that though he had every right to be, he wasn't heavy handed, forcing things on her before she was ready.

"Is it permanent?"

"No, the effects last for a day or two as the rune fades."

"Hmm. Ok, why not?" she said, shrugging. She'd been dying to explore, so if this let her do that, she was down. Poseidon edged closer, until their chests were nearly touching. She forced her breathing to remain steady and even, forced her muscles to lock into place as his scent enveloped her.

"Turn around," he said in a low voice. She obeyed. "Move your hair." Again, she obeyed immediately. Something in the soft timber of his voice compelled her to do so without question. What else could he command her to do, obeying without hesitation? Her imagination started to run wild: *grab the headboard...get on your knees...kiss me...watch.* She shivered and swallowed hard before banishing the thoughts.

"This will sting a bit, but it shouldn't be too painful."

Her lips parted on a soft gasp when he trailed his fingers down her neck to the top of her spine, but it wasn't from pain. Goosebumps erupted along her skin and she forced herself not to shiver at his soft caress. She knew he had to have noticed but she couldn't make herself care.

"So soft," he whispered. He cleared his throat softly and then heat flared on her nape. She gritted her teeth but remained still. It did sting but no worse than a bee, and it only lasted for a few seconds. He stood there for a second longer. She could barely feel his chest touching her back, but she could feel the heat radiating off of him, seeping into her bones. She would *not* lean backwards into him...

Poseidon stepped away before she could convince herself that leaning backwards was exactly what she should be doing. She got a grip on herself and decided she needed to ask Nerina to hook her up with someone again ASAP and she *would* make it work. Once she got laid, she'd be back to normal and this whole raging horndog persona she'd recently adopted would be gone. She could come to work every day and not have to physically stop herself from jumping her boss.

Beck rolled her shoulders. She didn't *feel* any different. She faced him and winged a brow upward.

"Do you trust me?" he asked, seeming to know exactly what she was thinking. She gave him a level look and he rolled his eyes. "Ok, do you half way believe that based on my past behavior where you are concerned that I wouldn't willingly do anything to harm you?"

"I...suppose so."

"Ok, good," he grinned. "Let's go."

BECK EXPECTED to merely be able to breathe underwater, but the mark Poseidon had given her had done far more than that. She felt the water pressing against her on all sides, otherwise she may not have even believed they'd actually left the dome, because she could breathe, speak, and walk as if she were in any normal room on land. She didn't float or swim, words weren't muffled, and the water didn't fill her mouth as soon as she opened it. *Weird. So cool, but so weird.*

They visited several communities within three different realms and she'd seen such wondrous things that she thought she had to be dreaming. Some beings were like Nerina or the mermaids, looking *mostly* human. Others were like sea creatures from a mortal science fiction or horror movie. Gills and fins and fangs, bright scales and big eyes, multiple heads and tails. Some were terrifying. Some were beautiful. All were fascinating.

She'd watched Poseidon as they'd moved through the realms and had honestly been in a bit of awe. He'd listened to all who wished to speak with him, helped those who needed it, raised glasses and shared laughs with his subjects. He'd never seemed condescending or bored, never acted irritated or made anyone feel like he was there solely for looks or out of obligation. He genuinely seemed to like and care about these beings. He exuded the perfect balance of powerful ruler and someone who could be your buddy. Though she knew it had been quite a while since he'd visited some of these settlements, he even remembered some of the creatures' *names* for crying out loud.

She had to admit she was a bit surprised. The part of her that had been told stories of the horrors the gods committed all her life expected him to rule with an iron fist, for his people to fear and despise him and for him to hate and resent them in return. The other part that knew he had a reputation for being the laid-back ruler who only thought with his cock, and someone like that couldn't be a true leader, could they? But neither one of those was accurate. He truly was a good king, one who Beck herself would be proud to serve.

For the thousandth time, she wondered why her mother had lied about all of this. Why had she filled Beck's head with such utter bullshit? Anger simmered in her chest. She vowed that she would be finding out soon. *It's time mom and I had a little chat.* Beck deserved to know the truth.

Finished with their work for the day, Poseidon walked beside her along the beach within the dome. The mystical sun within it was beginning to sink low in the sky and the sunsets here were something she'd never get used to. Vivid purple and pink light danced off of the turquoise water, the sand beneath glittering like thousands of diamonds.

"Thank you for coming with me today," he said after a beat of silence.

"It's my job," she replied automatically before wincing slightly. That sounded pretty cold. "Sorry. I...enjoyed it actually."

She made sure to keep enough distance between them as they strolled that their arms didn't brush, but she couldn't stop herself from glancing at him from under her lashes every few seconds as she pretended to watch the sun or the waves. She had to suppress a sigh. Sunset light in Aqueous *really* agreed with Poseidon.

"Can I ask you something?" he said, looking slightly tense.

"I won't promise I'll answer, but you can ask," she responded carefully.

"Why do you hate me so much?" She drew her gaze away from the sea to look at him. Big mistake. His eyes were even more golden in the setting sun and they seemed to be peering right to the heart of her. He seemed bothered by the idea of her hatred. Not annoyed like when she first arrived, but bothered, as if it...pained him?

"It isn't you, in particular," she hedged. She wanted to tell him that she didn't hate him, not anymore, but he continued before she could.

"Ok, fine. Us in general," he prompted. "What did we do to you?" That tiny edge of hurt in his voice did her in. She took a deep breath and let it out slowly before answering. Why not rip the band aid off the first experience of true sharing? Just get it over with. She wouldn't tell all, but she found she wanted to tell *some*. Was dying to, actually. She'd had no one to talk to about any of this before and the words tumbled over themselves in their haste to make it out first.

"Do you know what Beck is short for?"

He blinked, clearly not expecting that response. "Um, I assumed Rebecca?"

She shook her head. "Beckham."

"Beckham? I like it," he replied, still looking a bit confused. She refused to acknowledge that hearing him say the hated name elicited a completely different feeling than when her mother uttered it—or spit it with disdain, usually.

"The *reason* it's Beckham is that we lived across the street from Beckham Park." He frowned, not understanding. She ran her hands through her hair, fingers getting caught in a few knotty curls before tugging their way free. Beck exhaled roughly.

"My mother fled your world, but she hated every minute on the Mortal Plane. She blamed me for her self-imposed prison sentence there, living among those so far beneath her." Beck rolled her eyes. How many times had she heard that in her life? "She didn't want me, never did, and was never shy about making that fact clear. Do you get it now? She didn't even care enough to really *name* me. She just looked out the window and picked the first thing she saw." Beck barked out a humorless laugh. "I guess it's a good thing we didn't live across from a Taco Bell."

She rubbed her chest as a stab of pain suddenly flared. She'd come to terms with this a long time ago...or at least she *thought* she had, but talking about it now sliced through the scar covering the wound. She glanced away from him, staring down at her toes in the sand.

"She..." How to explain without giving away too much about who her mother was and what power she possessed? "...had her shit together long enough to secure us a place to live but not much past that. I was taking care of myself by the time I was seven and taking care of *her* by the time I was nine. I stole food, begged for money, lied about too many things to even keep track—whatever I had to do. I tried to keep up appearances as best as I could and most people just assumed she was a mortal woman with lots of demons she was dealing with and I was the poor daughter caught in the middle of it all. Many adults were kind to me because of that, actually, so that was nice, but I never had friends. I was always on the outside, never fitting in anywhere. I tried with mortals and supernatural beings alike, but I wasn't right for either world, not really. I didn't belong anywhere. It was…it was hard." *Gods, it really had been.*

She rarely let herself think back on it all, but now laying it all out together, she could really see everything and really *feel* everything. She forced the tears away and swallowed thickly, slowly raising her eyes to meet his once more. She was afraid of what she might see. Pity? She didn't want that, honestly thought she might die if he pitied her. *Why did I tell him all of that? Stupid, stupid, stupid.*

But it wasn't pity she saw when she held his gaze. It was blazing anger. *Ok, not what I was expecting.*

"Your mother…" He trailed off and clenched his jaw. The ocean behind him became tumultuous, the waves crashing with a dangerous force. Confused, she turned her gaze back to him.

"So, you see now?" she continued, "I blamed you all for the life I had. That's where the hate really came from I guess. It wasn't so much the stories mother told me, which yes, I'm starting to believe may have mostly been fabrications, and I have no idea why she would lie about all of that—that's something to figure out another day—but it was more that I hated you all for what you'd made *her*, which is what made my life a nightmare. And then there was the whole abandonment by my father thing, which I know now wasn't quite true either, but still—fuel to the fire for as long as I can remember."

Poseidon opened his mouth to respond again, but closed it promptly. He tried again, but once more snapped it shut. He was seething for some reason, but apparently had no idea how to respond. Which was fine, she was done talking for the evening. She hadn't imagined sharing would take such a toll on her. She honestly just wanted to curl up in bed and cry for a while, which she never did. Ever. She'd stopped crying when she was six or seven. She'd learned far too quickly that the tears did nothing but make her mother irritated. They didn't put food in her empty belly or keep her warm, so she'd all but banished them from her life. Now they threatened to start and maybe never stop.

"I'll see you tomorrow," she said and turned away, making her way quickly over the soft sand towards the castle.

"Beck," Poseidon called, finally finding his voice. She stopped and glanced over her shoulder.

"You...you could belong here," he said quietly. Her breath caught and her chest constricted. She wanted to belong here more than she would let herself admit and his words had speared her right through the heart.

Not sure how exactly to respond, she whispered a soft, "Goodnight," and hurried inside.

TWELVE

Dalton Pembroke began to swim up from the depths of unconsciousness. He was lying on something soft and giving. Not the floor of his cell? *What the...*

Memories flashed behind his lids: Skylar coming to see him; a flash of light and a pulse of power unlike anything he'd ever experienced; a strange woman with purple eyes and silver tattoos.

His eyes flew open. He was in what appeared to be a hut of some sort, a thatched ceiling above him. The most delectable smells invaded his senses. It reminded him of the Hawaiian Tropical Sunset candles Skylar had put all over the mansion—*they were buy three get one free, dad! I bought forty!*—but every note was slightly different. Stronger. More intense. Things he couldn't place but instantly loved.

He eased upward, prepared for his muscles and bones to scream in protest as they always did since his imprisonment, but he found he felt...good. Great even. Rested. Completely healed. Better than he had in years to be honest. *How long was I out?* He tilted his head, letting his heightened and honed senses reach out and explore the surrounding area. He heard the lap of soft waves outside, a waterfall somewhere nearby roaring quietly, a soft breeze rustling leaves and...

bells? No one else nearby though, no one waiting in the wings to attack.

Dalton rubbed his eyes and turned to plant his feet on the smooth wooden floor. A note was propped on the side table beside a pitcher of what looked like water. He was hesitant to drink, not trusting this dream yet. He poured some of the liquid into the glass, sniffing and swirling. He detected nothing indicating that it had been poisoned. Suddenly parched beyond belief, he decided it was worth the risk and took a tentative sip. His eyes slid shut in sheer bliss. It was in fact water, but it was the purest, crispest, coolest water he'd ever tasted. It was like every other drop that had ever touched his lips before this was mud.

He gulped down the entire glass, refilled it, and polished off the second as he opened the note:

Morning, sunshine! I hope you enjoyed your three weeks of rest and healing. Trust me: you needed it.

Weeks? He'd been out for *weeks*?? That woman must have mystically drugged him for him to have slept that long. He should be fuming about that, but after what he'd endured...well, he suspected he did, in fact, need it. He continued reading.

There are clothes in the closet, food will appear as soon as you wish it, and your room is comped. Consider yourself a VIP! There is another guest on the premises, but play nice with her despite how badly you might want to strangle her. She has that effect on people. I will be there to collect you soon, promise! –E

He frowned. This note was utter nonsense. Who was here with him? Why would he want to strangle them? Where was *here* anyway? And who the hell was E?? He scrubbed a hand across his chin and realized how badly he needed a shave. He glanced across the room towards what he assumed was the bathroom and another note caught his eye. He quickly moved to snatch it off of the door, pleased to find that his full speed had returned.

E stands for Emmie by the way. I'm Skylar's newest bestie and the perfect creature who rescued you. You can thank me later. XOXO

Skylar. The name sent his pulse racing and his heart thudding against his chest. The most important person in his entire life. She was safe? She was with this strange Emmie person? Could he trust this note or was it all some trick? He didn't understand why she would have taken him from that prison just to torture him more, but he'd learned long ago that motivations for vile acts rarely involved logic.

But the more he thought about it, the more his gut told him that this Emmie did not mean him ill. And he always trusted his gut. It was the first thing he'd taught his daughter, something he drilled into everyone who worked for him, and his had never steered him wrong.

But then why did he have to remain here? Why could he not see Skylar now? He wanted to roar in frustration. He was not in the mood to wait around wherever the hell he was for this Emmie person to come back to collect him. *As if I'm a piece of luggage left at baggage claim.* He felt himself beginning to change, his transformation on a hairpin trigger after being held so long in that place, unable to change fully to protect himself because of the onyx surrounding him and in the cuff of if they'd forced him to wear. Now, his beast was desperate to rise, ready to jump at the slightest provocation.

Dalton closed his eyes and took deep, settling breaths. Eventually, he calmed and came up with a plan. He would shower, definitely shave, dress, and explore. He would find a way to leave and he would find his daughter himself. He'd never encountered a problem that he couldn't solve, and he sure as hell wouldn't start now.

He found that the hut was more of a beachy cabin, comprised of a small bedroom, connected bathroom and closet, a living space, and small kitchen. It was decorated in shades of soft blues and white, sea glass and shells were collected in bowls and vases, and gauzy curtains fluttered in the breeze from the open windows. It was like pure heaven after that cell.

He showered and though he'd meant to do it quickly, he lingered, allowing himself to indulge in the hot water. After weeks—or maybe months, he still wasn't sure—of being held in that cell with his only chance to bathe in any way tied to his non-ending drowning, he allowed himself a few extra minutes to luxuriate in the stall. Eventually, he forced himself to leave and get rid of his scruff.

It was a common misconception that immortals couldn't change at all physically. They could, to an extent. They could heal, but scars could still be left behind when injuries were grave enough. They could get tattoos, if special mystical inks were used. Their hair could still grow, but only to the point where it had been when they'd transitioned into immortality. It was one reason many males left their hair, facial and otherwise, longer around the general timeframe of transition for their species—that way they always had a little wiggle room to change their appearance should they wish to during their un-ending lives. Dalton had transitioned with a full beard nearly down to his chest, full mustache, and hair so long it brushed his shoulders. He hadn't kept any of them at those lengths in centuries, but he liked having the option.

Feeling more like himself, he checked out the closet. He bypassed the Hawaiian shirts and swim trunks with a quirk of his brow, and donned utility pants, a black t-shirt, and boots—his personal uniform. No weapons to be found, but it didn't bother him. His entire *body* was a weapon.

His stomach gave a loud rumble as he crossed to the door and instantly, the small table was filled to the brim with so much food he could scarcely believe it. Meats, cheeses, fruits. Things he'd never seen before but that made his mouth water. He wavered, but forced himself to turn and walk out of the door. Exploration first. *Then* feast.

Dalton stepped outside into a certified paradise. He blinked several times, trying to make sense of what he was seeing. Soft golden sand stretched out to pale turquoise water. A bright purple tail cut through the water and disappeared beneath the waves a moment later. Lush foliage with vibrant orange and pink flowers and towering silver palms surrounded the curved beach. The clouds were swirls of purple and blue, the sky a light silver. *How strange. Beautiful, but strange.*

Everything gave off a very distinct *other* vibe. Dalton didn't sense anything threatening, but he kept on alert. He longed to explore the water, but made his way through the thick vegetation towards the waterfall he could hear in the distance. He discovered that the bells he'd been hearing were the palm fronds themselves as they blew in the wind. His lips curled upwards. He'd bet Skylar would love these. He ran his hand along several as he passed, wishing that his daughter was here with him. God—*or Gods, he supposed*—he missed her, and worse, he knew that she had to be hurting. To her, he had died all that time ago. She would be devastated.

He knew that Lucas and Zahara would be there for her, but he hated the idea of her hurting. She'd had enough hurt to last for more than one lifetime. She wasn't his blood, but she was his daughter in every sense of the word, every fiber of his being screaming that he was her father since the moment he saw her scavenging for food in that dumpster when she was eleven-year-old, looking like an adorable, though slightly deranged, raccoon. His lips curled slightly at the memory. *Don't worry, Rocket. I'm coming home.*

The soft roar of the falls grew slightly louder and he finally split a sheet of hanging vines to reveal an open-air temple settled in the middle of a lush meadow. Large and elegantly carved columns sat at intervals on a raised platform of white, glittering stone. More vines and ivy grew over the top, creating a living roof dotted with flowers. The falls were still strangely quiet despite his nearness to them. In the middle of the temple there was an ornate, gilded lounge.

And upon it: a gorgeous woman.

Was this the person the note had indicated? He made his way forward slowly as not to frighten her. She eyed him as she sipped deep red wine from a golden goblet.

"Ah, you've finally decided to grace me with your presence," she purred, somewhere between annoyance and amusement. Hair black as jet curling around delicate facial features, light blue eyes, and ivory skin. She was draped in a flowing white gown that revealed more than it covered. He just stopped himself from scrubbing a hand across his mouth. She was flawless. *Stunning.* And very much unlike anything he'd ever encountered. He floundered for a moment, but quickly regained his composure.

"Apologies for keeping you waiting," he said with a wry grin that made the woman's eyes widen for a moment in obvious appreciation. Dalton Pembroke was one of the fiercest and most-feared supernatural creatures on Earth, could be cold and merciless to a terrifying degree. But he was also a charmer when he wanted—or needed—to be. "Who are you? Where are we?" he asked, keeping his voice soft and even.

"I am a goddess and you are in my own personal realm...or, well, the realm that I borrow from time to time," she said with a slight frown. Like a...vacation home? Did gods have vacation *realms*?

"Goddess?" he whispered, incredulous. Though he knew the gods were real, hearing it confirmed was still unbelievable. He'd learned that all of the legends (at least in part) were true, that the gods *actually* existed and were alive and well living in other planes of existence. Which is exactly what had started this whole mess to begin with.

He shook himself, not ready to trudge down that road quite yet. He needed to find his way away from here, find his daughter, and then they would hash out the new, terrifying reality he'd discovered.

How exactly does one converse with a goddess? If some of the stories were to be believed, she could smite him down with the flick of a wrist if she desired. He cleared his throat and attempted a conversational but respectful tone, just the right amount of flirtation thrown in.

"Does the goddess have a name?" He smiled.

"She might," she said, her lips curling, but then she shook herself and straightened, a haughty air settling over her. Dalton arched a brow. "Emmie tells me that your name is Dalton and that I must share my paradise with you for a time." She said it as if she were put out by the news, but beneath the surface he could sense her excitement. He thought back to the note—it had only mentioned one other "guest." Perhaps the goddess was lonely, then, excited for the company. Why not leave then? *Unless she's a prisoner of some sort as well.* Who the hell is this Emmie that she could keep a *goddess* somewhere against her will?

"And is this Emmie a goddess as well?" he asked.

"Not that it is any of your business...but she did say I should, how did she put it? *Play nice* with you, despite the fact that you should be worshipping at my feet." Dalton's smile remained, but it took on an edge now. He would be doing no such thing. "So, no, she is not a goddess, but she is *of* the gods and beyond powerful."

"Can you get in touch with her? I need to leave."

"I can send a message, yes, but she comes when she wishes and *only* when she wishes. She said she would return soon. Until then, we are...neighbors." The woman took another long sip of her wine, studying him. He scrubbed a hand down his face. No. That answer wasn't acceptable to him.

"And should I wish to leave without her assistance? Is there a... doorway out of a realm?" Did he really just ask that? He would take the time to process all of this later, but right now, he cleared his mind of everything but the mission, a skill he had honed over centuries.

Her lips curled. "Usually, yes. But this realm was created specifically by Emmie and therefore, she is the only one with a key. Fickle things, keys. Always causing trouble..." she said in an odd tone, her eyes losing focus for a moment. She shook herself and gulped down the rest of her wine, returning her gaze to him. Her eyes looked a bit glassy. Was she dunk?

"What was I saying? Oh, yes—you're stuck here until Emmie returns for you."

"Surely a goddess could help me leave?" Dalton smiled at her again. Perhaps stroking her ego would be beneficial. She expected him to worship her after all, so she would surely like showing off her power.

"Of course I could," she scoffed, but he could sense something off. Had she faltered there for a moment? "But I wouldn't waste such power as mine on some lowly immortal creature as you."

That's the way of it then. He supposed she had every right to have that attitude—she was a goddess for fuck's sake—but it didn't mean he had to enjoy it. He'd always had a bit of a problem with authority. He was the ultimate alpha and didn't take well to being spoken down to. Even so, he tried to keep his temper in check.

"You'll not begrudge me looking for a doorway myself then, I'm sure?"

"Oh, by all means. Knock yourself out, as they say." She waved her hand grandly, inviting him to do what he would. He gave her a clipped nod and very shallow bow, and backed away from the temple, keeping his eyes on her until he was back in the forest again.

He spent the next few hours exploring every inch of his newest prison. He'd found that when he went far enough one way, he'd magically end up back where he started, like the old Nintendo game Skylar used to make him play. Mario would run off of the screen on the right and run right back on again from the left. So, the realm was circular, some sort of continuous loop.

"Fuck," he grated, but he didn't give up. He ran and ran and ran... but eventually, he relented. He wasn't giving up, but he decided to take a break. Hunger was gnawing at him as he walked back to the cabin and all he could think about was devouring every bite on that table. To his surprise, and slight annoyance, the goddess was lounging in a hammock just off of the small deck.

"I expected you back much sooner, I've been waiting for ages," she pouted. "You're quite determined."

Dalton wiped sweat from his brow and stalked past her, bounding up the steps.

"I am. I *will* find a way out of this place. I need to get back to my daughter."

"Daughter," she echoed. "I have a daughter as well."

He turned to face her. "Then you can understand the fact that I will stop at nothing to get back to her."

She pursed her lips and canted her head as if seriously contemplating his statement. She eventually hiked a shoulder.

"I wish you luck with that endeavor," she said in that haughty tone again. It grated on his nerves. The sooner he could leave here, the better. There was something off about this female. Not the fact that she was a goddess, but something else that he couldn't quite put his finger on, like something dangerous was brewing right below the surface. Her moods were mercurial and he had no idea what power she might possess—those two things could spell disaster. She seemed a little...unhinged.

She made her way out of the hammock, not nearly as graceful as she seemed to think she was. How drunk was she? It took special kinds of alcohol—or insanely copious amounts of mortal alcohol— to get immortals like him drunk. What would it take to get a goddess tipsy?

She straightened and blew a lock of hair off of her forehead.

"As I am sure you are simply dying to dine with a goddess and worship at her feet. I suppose I will allow it." She looked at him expectantly. He barely kept himself from snorting. Was she serious? Were all of the gods like this? If so, Dalton was just fine never meeting another one. Now he understood the other part of Emmie's note: he could certainly see himself wanting to strangle the goddess if she kept this up for long.

"I appreciate the invitation, but I respectively decline, goddess."

Her mouth popped open with a small huff. She narrowed her eyes, anger radiating from her. Would she attack him? The famous wrath of the gods coming to life? He tensed and prepared to shift into his full lupin form should he need to. He didn't care who or what she was, he would not go down without a fight. He bent his knees slightly, ready to spring. His nails lengthened into black claws and his teeth sharpened into fangs inside his mouth. Unlike a typical shifter who was all or nothing, as a born lupin he could call certain attributes of his full beastly form at will. Sometimes you didn't need to go full demonic wolf-like creature, you just needed a good set of claws.

He waited but...nothing. She merely sent him killing looks before huffing and turning to stomp off like Skylar used to when she was fourteen. Did she have no power then? Or she merely chose not to use it on him?

"When you change your mind, you know where to find me, dog," she called over her should. He narrowed his eyes at her retreating back. When she was well away, he straightened and went inside. He was ravenous and as soon as he walked into the living space, the table once again became laden with food.

Dalton sat and gorged on the most delicious meal he'd ever had. The tastes were much like the smells: intense and sharp in the best possible way. He sighed, knowing that he could never enjoy typical food the same way ever again. He made his way back outside and thankfully, he was still alone. He settled down in the sand and stared out over the water, taking a moment to be thankful that he was alive and out of that cell, that all his torture was behind him. He didn't allow the memories of that time to surface, though they tried. They would haunt him for a long while, he knew that, but for now, he kept them at bay. He just let himself relax in this moment, to feel joy at the sun on his face and the fact that he would see Skylar again soon.

He closed his eyes and smiled his first genuine smile in ages.

THIRTEEN

Poseidon had no idea how to do this. It had been so long since he wanted to actually get close to anyone that he was admittedly a bit rusty. His newfound desire was still just a small flicker and it wasn't enough to be helpful in guiding his way. But it was growing, bit by bit, and the surge of anger he'd felt towards Beck's mother had helped give it a boost.

His hands had heated and his power had surged listening to Beck share that piece of herself with him. The way Beck had been forced to live, how alone and unwanted she must have felt...He gripped his drink far too tightly, the glass threatening to shatter.

She tried to hide it but he had caught the hurt as she'd spoken the words. He wanted to soothe her, to make sure she never felt that way again, but...he had no clue how. He'd meant what he said. The voice had whispered in his mind and he'd voiced the thought without, well, thought. She *could* belong there...with him? He rubbed his temples and groaned.

Maybe Hades could provide some pointers. He'd managed to put his hatred of Persephone behind him and was falling deeper and deeper in love with Skylar every day. They'd even gotten married for fuck's sake. If Hades could pull that off, surely Si could make friends with Beck, right? *What if I want to be...more than friends?*

He frowned, the whispered thought catching him off guard again. Sure, he wanted something physical with Beck so badly he could barely stand it. So badly, in fact, that he couldn't even manage his usual favored activities as of the last few days. Every time he tried, all he could think was how badly he wished that *she* was the one kissing or stroking him, that it was *her* soft skin pressed against his own, *her* icy blue eyes boring into him as he rose above her. It had been a bit of a buzzkill, though he didn't mind too much if he were being honest. He'd grown tired of having to fake his way through encounter after encounter, pretending to love every minute. He enjoyed himself enough, he supposed, but not enough to compel him to want to keep repeating the half-hearted liaisons.

So, yes, he most definitely craved something physical with her, but more than that? An actual relationship? No. That was ridiculous...wasn't it? But what if it *wasn't?* What if this was what he'd been waiting for all this time? Finally something worth exploring. She wasn't his one true match, he knew that, but he couldn't deny that he was drawn to her. So, maybe he *could* do this. Maybe he could push through this wall and actually be something more with her, have some contentment for the first time in long memory. He could do casual dating, right? Zeus did it all the time. If Zeus could do it, so could he damn it.

His resolve became firmer by the second. Yes, he could do this, *would* do this. He would find a way to connect and explore this with her. If she wanted him, that is. He frowned. What if she didn't? The thought was...unwelcome. She was attracted to him, that was obvious despite her attempts to hide the fact, but could she ever want more with him? *Only one way to find out.*

Path set, Si tried harder to get to know her and, to his delight, she was thawing more and more each day. They'd told each other tidbits from their pasts and though her life on the Mortal Plane was far from ideal, she had a handful of not completely terrible experiences to share. The smallest of smiles played on her lips as she recounted the time spent with the poor souls from the boat. Even that tiny tilt of those full lips transformed her entire face. He caught the briefest hint of the dimples he longed to see with every fiber of his being. He recounted tales of his admittedly long life, which she liked to tease him about in her dry way. *Do you need a walker, Father Time. Do you miss the dinosaurs? Did you break a hip getting up too fast?* It was something he found himself looking forward to more and more.

They hadn't gotten into anything too deep yet, but progress was progress, so he'd take it. Beck had yet to tell him who her mother was, and he decided to finally ask Zeus about all of his past partners. Narrowing it down to roughly twenty-four years prior had to limit the possibilities, right? Si thought about his own numbers from that time frame and grimaced.

Ok, so maybe it would still take quite a bit of time to narrow down the list, but he was determined to. Not only was it a puzzle nagging at him, but he had the urge to have a chat with the woman. She needed to answer for how she'd treated her daughter all these years. Even thinking of it made his power roil within him, a caged beast begging to be let out. He had no children—unlike his brother, he'd placed a special rune on his body to prevent such a thing—but if he ever did, he couldn't fathom being anything less than doting. How had Beck's mother barely cared for her? Left her to fend for herself at such a young age, especially being in the position they were in? An outsider in every sense of the word, and a terrified one at that. He couldn't understand the woman, but she deserved to be told how very wrong she'd been in this. Si felt... protective over Beck.

Poseidon glanced sidelong at her now as they walked through the garden maze he'd recently added to the grounds. He liked to change things up within the dome periodically or he grew bored. He'd bet her a full week off from her duties and a ride on Pegasus that she couldn't find her way out of the maze within three hours on her own. She'd *almost* grinned when she told him to get the saddle ready because she *would* be going for a ride on that pony.

They rounded a corner only to find another dead end. He smirked and she scowled before holding up a finger to silence him.

"Shut it," she grumbled. She bent over to toss her hair into one of those loose knots on the top of her head that he was coming to love. She had such a casual sexiness to her when she had her hair that way. Effortlessly more beautiful than Aphrodite without even trying.

"Would you like a hint? You can still *pet* Pegasus if you finish with a hint," he offered. "Perhaps give him a few Salenia fruits. He does so enjoy them." The look she gave him could curdle milk and he smiled wider. This was *fun*, the most fun he'd had in quite a while with his clothes on. Or at all really, truth be told.

"I've still got one hour and twenty-two minutes left, thank you very much. So, kindly take your hints and shove them." She gave an exaggerated curtsey. "Your majesty," she mocked. He narrowed his eyes but couldn't stop his smile. This female was…he wasn't sure what. He knew she was of the gods in some way, but he had no idea of her parentage and he still wasn't sure about the mysterious powers the demon had alluded to. He hadn't seen any manifest as of yet. Could she not produce them at will perhaps?

When first learning to control their powers, many gods could only call them in times of stress or fear. It wouldn't surprise him if that were the case given the fact that she grew up in the mortal world and the complete lack of guidance provided by her mother. The thought threatened to sour his mood, so he halted it quickly. He was enjoying himself and didn't want anything to ruin it. So, he held his arm out, gesturing for her to continue on her way. He let her walk a bit in front of him and may or may not have let himself sneak glances of that magnificent ass a time or two. Ok, fine, forty-seven times in the last hour. Sue him.

A slight tickle against his mind let him know his brother was trying to communicate. He opened his thoughts.

-Si, if you can pull your dick out of whatever orifice it's currently stuck in, we could use some help over here.-

Si rolled his eyes.

-What's going on? And my cock is tucked neatly in my pants at the moment, thank you very much. I'm not constantly *fucking, you know-* Though as he watched the sensual sway of Beck's hips, he longed to be. He scrubbed a hand across his mouth and jaw. *Mercy.*

-Maynard here again. We're going to end this. Now.-

Si went rigid, all humor vanishing in an instant. That prick.

He turned to Beck and said apologetically, "I've gotta go. I'll explain later." He phased away before she could even respond.

"Where is that piece of shit?" he barked as he fell into step beside his brothers. Zeus clapped him on the back and Hades gave him a nod in greeting as they rushed down the hall. Power rolled through him, ready to fight Maynard and put an end to all of this once and for all.

"He opened a portal by the lake. I have to find Sky."

"Ah yes, the little missus. Been dying to meet her...or well, meet her again, I suppose." He frowned slightly. "How weird is this whole reincarnate thing anyway?"

"Totally weird," Zeus agreed as the rounded a corner. Hades' body was shot through with tension and Si didn't think he'd ever seen his brother so on edge, so worried. They passed by a large window and Hades' steps faltered before he sighed in relief. Si followed his gaze and saw who he assumed must be Skylar sitting on the steps of the palace eating ice cream with Jeff.

"Weapons," Hades grated. Si cursed silently, realizing he'd left without his trident. He was going to blame it on a combination of excitement to end Maynard and distraction caused by Beck's ass in those shorts. They all phased to the armory, each strapping on blades of every shape and size, and Si summoned his trident, the weapon appearing in his hand within a heartbeat. Hades paused and straightened, tension stealing through his body once more. He phased and Si look to Zeus in confusion.

"What now?"

"Fuck if I know. Come on."

They phased to Hades' chambers to find Conan, their demigod-trapped-in-the-body-of-a-cat friend, sitting on the bed. He inclined his head towards a note next to him, a black crown beside it. Hades stormed to the bed, snatched up the note and scanned the words. His expression turned bleaker with every second, his skin paling. What the hell was going on?

Hades crumbled the parchment in his hands, threw back his head and bellowed at the ceiling so loudly that the walls shook. Si flinched and met Zeus' gaze. Worry flared there and they both moved towards their brother.

Zeus laid a big hand on Hades' shoulder. "What? What the hell is going on?"

"She's gone. Maynard has her. She went to him somehow, I think. Maybe even summoned him here herself. But either way, she's gone," Hades croaked, voice deadened. Zeus frowned in confusion.

"But she's on the front steps with Jeff, we just saw her two seconds ago, man." Zeus looked to Si who shook his head in a *don't ask me, maybe he's losing it* gesture.

"No, we didn't," Hades growled.

"Uh oh..." Si said, knowing how close Hades was to losing his shit. Smoke and flames were swirling around him already, his power a bow string pulled almost too taut. This could turn really bad, really fast if his brother didn't get himself under control. Hades disappeared again and Zeus and Poseidon let out matching exhalations of annoyance. By the time the two of them phased to the steps, Skylar was no longer there. Emmie stood in her place, steady gaze locked with Hades'. She stood her ground but there was fear just beneath the surface as Hades glared, rage pulsing from him.

Emmie didn't know how this would play out, Si realized. She could see all futures except her own. She didn't know if Hades would end her right now, and still, she'd done...whatever the hell she'd done. Si was still trying to put all the pieces together, but mostly he was just confused as hell.

"What the fuck?!" Hades yelled.

"She asked me to and I agreed. She didn't tell me what she was planning."

"SHE DIDN'T HAVE TO TELL YOU, GODS DAMNIT!" Hades stormed closer to her, smoke and flames billowing in his wake, scorching the earth as he went. "You knew! You knew what she was doing! How could you let this happen!?" Hades towered over Emmie, glaring down at her with such fury it made Si wince. It was the tensest stand-off Si had ever witnessed. Zeus made a move towards them, but Si stopped him with a hand on his shoulder. Whatever was happening, they needed to let Hades and Emmie figure it out. They both had their power at the ready though, just in case they needed to contain their brother's. The two of them together were the only thing that could if Hades let it loose completely. They were each other's checks-and-balances as it were. Any two of the brothers working together could subdue the power of the third if need be.

Finally, the fury drained out of Hades as if someone had pulled a plug in a tub, and he dropped to his knees. He put his head in his hands, pulling at his hair so forcefully he was ripping strands free. The sight made Poseidon's chest ache. He'd never seen his brother like this. Never seen him this hurt or afraid, this raw. Even after Persephone, it was nothing like this.

"H, we'll get her back. It'll be ok." Si placed a hand on his brother's shoulder, wanting so badly to take this pain from him. "We'll fix this, I swear to you we will." Hades shuddered but then an odd sense of calm stole over him. He looked around at the small group gathered, meeting each of their gazes. He told them all what he was planning...and told them all goodbye.

Poseidon, Zeus, Emmie, Conan—who apparently was going by Dean now—and Jeff all waited anxiously for Hades to return or to send word for them. They'd reluctantly agreed to wait while Hades went to retrieve his wife. He was going to try to rescue Skylar and stop

Maynard, but didn't seem to have much hope that he'd succeed. He'd been fully prepared to give up his kingdom and die in the process so long as Skylar was safe. So, they were at the ready in case he failed and Maynard tried to move in with his armies to take over the Underworld. Charon arrived, pacing along with the rest of them, Cerberus at his side. Poseidon gave the mutt scratches behind all of his ears.

"That idiot. That fucking idiot," the ferryman muttered as he walked, running fingers through his unruly red curls.

Dante landed in a flourish of silvery wings to let Zeus know that Ares had his army at the ready should they be needed to defend against Maynard's forces or if they should decide to take the fight to him directly. Zeus looked pensive and every bit the King of the gods. His eyes flickered between sky blue and deep, stormy gray as his emotions ebbed and flowed with his thoughts.

"No, we wait for the threat of invasion or for Hades' word. We have to trust him in this."

"But isn't anyone else having déjà vu right about now?" Si asked, worry gnawing at his insides like a raging hydra. He couldn't stop replaying the last time this situation had occurred in his mind. His chest constricted when he saw Hades in his memories: chained and bleeding and broken, anguished and enraged, so close to being taken from them forever...

Emmie slumped on the stairs rubbing her temples. Her eyes were like silvered mirrors, her own power flowing through her. She was muttering to herself quietly.

"Come on...make the decision...do it..."

Zeus eyed her and she met his gaze. She gave him a small shake of her head, telling him she didn't know the outcome yet and that they must wait. The future wasn't a simple a thing as many people believed. It was fluid, ever changing. Smaller things, like two people having a meet cute over spilled coffee, were fairly set, but big things? They could be swayed by any number of factors. So, though Emmie saw what would come to pass, she saw *multiple* versions of it. She tried to steer outcomes as best she could without overstepping and angering the Fates, but in the end, it was out of her hands.

"We have to trust him," Zeus repeated, though he looked half tempted to ride in, lighting bolts a-blazing. Si sat heavily on the stairs beside Emmie, feeling antsy and useless and cut open to the quick. He kept seeing Hades as he'd been before he left, on his knees and overcome with such love and pain, and Si had felt...jealous. Of course he felt terrible for Hades and what he was going through, but he also felt so incredibly jealous of his brother for having that kind of love and connection with another to begin with. He wanted that for himself so damn badly. Would he ever get there again? He frowned as a strange thought arose: had he ever truly been there before, even with Callie? He'd never had doubts before, but now, well...he couldn't be sure.

She hadn't been his—he'd never felt the shattering of heaven and earth type feelings that were said to accompany finding one's true match—but he'd certainly loved her fiercely...hadn't he? When she'd left, he'd been so utterly brokenhearted...but now, when he looked back, something didn't feel quite right. The memories seemed to be hidden behind a strange haze, the feelings themselves sheltered behind it as well. He shook himself, not understanding and assuming he was just too keyed up about their current situation to think properly.

So, instead of thinking to the past, he let his thoughts drift to Beck. He felt a stab of guilt for leaving her in the maze alone like that with hardly an explanation to speak of. She was probably back to hating him again and any progress he'd made had been erased. *Great. One more thing to worry about.* But the fact that he was even worrying about it at all was a good sign, right? *Say it with me, kids: progress!*

They waited for hours or days or centuries more, and Emmie finally let out a relieved whoosh of breath and her lips curled into a triumphant smile. They all let out a collective sigh, the tension melting off of them like ice under a harsh sun. Emmie threw her arms around Charon and kissed him hard on the lips, Dean's tail swishing as he watched, and Dante slapped Jeff hard on the back. They received word from Hades himself a few minutes later, relaying quickly what had happened.

Turned out Skylar was half god-half fucking *phoenix*. If Si hadn't seen the proof in Hades' thoughts, seen her burned by Mynard and rise as a certified badass from the ashes in Hades' memories, he never would have believed it. Phoenix were thought to be completely extinct, and that's only if you believed in them at all, which many gods didn't. They were myth and legend even to them. That his newest sister was one? Beyond amazing...and a little terrifying.

A cruel smile spread across Zeus' face as Hades sent Gavril to Zeus' side for...handling.

"Hello, old friend. So nice to see you again," Zeus purred as he latched a hand onto Gavril's shoulder so hard, the bones shattered to dust. Gavril gave a strangled cry of pain.

"Yes, we've missed you *dearly*," Dante added, voice cold and sharp as steel.

Gavril had once been a member of the Elite. He'd fought beside Dante and protected Zeus with his life, had been created from Zeus' own blood and considered a son of sorts by the god. But then he'd betrayed them all and began working with Maynard. Until recently, he'd been locked inside a dungeon far below Mount Olympus. He'd managed to escape while Zeus was otherwise occupied with concerning business dealing with Pandora's Box. He'd assured Si and Hades that there was nothing to worry about—yet, but they'd be discussing it again more seriously soon. The Box equaled big time bad news.

For now, Zeus and Dante escorted Gavril away and Poseidon didn't even want to imagine the pain their former friend and ally would soon be experiencing.

"That was a bit dicey there for a hot second. The future kept changing," Emmie said, massaging her temples again. Poseidon pulled her into his chest, holding her tight and rubbing her back. He knew the true toll seeing so many possible fates took on her. There were days she had to fight tooth and nail to stay lucid, and some days where she lost that fight, having no idea when she was or what was happening. She hid it well and was the strongest being Si had ever met. She melted into him and when she finally pulled away, she wiped a quicksilver tear off of her cheek and gave him a weak smile.

"One down, two to go," she muttered. Her gaze unfocused for a second and he knew she was seeing far beyond him again. She shook herself and gave him a pat on the cheek. "She's the key to it all. You better figure it out."

"Who? The key to what?"

She simply winked and disappeared with Charon in tow. Jeff chuckled low and led Cerberus instead, promising treats. Poseidon went from comforting Emmie to wanting to strangle her in all of ninety seconds. That had to be some kind of record. He scrubbed a hand down his face. Today had been one of the most stressful days he'd had in at least a thousand years, but the silver lining? Maynard was gone forever. He felt no guilt for feeling no guilt that Maynard had finally met his end. He'd been nothing but trouble since the beginning, and now, they could all rest easier.

-Thank you for coming. Talk soon. Need to worship my Queen for a bit- Hades' voice rumbled through Poseidon's mind and his lips curled.

-Talk to you in a few days-

-…maybe weeks-

Si could hear the smirk in Hades' thoughts before the doorway between their minds slammed shut, a blinking neon *Do Not Disturb* sign burned into the front. He chuckled before saying goodbye to Dean, telling the demigod to come visit him soon, and heading home, wondering what Beck might be up to.

FOURTEEN

Dalton was going crazy. Sure, he was stuck in a certified paradise realm, the most beautiful place he could possibly imagine, but a very small part of him almost wished for that cold, dark cell again. The goddess would not leave him the fuck alone. She alternated between haughty demands for his company and incoherent rants about lost kingdoms and keys and how everything was "his" fault. Who *he* was, Dalton didn't know and quite frankly, didn't care. He'd almost take the tank over dealing with her day in and day out.

He ran the entirety of the realm, covering miles upon miles, at least three times a day. Partly just because he *could* run freely as his kind loved to do after being held in a cage for so long, but the other part was simply to get away from her.

Thankfully, Emmie had thought to bar her from entering his cabin, so he could escape her there, but when he did storm inside and slam the door behind him, telling her in no uncertain terms that he was done conversing with her for the time being, she would often lie in the hammock just outside and rant or, even worse, sing terribly off-key for *hours*.

He'd figured out pretty quickly that the goddess—she'd yet to tell him her name, but he couldn't care less at this point—had no real power to speak of. He didn't understand how that was possible, but he was sure she would have used it on him by now if she had the ability. She threatened it often enough, that was for sure. He rolled his eyes at the thought. Maybe this place negated all godly powers and that's why she couldn't do anything to him. Or maybe she was full of shit and wasn't really a goddess at all. He didn't care anymore. All he cared about was Skylar

He wanted so badly to see his daughter, to make sure that she was truly alright, that it was like a physical pain in his chest. He felt completely useless and helpless—two things Dalton Pembroke *never* felt. He worried for Skylar and he worried for the innocent girl that he'd given up to those demons. What had happened to her? Had they taken her as they'd taken him? Was she being tortured now because of him? Was she even alive? Whatever had happened to her, it rested squarely on his shoulders. It was his fault they'd found her. Her pain and blood were on his hands forever. He vowed to somehow make it up to her or her family. He knew that she lived with her mother in Florida, but he hadn't seen the woman in his time watching the girl. His guilt flared even hotter. Had they taken her too? Or was she just waiting and worrying, not knowing where her daughter was or if she was ever coming home.

On top of everything else, he'd begun to have nightmares almost every night about his torture. He would wake up in a cold sweat, disoriented, sometimes even half-turned and lashing out into the air at invisible enemies. He knew he needed to "deal" as Skylar would say, but he wasn't sure he was ready to, at least not consciously.

"Not now, goddess," Dalton growled when he returned from his morning run. He wasn't in the mood today. The nightmares had been particularly grueling the night before and he awoke feeling as if his skin was still burning, the stench of charred flesh thick in his nose.

"You think I like having a lowly dog as my only company here?"

she spit. "I was meant to be a queen you know! You should be obeying my every thought, entertaining my every whim!"

He turned on her, baring his fangs and she shrank back.

"I said. *Not. Fucking. Now,*" he growled, his voice going low and becoming rougher as his beast began to rise. He was exhausted, pissed, and feeling like he had no control. The wolf within him had been trying to rise for days, desperate to take charge and protect him from himself. He stomped into the cabin breathing hard, and suddenly he hated it. Every damn inch of it.

He gripped the edge of the table and tossed it across the room. It slammed into the wall, splinting into pieces. He let the wolf out of its cage, and finally transformed fully, becoming a monster. Though human cinema depicted them as overgrown, deranged wolves, *real* lupin didn't just sprout fur or run on four legs. They remained men, but also...not. He grew taller, reaching nearly seven feet tall, and his muscles grew larger, expanding as blood pumped and the wolf within him began to take hold. Six-inch-long, razor sharp claws burst from his hands and fangs the size of small daggers shot from his gums. His eyes shifted to reflective gold and the bone structure of his face changed, become broader, his jaws extending, everything about him entirely menacing and out of a nightmare. A fully turned lupin was a terror to behold. Dalton had once seen a fae warlord piss himself at the mere sight of him in his lupin form.

But something even more terrifying than the physical transformation occurred once he turned fully: the beast took over within his mind. He was still there, but the inner wolf took charge as he watched from the passenger seat. He was a slave to the beast's desires to fight and protect, every thought becoming primal, animal-istic. All that existed was his goal and his path to it, and nothing stood in his way. *Nothing.* There was a reason why born lupin were one of the most powerful and feared supernatural species on earth.

He completely destroyed the cabin, rendering furniture to dust, shredded the linens and leaving deep claw marks in the walls and floor. Windows and dishes were shattered, the shells and seaglass strewn across the floor in every direction. He howled in rage and anguish and despair as he tore through the place, taking out his frustrations and anger out on anything in his path over and over again. When he could do no more, he finally collapsed into a deep slumber in the middle of the wreckage.

When he woke, the cabin was completely repaired, not a single pillow or dish out of place. He stared in wonder before a note on the table caught his eye. He scrubbed a hand down his face as he trudged over and picked it up.

Go wolfly as much as you need to. I know this isn't easy. The house will repair itself each time—and I won't even charge you the cleaning fee! Skylar is totally safe I promise. I mean, she did die that one time…

His eyes bulged. *Died!?*

But she's totally fine now. Good as new! Better actually, with new tricks and accessories!

He pinched the bridge of his nose, wondering not for the first time what exactly was wrong with this Emmie person. But, he had no choice but to trust and believe her. She said that Skylar was ok, so he would cling to that. It was all that mattered. He continued reading.

And most importantly, she's beyond happy and in love. She knows you're alive and she misses you and wants to murder me sometimes for not bringing you to her yet (don't worry, she doesn't! She just thinks about it–often). You'll be reunited soon, pinky promise! Oh and the girl you ratted out is also fine. Trust me. XOXO - E

Skylar is in love? And happy? That was all Dalton had ever wanted for her, so if that was the truth, his heart was full. And the girl was alright? Though he was still dying to see Skylar and leave this place, he felt better than he had in weeks and decided he would trust in Emmie and try to bide his time here as best he could. With that in mind, he showered, dressed, ate until he was nearly bursting, and exited the cabin. Not surprising, he found the goddess waiting.

"What in the gods' names were you doing in there?" she demanded. "It sounded like a beast was on a rampage! I feared for my life!"

"It was," he said simply, not having the energy to run to get away from her this evening. He walked past her to the water and sat heavily in the sand. A few moments later, she followed. He got the feeling that despite her holier-than-though attitude, the goddess was extremely lonely. Even outside of this place, he didn't think she had anyone. She mentioned a daughter, but it didn't seem as if they were close. *Don't blame the daughter one bit there.*

"I'm...sorry that you're not happy here," she said quietly as she sat near him. He cast her a sidelong glance. Apologizing wasn't exactly the goddess' style. "I'm not a complete monster, you know. I understand that you've been through some sort of ordeal and that you didn't ask to be brought here, that you want to get back to your daughter. You love her very much."

"I do."

She nodded and stared out into the waves, looking sad.

"I'm not sure I know how to love anyone properly. I do try, but I think I was just...made wrong."

Dalton wasn't sure what to say to that or how to handle this strange facet of her. He knew how to deal with the drunk, petulant goddess who wanted him to worship at her feet. He knew how to deal with the angered, raging goddess who wanted to smite him (though for whatever reason, couldn't). He knew how to deal with the intoxicated, rambling goddess who was bent on regaling him with every story she could remember over her very, *very* long life. He even knew how to handle the flirtatious goddess who made it very clear that she would very much like to go a few rounds in the bedroom with him.

But this introspective, almost caring goddess? He hadn't a clue.

So, they sat in silence, watching the water as it crashed to the shore, retreating once more and leaving dark glittering sand in its wake. He supposed he actually would miss this place when he finally left. Perhaps he could come back, bring Skylar. He knew she would adore it. His lips curled at the idea and he held onto the vision of her discovering this place, green eyes wide and alight with excitement.

"I'm sorry I'm making this harder on you. I know that I'm...a lot to deal with at times. Sometimes it's as if I'm not even the one saying these things, like I'm watching it from outside my body and even I'm saying *what is wrong with her? She's crazy*. But I can't seem to stop myself. I...drive everyone away, in the end."

Dalton met her gaze and inclined his head, accepting the apology. He felt sorry for her. He still wanted to strangle her and knew there was something deeply troubled inside her, but he did feel bad for her. She gave him a small smile and they both turned to stare at the waves some more, a strange truce drawn between them for the time being.

They must have sat that way for hours, but eventually the goddess sighed and seemed to shake herself. *Truce over*, he thought.

Tilting her head to look at him, she beamed.

"Did I ever tell you about that time..."

FIFTEEN

Poseidon jolted awake, the sounds of screams echoing in his mind. A dream? He stiffened when he heard them again. No, not a dream. *Beck.* He wasn't sure how he knew it was her, but he did, deep in his bones, his instincts flaring in alarm. He phased to her room and pounded on the door.

"Beck?" he shouted. No answer. He pounded again, harder. "Beck!?" She screamed again in response and he busted through the door as if it were paper. He froze for a moment, confused by the scene before him. She was writhing on the bed, eyes squeezed shut and sweat plastering her hair to her temples and neck. Dark shadows swirled around her, every now and then taking different forms before becoming shadows once more. Some kind of shapeshifter? He had no idea what was happening or how these things had gotten into his home, but he wasn't having it. He struck out against them with his power, bright blue light filling the space.

They...didn't disappear? They didn't so much as react to his attacks. *What the fuck?*

Beck whimpered and then screamed again, thrashing on the bed. He eased closer and tentatively reached a hand out to grasp one of the dark creatures. It slipped through completely as if they it truly were made of shadow. He knew some creatures, like wraiths, could become incorporeal that way, but you could still sense when you passed through their bodies. This was as if he had merely passed his hand through air. One momentarily shifted to a bed of flames, licking towards him menacingly. Si tilted his head. *Illusions?* His eyes snapped back to Beck. Was *she* casting illusions in her sleep? Was that part of her mysterious power she refused to talk about?

He sat on the edge of her bed and gently shook her shoulders.

"Beck. Beck, wake up for me, sweet." Her eyes flashed open and she shot upright, one hand flying to her medallion and the other to his wrist. She was panting, eyes unfocused for a moment. "Shh, Beck, it's ok. It's me. You're safe. You were just having a nightmare."

She blinked rapidly and her gaze finally focused on his face. She sighed in relief and slumped forward to rest her head on his chest without hesitation. His eyes went wide in surprise but he didn't dare move. He slowly raised one hand to her back, rubbing gently in soothing circles.

"You're alright," he said. "Just a dream."

"A dream," she echoed, her breath tickling his bare chest. "I was... burning. Over and over they put me in the fire and I could feel my skin burning away, my bones turning to ash. Oh gods...it felt so *real*." Her heart was racing, her breathing erratic.

"You're ok. Just breathe, nice and slow. There you go. It was just a dream," he assured her again and again. She began to calm and they sat like that for long moments until she finally pulled back.

"I'm so sorry," she said, cheeks flushed now from embarrassment.

"Hey, don't be sorry. We all have nightmares." He almost mentioned the shadows, but decided to let it lie. She would tell him about that when she was ready. She might not even realize she projected them at all while she slept. She gave him a small quirk of her lips—her approximation of a smile—but then it faltered slightly as her eyes dipped.

They roved over his lips, down his chest and stomach. He hadn't wasted time putting on a shirt in his haste to reach her and she seemed to appreciate that fact now. His muscles clenched in response to her attentions. He loved when she looked at him this way and he was acutely aware of how close they were. Her breath hitched and her gaze shifted to where her hand still rested on his arm. She slowly moved it upwards, her fingers lightly grazing his skin and making him shiver. She moved it over his bicep and shoulder, down over his chest, resting briefly over his heart. He knew it was beginning to beat wildly under her palm as the air around them became thick and heavy.

She'd kicked the sheets off as she'd dreamed, and she was in nothing but lacy underwear and a silk camisole. He told himself not to, but he glanced downward. Her nipples pebbled as he watched, clearly visible beneath the light silk. Her chest rose and fell in quick bursts and he needed so badly to lean into her, to kiss her lips and pull her against him, to feel her breasts against his own chest, to tangle his hands in her hair and have her wrap her legs around his waist.

No. Not like this. Not tonight.

He took a deep breath and stood, letting her hand fall onto the bed with a soft thud.

"I'm sorry for barging in, I just heard you screaming and was worried…"

She frowned. "You heard me screaming all the way from your room?" He nodded, hoping she didn't push the issue because he had no idea how to explain how in the fuck it was possible. His senses were extremely heightened, but he shouldn't have been able to hear her as clearly as he had from clear across the castle. It made no sense.

"I'll let you get back to sleep."

"Oh. Ok, right." She shook herself. "I'll see you tomorrow. Thank you for…barging in."

He nodded and left, fixing the door he'd destroyed on his way out. He wasn't sure what the hell had just happened, but he did know one thing: Beck was far more powerful than she realized.

~

ANOTHER WEEK of working with Poseidon and Beck was feeling both great and uneasy. The absolute *ache* she was feeling for him physically was wearing her thin. She could barely keep her hands to herself when he was near. She'd slipped a few times, grazing his fingers as he handed her something, brushing her arm against his as they walked. Each time, electricity seemed to dance between them and she'd had to call on every ounce of her self-control not to do more. Don't even get her started on how close she'd been to crawling into his lap and doing gods knew what with him when he roused her from her nightmare that night.

They hadn't plagued her since she'd arrived in Aqueous, and she'd begun to hope that somehow being in a godly plane would keep them at bay forever. She'd been wrong. They'd returned with a vengeance, the worst they'd been in a long while. The dark figure had gotten so close to her that night, she would have sworn she could actually *feel* him, feel the rustle of air across her bare arms when he'd reached for her. She'd barely escaped, diving headlong into a new terrifying nightmare that had almost made her physically sick. Even now, she shuddered to think of the burning, of the flesh melting from her bones.

But then she'd heard his voice and it had somehow pierced through the darkness, opening up a doorway of light for her to climb through. Poseidon had pulled her free of the dream and then she'd lost her wits and stroked his skin, marveling at how soft and warm it was beneath her fingertips. He'd let her explore for a moment, but then *he'd* been the one to break contact. So maybe he wasn't as interested in her physically as she'd assumed, but she couldn't stop wanting him no matter how much she tried. She'd given another demigod a try, determined to force herself to at least make it to third base, but it had been a no-go.

She didn't understand what the hell was going on with her. What was this weird fixation she had for Poseidon? Was it just that he was the first god she'd ever met and she'd immediately latched on to him, like a baby duck imprinting on whatever it saw first and deciding that was its mother? Or was it because he was the first person she'd really started to let her guard down for? The first person she felt she could actually be herself with? Whatever it was, it was starting to piss her off to no end. She didn't *want* to only want him, damn it.

But it seemed to be her fate to be stuck only lusting after the one person she couldn't have. She'd decided that there couldn't be anything like that between them—*if he even wants it. Jury is still out.* It would just complicate an already complicated situation even further. No matter how much she enjoyed spending time with him, he was still a god who enjoyed sex (and lots of it) with as many beings as he could find, never wanting more than physical release.

And as much as she wanted him to stoke this fire burning within her, fantasized about it constantly and brought herself release with his names whispered on her lips more times than she could count, she knew she couldn't just be a plaything he tossed aside when he was done. She understood that he wouldn't do it cruelly, but it would still happen and...ok, fine, she knew it would *hurt* if he treated her like everyone else. She wanted...more from him which was absolutely absurd and just about the dumbest thing she'd ever wanted her in life.

"So, when do you want your ride?" Poseidon asked now.

"Huh??" she asked, snapping her thoughts back to him. Ride? Oh gods, could he read her thoughts? She *had* imagined riding him just moments ago...

"Pegasus? You made it out of the maze on your own...allegedly," he added with a suspicious look. Oh. Right. Pegasus. Not a dirty kind of ride that involved Poseidon's lap. She let out a shaky laugh and composed herself.

"Are you calling me a liar?" she asked, eyes glittering.

"Hey, you said it, not me."

"Why you little—"

Poseidon held up a hand to halt her.

"Let me stop you there, because I assure you: *nothing* about me is little." That damn half flirty-half sexy smirk that did things to her she couldn't understand slid across his lips. *He shouldn't be the God of the Sea, he should be the God of All Things Sexy.*

"As you well know actually," he added with a wink. Her cheeks heated as she recalled vividly how right he was, and he chuckled. She opened her mouth to respond with...something. She hadn't actually come up with anything witty to say, so when Cyril interrupted them, she wasn't mad about it.

"Sir, I'm sorry to interrupt but I need a word." He nodded to the soldier and gave Beck the *one minute* gesture. She inclined her head and continued picking flowers as she wandered a few feet away through the garden. Each one somehow smelled more amazing than the last and her arms were nearly full. They resembled hibiscus flowers on the Mortal Plane, but each bloom was the size of a dinner plate. They were the most stunning shades of purple with pink centers and teal with purple centers, and everything shimmered slightly as if dusted with white glitter.

She brought a purple flower to her nose and glanced at Poseidon and Cyril over the edge. The pair looked troubled and her stomach knotted. She grew tense, worry beginning to slither its way up her spine, twirling around it like a serpent. Poseidon finally sent Cyril away and made his way back to her.

"What's wrong?" she asked. He studied her for a long minute and the worry squeezed tighter, making it hard to breathe and threatening to break her. "Just tell me, please."

"I don't want to frighten you, but we've had more attempted

breaches into the kingdom. I thought it was Maynard before, but he's gone and we have reports of Lackey Demons asking questions on other planes, discretely trying to find beings who can enter this plane and hiring them to do just that."

"Lackey Demons?" she asked with a frown, but then it hit. "The ones after me??" she asked, panic rising.

"I think so. But hey, I don't want you to worry alright? Anyone stupid enough to make a deal with them will have to answer to me directly. You are safe here, I swear to you. We're tightening up security around the dome and the castle grounds just to be sure."

He was so sure, so strong. She gave him an absent nod as her mind raced. Could those things—or someone working for them—get in here, despite Poseidon's assurances? What if they somehow swayed someone that Poseidon trusted and would willingly let inside the walls? How had they found her at all? Did they know for sure she was here, or had they just put two and two together: girl goes in the water plus girl doesn't leave the water equals girl possibly ended up in the Sea God's plane?

"Hey," Poseidon said again, softly. He reached out and oh so gently pinched her chin between his thumb and forefinger, urging her gaze upward to meet his. The grip was somehow both sweet and sensual, commanding yet giving. It did things to her that she couldn't explain.

For a moment, everything disappeared. She had no idea what she'd been so upset about a moment ago, no idea why she'd hated the man before her at some point or another. She knew nothing except that his hand on her sent a jolt of desire through her so strong her knees nearly gave out. He inhaled sharply as their gazes collided. She could barely breathe, needed to get away from his hold but also needed to mold herself to him, not allowing even a breath of space between their bodies. Her eyes dropped to his lips and she licked her own as she imagined how soft they might be, what it would feel like to kiss him. She could just *kiss* him with no other expectations, right?

A kiss was nothing. People made out all the time. It was no big deal. *No strings attached, just an innocent kiss...*

He cleared his throat and dropped his hand before she could begin to tilt her head towards his. He took a quick step backwards, putting more distance between them. *Shot down again.* No, no. This is good, she reminded herself. She'd reasoned out a thousand times why anything happening between them physically was a bad idea.

Then why did she want to scream in frustration now? To throw herself at him and force him to keep touching her?

"I will protect you, Beck. Never doubt that." Was his voice rougher than usual or just her imagination?

She forced the lust-fog out of her brain. *He'll protect me,* she thought, but what about when he wasn't around? *This is a temporary arrangement,* she reminded herself. At some point she'd have to leave and return to the Mortal Plane—though the idea of leaving Poseidon sent a sudden flare of pain through her, that voice in her head screaming *wrong.* She forced the thoughts away. She *would* leave and find her mother and...she had no idea what. Run, she supposed. But either way, she couldn't rely on his protection in this forever. She needed to be able to protect *herself.*

An idea sprung. Would he agree?

"I believe you, but I have a favor to ask."

"Add it to your tab?" he asked with a small smile, trying to restore the equilibrium between them. She rolled her eyes and his grin kicked up. Yes, there we go. Back to the way it should be.

"Teach me to fight."

"What?" he asked, brows drawn, clearly surprised by where her thoughts had gone.

"Like you do. Teach me. You might not always be around and I'm basically defenseless. My power rarely works so I can't rely on it to help me."

His eyes light with curiosity when she mentioned her powers— she'd been tight lipped about that so far, not sure how to speak of them without making it obvious who her mother might be—but then he seemed to really mull over her request. A part of her relaxed as he seemed to take it seriously. She had been worried that he would brush her off as her mother often had when Beck had begged her to help her with her power. The answers ranged from "Mother is tired, perhaps later," to the more biting, "Why should I waste my time? You're too weak." Both versions hurt in different ways.

Finally, Poseidon nodded. "I think that's an excellent idea. We'll add training into our daily agenda. We start tomorrow."

Beck nodded in return and began to head back inside with her bouquet. She stopped, not sure why but feeling the need to mess with him back after his comment about her seeing him naked earlier. She called over her shoulder, "I like a little eye candy with my training. Can we invite the guy with the silver wings?"

His mouth popped open to respond then he shut it and ground his teeth, narrowing his eyes at her.

"You'll regret that request," he purred, lips curling into a smirk.

Yep, she regretted it.

Training with a god may have been just about the dumbest idea Beck had ever had. *Ever.* She leaned over, hands on her knees, trying desperately to catch her breath.

"One...minute..." she gasped between ragged inhalations. Could gods—or demigods or whatever the hell she really was—have heart attacks? Because she was fairly certain she was on the brink of one now.

"Twenty seconds. That's my best offer."

The cocky bastard wasn't even winded in the slightest after taking her through hours of rigorous training exercises. Or maybe they weren't *actually* that rigorous, but she sure as hell thought they were. They were learning basic combat skills to start with and in her opinion, there was nothing basic about them. She may be at least part goddess but her body seemed to think it was an out-of-shape mortal and nothing more. She straightened and raised her face to the sky, groaning. Everything hurt and muscles she didn't even know existed were now making themselves known only to whine about how sore they were too. *Little bastards.*

"...and twenty." Her eyes flew wide as his words registered. Too late. She was flat on her back in the dirt a second later without even seeing him move. Her breath left her in a whoosh, and she groaned as pain shot through her.

"I don't think...you knocking me on my ass...every other second... is really helping me!" she shouted between panting breaths. Starting to like him? Ha! Her hate was coming back in full force. He walked around her twirling his trident like a baton as she laid there like a slug, breathing like she'd just run a marathon.

"We have to build you up from the ground floor." He tilted his head as he studied her. "Or maybe from the basement, actually." She flipped him off with both hands and his laughter boomed around the space. Normally she enjoyed his laughter. Today, it made her want to stick his trident where the sun didn't shine.

"Where's my eye candy? I'd rather *him* teach me," Beck snapped as she pushed to her knees and, eventually, her feet again. He narrowed his eyes, something flaring there. Jealousy? She might like that a little too much.

"Eye candy, hmm? Is that what you require to actually follow directions and stay on your feet for more than a few seconds? Very well, I'll give you eye candy." Was he really going to call Dante? Her eyes widened. Nope. He wasn't calling anyone. He was...*Oh gods*. She gulped.

Poseidon held her gaze as he stripped off his shirt. Her mouth went dry and her panties did the opposite. She watched him stalk around her once more, not noticing much of anything except the way his muscles moved and flexed beneath that flawless brown skin. How could someone be so perfectly made? Perfectly sculpted pecs, rippling abs. *And those fucking indentions.* His leather pants were hanging indecently low on his hips and it made the Make Girls Dumb Buttons stand out even more. *Gods help me.*

She wanted to run her tongue along each one, wanted to feel his muscles flex beneath her fingers in reaction. Would he like that? Would he ask her to move her tongue...lower? She'd never done that before, but she thought Poseidon would be the perfect subject to learn on. Would he guide her, showing her what to do, how he liked it? She swallowed hard as she imagined his hands tangled in her hair, his hips arching forward as she sucked him down...

"Hmm?" she said, trying to pull herself back to the task at hand. Had he said something? She blinked a few times to clear her mind. He smiled, one hundred percent cocky male, and she kicked herself for being so transparent with her thoughts.

"I said: again."

With that, he knocked her on her ass once more.

TRAINING WAS SLOWLY BECOMING LESS her on her back and more her actually learning things. She was already stronger than she was only a week ago and she was actually excited for their sessions each day. Which had nothing to do with the fact that Poseidon had taken to conducting each lesson shirtless now. Nothing at all. Ok, maybe that was part of it. She truly did like learning how to fight, feeling strong and capable in a way she never had before, but seeing him strutting around shirtless, sweat and dirt dusting that delectable skin...Well, it didn't hurt.

Beck's resolve was starting to crumble. Maybe she *could* withstand being just a fuck buddy after all. She could handle a friends-with-benefits situation with the God of the Sea...right? She didn't know how much longer she could last *not* giving into the physical needs that reared up every time she was around him. Hell, every time she even thought of him. And she could admit that it wasn't only the physical that was making her feel this way.

He was tough during her training sessions, but not harsh. He seemed to genuinely want her to learn and become stronger. He was patient and explained things surprisingly well, teased and taunted and in between the times when she wanted to punch all the handsome right off of his face, she was having fun. Lots of it, actually.

She'd never had much time for exercise or training of any kind, never realized that though she was something more than mortal, she could still hone her body, make it stronger and better. She liked the feeling. When Poseidon praised her, it made her chest bow and her stomach flutter. She'd never made anyone feel proud before and she reveled in it, wanted to see that look on his face more and more often.

They'd fallen into pleasant rhythms between training and work, and her walls were showing signs of some serious structural damage. Soon, they'd be nothing but dust and rubble. *No. Can't let that happen.* She needed to keep at least some sort of protection up around herself. Not only was she still afraid to share too much of herself and her past, but if she let the walls shatter completely, she would be a goner. She could finally admit how easily she could fall for him if she let herself, was already well on the way. She tried to fight it, but that damned voice in her head wouldn't shut up!

And falling for Poseidon would be bad. It would lead to nothing but a broken heart for her. She'd heard rumors around the castle that he wasn't entertaining guests like he used to, and admittedly, she had seen no one coming or going from his chambers, but that didn't mean that he wasn't still fucking his way through every plane and realm, nor did it mean that he was at all changed and ready to have an actual relationship with someone, least of all her.

But...the idea of having a relationship with him, the kind that she'd seen in mortal television and movies over the years made her chest ache. She wanted it. She wanted it so badly she could cry. Damn it, ok, so no, she couldn't just be a fuck buddy. She wanted more. She *needed* more. She never had in the past, but her life was different now, and now she needed different things.

She was fairly certain that she could classify their relationship as one of friends, not just colleagues, and that in and of itself was a huge accomplishment for her. So, she wouldn't cross that line. They would stay friends—*sans* benefits.

Simple as that.

"Ok, so before I tell you this, I'm going to need you both to remember that I'm the King of the Gods and that is an automatic get out of jail free card..."

"What did you do?" Hades grated. He'd managed to pull himself out of his bed with Skylar for a few minutes and agreed to meet with Zeus and Poseidon.

"I didn't do anything, exactly..."

"Zeus," Poseidon said, warning in his tone.

"Ok, ok. So, the thing about it is...the walls of the Box are weakening and we don't know why."

"WHAT?" Si and Hades both sputtered at once.

Si shouted, "What do you mean? How? You said it wasn't anything to worry about!"

"Start talking right the fuck now, Zeus," Hades growled.

"Calm down, alright. Only the outermost ring is showing signs of it...for now. I've got Pandora working nonstop to fix the problem."

This could be bad. *Beyond* bad.

The story of Pandora's Box in the mortal realm was a bit off. In reality, the Box was a prison, the most heavily fortified prison in existence and Pandora was its creator and constant overlord. Some of the eldest of the gods had imbibed Pandora with extraordinary power in order to provide her with the necessary strength to create the prison. They'd given their *lives*, their essences merging with her own. Her power maintained the barriers of the Box. If they were failing...it meant Pandora's power was failing.

Si thought about the Box itself. It was housed in its own realm with a harsh atmosphere that was constantly either boiling hot or freezing cold at any given moment. It sat in the center of a treacherous wasteland seated in the middle of a basin of sorts, soaring stone walls surrounding it on all sides. The vast areas on all sides of the Box were filled with traps and obstacles—lava and quicksand pits, poisonous plants and all manner of deadly creatures just lying in wait, invisible portals to other deadly realms or directly into fortified dungeons. There was basically no chance of escape from the Box, but with the inhabitants within, Dora had taken zero chances.

The Box itself was a circular behemoth of a structure. Si had never understood why they'd started calling it the Box if it weren't square, but he supposed "the Circle" didn't have quite the same ring to it. Each ring within it was a labyrinth of hallways and cells that held the prisoners of the gods. The further in the rings went, the more terrible the inhabitants. In the innermost level, the Ring of the Damned, the most powerful and vile creatures ever to have lived in any realm or plane prowled, their crimes too terrible to utter. They were gods in their own right, but they had come from somewhere different than the rest of them, somewhere dark and unnatural. They fed on agony and suffering, delighted in pain and death.

The Dark Ones.

"Ok. Ok. Not good, but not terrible," Poseidon said as he paced, trying to calm his thoughts. "Even if the outer walls fall, the Ring of the Damned requires the key." The prison had been created so that even if Pandora's power did ever fail somehow, the Ring of the Damned holding the five Dark Ones would remain forever, a mythical key needed to open the door that was permanently placed with unbreakable magics. The rest of the prisoners didn't equate to rainbows and puppies by any stretch of the imagination—a great deal of life would be lost trying to fight those creatures if they were to be freed—but it was *nothing* compared to what would happen if the Ring of the Damned were unlocked.

"We'll just put extra protections on it and..." Poseidon trailed off when Zeus rubbed the back of his neck. His blood went cold.

"You *do* have the key, don't you?" Hades asked, tone as flat and hard as a godsblade.

"Well...um, about that..."

"Zeus!!" Hades roared as he leapt up. Black flames and smoke swirled around him. Si's hands flared with blue light and he could feel storms brewing over the seas across every plane.

"Look, I don't know what happened to it, ok? It was there and then it just...wasn't." He looked distraught. "I don't know how someone could have taken it though. Only a handful of people even know that the room existed, let alone what was inside. I don't know what's happened but I've got the Elite and the most trusted scholars trying to figure it out."

"When was the last time you saw it?"

"Well it isn't like I go check on it regularly. I'm not Gollum with his precious for fuck's sake. But it was there...a decade ago, surely?" Zeus said, not quite convincingly. "A century, definitely." Hades cursed and Zeus tapped his hands in the air in front him, willing his brothers to calm. "Look, it isn't time to freak out just yet. We'll figure it all out and I'll find the key, but...well, we need to begin preparing just in case. It's why I wanted to tell you about it finally. I didn't want anyone to panic prematurely but I wanted us to be prepared."

Hades ran his hand through his hair. "If the Dark Ones are released..." They all shared a bleak look. It would mean the end of the mortal world as they knew it, literally the end of days. The godly planes would be harder to take down, but the Dark Ones would come for them after they'd conquered the Mortal Plane and tortured, enslaved, or killed every being there. They couldn't allow the Mortal

Plane to fall to that kind of horror. The gods may not be worshiped as they once were, but the mortals were still *their* people, their responsibility.

It would be an all-out war. A bloody one. One that they...may lose.

The Dark Ones held unspeakable power and had legions of dark creatures in their armies. Some of those armies had been dormant for millennia, remaining hidden, while others fled to the Mortal Plane and stayed *mostly* under the radar ever since the gods and Titans fought together to imprison the Dark Ones eons ago. But Poseidon knew that any who remained would rise again the moment their masters were free.

"It won't come to that, I swear it. We'll find the key," Zeus insisted.

"How are the walls failing to begin with? Why is Dora's power fading?"

"We aren't sure but they think poison somehow. Though again, they have no idea how that would be possible. She never leaves that realm, doesn't see anyone except her friends and none of them would do this. She said that she felt completely fine, her power brimming as always, but when she woke one morning, something felt... off. She couldn't pinpoint what exactly, but she just felt like something was wrong. A few weeks later is when her power started to dim."

"How the hell is she fine when she goes to bed and then when she wakes..." Hades trailed off and they all tensed as the idea sprung between them.

"No. No, it couldn't be him. No way. He's dead. Dead and gone and good fucking riddance," Poseidon insisted.

The God of Nightmares was the only Dark One who had evaded capture all those years ago. He had been fatally wounded in the battle though, and although they had never found his body, there had been no sign of him in thousands upon thousands of years. And there *would* have been signs. He couldn't deny his nature for that long. He would need to kill, to torture, to destroy. To *feed*. They would have seen or heard if there was any sign of him. He was *definitely* dead! Si shuttered at the thought of any other alternative.

Balthazar was ruthless and sadistic. He had the power to not only invade your nightmares and manipulate them, make them more terrifying than anything you could possibly imagine, but the ability to bring them to life around you while you were awake. Even the gods were not immune to his power and more than one had gone insane or died in their attempts to escape their waking nightmares. The brothers had all had tastes of his "gifts," but thankfully their own power was enough to stave off the worst of it. Poseidon had seen his loved ones in pieces around him while under Balthazar's attacks, and even now, the terror of that sight made his blood chill in his veins. *It had been so real...*

"Look, like I said, it isn't time to freak out yet. We'll get to the bottom of it, but I thought it was time I fill you in," Zeus said, pulling Si from his memories.

Hades was stewing in his anger, but there was also fear there. Fear for his new bride. Si could clearly see the terror of losing her in the battle that would be coming for them should the Box fall and the key find its way into enemy hands tearing him apart inside. Again, Si was struck with envy for that feeling. To love someone that much? To fear for them like that? It was terrifying but gods damn it did he want it.

"Find the fucking key," Hades grated before he phased away, a cloud of smoke left swirling in his wake.

Zeus' shoulders slumped. He looked beseechingly to Poseidon. "I didn't mean to...I..."

"I know," Si said, embracing his brother. Zeus really was a good king and this failure was going to eat away at him for a long, long time. "You'll make it right," Poseidon added, believing that his brother would do everything in his power to do just that. "And if not...well, we'll deal with that when it comes. Together."

Zeus squeezed his shoulder. "Together."

~

THOUGH THE THREAT was potentially very real, Poseidon pushed it to the back of his mind. For now, it was nothing to worry about. Pandora was working to shore up the defenses as best as she could and Ares was stationing soldiers within the wasteland, just to be safe. All would be fine.

Still, every time he trained with Beck, the possibility of war reared to the forefront and he put even more effort into her lessons. Forget defending herself against Lackey Demons or whoever hired them, she needed to be prepared for much, much worse. *No, I will protect her at all costs.* The whisper again, clawing its way through the dense fog within his mind. The instinct to burn the world down to keep her safe surfaced with a ferocity that startled him, only to fade away just as quickly. What the fuck was happening? Perhaps he really was losing his mind, immortality taking its toll finally.

The other thing that reared to the forefront of his mind during training: his intense desire for the female. They'd moved on to weapons training and every time he touched her to re-position her hands or arms, every time he stepped close and inhaled her mouth-watering scent, he shot harder than stone, the need to plunge inside her whipping at him like a sail in the wind. Don't even get him started on when he'd positioned himself behind her, wrapping his arms around her small frame to demonstrate the correct grip and stance.

The air around them had electrified as every inch of his skin flared to life, his blood singing in his veins. He'd barely resisted the urge to lean his head down to nuzzle the soft skin below her ear, to kiss there lightly before licking and biting. He'd barely stopped himself from trailing his fingers down the length of her arm, over the creamy skin of her chest, cupping her soft breasts before kneading harder. Would she lean back into him then? Beg him to continue? Rub that magnificent ass against his cock as he slipped a hand beneath the fabric of her shirt to pinch her nipples?

Even now, his cock began to stiffen at the mere thought of rubbing his fingers over her tightened peaks, hearing her moan softly in his ear. He groaned to himself and forced the thoughts away. Despite how badly he wanted her, he couldn't do anything physical with her without the promise of more. He *wouldn't* do that to her. He got the sense that she would need more from him and wouldn't be interested in a merely physical relationship. *Although, the way she's been staring at me all day...*he glanced her way. *The way she's* still *staring at me now from across the table.* He arched a brow and she shook herself, cheeks flushing slightly. He'd kill to know what she was thinking of to make her eyes blaze like that.

"We should probably call it a night," Poseidon said, stretching his arms over his head. She nodded and he walked her back to her room. The halls were nearly silent, only the sound of the sea outside echoing quietly around them. He hadn't realized how late it was, though she didn't seem to mind. They walked along in companionable silence, but something hung in the air around them, building with every step. Did she notice it too? Her quickened pulse told him that she did.

"So, um...do you want to go to a party?" he blurted.

"Huh?" she asked, whipping her head towards him. *So smooth, dude. So smooth.*

"My brother and his wife are having a party to celebrate their marriage and the demise of Maynard. Would you like to go?"

"As like...your date?" she asked, hope and anxiety coloring her tone. How should he answer that? Would saying yes scare her or delight her? Did *he* want it to be a date? What did that even mean with Beck? *Ugh, why is everything so complicated?*

"As...whatever you'd like," he answered lamely.

She rubbed the medallion as she thought his offer through.

"I...maybe next time," she said with a small tilt of her lips. He nodded his acceptance and was only slightly disappointed. It would be expected for him to bring a date or five though, so he'd have to find someone to go with him. He found he didn't want it to be anyone but her, but he wouldn't push her. This whole being friends thing seemed to be as new to her as it was to him, and they were both figuring things out as they went. She wasn't pushing him either and he appreciated it.

They rounded a corner and she gasped, nearly toppling over as Conan—er, *Dean*—shot beneath her, tangling himself around her feet.

Poseidon reached out to snag her before she hit the ground, silently damning the cat that wasn't a cat.

-What the fuck, man?-

-Emmie says you're welcome-

Huh? With a mental wink, Dean darted away and Si quickly realized the position he was in. He had one arm wrapped beneath Beck's back, the other resting on her hip, and her hands rested on his shoulders. Their gazes locked and whatever had been brewing in the air around them before now erupted into a storm of lust and desire. She swallowed as her eyes drifted down to his lips. *Don't lick yours, don't lick yours, don't—Fuck.* Her tongue darted out, wetting her bottom lip and he groaned quietly. He should release her. He would. Truly he would as soon as his body began taking orders from his mind again.

But instead of releasing her, his grip tightened, his fingers curling against her more firmly. She didn't lower her hands, but gripped tighter with one while the other slid to his nape. They were both caught in this storm and neither of them could stop it. He didn't mind. It was the sweetest tempest he could imagine. He never wanted the gale to end.

He moved forward, walking her slowly backward, giving her time to rebuff him. Her back hit the stone wall and she gasped softly. He moved forward one more step, their bodies mere inches apart. He moved one hand and braced it against the wall beside her temple, the other still gripping her hip. Her breaths were coming quick and shallow, her chest rising and falling in rapid bursts. Their hearts were both racing, thundering loudly in his ears.

"We…shouldn't…" she barely whispered between ragged breaths even as she tugged his head closer. He couldn't stop himself from shifting forward and settling himself against her. He lowered his head, gently rubbing the tip of his nose against hers. That was all. He remained still, waiting for her response, letting her make the decision. It damn near killed him, but he waited. She held his gaze as she tentatively shifted her hips forward again, rubbing against him. A moan slipped from her lips and the sound made him impossibly harder. His cock strained against the laces of his pants, aching to be buried deep inside her. She widened her stance and rocked her hips forward once more, grinding harder against his erection and digging her fingers into his skin.

He closed his eyes in tortured bliss. He could feel the heat of her core against him, burning through his pants. She wore short cut-off denim shorts and the small amount of fabric between them lent little the imagination. She rocked again and gripped the nape of his neck tighter. Was she as pent up as he was? His fingers flexed on her hip as he desperately tried to remain still. She was both unsure and confident in her movements, as if she knew exactly what she needed but wasn't completely sure how to get it.

Was she…inexperienced? He'd thought perhaps that was the case before, remembering her adorable innocence as she took in the straps on his bed. He would be slow and gentle with her if it killed him despite the raging need burning through him to rip her clothes off and fuck her hard right here in the hallway. *No! No, they weren't fucking. Not now. Not yet. Not* ever. He gritted his teeth. He couldn't keep his thoughts straight when she continued to writhe against him.

"Poseidon…need…I…you…" she panted, not able to get a full thought out.

"Tell me, Beck. Tell me what you need," he growled quietly, his lips still so agonizingly close to hers, but not touching. She dug her nails into his shoulder as he shifted his hips forward the tiniest bit, pressing harder. She hissed in a breath and her eyes flashed wide.

Deep cobalt stirred there, boring into him unlike anything ever had before.

"Just…just scratching an itch. Nothing more," she rasped.

"Yes. Itch. Scratch. Agreed."

"Then kiss me," she demanded, breathless. He needed no further command. He swooped down, pressing his lips to hers finally. *Gods*, the feel of her lips against his. So soft, so giving. She splayed her fingers across the back of his neck, holding him to her as if she feared he would leave. *Never*, he growled within his mind. He tried to remember to keep things gentle but when she sucked his bottom lip in between hers, his control started to fray. She opened to him fully and he took her mouth, thrusting his tongue against hers. Her answering moans stirred more desire in him than he'd ever known. Again, she was timid but curious, stroking her tongue back against his and becoming more confident by the second.

The taste of her. The feel of her. The smell of her. Everything was overwhelming his senses and he only wanted more, never wanted it to end. He edged his hands under the bottom of her tank top and she moved against him harder, unabashed now as she tried to seek her pleasure. He moved his hands upwards, marveling in how soft and warm her skin was, scorching him as he touched. He cupped her breast over her bra and she arched her back, pressing more firmly into his palm. He couldn't stop himself from pulling the cup down, letting her breast spring free and into his waiting hand.

"Gods…" he moaned. He'd been dreaming of this for too long, imagining how she would feel. She was perfect, more than perfect. Her nipples were hard, rubbing his palm as he kneaded. She began grinding against him faster.

"Don't stop. More of that. Need this. *Oh goddddsss*," she groaned as he lightly pinched the bud between his finger and thumb, rolling gently. *Need to taste.* He kissed down her neck as he tore the front of her top in two. The bra went next and he took a half a heartbeat to appreciate how glorious she was topless. Creamy white breasts tipped with dusty rose nipples, heaving as her breaths sawed in and out of her. He licked his lips before he bent his head and flicked his tongue against one. She gasped loudly, bucking her hips as her hands flew to the back of his head, holding him to her.

"Yes! Oh gods, yes like that." He twirled his tongue around and around before finally closing his lips around the peak, sucking hard. "Need...more..." she panted. *More? Yes. Everything.* He ground his cock against her harder, unable to stop himself. He trailed a hand down her stomach before tearing at the button and zipper of her shorts. He shifted back enough that he could get his hand between them. He cupped his palm against her and inhaled sharply. She was so wet, her panties soaked through. For him. He wanted to beat his chest in satisfaction. He curled his fingers against the wall beside her head, gouging deep grooves into the stone. He ran a finger lightly back and forth over the small lacy barrier that stood between him and her hot, wet sheath. He moved his head to her other breast, licking, sucking, biting, all the while moving that finger back and forth, but never pushing forward.

"Si, please..." she nearly whimpered.

It was the first time she'd used the nickname that only his closet friends and family used. It...pleased him to hear it on her lips. More than pleased him. He took her nipple between his lips once more as he yanked her panties aside and thrust a finger deep inside her. She gasped and arched her hips at the sudden intrusion. He moaned against her skin. She felt like heaven. She was so slick, so tight. She wasn't...no. Couldn't be.

He pulled away and met her gaze.

"Virgin?" he panted, unable to form full sentences, all the while still thrusting his aching shaft against her hip again and again like a brute. He tried to stop but couldn't.

"No, no, don't worry. Don't stopppp..." Relief flooded him. He didn't want to hurt her if this was her first time doing these things. He captured her mouth again as he pumped his finger in and out, in and out. She widened her legs, hitching one leg up over his hip, giving him better access, allowing him to thrust deeper.

"Oh gods, I think I'm...I might be...close..." she whispered against his lips, as if in awe. He added another finger and she bit his bottom lip hard as she moaned. How did she know he loved that? He was warring with himself, unsure of what she would like, what might be too much for her. She might not be a virgin, but he knew for a fact that she wasn't nearly as experienced as he was. A bit of dirty talk wasn't for everyone, but he couldn't stop the words as they tumbled out of his mouth.

"That's right, Beck. Come for me. Soak my fingers," he rasped at her ear. She gasped quietly, but bucked harder, silently demanding more. He pressed the pad of his thumb against her clit, massaging with just enough pressure as he curled his fingers...

She threw her head back and screamed as she came in a rush. Her inner walls spasmed around his fingers, gripping him tight. *Dear. Fucking. Gods.* How could this feel so good, better than anything else in memory? He continued to thrust them in time with his hips, feeling himself getting close as well. *Already?* He removed his fingers and shifted his hips so that his cock now rested against her core. He arched his hips again and gritted his teeth as he felt her heat and wetness through his pants. She gripped the front of his shirt as she began to grind against him again, meeting him thrust for thrust, still coming down from her orgasm. Before he could stop himself, he held her gaze as he raised his fingers to his mouth. Her lips parted slightly as she watched him slowly suck each digit. His eyes nearly rolled back in his head. The taste of her was mind-numbing. So sweet, so intoxicating.

"Oh my gods..." she whispered, watching him raptly and biting her lip, cheeks flushing. Her pupils were blown, the black overtaking the blue almost completely. He used his other hand to massage her breasts as he thrust against her. She undulated her hips, seemingly desperate for another release. "A-again?..." she asked, wide eyed. Was this uncommon for her? *Oh baby, not on my watch.*

"You taste divine, Beck, so fucking good on my tongue," he whispered as he kissed her again. She made a sound that was half moan-half whimper, and he decided that she did, in fact, like a bit of dirty talk. What else did this angelic temptress like? He was desperate to find out, desperate to learn what made her purr, what made her scream.

She reached her hand downward, and after the tiniest hesitation, she rubbed his length through his pants. He bit back a groan as she handled him, gnashing his teeth to try to keep himself in control when he wanted so badly for her to grip him, skin on skin. He wouldn't push, though. She was in charge and could do whatever she wanted to do and nothing more. He couldn't stop rocking his hips though, thrusting his cock harder against her palm.

"Going to...come...if you keep that up," he ground out through clenched teeth. *Come?* From getting semi-jacked off through his pants?? *What the fuck?*

"Itch. Scratch," she panted with the tiniest curl of her lips. She *wanted* him to come? Sexy little vixen. He thrust harder and moved his hand down to massage her clit once more. He took her mouth again, dominating her tongue and she melted, surrendering to him. A second later, she stiffened and then yelled against his mouth as another climax rocked her. He couldn't stop himself from following her over and he threw his head back and yelled as he came so hard his vision blurred and his legs shook. He should probably feel embarrassed about coming in his pants like a mortal teenager, but he couldn't find it in him to give a flying fuck. He slowly stopped thrusting as his body began to calm. She was still breathing hard as he pulled away, letting a bit of space between their bodies, though he fucking hated it.

She looked lost in her pleasure, soaking up every last drop, a small smile playing on her lips. Lips that were red and swollen from his kisses. Lips he was dying to kiss again. She slowly pried her eyes open and met his gaze. She lost a bit of that after-glow haze and she dropped her eyes, beginning to right her clothing as best she could. She pulled the edges of her torn shirt together and crossed her arms to hold it closed. Was she embarrassed? Ashamed? That wouldn't do.

He pinched her chin between his finger and thumb and urged her eyes back upward.

"Hey, none of that. Itch. Scratch. Yeah?" She searched his gaze and he wasn't sure what she was hoping to find there. She gave him a tiny curl of her lips and nodded.

"Itch. Scratch," she confirmed. He leaned in and gave her one more soft kiss before he forced himself to take another step backward, giving her some space. She tucked a lock of hair behind her ear and took a deep breath.

"Goodnight, Poseidon." Back to Poseidon again. He tried not to let it bother him.

"Goodnight, Beck."

With that she walked on slightly unsteady legs the rest of the way to her room while he stood there and watched. He stared long after she was gone, committing every last detail of what had just happened to memory.

SEVENTEEN

Beck could totally do friends with benefits. She had managed to act completely normal around Poseidon after their...encounter in the hallway a few nights ago. He was acting like his normal confident-slash-sexy self, so she would do the same. Not that she was confident-slash-sexy, but yeah. She would act like her normal self and things would be completely normal. How many times could she say *normal* before it lost all meaning?

They'd agreed that they were merely scratching itches. Itches that in no way had been scratched. Oh no. If anything, she had opened herself up to So. Many. More. Itches. She had *never* gotten off like that before and the thrill of it still rattled her insides. He had been sensual and commanding all at once and the combination made her melt. He'd talked dirty and though she had never been sure whether she would like that or not, she was officially sold when he'd done it. His voice was like a silky caress against her skin, stoking the fire hotter and hotter. His tongue should be considered a deadly weapon, and don't even get her started on his fingers. She still couldn't believe she'd come not once, but *twice* from just his hand and his voice. She was aching to replay the scene again and again, to explore every facet of this new world she knew nothing about. She had no idea what pleasures might await, no idea what she liked or didn't like really, but she was desperate to explore it all.

Could she explore it with Poseidon?

Despite her slight apprehension at first, they'd fallen back into their easy banter and routine. He hadn't tried to touch her again past their usual contact during training, though he seemed to burn with the want to, and he hadn't invited her to his room late at night. What did mortals call that? A booty call? She didn't *want* to be a booty call, exactly, but she wouldn't have said no if Poseidon offered, she knew that without a doubt. Maybe he was waiting for her to make another move, to let him know she had another itch to be scratched. He'd let her run the show that night in the hallway, letting her make the decision to take things further or not.

So, maybe he really was leaving this all up to her. Which she actually really appreciated, but...she had no idea how to do any of this stuff. How did that even work? If she was interested, did she just drop it in casual conversation? *Oh hey, Si, you need to answer these three letters and also I could really use another orgasm or ten if you don't mind?* Did she show up at his door in nothing but a long coat over sexy lingerie like she'd seen in mortal movies? She thought that she could probably fumble her way through the physical side, but there was more to it than that.

More than the mind-blowing physical reactions to him, she'd felt such a connection with him in that hallway, unlike anything she'd ever experienced. She felt like she was in exactly the right place, exactly where she was *meant* to be, for the first time in her life. Did he feel it too? She thought that...maybe he did. It was impossible to tell though. She was so inexperienced with all this. Maybe he had that look with everyone while in the midst of pleasure, that look that said *you're mine.*

She scowled at the thought. She didn't want him to have that look with anyone but her, which she knew was ridiculous. *She* was the one who specifically said they were merely scratching an itch after all. *Shouldn't have said that.* Should have said what her mind was dying to scream which was that she…wanted him, damn it. *All* of him and only him. Should she admit it? *Could* she? It was a scary thought, too scary to focus on right now. She shook herself and focused on what was ahead. She was attending some sort of… sporting event? A *godly* sporting event.

"What is this again?" Beck asked as she walked with Nerina.

"We call it the Gauntlet. Think of it sort of like the mortal Super Bowl. It's an epic battle that happens every two hundred years. The gods pick teams and play a very extreme, very bloody version of rugby mixed with American football mixed with the gladiator battles of old. It's delightful," she said, looking eager. "Even Hades is taking part this year! He hasn't done that in almost three thousand years. Guess his new queen encouraged him." She nodded towards the field-slash-arena as they made their way down the steps towards their reserved seats on the front row. *I guess working for one of the brothers has its perks.*

An absolute stunner stretched her muscles next to who Beck knew without a doubt had to be Hades. She had golden blonde hair with streaks of red here and there, and it was plaited in two long braids that reached the middle of her back. She was grinning, small fangs glinting in the sunlight. *What was she?* Beck wondered. A siren like Nerina? Her skin did shimmer faintly in the sunlight, but it was a little different than Nerina's iridescent scale-like sparkle. Her emerald green eyes shined with mischief and cunning, but also an intense mix of lust and love as she looked at Hades.

As they made their way closer, Beck heard the woman—Skylar, she remembered now—talking to her husband. No, not talking, *taunting.*

"Are you prepared to be spanked thoroughly?"

"Didn't we already do that last night? And twice this morning?" Hades replied, lips curling into a smile that might be second only to Poseidon's. *Holy shit.*

"Hmm good point," Skylar said with a sultry grin. "Let me

rephrase: are you ready to have your ass handed to you? I'm taking the trophy home this year, no doubt about it."

"You'll regret choosing to play *against* me, love," Hades purred back, a sexy smirk on his face that promised all sorts of naughty things. *Dear gods* he was gorgeous. Hair black as jet with matching stubble along his strong chin and beautiful blue-green eyes that surely made panties melt at warp speed. He was every bit as muscled as Poseidon, but where Poseidon had a playful sensuality about him, Hades oozed raw, dark sexual energy. This male wasn't a *I'll have her home by eight, sir* type of guy. Oh no, he was a *she calls me daddy too* type. Beck nearly fanned herself.

"Do you recall the bet?" Hades asked, his voice deep and pleasing. He had a slight accent, reminding Beck a bit of the South African accent back in the Mortal Plane. *As if he needed one more check in the sexy column*, she thought.

Skylar moved closer to him and walked her fingers slowly up his chest. "Oh, don't you worry about that. I'll be ready to collect my— what did we settle on? One hundred big Os in a 72-hour period?—as soon as the game is over." She winked and then dragged Hades to her for a hard kiss. The easy back and forth between them, the unyielding affection there, made Beck's chest ache. She wanted that. All of it. She wanted to taunt and tease and love so hard it was plain for all to see. To *be loved* so hard it was plain for all to see.

And one hundred *orgasms in three days? Dear gods*. She quickly did the math and her mouth gaped. That wasn't physically possible... was it? She swallowed hard.

Poseidon caught Beck's gaze and smiled before jogging up to the stands.

"Nerina, Beck," he said nodding to each of them. "Are you excited?" he asked her.

"Umm, I guess? I have to admit, this will be my first time ever watching any kind of sporting event, mortal or otherwise." She knew the basic rules of mortal football—the American version anyway— because the games were often televised at the bar where she used to work, but she never really paid that much attention or actively watched a game.

"You're in for a treat...and possibly a shock," he added with a shrug. "We can get a little carried away sometimes."

His gaze shifted to Skylar as she smeared black paint under her eyes, using her fingers to pull the paint downward over her cheeks. She pointed at a hulking man standing a few yards away and brought her thumb to her throat and swiped it slowly across. The man's lips curled upward and he extended his hand, curling his fingers back toward him a few times in a *bring it on* gesture.

"That's her father, Ares," Poseidon explained helpfully. "They're almost as bad as her and Hades when it comes to, uh...*friendly* competition." Beck laughed lightly and then squealed as Emmie appeared right next to her, holding three boxes of popcorn.

"Would you stop that!" Beck hissed as she took one of the boxes from Emmie's outstretched hand. The smell of the buttery goodness made her eyes slide closed for a moment. If there was one thing she believed mortals had done right, it was buttered popcorn. Beck popped a kernel into her mouth and nearly moaned. This was the good stuff, straight from a movie theater.

"Never. It's too much fun." Emmie shifted her gaze to Poseidon, an expectant look on her face.

"Thank you, Emmie," he said with a smile.

"You are so welcome, my dear. More to come." Emmie winked at him and he just shook his head, a fond smile pulling his lips upward. "Now, I know the rules say that I can't place bets, but what if I just—"

"No," Poseidon and Zeus said at the same time. The King of the Gods had strolled over without Beck noticing. Zeus quickly put his brother in a headlock.

"No betting or helping others bet, Emmie," Zeus said as he rubbed Poseidon's head roughly. Beck believed it was called a noogie. "Ready to lose, brother? Skylar and I are taking you all down."

Beck was frozen. She'd never been up close and personal with Zeus before now and she didn't know how to feel. The familiar anger began to simmer. He was the reason her mother had fled to the Mortal Plane and treated Beck like dirt for her entire life, was possibly the reason demons were trying to kill her. Zeus' eyes shifted to her and narrowed slightly.

"You look familiar."

Her breath caught in her throat. The anger immediately transformed into fear and she curled her shoulders inward, as if she could hide from him. Though they didn't look extremely similar, she could see her mother in her reflection at times, something in the shape of her eyes and lips perhaps. Would he know who she was just by looking at her? Would Zeus kick her out of Aqueous immediately if he learned who her mother was? Did he have that authority as king of all the gods? Would he *kill* her?

His easy smile widened. "Oh I know why! It's because my brother is *constantly* fantasizing about you. I've seen your face in his head at least a hundred times this week…"

She relaxed slightly, breath huffing out of her with a shaky laugh. Poseidon's eyes went wide, meeting hers for a moment, and she would swear there was a slight blush in his cheeks before he moved quicker than she could even track, suddenly behind Zeus. They were about the same height but Si was built a bit more lithely. He was sleek and quick where Zeus looked to be more brawn and strength.

Poseidon knocked the king's knees out and wrapped an arm playfully around his throat. Zeus' laughter boomed around them, the sound big and hearty. Beck…liked it. She knew that this could all be some façade, that the cruel, uncaring, vengeful god that her mother had painted him to be could be his true personality, but…she didn't think so. Of course his wrath was legendary, but from the accounts in the books she'd read from Poseidon's library, it was usually justly deserved or meted out in protection of others.

She sighed. No, she was fairly certain that Zeus, just like Poseidon and Hades and the rest of them, were all…good people.

Funny and charming and caring and kind. *So why?? Why the fucking lies for my entire life?* The thoughts were beginning to wear her thin and make her head throb. Her entire life was starting to unravel, everything her mother told her becoming a suspicious web of confusion and deceit, and she was tired of being stuck in it.

"You're going down, oh great king," Poseidon said with an amused grin before Zeus worked his way out of the headlock and jumped up, shoving his brother playfully in the shoulder. They both adopted fighting stances, bouncing on their toes with fists in front of them. Beck wanted to laugh. Apparently boys were boys, no matter where they lived or what species they were.

An ominous gong sounded through the space and the gods waved goodbye as they jogged towards the middle of the large arena. The playing field itself was long and oval shaped, covered in silver sand, but boulders and strange puddles of black, oozing liquid, and other obstacles were set throughout the space. What in the hell kind of game was she about to watch?

Emmie, Nerina, and Beck took their seats and waited for the match to begin. The gods and demigods and who knew what else lined up in loose formations on opposite sides of the golden line drawn down the center of the field. Some looked deadly serious, some playfully taunting. Some wore full armor, others were shirtless. *That* part of the game, she could appreciate.

When the gong sounded a second time absolute chaos erupted. Beck didn't know where to look as she tried and failed to follow the glowing blue orb which was apparently an important part of the game. Wings, talons, swords, fire, fists—all clashed together on the field. Blood already splattered the ground, turning the silver to deep crimson in too many places.

"Oh my gods, is it supposed to be this...violent?" Beck asked, wincing as Dante's wings cut through the air towards the terrifyingly stunning woman Nerina informed her was Athena. A large spray of blood followed soon after. The goddess merely smiled and flipped over the warrior, grabbing his shoulders and tossing him twenty feet away, smashing through a boulder like it was tissue paper. Cheers erupted when someone threw the orb into one of the fiery rings on one end of the field. Beck hadn't even seen anyone get close to it, distracted by all the skirmishes.

"Get him! Slice his Him Tendons!" Emmie yelled before glancing to Beck. "See, because that's Achilles. Get it? His Him Tendons? Man, I crack myself up. Anyway, yes, it is supposed to be this violent and it's glorious, isn't it!? Not to worry though, no fatal wounds allowed. That's an automatic forfeit and no one's going to allow that to happen. Whoever wins holds bragging rights for two hundred years until the next game. It's very serious business. Big betting too," she grumbled. "But *I'm* not allowed to. Because of the whole already knowing the outcome thing." She threw her hands up in annoyance, spilling popcorn. "I mean, it's not *completely* set in stone. There is always a chance it could change, so I should be allowed to bet, really..."

Beck turned back to watch more, trying to keep Poseidon in her sights. He was an absolute force as he plowed through his foes. He spun and moved like water, landing blows with such lethal grace that she couldn't help but be impressed...and a little turned on. So, maybe the violence *was* kind of glorious. Each team managed to score several points or goals or whatever they were called—Beck was still fuzzy on all the terms and rules—and substitute players had been pulled in on both sides when injuries needed time to heal. It was pure insanity, but Beck decided that she liked it. Immensely.

She wished it was like mortal sports, occurring every week instead of every two hundred years. She would have liked to see another game. *But I'll be long gone before the next one*, she thought sadly. She shook herself, refusing to think about that right now. Instead, she actually let out a loud cheer when Hermes scored another point-goal-thing. Nerina gave her a surprised look. Beck simply shrugged and gave her a small smile.

Hermes somehow heard her over the melee and turned her way, giving her an exaggerated bow and winking when he straightened.

She gave him a wave in return, unsure what else to do. A second later, Poseidon careened into the Messenger God, the two of them flying half out of bounds and sending up giant sprays of sand as they landed. Poseidon stood, glanced to Beck with narrowed eyes before also giving her a sexy wink, one that was...possessive. This one made her toes curl and her pulse race. He turned back to help Hermes up, the other god shoving his blonde curls out of his eyes and giving Poseidon a quick and (she thought) playful punch to the gut. The two of them joined the game again, but from then on, Poseidon's gaze was constantly catching hers.

"I didn't think it was possible to eye-fuck someone whilst competing in the Gauntlet so fiercely, but here we are..." Emmie said, not taking her eyes off the field, but her lips curled upwards and Beck's cheeks heated. A second later, Emmie grew excited. "Oh! Oh, this part is so great! Just wait for it..." The Seer reached over Beck to steal some of Nerina's popcorn. A few moments later, an exceptionally brutal collision between Zeus and Hercules sent shockwaves through the entire arena, shaking the seats beneath them. *Holy shit.* Emmie merely bounced in her seat and cheered louder, cupping her hands to make her voice louder. Beck watched as the god and demigod grinned at each other, laughing together as Zeus rose and then pulled Hercules up. He slapped his son on the back fondly and then ruffled his hair.

Poseidon hadn't been lying. Zeus really was a good father to his children. She knew in that moment that if Zeus had had any idea that Beck could have potentially been his, there was no way that he would have banished her mother for it. It just didn't track. She sighed. Add it to the list of things her mother had lied about. But...of that was the case, why had her mother been banished?? Beck shook herself, not wanting the endless questions to ruin this day. She had all the time in the world to worry about them later. For now, she wanted to watch Poseidon body slam Ares again. Don't ask her to explain why.

Nerina leaned in towards Emmie. "It's going to be Hades' team, isn't it? He's been nearly unstoppable!" Emmie made a motion of locking her lips with a key and tossing it away. Nerina grinned. "Yep, definitely Hades for the win. I knew it was a good bet!"

Beck honestly wasn't sure who was winning and who was losing, so she couldn't really weigh in, but she had to admit that she was having fun. A lot of it. A time-out was called and the bloodshed stopped for a few minutes as both sides gathered near their respective benches on the grass ring that lined the playing field. Poseidon chugged something from a bottle and used the hem of what was left of his shirt to wipe his face. The muscles beneath were rippling and coated with sweat and sand and blood, though he seemed to have already healed from any wounds he'd sustained. Beck bit her lip at the sight and he noticed, eyes going deep whiskey. He licked his lips before hitting her with one of those panty destroying smiles. Her lips curled and she shook her head at him, laughing.

For some reason, the earlier trepidation about trying something more with him had all but faded as she'd watched the game. She didn't know if it was because she had let herself fully relax and enjoy the moment for once, or because of the way he'd watched her all the while, not seeming to notice any of the other fans—even the females (who Emmie had explained were demonesses but were not evil) who were clad in nothing but pasties and thongs. He hadn't even spared them a glance, though they were hanging over the edge of the wall, screaming for his attention every time he was near.

Instead, his eyes had always found *her*. Something was shifting, both inside of her and between them, and she was...ok with it. Eager for it, even. Beck was so damned tired of being so worried about every little thing, trying to keep everything hidden or locked away inside. She had nearly died, still had demons searching for her, and had the opportunity to finally live her life for the first time ever. *So, screw worrying. Just go for it.*

The game resumed. A goddess with flaming red hair got caught in one of those black puddles and disappeared from sight. More blood, more cheers, more points scored. Beck was starting to understand the rules a bit more and could follow the progress of the orb easier the longer she watched. She cheered with the rest of the crowd and even booed Zeus' team with Nerina. The siren had given her a strange look.

"What?" Beck asked, a bit more defensively than she'd meant to.

"I've never seen you laugh…or smile," she added with a tilt of her own lips. "It suits you."

Beck tucked a lock of her hair behind her ear, a bit self-consciously. She hadn't even realized she'd been laughing *or* smiling. *Have I really not done that here before now? How pathetic.* That settled it: she was going to start letting herself enjoy life. Starting with making the first move with Poseidon. Her toes curled at the idea of his lips on hers again, but she was pulled from the thoughts by a roar from the crowd.

Hades had distracted Skylar somehow before whipping around her and scoring again. Apparently the end of the match was drawing near and there wasn't much time left for Skylar's team to come back and win now. They would have to get the orb through the tallest and smallest of the burning rings to score enough points—and they'd have to do it in the next few seconds. Beck didn't see that happening. *Looks like it'll be Hades' team after all.*

"Here it comes…" Emmie muttered, bouncing in her seat again.

Skylar narrowed her eyes, fury radiating from her. Beck watched in absolute awe as the beautiful emerald darkened to nearly black and literal *flames* danced in her irises. Magnificent orange and yellow feathered wings erupted from her back, each wing tipped with black, and flames of the deepest orange and the blackest black danced along the edges.

"Holy shit," Beck breathed. "What *is* she?" Other than badass and gorgeous and mind-blowingly cool.

"She's a phoenix. Well, part phoenix anyway. One of the very last ones."

Nerina let out an awed sigh. "I'd heard rumors but *my gods* seeing it in person…" The entire arena seemed to share her same reaction. A stunned silence fell upon the crowd, punctuated here and there with awed whispers and gasps.

Everyone on the field seemed to be mesmerized by her too, entranced enough to allow her to tear through them in a blur of feathers and flames. Beings went down all around the field, grunts of pain and annoyance ringing out. At the end, only Hades still stood and Skylar met his gaze from across the arena as she hovered forty feet in the air and effortlessly dropped the orb through the ring for the win. The stunned crowd finally found their voices and began roaring and cheering and stomping their feet so loudly, it shook the stands. The gong sounded and the Gauntlet was officially over.

Hades gave her one of the sexiest smiles Beck had ever seen before phasing directly in front of his wife the moment she landed back on the ground. Phasing wasn't allowed during the game, but now that it was over, apparently the ban was lifted. He cupped her face gently, the look in his eyes so full of love and desire that Beck had to look away. Everyone else groaned as they rose to their feet, those that could anyway, and made their way towards the middle of the arena.

Zeus' blond hair was streaked with scarlet but he was grinning like an idiot as he slapped his teammates on the back and shook hands with the others. The crowd continued to cheer and applaud as the winners were presented with the biggest trophy Beck had ever seen.

"Woooo! Suck it, losers!" Skylar yelled, jumping up and down with the trophy though it looked like it outweighed her by at least fifty pounds. Beck couldn't help but laugh. This was quite possibly the best day of her life. Glittering explosions of light burst above them, raining harmless sparks down over everyone. More cheers, more jeers.

Poseidon met her gaze, grinning at her as she brushed soft, diamond-like confetti out of her eyes. She smiled back at him and his own faltered slightly, his eyes going wide. He absently rubbed the heel of his hand against the center of his chest. *What? Do I have some-*

thing in my teeth? His smile returned, even brighter than before and he phased directly to her, leaning his arms over the edge of the low wall separating the stands from the field.

"You have the most beautiful smile, Beck."

Si PHASED them back to his chambers and held on for a moment longer than necessary before stepping away. Beck decided that she didn't like that one bit, so she fisted his shirt and pulled him closer again. She wasn't sure what she was doing, but she found that she wasn't afraid to be doing it. She'd made the decision earlier to start living, and she was going to start *tonight.* The entire day had acted like a wrecking ball to her protective walls, taking them down to the studs.

It was a good day. *An even better night maybe?*

Poseidon arched a brow but grinned, stepping into her. He settled his warm hands on her hips and she shivered when her shirt rode up, allowing his skin to touch hers. She rose to her tip toes and used her grip on his shirt to urge him downward. He looked surprised but didn't fight her, giving a low *hmm* of appreciation when her lips met his. It was an innocent kiss, but there was something boiling beneath the surface. The promise of so much more, the *need* for so much more. Was he craving her as much as she'd been craving him? She sure as hell hoped so.

She pulled away enough to mutter, "Good game, as the mortals say."

He chuckled a little before leaning in to kiss her again, soft and languid. After a few more moments, he pulled back.

"I think I'm enjoying the after party much more." He gently cupped her face, and she leaned into his touch, rubbing her cheek into his palm. He lightly stroked her cheekbone with his thumb, but as he watched the movement, he wrinkled his nose. He stepped back and wiggled his dirty hands at her.

"I need to shower..." His eyes roved over and she thought that he was a few seconds from inviting her to join him, but he yanked his gaze back up and smiled. "Give me three minutes."

She nodded and he chucked her lightly under the chin before heading into the bathroom. She watched him go, enjoying the view and biting her lip as he pulled the remains of his shirt off as he went. Her fingers curled inward, the urge to run them over his shoulders and down his back nearly irresistible.

Beck smiled to herself. This was shaping up to be the best day she'd ever had, and, if she had it her way, the night would be even better. Something had shifted within her today and it was as if an entire life's worth of tension had eased from her shoulders.

She heard the water start in the shower and was half tempted to join him even without an invitation. His reactions to her gave her a strange jolt of confidence. The way he'd watched her all day...well, she was feeling confident as hell right about now. She took a step forward before shaking herself, and began to roam around the room instead. She lingered near the bed, peeking towards the bathroom door before she tugged on the straps, impossibly fascinated by them. Did Poseidon like tying up others? Or being tied up himself? Both? The thought of either scenario sent heat rushing through her.

She heard the water stop and quickly darted across the room to check out the book collection in the built-in shelves along the wall. Ancient looking volumes on subjects like war and various histories sat beside—

"Romance novels?" she asked aloud with a laugh. Mortal ones at that, the good kind with shirtless guys sporting super ripped abs on the front.

"And what, pray tell, is wrong with romance novels?" his voice purred from just behind her. She whirled, hand flying to her medallion out of habit. She smacked his chest with the other and was mildly disappointed that he'd put on a shirt.

"Don't *do* that," she scolded with a laugh. "Did all of you get together and decide that phasing to scare me was the new fun activity or what? And nothing, I just didn't picture you as the romance novel type."

"I'm full of surprises, Beck." She shivered at the promises that simple phrase held, the way his voice pitched low and sensual making her toes curl. He grinned and motioned towards the bar. "You should see Hades' collection."

"No way," Beck said as she followed him across the room. She couldn't imagine the God of the Underworld reading spicy romance novels.

"Oh yeah. Hades loves his smut." He jumped behind the bar with ease and threw a towel over his shoulder. "What can I get you, ma'am?" he asked with an insanely attractive fake southern accent. She laughed and told him to surprise her. He did his best Tom Cruise impression, flipping bottles and shaking cups, and eventually slid a glass of sparkling purple liquid towards her. She took a deep sip and gave a small "mmm" of appreciation. It was just the right mix of sweet and sour, the tiniest burn but in a good way.

He leaned his forearms on the bar and gave her that damned cocky grin she loved to pretend to hate.

"So…"

"So, what?"

"I was watching you all day." *I noticed and loved every minute of it.*

She ran her finger lightly around the rim of the glass.

"Shouldn't you have been paying attention to the people trying to almost kill you?"

"I'm an amazing multi-tasker," he said with a sensual smirk. "You had *fun*."

She tried to hide her smile as she took another sip. "Perhaps a bit…"

"Not a trace of disgust for me and my *ilk*…" Ah, she knew where he was headed. "So, what do you think of the gods after today?"

She wrinkled her nose and tried to stop her lips from curling upwards. She knew exactly what he was after. He was right: watching them out there today had solidified the fact that she had let go of her (most likely) completely unwarranted blanket hate of the gods. Despite the brutality and violence of the day, she'd seen so much love and comradery among them, it couldn't be reconciled with the terrible beings her mother had painted them as. She would get to the bottom of all of that soon, but for now, she was tired of holding onto hate that she just didn't feel anymore, that she had only been *forced* to feel because her mother had demanded it. She let out a long sigh.

"You're going to make me say it, aren't you?"

His grin widened, showing off those perfect pearly whites. "You bet your ass I am."

She narrowed her eyes at him, but she couldn't stop the half grin that spread. She reached forward and trailed her fingers along the back of his hand where it rested on the bar.

"So, *maybe* the gods aren't so bad…" She trailed off as he tensed. She glanced up to find that his grin had faded and he'd paled. He shot upright, ripping his hand from under hers, tension rolling off of him in sharp waves. Confused, she turned to find the most beautiful female standing in the middle of the room. She was tall and willowy and even standing still she had a sensual grace about her. Her hair was so blonde it was almost white, with streaks of blue woven within it. It was pulled into a loose up-do at the base of her neck, strands artfully pulled free to frame her high cheekbones. Her eyes were slate blue with striations of gold flaring around the irises, thick black lashes framing them, and her brows were perfectly shaped and manicured. She wore a gown of ocean blue glittering jewels, form fitted to her body perfectly but somehow still looking like it flowed like water across her skin. She smiled at Poseidon and she immediately reminded Beck of an Old Hollywood starlet. Graceful. Demur. Secretively sensual. Classic.

In a word: perfect.

Poseidon stood motionless, staring with an expression that Beck couldn't quite understand. She glanced between the two of them. What was happening? Who was this woman?

"Hey, Si," the woman purred.

"*Callie?*" Si choked out.

Callie? Beck's eyes flew wide. As in *Calypso*? This was the woman who'd had Poseidon's heart and then tossed it aside like trash? Nerina had told Beck all about it. They'd been in love, Poseidon head over heels so, but Calypso apparently couldn't be tied down for long and one day she just bolted. Just like that, gone with not much more than an "it was fun, see you around," note. And, as far as Beck knew, she hadn't looked back since.

Anger swirled within her. This woman had hurt Poseidon and every instinct was telling Beck to punish her for it. But on the heels of the anger was aching disappointment. She couldn't compete with this woman on any front. And now she was back? To be with Poseidon again and win his heart once more? Beck glanced to Poseidon, who was still staring at the former love of his life, as if Beck didn't even exist.

Or maybe she'd had his heart all this time, no need to win it again, she thought with another ache.

He moved towards Calypso as if in a trance. Beck's hand reached out for him, but she immediately pulled it back. Her chest constricted and she felt like such an idiot. She'd let herself think... well, it didn't matter. She stood there watching, unsure of what exactly to do. Calypso snapped her fingers in Beck's direction, not even looking at her.

"You there. Bloodberry wine in a chilled glass." The haughty tone grated on Beck's nerves. Of course she would assume that Beck was nothing more than a servant. *I'm a goddess too, damnit. Or at least partly.*

Poseidon shook himself and his gaze darted between Calypso and Beck.

"No, she's not—"

"Gods I've missed you," Calypso interrupted him in a breathy whisper. Beck began to back slowly towards the door. She wanted desperately to get away, to stop seeing the strange things passing between Poseidon and this woman.

"I...I..." he stammered. *Say you haven't missed her. Say you're...I don't know what with* me. *Say...something.* When he didn't, hurt and anger swirled within Beck's chest. Though it may not have been deserved, she focused all of that on the physical manifestation of every man's wet dream standing across the room. Heat flared in her chest and a second later, Calypso screamed and jumped backwards, clutching onto Poseidon's arms.

"What? What's wrong?" Si asked, looking around for whatever had made the woman so frightened.

"I thought I saw a hydraspider. You know how I hate those things!" She glanced around frantically trying to find the creature. Beck's eyes flew wide in alarm. Had...had *she* caused Calypso to see something? But she didn't even know what the fuck a hydraspider was. How could she make Calypso see something she didn't even know existed? "It...it must have just been a trick of the light," Calypso said, patting her hair and brushing off her dress.

Poseidon frowned, still glancing around and not stopping Calypso from manhandling him. With one more sting of pain, Beck turned and bolted silently from the room.

EIGHTEEN

Callie was here. Standing right in front of him. Clutching onto his arms in a way that was both familiar and unwanted. Why the *fuck* was Callie here, standing right in front of him, clutching his arms? The shock began to wear off and annoyance verging on anger took its place. He gently but firmly removed her hands from his body and stepped away.

"What are you doing here, Callie?" he said irritably.

"I can't just come visit you, love?"

"No, you can't—and don't call me that," he added with maybe too much bite. He'd thought about seeing Callie again at least a thousand times since the day she left. A thousand different versions of how this might play out should it ever happen had run through his head, and still, none of them had prepared him for this. He'd thought he'd feel pangs of loss and wanting, the remnants of his love for her pushing through the shards of his broken heart.

But right now, all he felt was pissed.

Callie tilted her head at him, calculation behind her slate eyes.

"Are you not happy to see me, Si?"

He didn't answer, just crossed his arms over his chest. She arched a delicate brow and began to stroll around the room, as if she'd never left. She trailed her fingers along the romance novels and he let out a low hiss. *Beck. Damn it.* He'd barely even acknowledged her existence once Callie had materialized. He hadn't meant to, he was just shocked. Beyond shocked. He'd stared at Callie, lost for words, but Beck must have seen it as relief and adoration. He had no doubts that Beck had learned about his history with Callie, so what she must have seen was the God of the Sea flooded with relief that his long lost love had returned. *Fuck!*

He clenched his teeth in frustration. Today had started out as one of the best in recent memory. Not only had Hades agreed to play with them again, something Poseidon had missed the last few millennia, but Beck had watched him intently during the entire match. He'd felt her eyes following him, admiring him, appreciating him. She'd seemed more relaxed and happier than she'd been in all the time since she'd come to the kingdom. He could see the joy in her features, the hatred completely gone. She'd *smiled* for fuck's sake. A real, full smile, and it had nearly taken him to his knees. His chest had constricted as she'd grinned at him, those achingly adorable dimples his new favorite thing in the universe.

It had caused that small whisper of wanting to transform into a roar within him, demanding he go to her, touch her, protect her... claim her. It had quieted again soon after, but he couldn't pretend he hadn't heard it this time. There was something between them, he knew it in his bones. He would fight through whatever his weird hang ups on relationships were in order to be with her.

But then he'd gone and fucked it up. All because Calypso had decided to show up unannounced after centuries? Heat flared in his palms and the ocean above them roiled, the water darkening to near blackness. He glared at Callie. She took in the state of the sea around them with interest.

"Oh come on, Si, don't be mad at me," she pouted, clearly assuming she could use her wiles to coax him from his anger and right back into her bed.

"Seriously? Don't be *mad*? You walked out the door without a goodbye, Callie. You left a fucking note and I haven't heard a word from you since. You...you ripped my heart out and couldn't have cared less. And you're going to tell me not to be *mad*?"

She gave him a look like he was crazy, hands on her hips.

"You knew it would happen eventually. I can't be tamed, Si, you knew it from the start."

It was half true. Part of him hadn't expected for things to last forever. She was known for her wild nature, after all. But he also felt so strongly for her, and thought she felt that way for him as well, so he believed she would settle down with him. But, even if she did decide to leave, he would have expected her to do it differently. Did she not even love him enough for that? It...hurt. He could admit it. It fucking hurt to be left like that by someone you would die for.

Si frowned.

Would he have though? Now he...wasn't sure. In fact, he couldn't even remember why he'd wanted to pursue her in the first place now. He thought hard to before they'd gotten together. He couldn't even remember thinking much of her. She was beautiful, of course, but he'd never paid much attention to her when she'd been at gatherings or the stray battle here and there. He had a flash of a memory of him turning her down when she approached him once, but then it disappeared, gone like smoke on the wind. *Why the hell had we even gotten together?* He...didn't know. All he could confirm for sure was that they'd crossed paths once or twice, and then suddenly he was nearly obsessed with her.

What the hell? Had he never really thought about it before? He supposed not. He was so happy with her, so in love, that he never needed to examine why they were together. After she left, he didn't care to remember the early days because it hurt too much. Now, his head began to pound as he tried to wade through the thick fog surrounding the memories. Si shook his head and pushed the thoughts away. He'd think more on it later, but for now, he had to deal with his ex.

"I am who I am. But that's why you love me."

"Lov*ed*. Past tense," Si grated. She canted her head to the side, her eyes full of challenge. She slinked towards him, so much sensual grace she was basically sex walking. He stood his ground as she neared and his muscles tensed when she stopped with mere inches between them. She ran her nails up his chest and around the back of his neck. His eyes slid closed, emotions warring within him. He didn't want her and yet...*something* demanded that he did. It was a powerful emotion, spreading through his entire being like wildfire, but it also felt...wrong. Thoughts of Beck poured through his mind, stronger than the other emotion. It slowly faded and his eyes flared wide.

He stepped away from her once more and she looked both annoyed and confused. *Thinks I can't be immune to her charms?*

"I'm going to ask you once more, Callie. Why are you here?" She glared for a second longer, calculating again, but she quickly wiped the expression away.

"I missed you," she said once more, tone pure innocence. He gave her a stern look and she relented. "And ok fine, there's also a bounty out for some mortal girl," she admitted with a wave of her hand. Poseidon's blood went cold and his muscles went stiff. *Beck. She's talking about Beck.* He wasn't sure how he knew, but he knew immediately and without a doubt.

His mind raced, the instinct to protect her flaring inside of him again. Thank gods Callie was so haughty that she refused to even look at anyone she believed to be beneath her. And she'd automatically lumped Beck into that category, automatically assumed she was a servant. That sent another flash of anger through him. *How fucking dare she?* Beck was beyond beautiful, beyond strong, beyond smart. *She's mine and Callie has insulted what is mine. I will not allow that to stand.* He didn't have time to deal with the whole *mine* aspect of that thought, he needed to handle the situation at hand.

Poseidon forced himself to calm and think rationally. Callie had called Beck a mortal, so the demons searching must not want it to be widely known who and what they were actually after. The bounty had to be hefty to attract Calypso's attention and to bring her snooping in Poseidon's kingdom.

Rage spiked but he kept his tone bored.

"And you think a mortal is hiding here? In Aqueous?" He arched a dark brow at her sardonically.

"Well, no, not exactly. But I want that bounty, Si, so I'm following every breadcrumb I can. The demons attacked her at sea, so they think a mermaid probably took pity on the poor girl and whisked her away to safety. I thought maybe…"

"You thought a mermaid rescued a dying mortal without a bargain being made first, and brought her back *here*?" He made the story seem too farfetched to even be considered an option. Mermaids were beautiful creatures to be sure, but they were also fearsome and wily. They rarely did anything for others without brokering a deal first, and those deals were usually clever and twisted. They were similar to the fae in the Mortal Plane in that regard.

"Did you forget mortals can't breathe underwater, Callie?" he added in a teasing tone, though it was hard for him to force. He didn't want to tease or flirt or even speak with her if he were being honest. He wanted her gone and he wanted to find Beck and apologize and get things back on track. Today had been a turning point, he just knew it, could feel it deep in his bones. When she'd pulled him to her and kissed him earlier, it was a big fucking deal.

He'd been waiting for her to express interest in more since the hallway. He hadn't wanted to push, had left it up to her to figure out if and when she was ready for anything else. But beyond the physical, something more had been brewing between them. Had that slipped through his fingers? *No!* No, he could fix it. He just needed Callie gone chasing leads on Beck's whereabouts somewhere far, far away from his plane.

She rolled her eyes. "Of course I didn't. Obviously she wasn't brought here. I was going to say," she met his gaze and nibbled her bottom lip, "I thought maybe you could…" She let the sentence linger around them and as realization dawned, he wanted to laugh though there was nothing funny about it. The absolute audacity of Calypso was staggering. How had he ever loved someone like this? Someone so cruel with other's feelings, so callous to their emotions. Did she not wonder what it might mean to him for her to come here after all this time? And then to find out that she only wanted to *use* him? Did she not care at all that she could be breaking his heart all over again?

And Si thought that...well, if not for Beck, she might actually be doing just that. If he hadn't been feeling this small flicker of connection with Beck, of the want to explore it more, he might have fallen right back into Callie's open arms, right back into her bed, and set himself up for failure and agony all over again. Even now, that strange longing for Calypso tried to rear its head once more but he banished it with a growl, too annoyed to let his past emotions try to take root.

He studied her as she willed him to help her with her pouty lips and bedroom eyes. Being the primordial Nymph, the one from whence nympheria demons, both sea and air nymphites, and the nymphs found on the Mortal Plane came, she was sexuality incarnate, every sway of her hips and coy gesture meant to drive men wild. And she had. Dear gods had she driven Poseidon wild. Is that why he'd loved her? He'd been blinded by lust and desire? No, surely not.

He'd felt actual affection for her, had been completely broken-hearted when she left. But, again, now he couldn't quite remember *why* he'd loved her so hard. He couldn't remember many redeeming qualities at all, actually, other than the physical. Did she make him laugh? Did they share secrets in the darkest hours of the nights? Did they comfort each other and protect each other? He...wasn't sure. He wanted to scream in frustration. Why were all these thoughts plaguing him now? Why did nothing make sense?

Focus, damn it. A plan was forming. A plan to keep Beck safe and right now, that was his only goal.

"I suppose I could help," he said at last, letting his panty-melting smile slide into place. It felt so wrong, but he needed to play this right. And if there was one thing Callie loved, it was being adored. So, he would let her think that he'd forgotten the hurt and was back to wanting to worship her. Her eyes lit with excitement and triumph. It took all his might to keep the sea calm around them as his irritation spiked. "For a price," he added, his voice low and husky.

She let out a shaky breath as her nipples hardened beneath her thin gown.

"Name it," she said, eyes hooded. He swallowed hard.

"A kiss," he purred, looking at her hungrily. She smiled a sultry smile and moved to him, wrapping her arms around his neck.

"That's better," she whispered almost to herself, a triumphant look in her eyes. "I thought you'd never ask, baby" she said just before her lips met his. She moaned softly as her eyes slid shut. His body rebelled, wanting to push her off of him and wipe every trace of her from his lips. But he forced himself to remain, forced himself to accept the kiss and return it, forced his tongue to thrust against hers. Callie moaned louder as she moved to press her body more fully against his. He lowered his hands to her hips to halt her.

His blood was pounding in his ears, an incessant whisper scratching against his mind: *wrong, wrong, wrong,* while another force was trying to tell him to deepen the kiss, trying to tell him how much he still cared for the woman before him. He heard a faint gasp but it sounded far away as he tried to remove himself from what was happening. *Just a bit longer. This is for Beck. You can do this.*

He allowed the kiss to continue for a moment, feeling sick the entire time, before finally pulling away. Callie was breathing hard, clearly aroused.

"Mmmm. Missed that so much," she said, sounding a bit lust-drunk.

"Me too," he whispered, hating how the lie tasted on his tongue, hating how *Callie* tasted on his tongue. She smiled and cupped his cheek.

"You'll always be mine, Si. *Always.*" It sounded almost like a threat, her eyes cold and serious. Then she softened and smiled. "Now, about that help..." she said sweetly. "We can play more after," she promised, ever the sultry seductress. He barely stopped himself from lashing out. She just really couldn't help herself, could she? She wanted to use his power, then his body, and then leave him again. *Stay calm, play the part*, he commanded himself.

He smiled and nodded. "Let me help you first, love. Anything to make you happy." He sounded like a sap even in his own ears. Was this how he'd always been with her? Her little lapdog, worshipping the ground she walked on and giving in to her every whim? How had anyone been able to stand being around him?

He tapped the tip of her nose and she grinned triumphantly.

"Well, if you insist." She all but fluffed her hair and he fought not to roll his eyes. He stepped away from her and closed his eyes, communicating with sea within the Mortal Plane. It held memories, as Callie well knew, but what she didn't know? He could *manipulate* them. It took a great deal of power and he began to build it up from deep within himself.

"When did she enter the sea?"

Callie rattled off the date and an approximate location, and Poseidon carried on his false search. He could feel Callie bouncing on her feet next to him in anticipation. He made his lips quirk.

"Patience never was your best virtue." He felt her run her hand under the hem of his shirt, splaying her fingers across his stomach as she giggled softly. *Don't cringe away, don't cringe away*

"One of the many things you love about me." He ground his teeth but forced himself to smile.

"I think I found her." His eyes flashed open and he waved a hand before them, a screen-like projection appearing. The picture looked as if it were being viewed through water, a slight wavy quality to it. The scene played before them:

A petite, brunette mortal was being pulled under the water by a length of rope attached to something heavy. She struggled to make her way back to the surface as she was pulled further and further down before her eyes slid shut and her body went limp. Sharks began to circle and it drew the interest of a coven of mermaids swimming nearby. They drew near, flashing fangs and claws at the sharks before they swam off in a rush, recognizing that for once, they were not the apex predators. The mermaids investigated with interest.

"Oh, oh. See! Mermaids! Guess the demons had that right. Wonder what's so special about this mortal? Probably made a deal with one of the higher demons and then refused to pay up. Little fool…" Callie prattled on and Si forced himself not to seem annoyed.

The scene continued:

One of the mermaids sliced through the rope with her claws while another gripped the unconscious mortal around the waist.

"What are you doing, Zelda? She made no bargain," a redhead said.

Zelda studied the girl. "She reminds me of Marena," she said with a sad shrug. "Call this one a freebie."

The others nodded sadly.

"What do we do with her, then?" a blonde asked.

"There are islands not far from here where mortals often venture. We'll take her there and someone will help her." With that, they swam off so quickly they were fluorescent-colored blurs in the darkness of the sea.

The projection faded away and Poseidon resisted the urge to sag after the use of such power. He'd need a good nap after this. Manipulating one or two small details of a water memory took a lot of effort, but fabricating an entire scene with enough details to make it convincing? It was staggering.

"There you have it. I would check what I believe would be the Florida Keys on the Mortal Plane. Hospitals perhaps. If someone found her after a near-drowning, I'm sure that's where she would have gone. I believe they call unidentified victims of accidents a "Jane Doe"—you could check for any of those having been treated around that time."

"You're brilliant, my love! I bet those moron Lackey Demons didn't even check there," she muttered to herself. "They've merely staked out her home and places near it. Worthless." She gave him a smile that would compel most men to give her anything she desired and laid her palms against his chest. "As much as I loved seeing you and as much as I long to do all manner of depraved things with you, I need to check this out before anyone else does. You understand, don't you baby?"

Wow. Wooowwww. Had she always been this way or was this a new development? His brothers hadn't particularly liked her in all the time they were together, but he assumed it was just because they knew how it would end and knew how hurt Si would be. Maybe they'd seen her true colors from the beginning? His head was throbbing and his body was fading fast. The use power had drained him and he knew he would collapse soon enough.

"I understand, of course," he said, kissing her temple. "Will I see you again?" he asked, forcing a hopeful, sensual tone, as if he wanted to see her again so they could do all the dirty things they didn't get to do this time around.

"Of course. Just as soon as I find this bounty, and square up a few other loose ends. I can come stay for a while," she said, sliding her hands up his chest and around the back of his neck once more. "We can make up for lost time," she purred before pressing her lips to his. He stiffened but quickly forced himself to relax.

"Can't wait," he whispered against her lips before kissing her back softly. She stepped away and smiled.

"Bye, Si," she said with a wink. With that, she vanished.

He sagged in relief and staggered to the bed, barely making it before his legs gave out. *Have to...do...one more thing...* He fought to keep his eyes open and his thoughts from going dark. He reached out to speak to his kingdom, the Plane itself answering his call. With the last bit of his strength, he issued an unbreakable command.

Calypso's open invitation into this Plane is hereby revoked. Indefinitely.

With that, he fell backwards onto the bed and knew no more.

Beck had tossed and turned all night, torn between hurt and confusion and anger. The way he'd...and the way she'd...and the way they'd...She'd shoved her pillow over her face and screamed in frustration until she eventually fell into a fitful sleep. Nightmares plagued her, but this time it wasn't the long corridor and the shadow man. Scenes of Poseidon and Calypso together played in her dreams, over and over. Them kissing, tangled up together. Him giving Beck a cruel smile, whispering, "Oh come on, Beck. You can't really have believed I'd pick you?" She honestly would have preferred the shadow man and the terror.

Now, she waited in the study for Poseidon to show up, growing more and more agitated by the minute. He was over three hours late. What the hell was he doing? *Actually, nope, I don't want to know.* That heat flared in her chest again. Her power? Twice in as many days? That was unheard of, but here it was, burning away. She wished she really knew how to use it, to practice or hone it into an actual useful skill like her mother's had been once up on a time.

She tapped a pen on the table, the speed increasing in direct proportion to her irritation. She'd already gone through all of the latest correspondence, sent responses to several invitations, and outlined a plan to help in construction of a new school within the Pathsiros' realm. She bounced her foot in time with her taps, counting the seconds in her head. She was giving him thirty more, that was it. No more. If he wanted to spend the entire day sowing his oats with his former flame then that was fine, but she wouldn't just sit here like a fool while he did it. She had other things she could be doing. Important things. Things like...*ah shit*. Guilt speared her. Things like trying to find a way to contact her mother. Yes, she really should do that. Emmie had said she was safe, but that didn't mean Beck shouldn't try to check for herself.

One hundred and forty-two seconds later, she threw the pen across the room.

"Fuck this."

She stormed out of the study and stomped down the hallway. She was halfway to the stairs when she heard him call her name. Her spine stiffened.

"Beck, wait," he called again.

She debated continuing on like a child having a tantrum, but she reminded herself that she was going to keep things civil. He'd technically done nothing wrong, after all. They were friends and nothing more, despite what she'd thought *might* have been shifting last night before the bitch showed up. She ground her teeth. *Civil. Friends. I can do this.*

Beck stopped and turned, trying her best not to glare at him. He jogged towards her, looking exhausted. *Do not think about why, do not think about why...*

"I'm sorry," he said in a rush, as if he couldn't get the words out quickly enough.

She coolly replied, "For what?"

"Last night."

"Why would you apologize for that? You have nothing to be sorry for." She tried and failed to keep her tone from being sharp and formal. Part of her wanted so badly to fall back into their comfortable banter. The other part wanted to rip Calypso's hair out.

"No, I do. It…it wasn't what it looked like."

Before she could stop it, the words whipped out. "Oh, so you *didn't* have your tongue down her throat then?"

He reared back as if she'd struck him. "You…you saw that?"

"Oh yeah, I saw it all."

After she'd left, she'd had the intense need to go back into that room and see them together again. She thought maybe he'd just been shocked to see Calypso there again and *that* was the reason for pretending that Beck didn't exist, not because he was still infatuated with Calypso. So, under the guise of delivering the drink that Calypso had requested, Beck had come back…only to find them kissing. And not just a kiss, but a *kiss*. Calypso had been draped over Poseidon's body like she owned it, like she couldn't get close enough, and his hands were gripping her hips as if he couldn't wait to tear that gown from her body. Beck had nearly broken the glass she was holding, wanting to use the jagged shards to flay the bitch.

She knew that Poseidon had sex with countless others, and she'd even fantasized about watching him while he did, but seeing him kiss Calypso right in front of her was different. It was too intimate, too…devastating. Beck knew that all the sex Poseidon had with others was just meaningless fun, physical release at its finest, but he had a *history* with Calypso. A very long, deep, connected history full of love and heartbreak and she had seen enough mortal movies to know that histories like that often repeated themselves. Beck honestly didn't know what she would do if he was back with Calypso. *Can't stay here. Can't see him with her.*

Anger rose, heat flaring once more. She wasn't doing so hot with this civil thing. She turned and strode away without another word, willing the tears in her eyes away. She would *not* cry in front of him! He phased in front of her and she collided with his chest, bouncing off hard enough to stumble and land on her ass. Or she would have if he hadn't caught her. She glared at his hands and he quickly removed them from her upper arms.

"Beck, please let me explain."

She held up a hand to halt him. "You don't need to explain, and I don't need an explanation."

"Yes, I do, and yes, you do. I was doing it to protect you."

She barked out a laugh. Was he for real? "To *protect* me? Let me get this straight. You sucked face with your ex after I thought we were...that we were...whatever. Doesn't matter." She blinked hard before starting again. "You made out with her *for my protection*? Is that really the story you're sticking with here?"

"It's the truth. I wouldn't lie to you, Beck." His gaze was intense. Serious. Earnest. She...believed him? Not about the make out thing, but that he wouldn't lie to her. How did that make any sense? She exhaled, all the anger draining out her. The only thing left was hurt and disappointment, two very familiar emotions. She'd felt them so many times because of her mother, she could hardly bear to feel them because of Poseidon. Because she...cared for him. Maybe cared for him *a lot* if she listened to that stupid voice in the back of her mind. Her shoulders slumped.

"Look, it doesn't matter, alright? Can we just forget about it?"

"No, not until you let me explain everything."

"I...I've gotta go." She stared straight at his chest, unblinking and willing the tears away, until he finally relented and stepped to the side.

"Boon!" he called from behind her, sounding desperate. She turned back slowly to face him. "You owe me a boon! I'm cashing in. You have to let me explain."

She narrowed her eyes. "You're using your favor, that could be anything in the world—within reason—to demand that I let you explain why you were kissing your ex last night? Do I have that right?"

He couldn't be serious. But if he was, he must really need her to understand what had happened. Why? Why did he care so much?

Her gut was telling her to listen to him, to let him explain, but her walls were trying to build themselves back up again already. She wanted to yell in frustration. She didn't know what to do, but thankfully, she didn't have to decide.

A second later Emmie popped into existence right beside her. Beck squeaked in surprise before sending the Seer a killing look.

"Could everyone *stop fucking doing that*!?" Beck bit out through gritted teeth.

"Emmie, what are you—"

She held up her hand to halt Poseidon's inquiry. "Not here for you, pumpkin. Although," she narrowed her eyes at him, "you are in trouble." Her smile returned. "I'm here because it's girl's night!!" she squealed as she wound her arm through Beck's. Before Beck could protest—she was definitely *not* in the mood to be social—the two of them disappeared.

"Where are we?" Beck asked in an awed voice, her annoyance at being whisked away for girl's night quelled. They'd materialized inside of an enormous room that was half arcade, half home movie theater, housed in an opulent stone tower of some sort.

"Welcome to the Underworld!" Skylar yelled as she rushed towards them, light pink liquid spilling over the sides of her glass. She hugged Emmie and then threw her arms around Beck. Beck tensed in surprise, but eventually awkwardly returned the embrace. "Nerina and Emmie have been singing your praises, so I insisted you be invited to girl's night." Skylar looked over her shoulder toward a circular couch, a table in the middle piled high with enough food and drinks to keep an army happy, and Emmie gave Beck a conspiratorial wink.

"I like to let her think she decides things on her own," Emmie whispered.

Skylar turned back with a grin. "Come on, come on." She dragged

Beck forward with almost too much enthusiasm. *Ouch.* Beck checked Skylar out as she tugged her forward. The Queen of the Underworld was in tight, hip hugger jeans, a black glittering crop top showing off a supermodel-esque stomach, and no shoes. Beck glanced down at her own jeans and plain white tank top, feeling a little underdressed.

"Ok introductions!" Skylar pointed around the table. "So, you already know Nerina obviously. This is Lillian, she's a harpy." Beck frowned as the petite beauty on the couch gave her a sweet wave in greeting. Lilac hair pulled into complicated looking braids, glittering rose-gold eyes, adorable pixie-like facial features, and pink, iridescent wings fluttering behind her. *She looks like Tinkerbell.* She smiled revealing small fangs and Beck noticed her nails were actually more like pink claws. *Ok, so maybe a killer version of Tinkerbell.*

"I thought harpies were...well, umm..."

"Heinous little bird creatures with faces so ugly any who looked upon them would poke their own eyes out?" Lillian asked with a roll of her eyes and a smile.

"Well, yeah, something along those lines," Beck agreed. She'd found a book among Poseidon's things in the study that depicted myriad mythological and mystical creatures. The description and sketches of harpies in that volume seemed nothing like the woman on the couch chugging...White Claws? Beck huffed out a laugh.

"Fucking Hermes," Lillian muttered.

Emmie explained, "Once upon a time, a harpy wronged someone that Hermes loved deeply." Sadness flared in her eyes, there and gone quickly. "He slandered the entire species across the godly and mortal Planes alike in revenge."

"Ahhh, got it."

"We thought about changing our name for a while, just to get away from the reputation, but we've found it actually aids us. Foes often don't realize what we truly are until it's too late. So, in some ways, he did us a favor." The harpy shrugged. "You can call me Lily by the way. And another by the way: these are delicious!" She wiggled her can in the air. "They come from the Mortal Plane, like you, yes?" Beck's brows flew upward, surprised to find everyone knew her story. Or a very small part of it at least. She laughed a bit, unable to *not* be charmed by Lily's sweet demeanor.

"Uh, yes to both. Those are all the rage there. I believe the phrase is 'Ain't no laws when you're drinking Claws'."

Lily screeched in delight, the sound making Beck wince. "No laws tonight! To mortals!" she cheered, holding her can high in the air. Everyone raised their own, Beck included as Skylar slapped one into her palm with a wink.

"Ok, so you've got Lily. This is my BFF, Soul Seer and general bad ass extraordinaire, Zahara, but we call her Z. Or bitch, or whore, or asshole, or—"

Zahara cut in. "Ok, she gets it. And I thought we agreed long ago that *you* are the asshole." Zahara grinned and inclined her head in greeting, and Beck gave her a small wave. Brown skin, shining black hair, and a glint in her eyes that would make men drop to their knees —to worship her or beg for mercy? Probably both. Beck wasn't quite sure what a Soul Seer was, but it definitely sounded cool...and maybe a little ominous.

Continuing, Skylar said, "And this is the infamous Medusa."

Beck gasped and automatically averted her eyes. Laughter erupted and she realized how stupid it was: obviously Medusa's gaze didn't actually turn everyone to stone seeing as how everyone in the room wasn't, you know, *stone*. She raised her eyes a little sheepishly to find the woman smiling at her. Beautiful alabaster skin, startling pale green eyes, the body of a fertility goddess, and...Beck canted her head, brow furrowed. Wasn't there supposed to be...

Medusa closed her eyes briefly and her blueish-black tresses transformed into ten deadly looking serpents. Black bodies with green patterned scales down their backs and blood-red eyes. They all raised up, hoods flaring and fangs bared. Beck flinched backwards and was met with more laughter. Even the *snakes* laughed, tiny little hissing sounds. Their small mouths curled into...smiles? *Whoa. Ok. Weird.*

"I can call them at will, you see." She stroked one and it closed its eyes, leaning into her touch like a housecat, before they disappeared, becoming curling locks of hair once more.

Skylar leaned in close to whisper conspiratorially, "If you're wondering about the hair downstairs like I was, the answer is no." She snorted and cackled. "Hades almost died when I first asked. Ahh, good times." Beck wasn't sure how to handle any of this. Perhaps she was in over her head with girl's night.

"And, um, the whole turning men to stone thing?" Beck asked, curiously.

Medusa's smile turned downright sultry. "I make men hard as a rock with one glance." She winked. "A simple *lost in translation* error." Everyone broke into laughing fits once again and Beck offered a tentative smile, relaxing a bit more and finding her footing with these females around her. So, maybe girl's night wouldn't be so bad after all.

"And everyone, this is Beck. She's...well, I honestly have no idea what she is, but we like her. She's working with Poseidon." Medusa and Lily both sighed, eyes going dreamy.

"He is so damned *sexy*," Medusa mused.

"Yummm. Have you slept with him? I haven't had the pleasure but my gods I've heard the rumors of the, well, *pleasure*," Lily said, practicaly drolling.

"No, of course not. I mean, one time we kind of..." Beck snapped her mouth shut. What was wrong with her? About to spill the beans on their sort-of-kind-of-but-not-really-*almost* relationship and one time orgasm exchange? "Nope. Definitely have not slept with him."

"Well, put in a good word for me, will you?" Lily said with a grin, tapping her tongue against one of those fangs that were somehow fearsome and adorable at once.

Emmie pulled Beck onto the couch and they all talked, ate, and drank. *Oh boy* did they drink. Beck hadn't ever really been drunk before—her mother had drunk enough for the both of them and between that and working at the bar, she'd never seen the draw of alcohol, seeing all the worst parts of it day in and day out—but she thought girl's night was the perfect opportunity to give it a go. She was feeling...*things* about Poseidon and their strange relationship, extremely confusing things, and she was still upset about the whole Callie debacle. So, yes, copious amounts of alcohol sounded like an excellent idea.

Soon enough, they were all feeling pretty good and the giggles and overall level of silliness were reaching new heights.

"Oh, oh, I have an idea!" Zahara shouted, halting her dance on the pool table. Skylar snorted as Z explained.

"Yessss. Ok, let's go! But we need to be sneeeakkkkyyyy."

CHAPTER

TWENTY

Poseidon lounged in Hades' study, drinking and spending some time with his brother. He hadn't planned on visiting the Underworld that afternoon, but just as Emmie had phased away with Beck, she'd tossed a note at him:

You want to go have drinks with your brother.

A few seconds later she momentarily reappeared to toss another note his way:

Hades, I mean.

At first, Poseidon planned to refuse the strange invitation. He wasn't sure he was in the mood for socializing. He had royally fucked up with Beck. Not only had he ignored her when Callie had arrived, but she'd seen them kissing for fuck's sake. On top of that, he'd stood her up earlier in the day, passing out so hard after using so much power that he'd overslept by *hours*. So, no, he wasn't in the mood to go have drinks with anyone.

A heartbeat later, Emmie returned again, annoyance clear on her face. She hurled another note at him and disappeared:

Get your ass to the Underworld. NOW.

Despite his lack of enthusiasm, he knew that not listening to Emmie when she was this adamant about something was never a good idea. He phased to his brother's throne room and Hades grinned.

"Emmie said you'd be showing up." They made their way to the study and had been drinking and talking ever since. It felt good to hang out with Hades again. He seemed so different now that he'd found Skylar, lighter and more at ease than Poseidon had ever seen him. Si realized now just how unhappy and unsteady his brother had been all this time. Pure contentment oozed out of Hades now, and Poseidon couldn't have been happier for his brother...and hoped maybe some of it might rub off on him.

"So, are you going to dance around the subject all night or are you going to tell me what's wrong?" Hades said, smiling over the rim of his glass.

Si exhaled roughly. He *had* been dancing around it all night, preferring to talk of just about anything else. But now, he thought maybe it might help to talk it out. Hell, it couldn't hurt or possibly make things worse.

Poseidon rubbed the back of his neck. "I might have fucked something up."

"Let me guess, you stuck your dick somewhere it shouldn't be, yet again? Is this a full scale going to start a war situation or something a bit less dramatic?"

Si gave him a dry look. "I haven't stuck my dick anywhere in... wow, it's been weeks actually."

Hades' brows flew upward. "Ok something is definitely wrong with you. Do I need to summon healers?"

"Oh fuck off." He leaned forward and rested his elbows on his knees. "There's a girl and we've been getting close. Close-ish anyway."

"The one you kept staring at during the Gauntlet?"

"I wasn't staring...that much," he finished lamely. "But, yes, her."

"Hmm. Close-ish?" Hades asked, surprised. "As in *physically* close?"

Yes. Sort of. That one glorious time. "As in getting to know each other."

"Huh. I didn't think you were into the whole getting to know you thing with any of your little playmates."

"I'm not usually. And she isn't a playmate. She's..." Si exhaled roughly, rubbing his short hair. He had no idea what she was now. They'd definitely been what he would consider friends, but that feeling had been growing and changing into something more. Last night, he'd thought that maybe there was truly the chance of something there.

"Anyway, things were going really well I think actually, and I felt like things were taking a turn into...*more* last night, but then fucking Callie showed up."

"What??" Hades shot upward in his chair.

"Yep, she just showed up in my room like she never left, like I would be glad to see her there after all this time."

"And were you? Glad?"

"I..." Si thought about it. He'd had that strange compulsion trying to *make* him feel glad, but in the end..."No, I wasn't. I was shocked more than anything."

"Wow, I can't believe she just showed back up like that after all this time. What did she want? A relationship again?"

"No, she just wanted to use my power to see some water memories. She's after a bounty," he exhaled roughly, deciding to just lay it all out there, "and it's Beck."

Hades furrowed his brows and Si explained all that had happened with Beck since the beginning: the demons after her, his rescue, their bargain for her refuge in his kingdom, everything.

"I still don't know all the details, but anyway, that's why Callie was there. Just to use me for that." Hades looked like he wasn't surprised and Si's suspicions from before sprang to mind. "Let me ask you something. Did you *like* Callie when we were together?"

Hades thought the question over as he took a long drink.

"To be honest, no, not really. I know I don't really have room to talk seeing as how my wife tried to have me murdered and all that, but...no, Callie was never my favorite person. She was just so self-absorbed and constantly preening. She wasn't kind to anyone she saw beneath her, which was almost everyone. She wasn't outright cruel, mind you, but she was never kind, and that's just as bad. She never..." He trailed off and looked at Si, seeming a bit uneasy.

"Just spit it out," Si sighed, hating how much he'd missed.

"She never seemed to love you. She loved how much *you* loved *her*, but it never seemed like she even cared about you other than for what you provided in the bedroom. It was like you were her trophy or something. I don't know man, it's hard to explain." He ran his hands through his hair and Poseidon was envious of the dark locks. Maybe he'd give longer hair a chance again one of these days.

Si groaned and let his head fall back, staring at the ceiling. "Seeing her again just brought up a lot of shit I guess. Looking back, it's hard for me to remember why I loved her, or...well, to remember if I was even *happy* with her." He looked back at Hades.

"Well as the mortals say, hindsight is 20/20. It's easier to see things for how they truly were after the fact. Had you never thought about it until now?"

"Not really. When she first left, I was so hurt I didn't want to think about her at all. Then after I recovered, it was just easier to keep her from my mind, you know? But now...I don't know." Si scrubbed a hand down his face.

"So, back to the Beck situation," Hades promoted, seeing that Si was clearly struggling with this train of thought.

"Yeah, so I think when I was dumbstruck by Callie's sudden reappearance, Beck saw it as joy and relief, and..." His neck heated. "And ok, so I promise there was a reason for it, but I had to kiss Callie even though I honestly didn't want to—don't give me that look, I swear to you I didn't—and Beck saw it. She's upset but acting like she's not and...man, I'm bad at this whole relationship thing, aren't I?"

"Relationship?" Hades asked, sounding more than surprised.

"Whatever. Just help me."

Hades smiled. "I couldn't decide if I wanted to kill Sky or bed her in the first few weeks she was here. I locked her in a dungeon for over a week for fuck's sake, man."

"And this helps me how?"

Hades reached forward and shook Si's knee. "What I'm trying to say is that every relationship has its challenges, especially at first. If you really want something more with her, then you need to go all in. I know that for whatever reason, you don't get close to anyone anymore, not since Callie, so if you're even wanting to try with this girl, then that's a big deal and you shouldn't give up. But no more of this 'oh we're friends but maybe more but maybe not and blah blah blah' bullshit. Commit, man."

Commit. Could he? Maybe. Did he want to?...Yes, he did. He was still working through the whole wanting more thing but when he got down to the bones of it, Si hated the idea of being with anyone else and could barely stomach the thought of Beck with someone that wasn't him. So, maybe Hades was right. He needed to go all in and really commit to this. But...

"I don't even know if she'll want anything to do with me now."

"I'm sure she does. I saw the way she was looking at you yesterday. You just need to do some major groveling."

"Hmm, groveling you say?"

Hades nodded, grinning. "Oh yes. A combination of grand gestures and lots of orgasms usually does the trick with Sky. *Lots* of orgasms."

Si rubbed his jaw, thinking that through. What kind of grand gesture would get him back in Beck's good graces? He needed to be back there first before he could offer the orgasms. But gods did he want to offer them. He'd been thinking about scratching their itch nonstop since it happened. The way she moved against him, the way she reacted so strongly to every touch, the way she tasted. *Fuck me.* He had to stop himself from groaning at the memory. *Ok, it's decided. I'm doing this.* He would make things right with her and then he would beg to touch her once more. To touch. To tease. To taste.

Feeling better, Si and Hades began talking of this and that, just bullshitting when a loud chime sounded, reverberating throughout the castle. Hades cocked his head to the side, brows drawn. It came again. Was that...

"Since when does the God of the Underworld's castle have a *doorbell?*" Poseidon asked.

Hades shook his head with a rueful smile as he unfurled his massive frame from the chair. Si followed and they made it to the front door just as the bell chimed again. Hades threw it open to find... nothing, though they heard giggling and not-so-hushed whispers coming from a cluster of statues off to the right.

"Did you really install a doorbell *just* so you could play ding-dong-ditch?" Hades called. The giggles turned into cackling. "You'll pay for this one, love." There was a sensual promise in the threat.

"Looking forward to it!" Skylar called from her hiding spot. Loud thudding smacks and shushes came on its heels. "Oh, right," she said not-quite-quietly. "You didn't hear that!" she yelled again. They cracked up once more as Hades shut the door, chuckling to himself.

"Girl's nights are always...entertaining."

SOMETIME LATER, Dean bolted into the room

-Quick! There's trouble! Follow me now!-

Hades and Si exchanged a glance at the strange message, but neither hesitated to bolt after the cat. They expected to find an attack of some sort in progress or something wrong with the castle, but they found absolutely nothing.

-Um ok so Emmie told me to get you guys here and tell you to be silent and to give you this- He inclined his adorable black head to a piece of paper folded into the shape of a...

-Is that an origami penis?- Hades barked with silent laughter.

-Emmie's talents know no bounds- Dean said, a smile in his voice. Si's lips curled. He knew that Dean had been in love with the Seer for centuries, but seeing as how he was a cat, he couldn't really do much about it. So, he resigned himself to being her friend and associate whenever she needed. That part made Si a little sad, but they'd all recently renewed their attempts to find the enchantress who had cursed him, determined to rid him of his feline form once and for all.

Skylar's shifter friend, Lucas, was aiding them with research in the massive archives of Willow Corp, the network of assassins, thieves, and spies that Skylar's father ran. He also had numerous contacts in the supernatural world in the Mortal Plane and he, Emmie, and Dean had been working almost non-stop to find a trail to the enchantress. Eventually, they'd find her, they'd get his curse removed, and then maybe he and Emmie could be something together. Dean was a dear friend, fiercely loyal and a warrior to his core. Si wanted him to find happiness after all these years of misery being trapped.

Hades grabbed the note and his lips quirked upward.

-Note is for you, loverboy-

Si raised a brow and Hades handed it over:

You've got groveling to do. Normally I don't condone eavesdropping...HA! Of course I condone it. Encourage it, actually. So, listen closely and take notes. I have faith in you. Tell Dean thank you for me. XOXO – E

-I'll leave you to it. Don't get caught or Skylar will somehow blame me and have my ass- Hades wiggled his fingers at Si in a mocking goodbye, inclined his head to Dean, and disappeared.

-Good luck, mate- Dean said as he strolled away, tail swishing. *-you're going to need it!-*

*Ok then...*Si decided to do as he was told. He leaned his head towards the door and listened.

Despite being fairly drunk, Beck still had the wherewithal to keep the important secrets secret. Mostly. No one knew the *really* important secrets anyway like her mother's identity or the details of their exile to the Mortal Plane. *Yeah, because I don't even know the true details anymore.* She'd given a condensed version of her history that was as accurate as she could make it: her mother had fled to the Mortal Plane for...reasons, Beck hadn't exactly been a welcome addition to the family, her mother kind of sucked in all things motherly, and Beck had despised everything about the gods her entire life.

Thankfully, the others hadn't been pitying, but they'd been indignant on her behalf and assured her that things would be better now. Did she have actual friends now? The thought made her drunken heart soar and she may have even gotten misty-eyed at their adamant declarations and offers to track her mother down and beat some sense into her.

"I'm serious, point me in her direction and she'll be sniveling at your feet for forgiveness," Z had quipped as she and Lily played darts —with daggers.

After a bit of mischief that included ding-dong-ditch and phasing to Mount Olympus to have Medusa scare the hell out of Zeus with her snakes, they'd settled back into the giant entertainment room. Music was playing low in the background and they were just having...girl talk. A novel concept to Beck, but she was enjoying it immensely. She was also immensely enjoying whatever fruity concoction Z had created. Her head felt light and bubbly and she *liked* it. *No wonder mortals liked getting shi-tanked so much!*

"Ok, so, describe the kiss again, but *slower...*" Lily said in a dreamy voice.

Beck giggled. In trying to keep the big secrets hidden, she may have spilled some of the other ones. Like her make out session with Poseidon and her maybe sort of almost feelings for him. Were those real or just drunken ideas? She'd heard too many mortals in the bar confessing feelings after too many shots. She'd never understood if they were just brought on by the alcohol or if they were true feelings that they merely felt comfortable to share with liquid courage running through their veins. She thought maybe the latter because her feelings for Si sure felt real as hell. So real, they were almost painful. Drunk Beck was also unable to tell the voice in her head to shut up, so it was yipping all night like a chihuahua. *Yours, yours, yours. Bark, bark, bark.*

"I've already told you three times," Beck said, tossing a pillow at the harpy.

"But I need to live vicariously! I'm in a bit of a…dry spell lately."

"Umm, that's because you straight *killed* the last three dudes you screwed, Lil," Medusa said as she fixed another drink. "*Viciously.*"

Beck's eyes flew wide. "Killed??"

Lily rolled her eyes. "Ok, that isn't exactly how it went down. It's not like I offed them as soon as we got off." She giggled for a second but then her eyes narrowed, the rose gold glittering with rage. "They all joined my sister's army. *Of course* I had to kill them to prove a point. I kill anyone I can find in her army. Those three just *happened* to have also spent time in my pants." Army? Were harpies warriors? Beck could scarcely imagine Lily killing anyone, let alone three men or fighting against a whole army. Beck had so much to learn about so much. "An-y-wayyyyy," Lily said, glancing around. "Z, aren't you supposed to be Zeus' plaything soon?"

"I will not be his *plaything*, thank you very much," Zahara said seriously. She looked around the circle and a wicked grin split her lips. "He'll be *mine*." Peeling laughter from the group and raised glasses to Z making Zeus her bedroom bitch.

Lily sighed. "You know, I really can't decide which of the brothers is the sexiest. It's impossible."

"You know who gets my vote!" Skylar yelled, tossing back a shot of some sort.

Zahara rolled her eyes with a smile, but answered the original question. "I'm not sure when he's going to call in his ten days. I honestly thought he would have already but...I'm still waiting."

Beck got the feeling that Z was tired of waiting. Beck had learned that while Skylar was in the Underworld with Hades, Z didn't think it was on the up-and-up. So, she made a bargain with Zeus to check in on Skylar and confirm that she was alright. In exchange for his help, Zahara had to spend ten days with the King of the Gods doing... who knew what. If Z had her way, lots and lots of sex, apparently.

"Well, I simply cannot wait to hear how that goes," Medusa mused.

Emmie cocked her head to the side, looking up from her phone, and then smiled one of her knowing smiles. Beck had been surprised to see an actual phone here and Emmie had explained that she used it to text with Lucas in the Mortal Plane. Lucas was like a brother to Skylar and Z, though they'd both slept with him at different times, but everyone was cool with it. *Who am I to judge?* Now, he and Emmie were working together with Dean—who was apparently a demigod trapped in a cat's body—to track down a missing enchantress...or something along those lines. It was all very confusing and Beck's drunken mind couldn't quite keep the details straight. She made a mental note to try again when she was sober.

With the way Emmie smiled at the screen every so often, Beck was pretty sure they were talking about more than strategy and enchantress-related things. What did mortals call that? Sexting?

"Ok, I need help here, this is a serious SOS," Skylar moaned, flopping down on the couch. Everyone looked at each other worriedly. "I need ideas of what to get Lucas for Christmas this year!" She threw her hands up in exasperation. "I don't think my usual funny boxer shorts or coupon book for free hugs and bikini car washes will work this year. I mean, I'm a Queen now and all." Everyone laughed. "I'm serious! I need help. I've only got five days until the party. HELP."

"Don't worry, you get him an excellent gift," Emmie assured her.

"Butttt you aren't going to tell me what, are you?"

"Where would the fun be in that? I'm so excited for the party! My first mortal Christmas! I've already got the required 'ugly sweater' though I think it's actually quite cute: it has a cat on it that looks just like Dean and he's wearing a big red hat!"

"Oh, he's going to *love* that," Medusa said with a chuckle.

Lily said, "I've always loved the idea of mortal Christmas celebrations. Everything looks so pretty with all the sparkly ornaments and lights and you get to eat those little men." She sounded almost… wistful? But wait, did she just say…

"Uhh…what now?" Beck asked, looking to Skylar who looked a mixture of confused and intrigued, hiking a shoulder at Beck to say *I have no idea, but that's Lily.*

"The red headed men that are eaten? I assume in some sort of sacrificial capacity. Is that not right?" Lily asked with a frown.

Red headed…? Beck's eyes widened and Skylar and Z busted out laughing. "Gingerbread men," Skylar said, between giggles.

"Oh my gods," Beck said, not able to rein in her own laughter. "Lily, they're ginger*bread* men. They're cookies!"

"Ooohhhh. You know, that does make much more sense. I never thought that mortals as a whole were cannibalistic but I just went with it." She shrugged, grinning, and Beck's stomach hurt from laughing so hard. "What!? It's an innocent mistake. You know I don't pay attention to details as often as I should." She threw a pillow at Skylar and flashed a fangy smile.

"We always went all out for it," Skylar said. "I think in the beginning my dad went overboard to make up for me having a complete shit sandwich of a childhood before he found me." Beck must have shown her confusion. "Oh, right, you don't know my tragic backstory. Condensed version is Ares is my biological father and he and my mother were attacked when I was just a wee little adorable half-goddess, half-phoenix. I got sent to the Mortal Plane for my protection, but found my way into the foster system and with some not-so-great foster parents before Ares could come for me and then I was all but lost. I escaped from the shitheads and my adoptive dad, Dalton, found and raised me. He's a full blooded, born lupin and runs a company of badass mercenaries and spies—like me and Z," she added proudly. "I didn't know about Ares until really recently. I'd *thought* my dad—Dalton—had died, but apparently that didn't happen and now I'm just waiting patiently for *someone* to cough him up." She glared at Emmie, her eyes momentarily turning black with flames in the irises.

"Don't you take that tone with me, young lady. I told you—*soon*. I'm playing a cosmic game of chess right now and all my players need to be exactly where they are for the moment. So, just trust me, will ya?"

Skylar rolled her eyes but smiled. "Only because you vowed that he's safe and that this is necessary to avoid a super big bad. Anywayyyy," she said, shifting her focus back to the group, "dad always went totally overboard for Christmas. Like the house was completely decked out with lights and a massive tree in the living room, the whole nine yards. He even dressed as Santa and hired shifters to be reindeer each year, even after I was way too old for it. It was amazing. How about you, Beck? You lived among the mortals like me and Z. What are your thoughts on Christmas?"

"Well, I always loved the *idea* of it. The little town where we lived would decorate the boardwalk and put lights in the palm trees, and everyone was always a bit nicer during the season, but I never got to really celebrate it myself." When the others stared on expectantly, Beck continued a bit self-consciously. "Well, um, my mom wasn't about to lower herself to taking part in mortal celebrations that were so far beneath her," she said, rolling her eyes. "And even if I did manage to find the extra cash for a tree and decorations, it wouldn't have been much fun celebrating alone—and mom probably would have just torn everything apart in a drunken rampage anyway. So, I never did." She shrugged.

"You never even had a tree?" Z asked sadly. "My dad's family didn't celebrate Christmas, but my mom was born and raised in New Orleans and insisted we at least had a tree every year. My dad gave mom anything she wanted, so we always had the biggest tree she could find, even if it didn't actually fit in our house most years." She laughed at the memories she was surely replaying in her mind.

Beck sighed. "Nope. I wanted one so badly though. I wanted the whole experience, something to feel...normal. Like I belonged there for once, you know? I would finally be the same as everyone else around us." Not quite sure why she was continuing, deciding to blame the booze, she added, "One year, my mom was in a surprisingly good mood and promised that not only would we get one, she would take me to see the giant one outside of Rockefeller Center. So, for weeks, I had my heart set on it and was actually excited. She kept promising, over and over, to make up for all her previous years of letting me down and blah blah, right? Of course, Christmas rolled around and she was back to being, well, herself, and that trip never happened and no tree magically appeared in our living room." She shrugged a little self-consciously when she found four sets of eyes looking at her sadly. "It's ok," Beck added hastily.

"No ma'am it is *not* ok. No offense, but I kinda wanna toss your mom across the River Styx by her hair," Skylar said.

"I second that motion," Medusa chimed in.

"She sounds like a Grade-A beeotch and I have very special blades that I reserve for Grade-A Beeotches," Z added.

"She's the worst," Lily said indignantly. "I don't like her at all. May I hurt her? Just a little?..."

Though it was probably totally fucked up, Beck's chest warmed at their support and kindness. It may be the alcohol talking, but she already loved all of these women.

"I appreciate the offers of violence, but it's ok, really," Beck assured them.

"Ok, fine, we leave your mom be—for now—but you are officially coming home with me for the Christmas party at the mansion," Skylar said. "We kept the tradition going and do it up right. Big ass tree, presents, eggnog, ugly sweaters, Christmas Vacation on repeat on every TV in the place. It's the best. No arguments. You can meet Lucas and fall in love with him like everyone else seems to as soon as they meet him. Oh and Castlebrock does this really inappropriate bit with a snowman and a carrot...well, you just gotta see it. And—" Skylar was cut off by Z yelling indignantly.

"I hate to rain on this holly jolly parade but: Who ate all the FUCKING Twizzlers? I specifically called dibs." She glared around accusingly.

Skylar's eyes widened for a moment but then a wicked smile curled her lips. She twirled a handful of red braided candy strings around in the air.

"Oh do you mean *these* Twizzlers? Hmm..." She snapped her teeth down and made exaggerated chewing motions and noises of delight.

"You little punk!" Z launched herself at Skylar. She laughed and flipped over the back of the couch easily before leaping to perch on top of a pinball machine. They chased each other around a bit as the others watched and continued munching.

"You know what I've found I quite like? Those extremely sour candies that look like gemstones," Medusa said as she rooted through the bowl of candy on the table. "Do we have any of those?

"Hmm I thought I saw...there!" Beck tossed a black cherry Warhead to Medusa. "There are these other candies on the Mortal Plane that are like tiny grains of fruity salt that explode in your mouth. They're soooo good. They're called..." She frowned. "Something. Why can I not remember the name?"

Emmie perked up, excitement thrumming through her. Z walked up then with Skylar on her back, their skirmish over the stolen Twizzlers forgotten.

"There was this one time that the lady down the street gave me like five bags because she felt sorry for me having to deal with my terrible mother, and I dumped them all in a bowl and poured a bottle of water of them. I thought it would be cool to see all of them explode at once. Damn it, what the hell are they called?"

Skylar's eyes flew wide and she gasped. Emmie smiled and whispered, "It's happening…"

Skylar leapt down and grabbed beck's shoulders.

"WHAT IF IT WAS A WHOLE POOL OF THEM?" She jumped up and down, her eyes shifting black with flames again in her excitement. "Oh my gods, oh my gods. Ok, ok. Castle!" she bellowed to the ceiling. "Get the water out of the pool immediately and fill it to the brim with Poprocks!"

TWENTY-ONE

Beck had survived her first girl's night—including an explosion of Poprocks and soda so large it had blown the roof off of the pool house in the Underworld—and her first subsequent hangover. She didn't see Poseidon the day after, which was possibly due to the fact that she spent most of it in bed, but she didn't see him the following day either. She found a note on her door from him telling her to take the rest of the week off. Was he avoiding her? She didn't like that at all but decided that maybe some distance was a good idea. It gave her time to really think about everything.

She was the first to admit that she had no actual idea how to navigate a relationship. She and Poseidon had never had a conversation about what they were or weren't, had never talked about wanting to be more with each other, had never discussed...ok, so she was sensing a theme. They needed to *talk*. Talking was the only way to get a clear idea of what they wanted, to see if they were on the same page with things. What would she tell him though? She needed to figure out her own mind before they had *the talk*.

Did she want a physical relationship with him? She closed her eyes and remembered how his lips felt against hers, his fingers dipping into her shorts...She groaned. Yes. She wanted something physical with him more than just about anything.

Next question: did she want more to go along with it? She thought about how they'd been these past few weeks. Working together, joking, talking about nothing when really it was everything. He didn't push her for information which he really had every right to do. He trained her voraciously, but seemed to truly want her to learn to protect herself. He was patient with her, giving. He made her laugh. She felt comfortable around him, more so than with anyone else in her entire life. And there was the matter of that stupid voice constantly telling her that she was...*meant* to be with him, that he was meant to be with her, that they were connected on some level she couldn't even begin to understand. And she was tired of fighting the voice.

So, yes, she wanted more. She wanted everything. She wanted them to...date? She threw her arms over her eyes. How lame did that sound? But as lame as it was, it was true. Did he want that? Was he really done with Calypso? Because as much as Beck wanted Poseidon, she didn't want to be a consolation prize, just a fill-in for the person he really wanted. The thought soured her mood but a knock on the door thankfully pulled her from her thoughts.

"Nerina, I'm not really in the mood to—oh!" It wasn't Nerina at the door, but Hades. *Holy shit.* "I...I'm sorry. I thought...um, hi?" she squeaked.

The god grinned at her with a smirk that was almost as sexy as Si's. *Si?* Already calling him the nickname reserved for his friends and family? She'd let it slip once when they were scratching their itch, but not since. Beck had never been this up close and personal with Hades, only seeing him from a far at the Gauntlet and peeking him drunkenly from behind a statue when they played ding-dong-ditch, so she took a moment to really take him in. Tall and lean, with a broad chest, and rippling muscles that stretched his black t-shirt tight. Black, tousled hair and blue-green eyes, the color of sea glass that sparkled with amusement. He had a dark sensuality clinging to every inch of him. Dear gods he was...*wowza.*

"Poseidon has requested I conduct your training today." She'd been momentarily distracted by his pecks but jerked her head up.

"Huh?" she grunted ineloquently, and promptly wanted to die.

"Your combat training? He's...otherwise occupied," Hades said with an amused smirk. Her heart clenched. Was Poseidon screwing someone else right this very second? She wanted to be pissed but she couldn't, not really. He had every right to screw whomever he wanted, however he wanted, whenever he wanted. But would he agree to stop if she asked him? Could he do exclusivity with her? Would she be ok being with him if he couldn't, or wouldn't? *Ugh, too many questions.*

"Training. Right. With...you?" Beck gulped. She couldn't deny that she was intimidated as hell by the thought. She knew that Poseidon was powerful and lethal beyond measure, but his easy-going personality made it easy to forget that fact. Hades, however, simply oozed raw power, giving a constant *fuck around and find out* vibe that anyone within a twenty-mile radius could see.

"I'll go easy on you, I promise," he all but purred with a smirk. *Gods his voice...*She barely stopped a shudder.

"I won't though!" Skylar said with a brilliant smile as she popped around Hades' back and wrapped an arm around his waist. Hades smiled widely, and Beck got the feeling that he'd been messing with her just a bit. When Skylar winked, Beck was positive about that. She narrowed her eyes at Skylar, but the Queen of the Underworld only grinned in response saying *oh come on, it was fun, can you blame me?*

Beck wasn't sure if it made her more or less nervous to know that Skylar would be helping in her training as well. She thought back to the Gauntlet and what she'd seen Skylar do was indescribable and terrifying. Absolutely amazing and cool, sure, but fucking terrifying all the same.

"Umm..."

Skylar rolled her eyes. "Come on, get dressed. You have five minutes or I'm dragging you out regardless of whether you're clothed or not—though if we're having a half-naked training session, I'm going to insist that we sell tickets. And possibly add mud to the mix." She grabbed Beck's shoulder, turned her around and swatted her butt to force her back inside the room, closing the door behind her. "Four minutes, fifty-eight seconds!" her voice rang out from the other side of the wood. Beck sighed and hurried to get dressed, accepting her fate.

"YOU'RE MUCH BETTER than I expected," Skylar said as they took a break to get some water. Beck was covered in dirt and sweat and, yes, blood, though most of her cuts had already healed or would be there soon. Skylar had been truthful when she said she wouldn't take it easy on Beck. She'd been ruthless and demanding but Beck hadn't been cowed. Instead, Skylar's barks and taunts had lit a fire in her chest. She fought back with a grit and determination she honestly didn't know she possessed. She was still no match for the demigod Queen when Skylar stopped pulling her punches, but Beck had spent more time on her feet than her ass, and had even landed a few glancing blows, so she was calling that a win. Hades had mostly observed and provided instruction. He was an excellent teacher. Calm and calculated and surprisingly patient with her. So, all in all, it was a really good training session.

Skylar wiped her mouth with the back of her hand tossed her bottle down.

"Now, why don't we work on your power?"

Beck's eyes went wide before glancing around nervously.

"M-my power?"

Skylar looked at her like she had a few screws loose. "Yeah, your power. You told me the other night that it only half-ass worked, so let's fix that." Beck frowned. She'd talked about her power? *Damn White Claws...*

"I..." Beck hesitated. Should she speak about her power? It might lead them to suspect who her mother was, though their powers were slightly different. Her mother could make people believe the things she wanted them to, blurring their thoughts and memories for a time, but the few times her power had worked properly, Beck had been able to actually make people *see* things she wanted them to and produce full illusions out in the world, not just a trick within their minds. On the boat, that demon hadn't just thought Beck and Oscar had disappeared, she had actually created an illusion, making their bodies disappear from view.

Did she want to learn how to harness and control her power? More than anything. Did she have the guts to do it? She took a deep breath and pushed her shoulders back. She was tired of being afraid. If they found out who her mother was, so fucking be it. If they wanted to punish her simply because of it, then they weren't the beings she'd grown to think they were and she would deal with it.

She set her shoulders back and gave Skylar a hard nod.

"Ok, yes. Let's fix it."

She spent the rest of the afternoon working on her illusions. Thankfully, Hades showed no signs of connecting Beck to her mother, so she began to relax as time went on. Hades and Skylar were both able to help her understand her power better in different ways. Skylar knew what it was like to have to learn to find and harness new power—she'd activated her phoenix powers once she died and rose from the ashes very recently—so she was able to understand that aspect of it. Hades had eons of experience dealing with his unfathomable power, so he had an insight that few others did.

"You have to banish fear of your power. I believe that is why you've never been able to use it to its full potential before now. Being raised in the Mortal Plane may have dampened it a bit, it's true—we're far stronger when we're on a godly plane—but I believe that you've mostly held yourself back, shackled by fear," Hades explained. He wasn't condescending or cruel, and Beck knew that he was right.

She'd been terrified of using her power growing up, terrified of someone finding out who and what she was, or at the very least realizing she was different which would lead to her ending up in a cell or a lab somewhere.

"You can't think of your power as something separate from yourself. It's a part of you. You can't harness and control it if you think of it as anything other than *yours*."

"Like an extra arm," Skylar supplied somewhat helpfully. Beck tried and tried, and though she didn't have a *ton* of success creating illusions that lasted more than a few seconds, she felt excitement about her power for the first time in...ever. She finally felt safe enough to actually embrace and explore it and that was huge. She may not fully understand it yet, and she was still having trouble reaching it fully within herself, like she still had some kind of mental block against it, but she could at least think of her power as something that was an important part of her, not something she had to fear and hide and hate.

"That was better!" Hades praised before cocking his head to the side. A smile pulled across his lips. "Ah, I believe our lesson has come to an end for today. Si has a surprise for you."

Beck felt the heat in her chest recede as she stopped trying to wield her power, and she straightened.

"A surprise?" she asked with a frown. Skylar grinned, bouncing with excitement, obviously in the know.

"Good job today, Beck. I'll see you later," Hades said with a smile. Before she could even respond, Skylar latched a hand on her wrist and phased them back to Beck's room.

"Ok, get showered and changed and I'll see you in a bit."

"Wait. Just wait. What's going on? What surprise? What's happening?"

"My lips are sealed but it's...ahh it's the *sweetest* thing! Ok, ok, I'm not going to ruin it. Just trust me, Beckalicious!" Beck smiled at the ridiculous nickname (though she secretly loved it), and with a wink, Skylar phased away. Beck wasn't sure what the hell was going on, but she couldn't deny that she was curious to see what kind of surprise Poseidon had prepared for her that had Skylar gushing. And, ok, she was also excited because this was the first time anyone had surprised her with anything in her entire life.

She showered and frowned when she entered the closet. All of her clothes were gone. A single outfit was left, a note pinned to the front:

Wear me.

She grinned despite herself. She donned the jeans, cream colored sweater, and brown leather boots that were just about the most comfortable shoes she'd ever put on her feet. Just as she was wondering what to do next, a knock sounded.

She tugged the door open and her heart sped up. It had only been a week since she'd seen Si, but staring at him now, it seemed like an eternity. Something relaxed in her chest. An extra strain had crept inside it in the days she'd been apart from him without her even realizing it. She drank him in, eyes roaming over him, attention snagging here and there. His dark green sweater was pulled tight over his chest and arms, and his dark pants hung perfectly on his narrow waist. She forced her eyes up before they dipped lower. As her eyes lifted, she found him staring at her as well, looking...hungry. He rubbed the back of his neck and snapped his eyes back to hers.

"Hi," she said a little breathless. He smiled that heartbreakingly gorgeous smile, though it seemed a tiny bit unsure.

"Hi," he said back. He cleared his throat. "Would you...I mean, I have something to show you, if you wouldn't mind..." He fidgeted as he spoke. Was he *nervous*? The idea of the God of the Sea being nervous to show her whatever it was he'd done made her want to laugh. No, not just want to. The giggle burst from her lips. His smile returned, more like his usual self, and he narrowed his eyes.

"Just come with me, damn it."

"Well, when you ask so nicely," she said with a smile. A real smile. He seemed dazed by it, lost in it. She felt herself blush slightly and she rubbed her medallion. She'd been worried about whether things would be strained between them, but all that worry just fell away the moment she saw him. She was so damned happy to be near him again that her path was set in stone: she was going to lay her thoughts out there and they'd figure out where they stood. Tonight. She'd do it tonight after she saw whatever this surprise was.

They walked in silence but it wasn't uncomfortable. She got the feeling that he was just happy to be near her again too.

"I'm sorry," he said finally as they stopped in front of the massive doors leading into one of the ballrooms that didn't seem to ever be used. "About...everything. I'll explain it all later if you'll let me, but just know that what you saw was not what it appeared, I swear to you. I don't want Calypso." Though she wanted to kick herself for completely forgetting about the whole Calypso incident until this moment, his words sent a thrill through her. He seemed so earnest. *Truth? He truly doesn't want her?* "I want—"

He was interrupted as the door creaked open and Skylar peeked her head out.

"Ok, I'm sorry to intrude and Hades told me to make sure you knew that he tried to stop me but that I am a force to be reckoned with, so he has no control over me, which—duh," she said with a grin and a roll of her eyes, "but hurry upppp!"

Si looked upward as if praying for patience. Beck looked between them, bewildered and amused. He finally shook his head and shrugged. Skylar squealed, bouncing up and down and then stepped back as Poseidon commanded the towering doors to swing inward revealing—

"*Oh my gods,*" Beck said, staring in awe. The entire room had been transformed into a Christmas wonderland straight out of a Hallmark movie. The biggest Christmas tree she'd ever seen stood in the middle of the back wall, reaching the three-story ceiling with ease. It was trimmed expertly all in blue and silver, the lights glinting off of the glittering ornaments and tinsel. Wreaths and garland adorned the walls, and mortal Christmas music played in the background.

Skylar bounded over as she pulled a Santa hat on her head. It had two tails, giving her the look of Santa-esque pigtails. She held up another hat in one hand and a headband with antlers attached, covered in jingle bells and glitter in the other quirking a blonde brow in question.

"Uhh...the antlers?" Beck said, a little unsure. Skylar smiled and tossed the hat to Poseidon. He dutifully put it on as she placed the antlers on Beck's head and jumped up and down, clapping and squealing.

"Isn't it amazing??" Skylar asked, looking around and beaming. "Si totally rocked it. And check it! I even got Hades to wear an ugly Christmas sweater! Tell me this isn't the most amazing day in the history of history!"

Beck was at a loss but huffed out a laugh when a scowling Hades raised his glass from where he leaned against the mantle above one of the many fireplaces in the vast room. He was indeed wearing a bright green sweater with a three-headed dog wearing antlers and Rudolph noses on it. *Cerberus?* Beck looked back to Skylar and realized that her sweater matched. She leaned in and gave Beck a quick peck on the cheek.

"Talk soon! I need more eggnog!" She flounced off towards Hades, a glass magically appearing in her hand just as she wrapped her arm around the god's neck and pulled him in for a hard kiss.

"This is...you did all this? *For me*?" Beck asked, still unable to tear her gaze away from everything. There was a certified Christmas feast set out along an obscenely long banquet table on one side of the room, complete with one of those terrible fruitcakes that no one in existence actually seems to like but for some reason are a staple of mortal holiday celebrations. Beneath the tree were hundreds of gifts, and she wondered if they were real or just for decoration. In one corner a couple of couches had been set up around a giant flatscreen. Comfy looking oversized pillows and beanbag chairs were spread around in front of the couches and *Christmas Vacation* was playing to raucous laughter.

Something wet landed on Beck's nose. She frowned and glanced upward, gasping in shock: it was snowing. *Inside* the room. The flakes disappeared just before they hit the floor, but it made everything so magical she could barely stand it.

"But how...why..." She glanced to Poseidon, unable to form a coherent sentence.

"I *may* have overheard a bit of girl's night conversation," he said, rubbing the back of his neck again.

Her face heated. "Which bits?" Had he heard her gushing about their hallway encounter or about her possible feelings for him that she was pretty sure drunk Beck had left the "possible" out of completely?

"Only the part where you talked about never having Christmas, but always wanting to," he assured her. "Promise." He was studying her, waiting for her reaction. "I...well, I thought it was time you had one. I had to get help from Skylar and Emmie and Zahara. They forced me to watch about a hundred Christmas films, insisting that it was crucial research, but I swear almost all of them were the *exact same* movie just with different actors..." Beck stared at him and he shook himself. "It took me a while to figure out the snow, and to find the right tree, and wrapping presents is *way* harder than it should be, and what the hell is fruitcake even?? Is that real or was Skylar just messing with me?..."

He trailed off, looking...*worried*. Could he possibly think that she wouldn't like it? Her heart twisted. No one had ever done anything even remotely close to this sweet for her before. She had no idea how to feel, how to react. Tears pricked her eyes, but, for the first time in her life, they weren't from pain or anger or sorrow. They were from *joy*.

"This is...Poseidon, I...I don't even have words," she said in awe. She gazed around once more, not understanding how it could possibly be so beautiful, so perfect. It was more than she could ever have asked for. His shoulders sagged in relief and he gave her a heartrending smile.

Before she could say more, Lily screeched and barreled into Beck in a surprisingly strong hug, almost knocking all the air from Beck's lungs in a whoosh. *Gods, was that a rib cracking?* Beck decided that Lily was indeed a terrifying little creature and made a mental note never to mess with harpies.

"This is so cool!! I knew mortal Christmas was amazing, even without the cannibalism!" She flew into the air, wings fluttering behind her, and caught flakes of the magical snow on her tongue.

"Cannibalism?" Si asked, leaning close to Beck's ear.

"Don't ask," she said chuckling and loving having him so near her again. She inhaled and had to stifle an *mmm* of satisfaction. She was shocked that so many people were there, but she smiled in greeting as she and Si roamed around. She wasn't sure whether they were all curious about Christmas or just couldn't pass up a good party. Beck didn't have much of a frame of reference when it came to parties, but she was fairly certain this was one for the ages.

Beck laughed out loud when she saw Zeus. He was wearing silk shorts made to look like Santa's pants, a red, fur-lined coat open over his bare chest—which he'd smeared with body glitter—and a Santa hat. He lounged in an enormous green chair, string lights hanging all around it.

"Beck! Come sit on my lap and tell me what you want for Christmas," he yelled, patting his thigh and giving her a flirty smile. "I bet you've been naughty..." Before she could even respond, Hercules took a running leap and landed hard in Zeus' lap. Zeus let out a loud "oomph" and Hercules wrapped his arm around Zeus' neck.

"I want a sword, and a new saddle for Pegasus, and a llama, and..."

Everyone laughed as Zeus dumped him unceremoniously onto the floor and the two started play fighting with giant candy canes. Beck shook her head but couldn't stop grinning. How had her mother ever called these people monsters?

They mingled and ate the most amazing food—fruitcake not included. Beck laughed as Skylar attempted to channel her inner Mariah Carey in the karaoke corner, and Hades grimaced lovingly, covering his ears. Zahara tossed popcorn, booing loudly, and Skylar chased her around the room, still singing at the top of her lungs.

Beck was even coaxed into playing *Pin the Nose on Rudolph* with Hera, Nerina, Medusa, and a handful of the Elite. She'd just pressed the paper nose to what she thought was semi-close to the right spot, when Poseidon stepped behind her.

"Dance with me?" he asked low in her ear again, making her shiver. Beck yanked her blindfold off and turned to see if he was joking. She'd never done much dancing, but when he arched his brows and gave her a pleading gesture, she couldn't say no. She didn't know if it was the eggnog—which Skylar had spiked to high heaven—or just the amount of fun she was having, but she grinned at him and nodded, letting all of her inhibitions go for just one night. Medusa catcalled her as Si led her onto the dance floor.

He pulled her close as *I'll be Home for Christmas* began and her heart started to beat wildly in her chest, heat pooling in her belly. She gazed up at him and that voice in her mind sighed in pure contentment. She was where she was meant to be. She was *home*. She couldn't explain it and didn't care to try. She just wanted to luxuriate in this moment, to remember it forever. After the first chorus, Lily flitted above them with mistletoe dangling from her fingers.

"Kiss!" Skylar yelled from where she danced with Hades. "It's the rules!"

"Yeah! Kisssssss!" others chimed in.

"I will toss all of your asses into the sea before you can blink, you know that right?" Si called, but Beck, caught up in the night, went to her tip toes and drew him in for a soft kiss. He seemed surprised at first, but returned it tenderly before the room broke into cheers and jeers, and they both pulled away, laughing. The evening went on and on and it was the most amazing night of her life by a mile. After what had to be the biggest White Elephant gift exchange in history, with some of the strangest gifts in history, the guests all eventually took their leave until only Si and Beck remained. He brought her a glass of sweet wine and they lounged on the couch in front of the largest fireplace.

"This was the most amazing day of my entire life," she said quietly. She turned to meet his gaze. "I can't believe you did all this for me. Thank you, Si."

His breath hitched slightly. He reached out to run his fingers over one of the jingle bells dangling off of her antlers, something intense burning in his eyes.

"You're welcome, Beck."

TWENTY-TWO

Hades had said grand gesture, so Si had pulled out all the stops, and man oh man had it been worth it. Watching Beck's walls crumble, seeing tears of joy turn her eyes glassy, and seeing her allow herself to have fun made his chest ache in a way he couldn't describe. It felt so utterly *right* making her happy, like it had been his job all along and he'd never fulfilled his obligations until now. A profound sense of satisfaction settled deep in his chest. She'd kissed him in front of everyone like it was nothing. She'd danced and laughed and smiled. *Those fucking dimples...*

"I'm cashing in my boon," he finally said as she sipped her wine, staring at the fire. She tensed for a moment before turning to face him fully on the couch and nodding. He let out a long breath before starting. He was eager to get this all out, to make her understand, but he was worried about what her reaction would be. He hoped she'd believe him, and he'd be lying if he didn't also hope the big Christmas surprise had buttered her up a bit.

"Calypso showing up was the last thing I could have ever imagined. I haven't seen her in almost two centuries, since the day she left me. I was shocked to see her, but I wasn't *happy* about her sudden reappearance in my life, in my fucking bedroom," he all but growled. He paused to curb his anger before continuing. "Anyway, I don't want you to freak out, but there's a bounty out for you." She sucked in a harsh breath and her shoulders tensed. "Don't worry, please. You're safe here, I swear on my life, but Callie was after the bounty. She didn't notice you when you were in the room and the demons only said that you were a mortal of interest to them, so she doesn't know who or what you are, not really. She wanted me to pull the memories of your escape from the sea to help in her search."

She swallowed hard. "And did you?"

"I did but I didn't." At her confused look, he explained, "I manipulated the memory. She has no idea I can do that, so she has no reason not to believe everything she saw and go chasing her tail for the next few months. I made it seem as if mermaids had rescued and delivered you to an island in the Keys somewhere. She's probably still combing the islands and searching mortal hospitals. That's why I was late the next day, too. Using that much power to manipulate the memory completely wiped me."

She was quiet for a moment, seeming to sort through everything he'd just told her. Finally, she asked, "And the kiss?"

"I had to make her think I was back to being putty in her hands so she wouldn't be suspicious. She *expected* me to be. She isn't used to anyone not being obsessed with her, especially me. But I'm not. Not anymore. Maybe wasn't ever..." He frowned and shook himself. He was rambling, fucking this all up. He needed to focus. "All I wanted was for her to *think* I was still the love sick fool she left high and dry all those years ago, and leave as soon as possible. As soon as she was gone, I revoked her ability to enter the kingdom without my permission."

Beck nodded and stared at her wine, as if it held all the answers in the universe. He tried to wait patiently, but worry was gnawing at him. Would she believe him? Forgive him? He knew that *technically* there wasn't anything to forgive, but he also knew damn well that he'd hurt her, however inadvertently, and that made his stomach churn.

"Why did you do all this for me?" she finally asked. Ok, not quite what he was expecting her to say.

"Didn't you like it?" His brows drew down in confusion.

"No, no I did!" she blurted. "It was absolutely amazing. I can't even begin to tell you how amazing and perfect it was, but I just want to know *why* you did it. Why you've done all of it, really. Rescuing me in the first place, putting up with my…irritation at the beginning, letting me stay. Why did you do any of it?"

Ok, this was it. Time to cut the shit and lay it out.

"I did it because…since the beginning, there was something drawing me to you. Even your call when you were in the water that day. It jolted me from my bed like it was the most important thing I'd ever heard. I don't understand it and I'll be the first to admit that I haven't done *more* in a long time, but I want to try. I want…you, Beck. All of you." Her lips parted on a soft inhale. So many emotions flitted across her face: surprise, joy, desire, a touch of guilt?

"You want to be with me?" she whispered.

"Yes, I do. I want to try," he said, emphasizing the *try* part. He wanted to try more than anything, but he needed her to understand that he wasn't sure what he was capable of giving her. "But, Beck, I need to tell you something. For years, I've felt basically nothing for anyone but my brothers and a handful of friends. I had no desire to get to know anyone, to be more than the barest of acquaintances or bedmates." She frowned and he quickly continued, "I wanted to though. I wanted to so damn desperately, but it was like I just… *couldn't*, like something was blocking me."

"And now, you…feel things again?"

"A bit, yes. It's there but…it's still just a flicker. That's the problem—I don't know how much *more* I can offer you. I want to try, gods I want to try so badly, but I don't want to get your hopes up only for you to be hurt when I can't give you what you want and need. I honestly thought that something inside of me was broken, like I was physically incapable of feeling anything for anyone, but with you I feel...*something*." He sounded pleading in his own ears, but he was desperate for her to understand. "Damn it, I'm not explaining this right at all."

She studied him and he held his breath.

"I want to try more with you too," she finally said, sounding a little shy. "I can't promise how I'll be with this either. I've never been good at opening up or, well, peopling in general as the mortals say. I've kept myself closed off for so long, I don't even know if I know how to be with someone like that." She took a deep breath and let it out slowly. "But...I feel like this is right. I've been feeling drawn to you too, even at the beginning when I hated you...So, it might be hard and I might be really bad at this whole relationship thing, but I want to try if you do."

He smiled, relief flooding him and warming his chest. He leaned forward to kiss her, but she stopped him, blurting out, "But we're exclusive. No more sex parties or orgies or whatever you call them. No more different hookups every other day. No one in your bed but me."

Wait. Shit. She hadn't meant to say that. Well, she had but she hadn't. She did want to make the fact that she wanted to be exclusive clear but she didn't mean to insinuate that she'd be jumping in his bed in a nanosecond. *I might jump in his bed in a nanosecond.* No. They should take things slow, right? Get to know each other and work on this *more* thing together before they got physical, especially since neither one of them knew if they could even do a relationship.

She had all kinds of baggage and he had literally been unable to feel anything or want more in hundreds of years. *What is* that *about?* But he claimed he wanted her and he'd seemed so earnest, so desperate for her to understand and believe him, that she couldn't help but do it. She didn't think he was blowing smoke just to get what he wanted. After all, he'd just thrown this entire Christmas party for her, basically shouting to everyone in attendance that she was more than his employee or friend.

To her relief, he didn't balk or try to argue. No, his smile turned sultry and holy shit it was like a drug. The chances of her jumping in his bed were skyrocketing.

He curled a lock of her hair around his finger and purred, "So, *you'll* be in my bed then?"

"I...um...I..." She was lightheaded. She couldn't focus with his skin so close to hers, his heat seeping into her despite the small distance between them, his intoxicating scent surrounding her.

He dropped her hair and leaned back. "I'm messing with you, Beck. Don't get me wrong, I'd love to have you in my bed more than just about anything in the world right now, I won't lie about that, but I think we should..." He swallowed hard and then, almost as if it pained him, he said, "We should take it slow with that."

She exhaled shakily. Yes. Slow. That's what she wanted... wasn't it?

"That's probably a good idea," she reluctantly agreed. "So, are we like...dating?" She scrunched her nose, hating how dumb she sounded. He laughed out loud, the sound carefree and sexy.

"I guess so," he said after a moment, seeming surprised. He huffed out another laugh and slung his arm around her shoulders, tugging her close into him. She snuggled deeper into his side immediately, melting against him and relishing how safe she felt within his arms.

"So, good surprise, then?" he asked after a few minutes.

Beck smiled. "Pretty damn good."

THE NEXT TWO weeks passed in bliss and intermittent bouts of awkwardness. Thankfully, they were both able to find the humor in the awkward, and the moments always passed quickly. They were both trying to figure this whole thing out in the midst of life continuing all around them. She'd gone to Christmas at Skylar's home in the Mortal Plane, though Poseidon had been extremely loud in his protests about it. Skylar had assured him that she'd be beyond safe within the mansion, surrounded by hundreds of highly trained and lethal immortals, plus herself, Emmie, and Hades, and the entire place was warded by some of the most powerful enchantresses in the world.

"How the hell am I going to explain why Derek Morgan himself just randomly showed up at our Christmas party, Si? Come on!" Skylar had said, throwing up her hands in exasperation. "I'm going to have a hard enough time trying to cover up Hades' true identity with all his godly mojo flaring off him like a nuclear reactor for fucks sake." She shook her head and muttered, "no one is going to believe he's a freaking shifter, even with all the booze in the world."

Though he'd pouted about it—which was actually incredibly adorable—Si had eventually begrudgingly agreed that Beck would be perfectly safe at the party.

"Just don't go kissing anyone else under the mistletoe," he said in a low rumble before kissing Beck thoroughly enough to make her forget her own name, let alone want to ever kiss anyone else again.

The party had been just as amazing as Skylar had said, though there was a bit of a somber quality to it at times whenever Skylar's adopted father, Dalton was brought up. Skylar knew that he was alive and well now, but, per Emmie, she had to wait to see him and spread the good news. Beck could tell Skylar was missing her dad, but did her best to throw herself into making the party amazing for everyone. Beck met Lucas and had indeed immediately fallen in platonic love with him, just as Skylar had predicted.

Seeing Emmie and him together in person, Beck now knew without a doubt that there was something intense between them, more than just searching for a missing enchantress. Dean had also been at the party, stealing food from the tables and hanging around Lucas and Emmie most of the evening. Si had told Beck that Dean had been in love with Emmie for ages, but seeing as he was stuck as a cat, he couldn't do anything about it. She wondered if it was hard for Dean to see Emmie with Lucas now, but as she studied them, she got the feeling that they were all friends. Dean didn't seem angry or upset, and Lucas and Emmie both grinned and laughed, eyes sparkling as they talked telepathically with the demigod. So, maybe Dean was perfectly fine with Emmie and Luke together, just happy that his friends were happy?

Poseidon met with his brothers a few times and always came back looking tense and worried. After every meeting, he threw himself into her training sessions with even more vigor, and encouraged her to continue to work on her power as often as possible.

"Is there a war coming that I'm unaware of?" she teased once as she dusted herself off in the training ring. He'd stiffened, lips pressing into a hard line. She straightened and went tense, all teasing gone. "What? What's happening? Is there really a war??" He hesitated but told her that a war, indeed, could be coming for all of them. He didn't give her too many details, but he'd looked serious and worried enough that she knew it wasn't something to be taken lightly. If a god as strong and powerful as Poseidon was afraid of something, she knew it was the baddest of the bad.

In between training and working and navigating their new relationship, there was the tension. *My gods the tension.* Si had held true to his word and was taking things slow in the physical department. He hadn't initiated anything more than cuddling while they watched movies or the sunset, or holding her hand while they walked. They'd kissed, but each time he'd been the one to break it off just as she was about to jump his bones and toss the whole *going slow* thing right out the window. He never pushed her for more, never even brought it up. She knew it wasn't because he didn't want her. The way he looked at her, the way his golden eyes would burn and darken as his gaze raked over her body made it perfectly clear: he definitely wanted, he just had more self-control than she did.

Beck on the other hand was about to combust. Every touch, as innocent as it may be, burned with something so much more below the surface and made her ache in the worst way. Her entire body jolted to attention every time he came near, every inch longing to touch every inch of him. She had never reacted so strongly to anyone before and had no idea how to handle it.

"Dude, just make the first move," Skylar said as she tossed a popcorn kernel into the air and caught it effortlessly in her mouth.

"I don't know *how* to make the first move," Beck admitted. "I'm not good at this stuff. I have basically zero experience and the experience I do have is absolute crap! I've never done much of...anything." She ran her fingers through her hair as she paced. She'd run into Si coming back from a swim earlier, had taken one look at his bare chest, damp with rivulets of water slowly making their way downward, and had promptly turned and sprinted away without a word. Skylar had been wandering the corridor looking for Emmie when she'd spotted Beck. She'd yanked Skylar into an empty study and confessed her predicament. Emmie strolled in a moment later with popcorn. *Great. My sex life—or lack thereof—is a spectacle in need of popcorn.*

"I don't know what I'm doing," Beck groaned. "How the hell do I seduce someone like him when I'm barely a step above being a virgin?"

"First off, I'm going to need you to explain the *barely a step above a virgin* thing," Skylar said with an arch of her blonde brow.

"And two," Emmie continued, "with the way he looks at you, I'm pretty sure all you need to do to seduce him is to crook your finger. He's very smitten with you, little goddess of unknown origins." She smiled and winked, as if they were in on some joke. Being friends with a strange, sometimes befuddled oracle was really weird sometimes. Beck shook her head and brought her attention back to the topic at hand.

"Ugh, ok to answer question number one: I've had sex but, well... nothing else. I'd, um, never even been fingered until Poseidon," she said in a quiet rush, feeling ridiculous saying the words *fingered* and

Poseidon in the same sentence. Emmie and Skylar both gasped in horror and Beck's cheeks heated.

"*No* foreplay?" Skylar asked, incredulous. "But that's just...that's just...not ok!" she sputtered, outraged. "Names. I want names of these fools. The Queen of the Underworld shall smite them on behalf of your lady bits. You think I'm joking? I'm not joking. This is some serious criminal activity."

Beck couldn't help but laugh before continuing on, though she knew damn well that Skylar was only half joking.

"And the sex I *did* have was...not good. At all." She rubbed her medallion and bit her lip, embarrassed. She'd always had the fear that maybe *she* was the problem. What if she was the one who wasn't good? That wouldn't do for Poseidon. If the rumors were true, he was beyond epic in all things sex-related, so surely he expected the same out of his partners? She shook her head in frustration. "And to your point, Emmie: I'm serious! He's a certified expert and I'm absolute novice level. I agreed to take things slow but..."

Around a mouth full of popcorn, Skylar said, "Trust me, been there. Slow is sometimes a dirty word. But you just gotta get out of your head." *Get outta my head. Oh sure. Great advice.* Beck's irritation made her chest heat and she seriously wanted to wring Skylar's neck. Beck cast her a dark look and Skylar gasped, leaping up onto the back of the couch and spilling her popcorn on Emmie's head as her wings flared out behind her and she bared her fangs.

"What? What's wrong!?" Beck asked panicked, whirling around ready to face whatever it was that had made Skylar wig out. Emmie just calmly picked kernels out of her hair.

Skylar slowly calmed, her wings disappearing. She glared at Beck.

"You just tossed an illusion at me, bucko. A really fucking freaky one at that, you jerk! I *hate* clowns!" *What!?* Beck hadn't meant to do anything at all, hadn't even realized she'd used her power. Disappointment flared. She really thought she was getting better with her power, but apparently not. It still just had a mind of its own...and how the hell did she even know that Skylar didn't like clowns? Had she mentioned it during girl's night? They'd talked about all kinds of things and Beck admittedly could only remember about half of it clearly, but she must have, right?

Emmie giggled. "Did I ever tell you about the time I shifted into Pennywise and Hades nearly took my head off? Ah, good times. It's so adorable that you two share your fear of clowns, you know. As if you weren't perfect enough for each other, you can pee your pants together when we go to clown-infested haunted houses!"

"Sorry, Skylar," Beck muttered.

"Forgiven." She eased back onto the couch, still eyeing the spot behind Beck a little warily. "Ok back to the important topic at hand: from what I've learned about Si, and Emmie can back me up on this since she's known him since forever, he *will* stick to his word and won't push things in the physical department unless and until you ask him to...or until you take matters into your own hands. So, you gotta decide if you're ready for that and if so, go get him, girl. Simple as that."

"Simple as that," Beck muttered. As if it could be that easy.

Skylar stood and placed her palms on Beck's shoulders, bending down slightly so they were eye to eye.

"You have *nothing* to worry about. You're a certified lady smokeshow and you'll figure out the physical side of things. From what you told us about that hallway incident, you've got more skills than you think. Plus, I *guarantee* if he finds out he gets a few of your firsts, his male pride will practically catch fire. Hades got my first big O with anyone but myself, and he's *still* riding that high."

Beck exhaled roughly. "Ok, I guess. I'll...try."

"Come on, Ems. We got places to go and demons to torture." Beck's eyes widened and Skylar grinned. "Not really of course." But when the blonde bombshell gave her a conspiratorial wink, Beck knew for a fact that she wasn't kidding. Sometimes she forgot how truly terrifying and lethal Skylar could be.

Emmie rose from the couch, a few pieces of popcorn still stuck in her silver locks. She patted Beck on the head with an encouraging smile and walked towards Skylar, but then she whirled around.

"Oh, I forgot to tell you! I'm going to see your mother tomorrow. Any messages you want me to deliver?"

"What? You're going to see my mother?? Where? How?"

"I've left an important package with her that I need to grab real quick like. She's still safely hidden from the naughty demons after you, promise. So, a note perhaps?"

"I…" Beck had plenty to tell her mother. Yell at her. Demand of her. But it couldn't be done in a note or through someone else. They needed to have a face-to-face conversation. "Tell her I'm looking forward to hearing the truth from her soon," Beck said, sounding colder than she'd meant to.

"Done and done. Good luck," Emmie said with a waggle of her brows. "Not that you'll need it," she added as she and Skylar disappeared from sight.

TWENTY-THREE

Keeping his hands off of Beck was the hardest thing Poseidon had ever had to do, but he'd promised her they would go slow and he was determined to keep to that path until she said otherwise. He wouldn't push her in this, but dear gods it was getting harder and harder with every moment he spent with her. Every time she laughed, every time she smiled, every time she seemed to be *begging* him to kiss her or more. He'd forced himself to pull back before he could get carried away every time they did kiss, knowing full well how close he was to losing all control.

When they'd spent the afternoon exploring the hidden waterfalls on the other side of the kingdom, seeing her in that tiny excuse for a bathing suit had nearly done him in. He'd longed to trace the rivulets of water that cascaded down her neck and chest with his tongue, to place her atop the jutting stones over the small pool and move that miniscule triangle to the side, lick her until she screamed...but somehow, he'd resisted. He didn't know how much longer he could, though.

He'd kept his hands off of her, but that didn't mean he didn't fantasize about her every single night, bringing himself release after release with her name on his lips. And still, he was never satisfied, hard again minutes later when thoughts of her fluttered through his mind once more. He felt like he had when he was young and first racked by these types of physical urges. It was getting ridiculous. Whatever was telling him that he wanted more with her, his cock agreed one thousand percent.

He finished dressing and was just about to phase to her room to escort her to dinner when a soft knock sounded at his door. He opened it to find Beck.

"I was just about to come get you. Couldn't wait to see me? Or are you just that hungry?" he teased.

"Si..." she rasped before launching herself at him. He caught her around the waist as she wrapped her arms around his neck. His eyes flew wide and then slid closed in bliss as her lips descended upon his own. The kiss was scorching, turning his blood to fire and burning through every inch of him. Without thinking, he lifted her higher and she wrapped her legs around his waist. His hands rested on her magnificent ass and he lightly kneaded her giving flesh before he could stop himself. She moaned softly before sucking lightly on his bottom lip. He gasped quietly and she delved her tongue into his mouth, lightly tangling it with his own. He reminded himself to keep things soft despite the savage need thrumming through him. He phased them to the couch, sitting with her in his lap.

She spread her knees and settled herself down on top of him and he hissed in a breath.

"Beck..." he whispered, "are you...ok?..." He could barely get the words out as she shifted her hips. He was hard as steel beneath her and needed her to keep moving like *that*. He needed so much more but he mostly needed to keep himself in control.

"More than ok," she responded, kissing across his jaw. "I couldn't wait anymore." She pulled back to look at him. "No sex yet but...I *had* to touch you." As if to prove her point, she ran her hands down his chest.

"Touch as much as you want then," he panted, capturing her

mouth once more. Things were still fevered but also slow and savory. She was both timid and demanding, and it was an impossibly sexy combination. They took their time, exploring and kissing and just enjoying the feel of their bodies pressed so tightly together. She rocked her hips slowly on top of his throbbing shaft, moaning softly against his lips. Perhaps she was as desperate as he was after all.

She reached beneath the hem of his shirt to trace her fingers up his stomach and over his chest. His skin burned deliciously everywhere she touched and he needed her to keep touching him, never stop. Gods, when was the last time he felt like this? He couldn't recall. The need burned within him so hotly he wasn't sure if he'd ever be able to put the fire out. She pulled upward on the fabric, asking him to remove it without words. He obliged. He would give her anything. Everything.

She sat back and admired him after he tossed his shirt aside. She slowly licked her bottom lip as she traced her fingers over his skin once more. He closed his eyes, letting the sensation rock through him. Her touch was so light, so unsure, so full of longing.

"So soft," she murmured. "So warm." Surprising him, she leaned down and planted a soft kiss just above his heart. His chest clenched. He eased his hand into her hair, pulling the strands back from her face.

"Beck," he rasped. She met his gaze. She looked rapturous, hungry, gorgeous.

"Yes?"

"Am *I* allowed to touch?"

"Please..." she begged. He kissed her again, nearly undone by her soft plea. He ripped her dress down the middle, unable to stop himself, though his touch was soft as he ran a finger along her jaw, down the column of her throat, between her breasts. She shuddered beneath his fingertips and it drove him wild. He unclasped the lacy blue bra she wore and slowly dragged the straps down her arms. He stared in awe, taking the time to properly admire her this time. *Perfect. She's fucking perfect.*

She was trembling by the time his hands covered her exposed breasts. She arched her back and pressed herself more firmly into his grasp and he groaned. He ran his thumbs across her hardened nipples and she gasped as he kissed her again, timing the thrusts of his tongue with the movement of his fingers. She rocked her hips against him, the friction driving him mad. His cock grew impossibly harder as she ground herself over him, so hard it was verging on pain.

Si trailed kisses across her jaw and down her throat. He could feel her pulse hammering beneath his lips. He bit lightly at the base of her neck, just where it met her shoulder, and she moaned roughly. *Like that spot, then?* He grinned to himself, cataloguing every tiny sound she made, every single reaction. He would re-live them over and over, would memorize how she liked to be touch, what made her whimper, what drove her to the brink. He would learn and master it all. When she thought of pleasure, he wanted her to think of him and him alone. He would erase any other male from her memory, and should she ever have another after him, she would only ever see him in her mind, would only ever recall his name to her lips as she came apart. The thought of her with anyone else immediately made him want to lash out, a surge of power jolting through him.

No one else. Mine.

The thought ghosted along the back of his mind, but was quickly drowned out by her soft panting breaths as he kissed and licked her breast. He deliberately didn't touch her nipple, making her tremble with want every time he got near. He traced his tongue around and around, before blowing lightly on the tight peak. She was undulating in his lap now, digging her nails into the back of his neck.

"Oh gods, Si...Please...." *Si. Yes.* He loved when she called him that. Loved it even more when it was in her raspy whisper, drugged by desire. He finally flicked his tongue where she wanted him to and she bucked her hips hard as she spread her knees wider, pressing more firmly against his lap. He was so hard beneath her, dying to bury himself inside her. *No. Not yet.* He closed his lips around her nipple and sucked hard while kneading the other.

"Yes, yes, yes."

He moved to lave the other nipple as he shifted them, lying her down on the couch beneath him. She gasped in surprise at the quick movement but groaned when he settled firmly over her. He rocked his hips and her hands flew to his waist. He thought for a moment she was going to stop him, but she pulled him against her harder, hitching her right knee over his hip. The movement opened her up more to him and he settled between her thighs. She cradled him there as if she were made for him. They fit together perfectly and he couldn't stop himself from rocking against her over and over as he licked and sucked and nipped. A wave of her enticing scent hit him and he remembered her taste. He had to have another, right from the source.

He trailed kisses down her breasts and stomach. Her hands clenched against the back of his head as he lightly ran his tongue along the top of her barely-there panties. She stiffened and he glanced upward, catching her gaze as he planted another soft lick and kiss in the same spot.

"Is this ok?" he asked, his voice rough. *Please say it's ok. Might die if I can't do this.*

Her throat bobbed as she swallowed. She looked dazed with lust but there was also a gleam of apprehension there. "I...I've never...I mean, no one has ever..." She blushed. Was she saying what he thought she was saying?

"This..." He swallowed hard. "This will be your first time?" She bit her lip and nodded. *Godssss.* To capture one of her firsts for himself? To have her always think of him when she thought about this pleasure? He wanted to roar with satisfaction. He had to make it perfect. He planted another soft kiss as the top of her panties and she sucked in a breath. "Do you *want* this to be your first time?" he asked, voice low and rough.

"Yes, please," she said automatically, eyes wide and pupils

blown. He could tell she was still nervous, but her want was obvious. She might be new to this, but she was eager. He licked his lips before he grinned at her.

"Well, since you asked so nicely…"

Oh gods. It was going to happen. Beck was torn between utter terror and desire so strong it was making her thoughts jumbled. She'd always been so curious about the act, had watched countless videos of it, if she were being honest, and had tried to imagine what it might feel like. But to finally have it happen? She wasn't sure what to think or expect.

Si dipped his head to trail light kisses along the bottom of her stomach again, just above the top of her panties. She tried and failed not to squirm. Even this was enough to make her want to explode. How would she handle his tongue actually on her? She couldn't even imagine it. But she wanted it. Gods how she wanted it. She'd fantasized about him doing it more times than she could count and now she was actually going to have it.

He kissed downward, his lips pressing on top of the lace and her breath hitched. She could feel his lips through the fabric, could feel the heat from him. *Oh gods*. She couldn't handle this. But she would. She would if it killed her. He inhaled deeply and his eyes slid closed with a moan. When they flashed open again, they were nearly black, the gold forking out like lightning around his pupils. He didn't linger long, though it looked like he was dying to. He continued downward, kissing and licking down her inner thigh. He pushed up to his knees and hooked his fingers in the strings resting on her hips. He swallowed hard as he slowly tugged the material down. She raised her hips off of the couch as he slid her panties out from under her.

She squeezed her thighs together as he tugged them all the way down and off her feet, shyness suddenly bombarding her. No one had ever looked at her like this before. What if…what if he didn't like what he saw? He stared intently at the apex of her thighs, lightly grazing his fingertips up her legs to her knees. He stopped there and met her gaze. He was asking silently, giving her the opportunity to tell him no, to stop this. The thought made her want to scream. She didn't want to stop this, *never* wanted to stop this. She forced the shy feeling away. She was proud of her body and if he didn't like it then...well, too bad for him. With the hungry look in his eyes, she didn't think she had anything to worry about anyway. His gaze bore into hers and she felt completely safe, completely comfortable. The last tiny bit of apprehension faded to nothing and she relaxed her muscles, letting her knees fall slightly apart.

He understood the permission and pressed them wider, his gaze falling directly to her core. He cursed quietly and scrubbed his hand across his mouth. She bit her lip, watching him as he watched her. She tried not to squirm but couldn't help it. Finally he seemed to not be able to hold himself back any longer. He lowered himself down between her legs, hooking her thighs over his shoulders, and dipped his head towards her.

She stopped breathing, her body going tense as she waited...and then a lash of the most intense pleasure she'd ever experienced cracked through her like a whip as he slowly licked her. Her hips rocked upward, her entire body bowing from the ecstasy of it, and she gasped out, throwing her head back.

"*Fuckkkkkk,*" he rasped. He licked again and moaned against her. The sensation was unimaginable. His tongue was hot and soft against her as he licked again and again, slowly, so deliciously slowly. Her eyes flew open and she saw streaks of blue lightning flaring above the water. He waved a hand, quickly turning the ceiling into the mimicked night sky instead of the ocean above them. He lapped at her over and over, not seeming to able to get enough, before finally flicking his tongue over her sensitive clit. She cried out, her hands flying to his head. He closed his lips around the sensitive spot and sucked gently. A strangled moan escaped her and she raised her head to look at him. He seemed to sense her eyes because he pulled back and held her gaze as he licked her again, long and slow.

"Oh my gods," she rasped, entranced. She couldn't have looked away if her life depended on it. Watching him as he did this to her was the sexiest, most erotic thing she'd ever seen, ever imagined. He continued to watch her watching him as he used his thumbs to spread her wider and thrust his tongue inside. She whispered his name over and over, the pleasure so intense she thought she might die from it.

"You taste so fucking good, Beck. Will never get enough of this."

His words made her impossibly wetter and he growled in appreciation. It was too much. It wasn't enough. Her head fell back as the tension began to build higher and higher. She was going to come. *Hard.* So hard that it scared her a little. But she couldn't stop it, wouldn't even if she could. As if reading her mind, or perhaps he could just tell these things, he whispered, "I want you to come on my tongue, Beck."

He licked again, faster, and she felt herself careen over the edge, her orgasm ripping through her so hard she saw stars. He kept licking, his tongue a frenzy as if he were the one shattering, not her. Her legs were shaking and her heart was beating so wildly she thought it might break through her chest. He wasn't stopping.

"Si," she panted. "Si, you can stop..."

"Never," he growled, reaching up to knead her breast as he continued licking, slowing things back down again. Could she go again? As she watched him slowly savoring her, looking so sexy and so turned on, she thought she absolutely could. She didn't want him to stop. *Never* wanted him to stop. She was sensitive, but he seemed to know exactly what her body needed. He licked softly while he tweaked her nipples, then ran the pad of his forefinger around the aching peak. So slowly it was driving her mad.

"Yes, just like that. Oh gods..."

Sensation after sensation bombarded her, everything so new. She tried to focus on each individual stroke of his tongue, each hum of his approval against her, each brush of his fingers. She wanted to memorize everything about this night, wanted it crystalized in her mind forever. He trailed his hand downward again and slowly pushed a finger inside her while he gently licked her clit. She writhed, the pleasure mind-blistering. He pumped his finger slowly and she moved her hips in time with his thrusts. She was already beginning to crest the hill again, the tension building, building, building...

She could feel him grin against her.

"You're driving me wild doing that, Beck. I love the way you move, riding my tongue..."

She whimpered, nearly coming from his words, and he added a second finger. She cried out in bliss, back bowing off of the couch again. *Oh gods.* The feeling of his fingers inside her, filling her, while he licked her, it was too much. Not enough. She was close again, her release coiling deep in her belly, tighter and tighter as he pumped his fingers. He sucked her clit again, harder as he moved his fingers faster. She lifted up again, unable to help herself. She had to watch.

He held her gaze as he sucked, and she exploded again, spasming around his fingers.

"Gods, Beck. You're squeezing my fingers so gods damned tight," he groaned, voice deep and hoarse. She fell back as the orgasm rocked through her, scorching her, leaving nothing but ash in its wake. Eventually, the tremors stopped ricocheting through her body. He kissed the inside of her thigh, his stubble rasping over her sensitive skin, before he raised up to his knees again, looking dazed and so sexy she could barely stand it.

She reached up and grabbed him around the neck, yanking him to her for a searing kiss. She could taste herself on him but she couldn't have cared less. He groaned and kissed her back so fiercely it staggered her. She reached downward and before he could protest she'd yanked the laces of his pants and freed his erection.

Dear. Gods.

She'd known he was big, she'd seen him in all his glory before, but her memory hadn't done him justice. She wrapped her hand around his shaft and he hissed between his teeth. She loved the feel of him against her palm. Hot. Hard. Smooth. She brushed her thumb over the head, a bead of moisture wetting her finger. She stroked him, softly at first, not sure what she was doing, but instincts began to take over.

"Ah fuck," he grated, as she gripped him tighter and moved a bit faster. "Yes. Gods, don't stop, Beck. *Please*..." He was begging her not to stop. It sent a thrill through her. She didn't want to stop. She never wanted to relinquish this prize. He held himself above her on straightened arms and his muscles began to shake.

"Already...close..." he bit out. She drew his mouth back to hers and sucked on his bottom lip as she moved her hand. Up. Down. Up. Down. Swirling her thumb around the slick head and rubbing the moisture down the shaft, her palm gliding faster now. She wondered if he could possibly come just from her doing this.

In answer, he grated, "Going to...come...fuckkkkk."

She felt his entire body tense and still for the span of a heartbeat before he bucked his hips forward into her hand once, twice. She felt hot jets of his cum land on her stomach, searing her. She didn't know if she was supposed to be grossed out by it, but she found that she... *liked* it. Was that weird? She instantly decided that she didn't give a shit if it was. He eventually spent everything in him and rested his forehead against hers, breathing hard.

"Ah fuck, Beck...I'm sorry, I shouldn't have..."

She silenced him with a kiss. "I...liked it," she said, a bit embarrassed. "It's kind of...sexy?" He leaned back to stare at her, studying her expression. He arched brow. "Is that weird?" she asked, biting her lip. She'd told herself she didn't care, but if he was grossed out by it...

"Not at all. It's...hot actually," he admitted, looking at her like she wasn't real. He kissed her again and sat back, a towel suddenly appearing in his hand. He wiped the mess away and then tugged her up into his lap. He brushed her hair back from her face and lightly trailed his thumb along her bottom lip.

"So…"

"So…" she echoed.

"How was your first experience?" he asked in a teasing tone, but there was a slight edge to it. Was he honestly worried about whether or not she'd enjoyed herself? The thought made her chest twist…but she decided to have a bit of fun. Now that she'd discovered how much *fun*, fun could be, she had vowed to have it more often, as much of it as possible.

"It was…adequate, I suppose," she said, feigning indifference.

"Adequate?" he repeated, eyes going wide. She smirked at him.

"You know, I really shouldn't make a determination after just *one* experience. Not very scientific. Perhaps you should try again." His lips curled into that cocky, sexy grin she loved.

"Oh really? Just once more then?"

"Maybe an encore performance…every day for the rest of forever?" she said with a lust-drunk smile. His laughter was warm and husky, wrapping around her like a cocoon.

"Deal," he said, running his hands through her hair again. It was like he couldn't stop touching her. And she wasn't complaining. She didn't want him to stop either. He leaned in and kissed her softly and she was seconds away from breaking the no sex decree from earlier. Why the hell not? *Because if you do that with him, you're a goner for good.* She may already be sort of on the verge of…falling for him. If she had sex with him, if they shared something like that and it was even close to what she'd experienced tonight, there would be no going back. She wasn't ready for that yet. Though she yearned for it so badly she wanted to scream, she was also still utterly terrified of it.

"Will you stay with me tonight? No sex," he added quickly, "I'll be on my best behavior, I swear. Just…stay the night with me." He sounded…vulnerable. She realized then that in all the partners he'd had in the past, he hadn't wanted to spend the night with one. To actually *sleep* with one.

She gently ran her palm along his stubble and he leaned into the touch.

"Yes," she whispered.

He grinned that heart-stopping grin that she loved and he drew her in for a soft kiss.

"How about a bath first?"

"Ok, this isn't a bath tub. This is a freaking *pool*. Will there be a lifeguard on duty?"

Si chuckled as he waved a hand, filling the massive tub in seconds. She watched in fascination and began exploring the room. The bathroom was all white marble with deep blue accents, and the tub itself was an obscenely large rectangular basin of the same white marble raised on a small platform, sea glass tiles surrounding the edges. The water flowed in from the stone wall to the right, making it seem as if it were being filled by a small waterfall. He watched Beck like a hawk as she trailed a finger over the cool stones, seemingly over that first bout of shyness with her nudity. Now, she almost *strutted*, he hoped feeling empowered by the way he couldn't stop devouring her with his eyes, and he fucking loved it.

Si waved a hand and the wall behind the tub disappeared, revealing a breathtaking view of the beach and sea beyond. Beck gasped quietly.

"It's beautiful."

The sun was setting and the deep pink and purple light reflected over the waves. He added some oils to the water that sent tendrils of bell palm-scented steam swirling into the air. He'd noticed she loved the trees, always running her hands over the fronds to make them tinkle like the bells they were named for, inhaling deeply when the rustling of the leaves released their sweet scent.

She inhaled and made an adorable noise of appreciation. He watched her as she stared at the view, but when he started taking off his pants, she immediately shifted her gaze to him. He smirked and let her enjoy the show. He made short work of the laces, barely having tied them when they left the couch anyway, and slid them slowly off. He stood when he was done, letting her look her fill. Her eyes widened as he grew hard under her gaze, and she absently licked her lip before biting down on it. Gods, to know what she was thinking about in that moment. Her nipples pebbled and her breaths grew shallow. He shuffled his feet wider and groaned. He'd been ogled more times than he could possibly count, but no single look had ever affected him like this. He could practically feel her eyes on his cock and he barely stopped himself from stroking it before her eyes. He was fairly certain she might enjoy that actually, but he reminded himself to take things slow. For now.

"Gods, Beck," he whispered hoarsely. "You keep looking at me like that and I'm going to lose my mind…"

She raised her eyes and gave him a sheepish grin.

"Oops?" she offered with a shrug.

He grinned. "Just get in the damn tub."

She quickly obeyed, moaning with delight as she lowered herself into the hot water. He entered just after, moving her up so that he could slide his body behind hers. She leaned back against his chest, resting her head against his shoulder, and sighed. He wrapped his arms around her, one over her chest, one over her stomach. She rested her hands over his arms, tracing idle shapes. Gods this felt so good.

Right that voice whispered in the back of his mind. And it did feel right. It felt so fucking perfect, like he'd been waiting for this his entire existence. To have her here, in his arms, lying against him so trustingly. He got the strange feeling that he should be feeling *more,* that this, as amazing as it was, was just a hint at the sensation he should be experiencing. *Fuck, maybe I really am broken or something.*

They sat like that for ages, staring out into the now star-strewn sky reflecting off of the waves.

"The nights are so beautiful here," she said quietly.

"They are," he agreed. He'd always loved the nights here, the way the stars danced and twirled, reflecting over the water. The night creatures often got a bad rap, but they were some of his favorites. Unlike their land-dwelling cousins, the water basilisks' scales were luminescent, sending streaks of blue and green light dancing beneath the waves as they moved.

He'd thought she'd fallen asleep until she said, "If this were my bathroom, I'd never get out of this tub."

"Who says we have to leave?" he murmured softly against her neck before planting a kiss just below her ear.

"Mmmm," she moaned quietly.

He kissed her temple and sighed. "This is...I haven't felt this content in I don't know how long." *Maybe not ever,* he added silently. Another soft kiss on her cheek. "I do believe I'm a fan of *more* with you, Beck."

"Ditto," she said a little breathlessly as she subtly moved her hips, rubbing that perfect ass against his lap. He bit back a groan and she tilted her head to the side, giving him better access to her neck, giving him the permission and invitation he needed. He continued placing kisses, licking and nipping softly, and she reached back over her shoulder to grip the back of his head. He moved his arms, slowly trailing his fingers across her belly. He took his time, driving her wild. He knew she was wondering which direction he would move, her muscles tense with anticipation. He grinned and continued to trace his fingers over her skin.

"Is this alright?" he asked quietly at her ear. She nodded eagerly before turning to capture his mouth in a kiss. Surprised but delighted, he kissed her back as he finally moved his hands upward.

He cupped her breasts as his tongue gently tangled with hers. He rubbed and kneaded softly, knowing damn well he was torturing her. He couldn't help it. She was so responsive to him, he loved every second with her. She whimpered quietly as she arched upward, begging him. He took mercy on her and finally rubbed the pad of his finger gently over her nipple. She cried out in pleasure, arching her back harder and digging her nails into the back of his head. He chuckled against her lips.

"*So* sensitive. The things I have in mind for you, Beck..." The words made her squirm over his lap and his cock shot even harder under her. He growled low in her ear before taking the lobe softly between his teeth. "You keep that up and I'm going to come again."

"I *want* you to," she panted. Her words almost did him in. Where was his legendary stamina? He'd had sexual encounters that had lasted hours, *days* nearly, but here he was, about to spill just from her gyrating in his lap and telling him that she wanted him to come. *Get it together, man.* He steeled himself, pulling on his self-control and commanding himself to hold out.

"Not yet..." He flattened his right hand on her stomach and slowly began to move it downward. He knew she expected him to tease her once more, so instead he quickly sank a finger deep inside her. She gasped and then groaned loudly against his mouth.

"So slick," he murmured before sucking on her bottom lip. He added a second finger and she arched her hips upward as he thrust. He kept working his fingers, twisting and curling them, hitting her in spots that made her make the most delicious noises. She was growing desperate and he could tell her climax was already close.

"Si..." she panted. Gods he loved hearing his name on her lips that way.

"I'm beginning to know what that tone means," he said with a smirk. "My woman is close." *My woman.* He frowned slightly at how easily the words had floated from his tongue, how much he liked them. An idea sprang to his mind. He'd told himself to go slow, not to push her too far too fast, but something was telling him that she wanted to explore this with him. *So, let's give it a go...*

"Do you trust me?" he whispered against her lips. She nodded immediately and something about that made his chest clench. She writhed harder against his hand, pressing her clit against the heel of his hand, begging him to keep going and his cock pulsed beneath her ass in anticipation. "Then look at the window."

She stopped kissing him and did as he asked, clearly a little confused but also intrigued. A moment later the windows disappeared, the wall taking their place once more.

"Hey!" she protested, but then she sucked in a breath. A large mirror appeared on the wall. They both stared at their reflection, her lips parted in shock...and appreciation, he thought. The view was spectacular and so damned arousing he could barely stand it.

She looked so small in front of him, her skin light where his was dark. Her hair was pulled back, but strands had fallen and clung damply to her neck and temples. Her pupils were wide, the deep, cobalt blue nearly gone completely. His eyes had darkened as well, black with amber streaks, and as their gazes collided in the reflection, something intense began to build heavily in the air around them. He could practically see the electricity dancing between them. He cleared the water of the oils, making it completely transparent so she could see *everything.*

Without taking his eyes from hers in the reflection, he whispered, "We can stop anytime you want. We don't even have to try..."

"No," she breathed. "I want to. Show me everything..."

His heart thudded against his chest. She was eager to explore with him, eager to trust him. *And why is that almost as arousing as what I'm seeing in the mirror right now?*

Her chest rose and fell in quick shallow breaths. He held her gaze and breathed against her ear, "Watch, then." He ran her earlobe between his teeth. "Watch as I make you come, Beck."

∿

BECK NEARLY COMBUSTED RIGHT THEN, his words so dark and sensual, the idea of watching herself come by his hands...She shuddered, eyes sliding closed for a brief moment before snapping open again. How did he know exactly what she wanted, what she needed, without even knowing herself? She knew so little about all of this, but she wanted nothing more than to explore it with him, to have him show her and teach her.

She watched as he kissed her neck, running his tongue lightly up the entire column of her throat. Her eyes were riveted to the reflection as he rolled her nipple between his fingers, making them both harder before her eyes. She gasped quietly and he met her gaze again. He grinned and then kissed her shoulder. He used his knees to spread hers wider and seeing herself spread this way, his fingers deep inside of her, was so damned arousing she could barely stand it.

She should feel shy, surely? Being in this position, seeing herself so open and vulnerable this way? But she didn't. She felt empowered and sexy and needed *more*. She gripped his head harder, pressing her breast more firmly into his hand and rocking her hips towards his fingers again.

"Do you like this, Beck? I want you to be honest with me about anything we do. If you don't like something, we'll stop immediately. I never want you to feel like you can't tell me exactly how you're feeling." She nodded and moved her legs even wider, fascinated with the sight of his fingers pumping in and out of her body.

"I—I like it. I *more* than like it." She swallowed hard, but then said the words that were on the tip of her tongue, trying them out. "Make me come, Si. I want to see it." She had never been this aroused, never felt anything close.

He growled against her skin and began thrusting his fingers faster. He moved his other hand to her other breast, rubbing and pinching and driving her mad. She was so close. She just needed...he pressed the heel of his hand against her clit and she gasped.

"Oh godssssss...." She fought not to throw her head back or close her eyes as she crested that hill and began plummeting, her orgasm ripping through her. She watched raptly as her muscles quaked, as his hands continued to work. Her instinct was to squeeze her legs together, but he used his knees to keep them apart. It heightened the sensations, making everything hit her even harder. It went on and on and she thought she might pass out from the sheer force of the pleasure when it finally began to subside.

"Fuck, I love feeling you come, Beck," he rasped, meeting her gaze in the mirror. "I love *watching* you come even more. So gods damned beautiful." He'd started softly thrusting his hips beneath her as if he couldn't help himself. He was so hard against her ass, she bit her lip at the thought. She pushed his hand away and quickly turned to straddle him, throwing her arms around his neck and dragging him to her for a soul-searing kiss. She settled more firmly on top of him and though he didn't penetrate her, she moved so that his shaft slid against her, through her lips.

"Fuuckkkk," he groaned, hands flying to her hips. She continued to move, gliding him back and forth against her. She wasn't sure what possessed her to do it, but she gripped his wrists and moved his arms, pinning them along the edge of the tub to his sides. He let her and his head lolled back with the sexiest moan as she took control from him. Did he enjoy relinquishing it? She could understand why that might be the case. He was a king, constantly in charge of making decisions and fixing problems. To be able to let go for a while, to let someone else take the reins? She saw the appeal.

She was so damned tempted to maneuver him so that on her next slide downward, he slid straight to the heart of her, but she resisted. Somehow. Barely. Instead, she kissed his throat and continued to ride him, the friction already making her want to come again. He gripped the edges of the tub so hard the tile began to splinter and crack beneath his hands.

"No breaking my tub," she chided as she nibbled his ear.

"I'll make you a new one," he growled, bucking his hips upward.

She gasped when he whipped his head forward and took her

nipple into his mouth again. He wasn't gentle this time and she loved it. He sucked hard before biting down softly.

"Oh Gods, Si! Just like that." He bit again before sucking hard and she gripped the back of his head, holding him to her. "Mmmmm," she moaned as she continued to grind on top of him.

"So close...going to...come!" he growled around her nipple as he came hard. She could *feel* his cock pulsing beneath her as he lost himself completely. It was enough to send her over once more.

He rested his head against her chest and she felt like something akin to jelly as she draped her arms over his shoulders and sagged against him.

"Whoa," she whispered between panted breaths.

"Whoa is right," he said, equally breathless. He pulled back and she raised her head. He cupped the back of her neck gently, staring at her with the most intense and curious expression. What was he thinking? She would kill to know what thoughts were spinning in that head of his. He shook his head faintly and then kissed her tenderly.

"Time for bed, you."

He instantly replaced the water in the tub with new, fresh water, and they cleaned themselves up quickly, exhaustion bearing down hard on her. He helped her towel off and kissed her nape softly, making her shiver. He scooped her up in his arms and she squealed as he phased them to the bed.

"Now, as much as I loathe saying this, I do believe you need some clothes, Beck." He grinned and she was secretly relieved. She knew damn well she wouldn't be able to sleep beside him naked all night and wake up with the no-sex rule still in place. It didn't matter how exhausted she was, she would lose that battle, she knew it without a doubt. A super soft t-shirt and matching shorts appeared and he donned a pair of matching lounge pants. He hopped into the bed and she hesitated, rubbing her medallion.

"So, uh...I have a confession to make." He arched a brow in question. "I've never actually slept with anyone before. Like, *slept* slept."

"Well, the mechanics are fairly simple. Step one: get in the bed. Step two: sleep. I think even you can handle that."

Beck grabbed a pillow and tossed it at his face as she crawled into the bed beside him.

"Smart ass."

He moved the pillow and grinned at her as he pulled her towards him by her hips and...tickled her? She laughed uncontrollably, the sensation new and not completely unpleasant as he squeezed her sides and then inner thighs. She'd never been tickled before in her life and she had a feeling he didn't do this often either. He laughed at her laughter and she could barely breathe.

"Oh my gods...st-stop. I can't br-reathe." He finally relented and pulled her in for a kiss as she gasped for air. She couldn't help the stupid smile that crept across her lips as she kissed him back. She reluctantly pulled back and he kissed the tip of her nose.

"I like this with you. Having fun. Laughing. It's...refreshing."

She settled in beside him. "Well, rumor has it you have plenty of fun, oh great God of the Sea."

He elbowed her playfully and she stuck her tongue out at him. Who was she? Giggling? Being flirtatious and playful? He was right, it *was* refreshing. She liked being this way. She felt so free, more so than she ever had in her life. When she was with him, she didn't feel like the weight of the world was on her shoulders, she didn't feel like she had to worry about her mother or the demons still after her or anything at all. Was this what normal people felt like all the time?

Si stiffened slightly and tilted his head. She'd figured out that that meant he was communicating with his brothers. A gorgeous smile bloomed.

"What?" she asked.

"Skylar has just been reunited with her father."

She felt a lump in her throat that she couldn't really explain. She felt such overwhelming joy for Skylar and also a sense of...longing? She was jealous of Skylar in a sense, jealous of the reunion she just had with her father, the relationship and bond she knew they had.

Would Beck ever know the truth about her own father? The burning urge to confront her mother about all of the lies was growing more and more every day. The time would come soon. Emmie apparently knew how to find her, so Beck would put on her big goddess undies and demand a meeting.

But not tonight. Tonight, she was luxuriating in the universe's most comfortable bed next to the universe's sexiest man.

"This bed is unfairly comfortable." She sank deeper into the mattress, not understanding how it could be so soft yet perfectly firm all at once.

"Then we should never leave it," Si said with an easy smile as he pulled her into his side, wrapping an arm beneath her and throwing the other over her hip. She snuggled into his side, nearly moaning at the warmth and the smell of him. She rested her head on his chest and draped her arm over his stomach, a little tentatively at first, not knowing if there was a right and wrong way to...cuddle? That's what they were doing, right? But then she found that it felt right. She hitched her hip over his leg and he gave a low rumble of appreciation. She tried to tell herself that everyone fit together this well when snuggled up in a bed, but a part of her wouldn't listen. It insisted that *they* fit together this perfectly for a reason.

"I'm ok with that plan," she whispered before yawning widely. He chuckled and she could feel the vibration deep in his chest beneath her cheek.

"Good night, Beck," he said softly, kissing the top of her head.

"Night," she mumbled before sleep pulled her swiftly under.

TWENTY-FIVE

Poseidon was torn between wanting to stay awake and savor every moment of this night, Beck draped over him like she'd been born to fit there, and feeling more relaxed than he ever had in his entire existence, so relaxed that the most peaceful sleep was beckoning him like a siren's song. In the end neither won out: Cyril had apprehended someone trying to enter the plane.

Good. Poseidon had been anxious for the bastards to try again. He wanted to...*chat* with them.

He gently disentangled himself from Beck and, after staring at her for a few long moments looking so peaceful and beautiful in slumber, he dressed in black leathers and a black shirt, with leather gauntlets over his wrists. He slipped into his godly persona, hardening his features and letting his power flow freer, just enough that anyone near him could feel it pulsing from him and, if they were smart, would cower. He summoned his trident and phased to the dungeons.

"Where is he?" Poseidon demanded.

"We've got him in the cell at the end of the corridor," Cyril replied with a jerk of his head towards the room in question. "He's chained and ready for questioning."

Si sensed unease radiating out of his general. "What is it?"

"Well...he looks to be a...well, a *wraith* halfling."

"That isn't possible," Si said, even as the hairs on the back of his neck rose and a foreboding feeling unfurled in his belly. Wraiths were dark creatures, loyal servants to—and solely controlled by—the God of Nightmares. They'd disappeared when their master had. *When he'd* died, Si insisted to himself. He was dead. He *had* to be.

With the exception of the king of the wraiths, whom Poseidon had captured prior to the end of the war with the Dark Ones and imprisoned in a mystical sphere in his study, they had all either been destroyed in the war, or had disappeared shortly after. Even halflings hadn't been seen in millennia.

"I didn't think so either, sir, but..." Cyril gave him a weary look. "He can't fully dematerialize, but he can half turn to smoke, just as the wraiths. I've never seen another creature that turns like that. I think perhaps his other half keeps him from being able to turn fully to his smoke-state, but he can turn enough that the wards didn't recognize him as a full-bodied being and he doesn't need to breath in that state. It's how he was able to get into the Plane to begin with."

"How far within the dome did he get before we caught him?"

"Not far. The outer gardens." Cyril clenched his jaw, clearly pissed with himself that the supposed halfling had made it even that far. Poseidon wasn't thrilled with that fact either.

He gave Cyril a hard nod and told him that they'd be discussing the breach later. He turned his head one way and then the other, popping his neck and preparing to tangle. Hades and Zeus were better known for this type of thing, but Si could be just as ruthless and vengeful when he needed to be. And now? Someone had entered *his* kingdom without his permission. Someone was after *his* woman (because yes, though this thing with them was new, he felt like she was his). He couldn't think of a more apt time be that version of himself. *No one threatens what is* mine.

He strolled into the cell and the creature glanced up. Black blood trickled from his lip and temple. His eyes were crimson, just as the wraiths were, his black-blue hair was spiked, and tattoos covered his forearms. Tattoos in the ancient language of the Dark Ones. That ill feeling redoubled in Si's gut. He was indeed a halfling of some sort, Poseidon could tell that much, but he refused to accept what Cyril believed.

"Why did you trespass into my kingdom?" Si asked without preamble, voice cold and hard as ice. The halfling lifted his chin in defiance.

"Just fancied a swim. Took a wrong turn at Atlantis I suppose," he replied with a sarcastic sneer, red eyes flaring with malice.

"Who do you work for?" Si asked, twirling his trident as if bored, slowly pacing before the creature.

"Oh come on," he scoffed. "I'd heard you were nothing but a walking fuck-stick, but you can't really be *that* stupid, can you?" A black brow rose in condescension. *This little prick is grating on my nerves already.*

Ignoring the jab, Si continued, "What are you? Wraiths are gone, have been for thousands of years." He let more of his power free and the floor beneath them disappeared save a small circle beneath the halfling's chair. The sea churned below them and dark shapes began to swarm. The boy's eyes widened and he flinched when a barbed fin broke the surface of the water just to his left. He swallowed hard, some of his bravado slipping.

"Not as gone as you might think." Si could tell he was trying to keep his tough façade in place, but he visibly paled as more shapes began to join the melee below him.

"Not the smartest idea to send someone who's afraid of the water and all the beasties within it into a plane full of them."

The halfling's chin rose an inch, a bit of pride overshadowing the fear for a moment.

"My master chose me specifically. His other worthless demon servants couldn't penetrate your kingdom, but *I* could."

"You didn't penetrate very far, I'm afraid. Probably a problem you're used to having," Si taunted, giving him a sympathetic look.

The boy sneered, looking ready to spit something back, but then he stopped. He cocked his head to the side and grinned.

"I can sense her, you know." He closed his eye briefly, as if in... ecstasy. "Mmmm. *Delicious.*" He opened his eyes, looking smug. "I've already sent word. You can't hide her here forever, Poseidon. We will find her...*he* will find her."

Rage exploded in Poseidon's chest, so strong and forceful it staggered him, even as a dark dread settled over him. He lashed out with a tendril of power without even thinking. It sliced through the halfling's chest, making him cry out in agony. The sting was similar to that of a jellyfish but about ten thousand more times powerful. One touch would be enough to kill a mortal. He sent another lash at the boy, then another. The halfling bucked against his chains, sweat and tears running down his cheeks as he screamed in agony. Black blood welled and slid down his ravaged chest. He shifted to his half-smoke state over and over, but couldn't escape the bonds.

"Let me go ahead and explain how this is going to go down: if I don't get answers, what you've just experienced will be a mere glimpse into the anguish in store for you. And when I finally get bored, my friends here will enjoy a nice, *slow* meal of you."

At that moment, a hydra reared out of the water beside Poseidon, its numerous heads all snapping razor sharp fangs within inches of the halfling, and screeching before sinking back below the surface.

"Now, I'll ask again: who do you work for?"

Hours later, Poseidon returned to his room, weary and beyond disturbed by everything that he'd learned. He'd share everything with his brothers in the morning, but for now, he wanted Beck. He *needed* her. She soothed him unlike anyone else in the world, and though he had that strange feeling that he should be feeling *more*, it was enough for him for now. It was...everything.

He entered the room and froze, body going rigid. Though she wasn't screaming, she was thrashing on the bed and dark shadows surrounded her. Just as before, they changed shapes quickly before morphing back into blackness, and within the dark clouds, images would flash. Fire again, a man holding a wicked looking blade and grinning, some kind of glass cage. Si frowned. Was this what she was dreaming of? Were the illusions just manifestations of her dreams? The halflings words rang in his ears *I can sense her...*

Si quickly crossed to the bed and slid in beside her. He pulled her against his chest, smoothing back her hair and muttering to her over and over.

"Beck, it's alright. I'm here. I'm here. You're safe." She slowly calmed and the shadows began to fade. She snuggled deeper against him and sighed. "There you go, love. I will always keep you safe," he whispered, holding her tight.

To his surprise, the shadows didn't disappear completely. They lightened, soft wisps of lavender and pale blue swirling around them instead. He couldn't see shapes or flashes this time, but he began to think that the shadows were, in fact, tied to her dreams. Black equaled nightmares, lighter colors equaled pleasant dreams? He watched them for what felt like hours, intrigued beyond imagining. He longed to see what she was seeing, to understand what images correlated to the colors. At one point they turned a deep, pulsing red, and then he caught a hint of her desire. He groaned and tightened his grip on her. He now knew exactly what red meant and it was his new favorite color.

He eventually dozed off, only to be awoken by warm, curvy Beck nuzzling his bare chest. He pried his eyes open to see her planting soft kisses just over his heart. She glanced up at him, her hair a tangled mess but looking so unbelievably beautiful. She gave him a sexy little grin, those dimples peeking through, and he arched a brow in response, his own lips curling upward.

"I think I like sleepovers," she whispered before kissing him again...and moving downward. His body immediately stood at attention—in every sense of the word. His cock immediately grew hard, waiting (somewhat) patiently for what his little minx might have in store. "I'd like to try something..."

His heart stilled before thudding against his chest. He bit back a groan as she inched lower and lower, her warm breaths tickling his skin. Was this what she had been dreaming of when the shadows had turned red? *Gods...*

"I might be amenable to you trying something..." he said, trying to keep his voice from sounding so husky. She glanced up again, biting her bottom lip before smiling. He'd never tire of the sight. She seemed different now, lighter somehow. It was as if all of her walls had finally tumbled down and she was allowing herself to be, well, *herself*, for the first time. His chest swelled when he thought that he might have something to do with that.

She kissed lower still, tracing her tongue below his navel before hooking her fingers in the top of his pants. She sat up and tilted her head, staring downward. Her brow furrowed slightly.

"These are not what you were wearing when we went to sleep."

"I had some business to take care of during the night." She arched a brow in question and suspicion, but continued to trace her fingers slowly just under the waistband of his pants. "I'll tell you about it... later..." he choked out the last word as her fingertips brushed the head of his cock. She bit her lip and then brushed them again. He groaned and dug his heels into the mattress. Gods, you'd think he never had someone touch his dick before. He needed to get a hold of himself.

"You'll have to help me. I've never done this before," she said, voice breathy. Never? So many of her firsts belonging to him sent a primal male pride surging through him. He nodded eagerly and she chuckled before unlacing his pants. His shaft sprang free and her eyes widened. Was she nervous? Or excited? Her eyes shifted to cobalt and her tongue darted out to run along her full bottom lip.

Oh, she was definitely excited. She moved to tug his pants further down and he helped her, tossing them off the bed. She settled back over him, eyes rapt as she reached out to stroke him.

He shuddered at the contact, his eyes sliding shut, but they snapped open a moment later. He'd be damned if he missed a single second of this. She wrapped her fist around his cock and slowly moved it upward from base to crown.

"So big," she murmured. "So warm." She circled her thumb over the head and seemed amazed at the bead of moisture she found there already. She was exploratory in her movements, but also sure and sultry. It drove him mad. She was the most delicious contradiction.

She leaned her head down and he held his breath. She tentatively licked the head and the tiny moan that passed her lips made his cock pulse in her hand. She licked again, running her tongue over the swollen crown again and again, dipping it into the slit.

"That's it, Beck. *Gods*, that's good." He forced himself not to flex his hips upward. "Now, close your lips around it." She did as he said, wrapping her perfectly bowed lips around him. It was the most sensual sight he'd ever seen. She slid her mouth downward, taking him more fully inside.

"Fucckkkk," he rasped. He reached out and gathered her hair into one fist, holding it out of her face and keeping it from obscuring this absolute vision.

"Mmm," she said. She released him long enough to say, "You taste good," before taking him in again, deeper this time. He could come already, watching her work him with her hot little mouth. She twirled her tongue around him again as she moved her mouth up and down, up and down.

"Gods, Beck. Don't stop. Just like that..."

She didn't let up, continuing to suck him harder, deeper, faster. She began stroking him as she moved her mouth, the slickness almost too much. She curled her fingers of her other hand over his stomach, clutching him, as if daring him to move away and take this from her. Like he would even dream of moving right now.

She pulled back to watch as she moved her hand up and down again, the way it glided effortlessly over his wet flesh. She bent again to run her tongue along the underside of his shaft, from base to tip and his hips shot upward. She was a fucking natural, somehow knowing exactly what he liked, exactly what would drive him crazy.

"Again," he demanded, barely recognizing his own voice. She grinned and granted his wish, this time cupping and then gently pulling his sac while she did. He yelled out, tightening his hand in her hair.

"Seems like I'm a fast learner," she whispered, a grin in her voice. She met his gaze.

"Ah, that's right, sweet. Eyes here..." She inhaled sharply, eyes flaring. She obeyed, holding his gaze as she ran her tongue over the head of his cock once more. The sight nearly sent him over the edge and he felt that familiar tightening at the base of his spine. *Already?*

"Gods. Going to make me come, Beck."

"Want you to," she said, continuing to hold his gaze as she took him deep into her mouth once more. He couldn't stop his hips from arching upward now, thrusting gently into her waiting mouth, down her throat. Her cheeks hollowed as she sucked him hard, moaning and subtly rocking her hips. Her scent hit him and he nearly lost it. She was aroused by doing this to him? *Fuck. Me.*

"That's it Beck, just like that. Gods, look at you..."

She moaned around him again and the vibrations sent new sensations coursing through him. *Can't last much longer. Going to...*

"Pull back, Beck. I'm going to come...pull back!" he said louder when she didn't release him, pulling gently at her hair. He didn't know if she was ready or willing to take him like that yet. She...*glared* at him, digging her nails harder into his stomach and sucking him deeper than ever before. He felt himself hit the back of her throat. She froze for a second, but then continued after she got used to the sensation, taking him out and back in, just as deep, over and over. *Oh fuck.* His muscles quaked as he tried to keep his release at bay but it was no use.

"I'm...coming!" he roared as his orgasm tore through him. He dug his heels into the mattress and arched his hips upward. He came hard and hot and Beck took it all. She swallowed everything he gave her, seeming to...relish it? She was writhing her hips even harder now and had even begun to move her hand downward—to pleasure herself? She stopped though, perhaps not ready for that yet. That was ok. He was ok with whatever she wanted, however slow or fast she wanted to go. But he could see how hard her nipples had become beneath her thin shirt and he inhaled deeply. His eyes nearly rolled back in his head. *Oh yes, she was enjoying this.* He could smell how much and he needed to get his hands and mouth on her soon or he might die, but she continued to suck and pump her fist until she'd wrung every last drop from him. His breaths sawed out of him and his muscles went to jelly as she pulled back with a wicked grin.

"Not bad for my first time?"

"Not bad? Not *bad*?" He snagged her around the waist and pulled her to him before she even knew what was happening. She gasped and he kissed her hard, taking advantage of her parted lips. She quickly wrapped her hands around the back of his neck and returned the kiss, thrusting her tongue against his. Gods, this woman.

She drove him mad in the best possible way. Everything was so different with her and he couldn't explain why. A delusional part of his mind supplied that maybe it was because she was his, his one true match, but he quickly discarded the idea. He would be feeling far more if that were the case. Hades had explained what it felt like with Skylar and he wasn't feeling anything like that. He scowled inwardly at that. He *wanted* Beck to be his, wanted her to be made for him and him alone. Either way, he had already decided he was never giving her up.

They finally pulled apart, both panting.

"Good morning," she quipped.

He grinned and pulled her in for another kiss as he jerked the material of her shorts and panties aside. She gasped when he quickly thrust a finger inside her. He groaned at how wet she was. Wet from pleasuring *him*. She couldn't be more arousing, more enticing, more...perfect.

"Best morning," he corrected before adding another finger.

TWENTY-SIX

"I can't believe you're really here," Skylar said, handing her dad another drink. Her *dad*. He was alive and whole and here. She flopped down on the couch beside him, trying to convince herself that this wasn't some crazy dream.

"I'd never leave you without a goodbye, Rocket," he said, reaching out to chuck her under the chin. Gods she'd missed him so much. Emmie had delivered him to the Underworld as promised, and he was taking everything in surprisingly well. Skylar knew that he'd discovered that the gods were real before he'd disappeared, but to know it and to experience it were totally different things. The introduction to Hades had been equal parts awkward and hilarious.

"Um, dad, this is my husband, Hades. God of the Underworld and all that jazz," she'd said flippantly.

Her dad had looked incredulous, slightly fearful, and highly annoyed. He sized Hades up and, to her immense delight, Hades had looked *nervous*, like a teenager picking his date up for the prom.

They'd shaken hands and her dad's eyes had widened slightly as he felt Hades' power rush over him.

"Do you love my daughter?" Dalton had asked.

"More than my own life," Hades had replied immediately.

"And I suppose being...a *god*, you can protect her?"

"I would quite literally burn down this world and any other to protect her," he'd said easily, "but in my experience, Skylar is perfectly capable of protecting herself," he'd added with a quick grin at her. Her dad had given Hades another long, measuring look, but finally gave him a hard nod and then a smile. He slapped Hades on the shoulder like they were old friends and everyone relaxed as the tension disappeared.

"Ain't that the truth. Kid was picking fights with viper shifters when she was still in pull-ups."

"Dadddd," Skylar had groaned, torn between joy and embarrassment. "You didn't even know me when I was in pull-ups." She rolled her eyes but couldn't stop smiling.

To her delight, Hades and her dad fell into conversation easily, talking battles and tactics, becoming fast friends. Luke had sent a message telling Dalton that he'd come see him as soon as he returned. He, Dean, and Emmie had gone off on some adventure to find the enchantress who had cursed Dean all those years ago. Skylar was only slightly put out that she didn't get to go along—it sounded like it might be fun—but she knew that something bad was brewing here on the homefront, could feel it in her bones. Plus, her spidey-sense was tingling that there was definitely some sexy fun times on the horizon between Emmie and Lucas and Skylar didn't want to cramp their style.

Her dad was utterly fascinated with this new world and Hades' tales from his long life. The introduction to the rest of the gods, including Skylar's birth father, Ares, would be happening later. She didn't want to overwhelm him too quickly. She could only imagine everything he'd been through all these months, though Emmie had assured her that he'd been in a certified paradise for the last few weeks while he recovered.

"So, how is your first experience with a god living up to your expectations?" Hades asked as he settled into the oversized chair across from Skylar and Dalton.

"Actually, you aren't my first. Sorry, buddy," Dalton added with a sly grin. "There was a goddess in that...realm with me, and there was something...off with her. I'm glad to see it isn't a trait shared across the board."

Hades quirked a brow. "Off? How do you mean? What was her name?"

Dalton shook his head. "She never would tell me, but she just seemed...unhinged? A bit delusional maybe? She acted like a queen but she had this strange look in her eyes, like there was something unstable below the surface. She had flashes of normalcy and was fairly decent in those rare times, but then she'd flip again and would mutter about lost thrones and something she'd stolen that *hadn't been worth it after all* and all sorts of nonsense when she was drunk. She nearly drove me mad honestly."

"Very strange. But, on the whole, most of us are fairly normal I'd say."

"Normal," Dalton laughed. "*Gods* being normal. I still can't quite get used to the idea of this all being real."

They talked more about what exactly had happened before Dalton's "death"—who had hired him and for what, but before they got into the deep details, Hades stilled and tilted his head, his entire body going tense. Skylar immediately went on alert.

"What? What is it?" Dalton tensed as well, reacting to his daughter's change in demeanor, glancing around for a threat.

"Looks like we need to have a little family chat," Hades said, downing his drink.

TURNS OUT, Si wasn't the only one with news to share. They all sat around the massive round table in Hades' war room. Dalton Pembroke, Skylar's dad, among them.

When Si arched a brow in question, Hades told him, "If war comes, I know that he'll want to be a part of it. They aren't gods, but he's got some of the most skilled and vicious supernatural beings in the Mortal Plane under his command. They could help...and I fear we'll need every bit of it."

They got through introductions and got Dalton up to speed on as much as they could. Zeus took a long drink before he finally addressed them all.

"The outer walls have fallen."

"Shit," Skylar whispered, looking to Hades with a worried expression.

"Between the wasteland and Ares' army, most prisoners have been taken care of, but..."

"The next level is starting to crumble now?" Hades guessed.

Zeus' lips pulled tight in a grim line. "The next *three* levels."

"Fuck," Si said, running a hand over his face. "How is Dora?"

"She's weakening more and more each day. They...they don't know how to stop it. They think that she's going to die from this." Die? What the hell had happened to her? In most instances, gods could only be killed with a godsblade or by mystical fire. A poison that could kill a god? *What the fuck??*

"Well, since we're sharing good news," Si said with a sigh, "a *wraith* halfling broke through my barriers last night."

"What did you say?" Hades asked, his voice a cold, sharp whisper.

"I didn't believe it at first either but, it's true. I saw it with my own eyes. He claims that Balthazar is alive, that he's working for him. Halfling said that Balthazar is weakened, so he can't raise all of the wraiths from where they've supposedly been hiding in hibernation all this time, waiting for their king and master to both return, but he's gaining strength, and," Si clenched his fists as rage and worry seared him, "he wants Beck. I don't know why, and neither did the halfling. Just said that the God of Nightmares would stop at nothing to have her. She's somehow the key to him returning to full power."

"What the fuck? I don't believe that for a second for starters, but obviously he'll have to come through all of us to get to our little Beckalicious, and I don't know if you know this or not, but I'm pretty badass. Oh!" Her eyes lit with excitement. "Ohmigosh, dad! You haven't seen me in all of my glory yet! Check it!"

She leapt from her seat and let her wings burst free from her back, the flames dancing along the edges, and Dalton's jaw went slack as he reeled backwards.

"Holy shit," he whispered. They all stared in wonder. The sight of Skylar in her full phoenix form was always staggering, even to the rest of the gods.

"I know, right? I'm super powerful too. Already iced one god. I can do it again if this one so much as tries to touch a hair on Beck's head or steps one toe inside of any of our kingdoms. You don't fuck with me and mine."

Her wings disappeared and the flames within her irises dimmed. Si's chest swelled at how much Skylar cared for Beck. It made him feel again like Beck really was meant to be with him, meant to be a part of his life with everyone else here, not just something he longed to be true. *So why the fuck don't I feel* more? It was an unsettling mystery that Si couldn't solve and it was driving him mad. He felt for Beck, stronger than he'd felt for anyone in far too long, but he didn't feel *enough*. It was like his heart felt it, but his mind wouldn't acknowledge it. Or vice versa. *Damn it!*

"You are a fearsome little creature to be sure, love, but Balthazar is unlike anything you've faced. Maynard had more in common with the Dark Ones than the rest of us for reasons we'll never understand, but he pales in comparison to them. And if the other Dark Ones somehow escape? Well, it will be a war that could end *everything*. We barely defeated them before." His eyes were dark, remembering those never-ending battles. They all were. The blood and screams and death.

"We won't let that happen," Si said confidently, not ready to relive those days again. Not even wanting to think about what it might mean for Beck. "They can't escape without the key, and I know we don't have it, but what are the odds that *he* does?" He was still trying to wrap his head around how Balthazar was alive at all, let alone how he'd survived all these years without them knowing. But even if he was somehow alive and in hiding in the Mortal Plane, there's no way he would have been able to reach the key. *Unless we have yet another traitor in our midst.* Si banished the thought, refusing to let it take root.

"Key?" Dalton said to himself, brows furrowing.

"What is it dad?" Skylar asked intently.

"Well, could be nothing but...that goddess, the one I was on the island with. She kept talking about something she'd stolen and muttering about *keys*. Think it could it be the same key? Could she have stolen it somehow?"

They all exchanged glances. Surely not...but then again, they had no other leads and it was always possible that a minor goddess had managed to sneak in and steal it. Zeus admitted that in an effort to not draw attention to it, he'd kept it in a nondescript room without guards outside. Perhaps a servant had stumbled upon it while cleaning and had somehow realized what it was? Either way, a small flicker of hope began to rise in all of their chests. Could they have found it? Or at the very least, someone who knew of its whereabouts?

"Do you remember anything else about the realm where you were recovering? Anything that could help us find it?" Hades asked.

Dalton shook his head. "The goddess said that it was Emmie's and that only she could open the doorway in or out."

"Where the fuck is the Seer?" Zeus growled.

"Umm they're gone. They're on Mission: De-Kittyfy Dean, remember?" Skylar said, chewing on her bottom lip. "I don't know when they'll be back." Hades sighed in irritation and thunder rumbled outside. Dalton looked around at everyone, taking in the stress of the situation.

"Well, when the time is right, I'm going to contact my guys, get the word spread that we might just be prepping for war."

"Dad," Skylar said, worry clear in her voice.

He held up his hand to stop her. "I know you're worried, but I won't just sit on the sidelines, Rocket. This is bigger than me, bigger than all of us. If you're fighting, so are we. End of story."

She studied him before sighing, knowing he was right and that she'd never change his mind anyway. She wrapped her arms around him.

"I just got you back. You better believe I'm not losing you again." She raised her head to the rest of them. "We need to find that fucking key."

"I'm...I mean, I think I might be...well, see the thing is..."

"Oh my gods, just spit it out," Lily said, splashing Beck with water. The girls were all swimming in the small lake fed by the falls near the emerald caves. Beck glanced to the jutting flat stone where Si had wrung so many orgasms from her with his tongue that she'd lost count just days ago, and her cheeks heated. *I wanted to do this last time we were here*, he'd rasped in her ear. *Been dreaming of it ever since...* With that, he'd sank to his knees in the shallow water...

She shook herself as more water splashed her face.

"Ok, fine! Cut it out with the splashing!" Another splash hit her and she sent Lily a killing look. The harpy merely grinned back. Beck took a deep breath and let it out before admitting, "I'm falling for Poseidon. Like, *hard*."

"I'll take *Things Everyone Already Knows* for $2000, Alex," Skylar said with a roll of her eyes, swimming the length of the small pond to sidle up right beside Beck again. She had been weirdly clingy in the past couple of weeks. It seemed like any moment Beck wasn't with

Si, she was being whisked away to the Underworld to hang out with Skylar who "needed Mortal-Plane-dwelling friend time" or having girls' days or nights. A bad feeling was starting to claw at Beck's chest, like something terrible was going to happen and soon. That first night she'd stayed with Si, she'd had a jolt of...*something* go through her in the middle of the night. She thought it was just a dream, but now, she wasn't so sure. It was like a strange sense of awareness that crackled through her body like electricity. And now Skylar's weird almost over-protective new attitude? Something was definitely up, but at the moment, that wasn't important.

Beck's mouth popped open. "*Everyone* knows?"

"Well, *he* might not because experience has taught me that men, as a whole, are exceptionally stupid," Z supplied from her sunbathing perch on another low rock near the water's edge. Beck tried not to be jealous of her body, long and lean and though not flawless, her scars somehow made her look incredibly badass and sexy. "But anyone with half a brain can see it," Z finished.

"What makes it so damned obvious?" Beck demanded indignantly, hands on her hips.

"You smile when you're with him, like a full-on dopey smile showing off those adorable little dimples of yours," Medusa said.

"You just seem...lighter now. Happier. More like your true self," Lily added.

"You look at him the way Skylar looks at Hades," Nerina said as she floated in the water.

Well, hell. Beck exhaled in exasperation.

"Ok, fine. So it's obvious, whatever. What am I supposed to do about it? He still seems like he's holding back. Not purposely, though. He gets this look sometimes like he's *trying* to feel more, like he's expecting to, but then gets frustrated when nothing comes." She shook her head, realizing how stupid it sounded now that she said it out loud. "It's hard to explain."

"Enchantments are tricky, aren't they?" Emmie asked airily, appearing out of nowhere and making everyone scream. Skylar immediately shoved Beck behind her and a summoned a sword with golden flames etched along the blade to her hand in an instant. Something was *definitely* up.

"What the fuck, Emmie!? You're supposed to be off on a grand old adventure with Dean and Lucas, like going full on Frodo Baggins right now!"

"We are and having a smashing time of it, thanks for asking. But I just wanted to pop in and say hi and to tell Lily that she's going to have to call a truce with her sister. We're all going to be fighting on the same side soon and we need all hands and claws and wings on deck. Soooo, good luck with that! Bye!" The Seer blew a kiss and disappeared.

"Wait!" Skylar yelled, but Emmie was already gone. She slammed her palm against the water, sending the spray right into Beck's face. Again. This was getting old.

"Damn it," Skylar growled, "we *need* her." The flames were burning in her eyes, and Beck was surprised. This was *real* irritation, not the typical, friendly kind she often got with Emmie. What on earth was going on?

"Make amends with my sister?" Lily huffed incredulously. "Fat freaking chance! What could she possibly be talking about fighting on the same side? I'd rather die!"

"Oh, well, about that..." Skylar said, "We're keeping it quiet, but I think you deserve to know, so I'm making the executive decision to tell you as Queen of Do Whatever The Fuck I Want. Pandora's Box is failing."

Lily and Medusa stilled and tensed. Zahara and Beck looked confused.

"This is...not good," Lily said, glancing around nervously.

"How?" Medusa demanded.

"They aren't sure. Apparently Dora's power is failing. They think she was poisoned somehow."

"Ok, can someone explain to the rest of the class?" Zahara asked, motioning between herself and Beck.

"Pandora's Box is a labyrinthine prison for the baddest of the baddies in the universe. The absolute worst reside in the very center ring. They're gods as well, but they're dark and pure evil. Like too evil for words apparently. The good gods and the Titans managed to trap them there millennia ago, but now I guess the prison itself is failing because its power is tied directly to Pandora's? I'm still not one hundred percent on all the details either, honestly."

"So...these bad guy gods are going to be freed now?" Beck squeaked.

"Well, *hopefully* not." Skylar explained how a key was required to open the gate to the ring where the Dark Ones resided, even if the rest of the prison failed.

"So, then it's ok, right? I mean, still not good about all the rest of the baddies escaping, but if you need a key to get to the rotten center of the Tootsie Pop, then no worries," Z said, looking to Skylar.

"Welllll, about that...the key is missing."

"What?!" Lily screeched, making Beck wince. Her skin prickled uncomfortably, some dark ominous feeling settling in her stomach. She rubbed her medallion, not liking the feeling at all and wanting to find Poseidon immediately. *Needing* to find him. Her instincts were screaming at her to be with him, that he would protect her, and...that *she* needed to protect *him* in turn?

Yours...protect...

The strange whisper she'd been hearing since she arrived fluttered through her mind again. But how in the hell could she protect someone as powerful as Si? She didn't understand that part of the whisper but she thought she understood the other part perfectly fine: he *was* hers. She felt it so deep in her bones that she couldn't even pretend it wasn't true anymore. She was meant to find him, she was meant to be with him. The only real question was: could she be *his* as well?

"We might have a lead, but we need Emmie's elusive ass and she's not helping us out at the moment," Skylar said with a roll of her eyes and a gesture to the spot where the Seer had just been. "I know that everything she does is for a reason, but damn it if it isn't frustrating as hell sometimes! And...there's more..." She glanced at Beck with a strange expression but quickly looked away. "The God of Nightmares is supposedly alive."

Medusa's snakes appeared, rearing back and hissing. Lily paled. Beck didn't know who that was but based on the reactions, it was no one she ever wanted to meet.

"That can't be true. It isn't possible," Medusa said, shaking her head in denial.

"That's what everyone thought but...yeah...and he's, um, searching for something that will supposedly help bring him back into his full power." That bad feeling felt like it was going to rip through Beck's chest and her need to find Si was starting to overwhelm her, like she couldn't breathe until she saw him.

"I...I think I'm going to head back. This is all...kind of freaking me out, I guess. I want to be back in the castle," Beck said quietly as she made her way out of the water. The others looked at her worriedly but she waved them off, telling them she was ok. She toweled off as they continued to talk about the alarming news and what it might mean.

"Fuck, I really might have to make nice with my sister," Lily said sullenly. "My troops will not be pleased." Beck still found herself forgetting that Lily was a badass warrior with a whole army under her control.

"Here, I'll phase you back, Beckalicious," Skylar said, rushing forward. Before Beck could protest or even say goodbye, Skylar whisked them back to her room within the palace. She'd been spending most nights with Poseidon now, but technically this room still belonged to her.

"Ok, out with it," Beck said with narrowed eyes. "You are acting super weird lately."

"I have no idea what you could possibly be talking about," Skylar replied, all innocence. Beck crossed her arms and glared.

"I am perfectly capable of walking back from the caves by myself and you know it. So, spill it."

Skylar tilted her head to the side and her eyes widened. "Oh no, Hades is contacting me. Must go!"

"You're so full of—" Skylar disappeared with a wink. "—shit," Beck finished to an empty room. She would get to the bottom of it at some point, but right now, all she could think about was finding Si. She needed to see him, to touch him to...*claim* him? *Where had that thought come from?* She didn't even know what that meant exactly, though her subconscious was quickly filling in all the blanks in salacious and delicious detail. She needed to make him hers. *Fully.*

No more doubts, no more waiting. She wanted him, all of him, and wanted him to have all of her. She was tired of dancing around the subject. Sure, she'd been terrified and hesitant to even try something more with him at first, but now? She had never been so sure of anything in her life and she didn't want to keep holding anything back. She had the strange feeling that they were on borrowed time, and after Skylar's revelation about Pandora's Box and what might be coming for all of them, she didn't want to waste a second more.

She took a quick shower and marched to her closet. A thrill of excitement shot through her when she asked the room for something special to wear, something...sexy. A beautiful ocean blue corset appeared. Lace with silk ribbons running up the front, and a matching thong lie beside it. She picked up the corset, unsure if she could pull it off, but as she donned the item, lacing the ribbons tightly up the front, she suddenly understood why woman loved lingerie.

She felt *fierce* in this. Sexy. Seductive. Powerful. It wasn't over the top but damn if it didn't make her look *good.* She stared in awe at her breasts: they looked what could be described as "ample" for the first time in her life. She ran her hands down her sides over her waist, liking the way the corset cinched her in just a bit there and made her hips seem to flare out a touch more than usual. She turned to admire the back view, adoring the tiny bow that rested just at the T of the thong. She had a feeling Si would adore it even more and her lips curled into a devious smile at the thought.

She dried her hair into soft curls and threw on a pair of jeans (she knew how much Si liked to ogle her ass in them, though he tried to hide it) and a t-shirt. She wanted her underthings to be a complete and total shocker. With a mischievous grin and her stomach turning flips, she took off towards his room. She knocked on his door but no answer. Damn it. She glanced inside the darkened room, but there was no sign of him.

Chewing her lip, she headed down the hallway and saw light streaming out from one of the mostly unused lounges. She padded towards the door and peeked inside. He was standing with his back to her, leaning over a table laden down with what looked like maps and notes. Journal entries maybe? A fire was roaring in the large hearth on the other side of the room. He looked tense, his muscles bunched and strained. He hung his head as she watched, his fingers curling into fists on the table. He was upset and she needed to fix it, to ease his strain.

She eased into the room and he sighed as she approached, knowing without looking that it was her. She didn't say anything, just stepped behind him and leaned against his back, wrapping her arms around him and placing a soft kiss against his spine. He relaxed as soon as she touched him and her heart thudded. Just being near him soothed her and it seemed it was the same for him.

"Are you alright?" she whispered.

He straightened and pulled her in front of him, trapping her between him and the table. He brushed the hair from her face.

"I am now," he said, leaning in to give her a soft kiss. She wrapped her arms around his neck, gently stroking the skin at his nape. He exhaled roughly and leaned down to rest his forehead on hers. She wanted to ask him what was wrong, wanted to get the full story of everything that was going on, but all of that could wait. She leaned up to kiss him once more, gently but with a palpable fire beneath the surface. He kissed her back, recognizing the fire and adding his own. She tilted her head to deepen the kiss, beginning to thrust her tongue against his harder, faster. His hands trailed to her waist and he lifted her easily onto the table, wedging his hips in between her thighs. She gasped and he hissed when he shifted forward, putting their bodies so achingly close together. She ran her hands down his chest and quickly under the hem of his shirt.

"I love your hands on me," he whispered as he kissed across her jaw, down to her neck. She loved her hands on him too, never wanted to stop touching him. His skin was so warm she felt scorched everywhere her hands traveled. She ran them over his stomach, loving how the muscles jumped beneath her fingers, before she moved them up his chest. She felt his heart beating steadily beneath her palms. She trailed them downward once more, curling her fingers into the top of his pants and yanking him closer.

She pulled on his shirt, pushing it upward and he reached over his head to yank it off from the back. *Why was that so sexy?* He leaned back in and she pressed herself fully against him, luxuriating in the heat coming off of him even through her clothes. *And sexy corset*, she thought with a sultry smirk. She bit his bottom lip, the way she knew he loved, and just as she wanted, he gave her a sexy growl in response.

She yanked on the laces of his pants and quickly pulled his cock free. She wrapped her hand around his shaft and he groaned, bucking his hips forward. It never failed to amaze her how big he was, how hard and ready he'd get for her. She stroked him over and over, making him mad with lust. He groaned again and made her gasp when he dropped to his knees suddenly.

As much as she would love to let him do exactly what she knew he was planning, she didn't want him ruining her big outfit reveal. She raised a foot to his chest to halt him. He arched a brow but whatever look she gave him had him licking his lips in anticipation. She slid off the table and took his hand, leading him slowly towards the fireplace. She was going to be the biggest cliché in the world, getting busy with her man for the first time on a fur rug in front of the fire-place—and she was going to love every fucking second of it.

He followed her without question, clearly intrigued by what was happening. She released him and took a step back, putting a bit of distance between them.

"Si," she said, voice shockingly steady despite how nervous she was. "I want you. *All* of you. Tonight."

He'd been letting his gaze roam over her body but his eyes immediately snapped back up to hers, going wide.

"All of…" He trailed off and scrubbed a hand over his mouth. "You're sure? We can wait as long as you want, Beck."

"I'm beyond sure," she said as she crossed her arms, reaching down for the hem of her shirt. She slowly drew the fabric up her body, revealing her corset.

"*Fuck. Me*," Si rasped before swallowing hard.

"Well, that's kind of the plan," she quipped with a smirk.

He licked his bottom lip and then hit her with the sexiest grin she'd ever seen. The absolutely devilish things that grin promised made her toes curl. He took half a step forward but she shook her head slowly.

"Ah, ah, ah. I'm not done yet."

He stopped and waited patiently as she trailed her fingers down her body to the button of her jeans. She took her time unbuttoning and unzipping, loving the way he his attention never flickered from her movements. She knew he'd seen a show similar to this thousands of times, had been with countless others, and yet, as he stared at her, you would think it was his very first time, that she was the only one. It filled her with even more confidence, more thrilling anticipation. She pushed her jeans slowly down her thighs and finally stepped out of them. She stood as he stared, eyes turning black with those mesmerizing gold striations seeming to pulse.

"Turn around," he said, voice low and gruff. She held her breath and turned. "Gods have mercy," he hissed. Before she knew it, he was behind her. He trailed his hands down her bare arms as he leaned in and skimmed his nose down her neck, inhaling deeply. He gathered her hair and shifted it over one shoulder, baring her nape. Goosebumps erupted over her skin when he planted a soft kiss there.

"Beck," he whispered at her ear, making her shiver once more, her entire body tingling. "You are the most beautiful." Another kiss on her throat. "Enticing." Another kiss on her shoulder. "Arousing creature I have ever beheld."

"Most arousing?" she asked, voice breathy.

"You make my cock so hard it feels like hot steel, Beck. Make me want to bury it in you so deep, pound inside you until you scream with so much pleasure that the entire kingdom trembles with it."

She shuddered at his words, reminded all over again of just how many skills that tongue of his held. He kissed the back of her neck again, slowly moving downward, licking and kissing down her spine. He dropped to his knees and trailed his hands up her thighs. She inhaled sharply and bit back a gasp of pleasure when he palmed her ass, kneading gently. His hands were so soft, so hot, scorching her to her core.

"Gods your ass could bring entire worlds to their knees." He kissed the base of her spine, just over that delicate little bow. Her knees trembled in anticipation. What would he do next?

"Spread your legs for me," he rumbled. "Grab the chair." *Oh gods.* She loved when he commanded her like this, loved that they could share these roles. Sometimes she wanted to take the reins and he let her. Other times, she wanted him to be in charge, wanted him to lead her and she wanted to be lead without question. She trusted him in everything they'd done so far, would trust him in everything to come. Always.

He made a sexy growling sound, rumbling from deep in his chest as she obeyed, widening her feet and bending to rest her hands on the oversized leather chair. At one point, she would have felt unbelievably shy and vulnerable in this position, but now? With the way Poseidon reacted to her? She *loved* it. He ran his hands over her ass once again, slowly kneading her flesh. He slid one hand in between her thighs and ran his fingers gently over her core. She tried not to squirm. She failed miserably.

"So wet for me already? Oh baby, we haven't even started yet. I've got to get you ready for me."

His voice was a silky caress, a dark promise that made her stomach and pussy both clench. He continued to stroke, the tiny piece of silk the only barrier between his fingers and her skin. She gasped when he bit her ass cheek lightly, and her knees nearly gave way when he leaned forward and ran his tongue over the silk...all the way up her ass.

"Oh gods," she whispered. He ran his fingers along the same path his tongue had taken, lightly tracing the tiny silk string. Her heart thudded against her chest, her pulse beating wildly. Would he...? Did she *want* him to? He gently circled that spot with his finger and her pussy *throbbed*. Ohhh yes, she did want him to. It was so forbidden. So erotic. She wanted it. *Badly.* He had the uncanny ability to awaken desires in her that she had no idea she harbored, not until he unlocked them as no one else could, as no one else ever had or ever would. He continued to circle his finger as he kneaded her ass cheek with the other hand.

"One day, I want to take you here, Beck. Would you like that?" Her pulse raced at the thought.

"*Yes,*" she breathed.

"Mmmm good. But for now," he whispered, leaning forward. He slowly licked where his fingers had been, circling so gently. She gasped and then moaned, legs trembling, heart pounding. She was so sensitive there, each soft lap of his tongue sending explosions of pleasure through her. He continued to lick as he shifted her panties to the side and slid his finger through her slick folds. She made some unintelligible sound, her head lolling forward. He spread her wetness upward, circling her clit and she rocked her hips, seeking his hands, needing more. He chuckled lightly and quickly thrust two fingers inside her. She cried out and spread her feet even wider, inviting him to do whatever he wanted. She dug her fingers into the arms of the chair as he moved his fingers in and out in slow rhythm with his wicked tongue.

"That feels so good," she murmured.

He removed his fingers and though she nearly whimpered at their loss, she immediately groaned in abandon as he licked her pussy. Having him do this from behind her, the angles so different than they'd been before, she almost couldn't stand it.

"Oh gods, just like that," she moaned loudly. He started to lick faster, deeper.

"You taste so fucking good," he growled against her flesh. "Could eat this pretty pussy for eternity."

"Oh gods, Si. I'm going to...almost...just like that..."

The pleasure became almost unbearable. He ran the pad of his finger over her ass once more and applied the *tiniest* bit of pressure in just the right spot. Her orgasm exploded through her like lightning. Her legs began to quake as she cried out, nearly tearing through the leather as she dug her nails in deeper and deeper. Before she'd even come down from the terrifying heights he brought her to, Beck turned to face him. He was still on his knees and he was looking up at her like he was worshipping her, and the sight made her chest twist.

She sank to her knees before him and he gazed at her so intensely it made her insides melt. He reached forward and slowly began to unlace the ribbons of her corset.

"I'm going to get you one of these in every color imaginable," he muttered. "Never seen anything so sexy. Nearly came just from looking at you."

She was panting by the time he was finally done unlacing. He tossed the corset away and immediately covered her breasts with his palms, rubbing, kneading, pinching. She pulled him into a scorching kiss, needing him unlike she'd ever needed anything.

"I want you, Si," she whispered against his lips. "*Now.*"

TWENTY-SEVEN

This had to be a dream. A fantasy. It couldn't be real. Si was finally going to take Beck the way he'd been craving to since nearly the moment he saw her.

"You're sure?" he asked her once more as he laid her down beneath him on the rug, ripping her panties off and ridding himself of every stitch of clothing as well. He knew this was like a scene from a cheesy romance movie, but he didn't care. It was fucking perfect. For the first time in recent memory, he felt like he was in the right place, at the right time.

"Yes, Si. *Please*," she begged as she sucked on his bottom lip. She cradled him between her thighs, yet another way they fit together as if made to be this way. He held himself over her with one arm and grasped his cock with the other. He bit back a groan as he stroked. He was harder than he'd ever been, to the point of pain. He needed to be inside of her so badly he could barely breathe. He ran the swollen head in between her lips, gritting his teeth at the sublime pleasure, the heat nearly burning him. He did it once more and she arched her hips forward, as if begging him.

He positioned himself at the right spot and slowly moved

forward, not able to hold off any longer. His eyes nearly rolled back in his head at the feel of her surrounding him, hot and wet and so fucking tight he hissed in a harsh breath between his teeth, the pleasure so intense he could barely breath. It took all of his willpower not to shove his hips forward, burying himself so far inside her, but he forced himself to go slowly.

He fed his shaft further inside her slowly, inch by inch. She tensed and gasped, but after a few seconds and shifting a bit, she groaned, digging her nails into his back.

"Alright?" he bit out.

"More," she half moaned, half begged. He gave it to her, pushing inside her as far as he could go in one slick, hard thrust. She cried out, back bowing, and he stilled.

"Hurt?"

Gods, he couldn't even form full sentences. His every brain cell was focused on the fact that he was buried to the hilt inside his woman, her sheath so tight and wet around him that he nearly came instantly.

"No," she whispered. She held his gaze, her eyes that beautiful cobalt that meant she was feeling strong emotion. Just arousal or... more?

"More, Si," she said and he started before realizing that she hadn't read his mind, she was asking him for more of him. No, not asking. She was *demanding*. He leaned down to kiss her hard, thrusting his tongue against hers. He shifted his hips back and thrust them forward again. She cried out into his mouth and he did it again. Slow, measured thrusts. Deep, so fucking deep. Perfect. This moment, Beck, the feel of her surrounding him, squeezing him like a glove—all of it. Fucking. Perfect.

"More. Faster. *Godsssss*," she panted, head thrashing as he kept up his slow torture.

"You want me to fuck you harder, Beck?"

"Yes!"

"Tell me. Tell me what you want."

Her eyes flared wide but then her lips curled upwards.

"I want you to fuck me so hard, Si. So fucking hard," she rasped, half command, half plea.

He'd honestly intended to keep things slow, telling himself that this should be gentle for their first time, but he couldn't. His instincts —and Beck—were demanding that he take her hard, that he bury himself in her and claim her as his own. So, he began to do just that.

He took her hard, slamming into her over and over, the slaps of their flesh against one each other lost among the sounds of the ragged breaths and moans and screams of pleasure and the roar of the fire. She arched her hips, meeting him thrust for thrust, sending him deeper and hitting spots that made her bite her lip, eyes sliding closed in bliss. He pinned her hands over her head with his own, intwining their fingers as he pounded his hips forward.

"You're so fucking perfect, Beck."

She gripped his fingers tighter, so tight the bones creaked, but he didn't care. She could break him into pieces and he wouldn't mind.

"Don't stop," she begged. "Ah, fuck, right there..."

Si didn't dare stop, didn't dare change a single thing. She tensed for a moment, every muscle seeming to go taut, before screaming his name in ecstasy. *His* name. He wanted to beat his chest.

"Gods, I can feel you coming, Beck. Squeezing my cock so fucking tight." With each spasm, her inner walls clenched around his shaft, maddening him. He was done for. His own body went rigid before his release tore through him, stronger than anything he'd ever felt before.

"Beck!" he roared so loudly he would have sworn the entire palace rocked.

Her eyes widened. "I...I can *feel* you..."

The way her eyes burned, he would bet anything that she liked that fact. When he'd finally given her everything he had, he collapsed on top of her. She rubbed her hands up and down his back as they both caught their breath, their bodies slick with sweat. He eventually found the strength to shift to the side, pulling her into his side and wrapping his arms around her. He kissed her temple, brushing sweat soaked hair from her brow.

"That was unbelievable. Or, well, for me it was. I don't really have a great frame of reference, but for me, that was mind-altering. Um...what about for you?" Beck asked, a bit timidly.

Poseidon nearly laughed. How could she possibly think that wasn't incredible for him? He knew he had quite a bit more experience but how to explain to her that this was so unlike anything else? He shifted her so that she met his gaze, arms still wrapped tightly around her.

"Beck, I have been with too many people to even remember, done anything you could possibly imagine, and fifteen additional things you couldn't." She frowned, brows knitting together.

"Hmm, this isn't really making me feel any better," she pointed out. He did chuckle at that, leaning up and cradling her cheek gently.

"All of that, and yet everything with you is completely new and different, Beck. It's like I'm experiencing everything for the very first time because with you, it *is* the first time. It's the only time that I can recall, the only time that matters."

"Oh," she said with a sweet smile, those dimples making his stomach dip. She bent down to kiss his chest, right over his heart. She did it again, and again, and he was already getting hard again. She glanced down and then back at him with a quick of her brow. He gave her a wicked grin.

"You can't possibly think I was done with you for the night?"

"Good, because I'm not nearly done with you either," she purred.

THEY BARELY LEFT Si's bedroom over the next...Beck had lost track of how many days. Five? Eight? She couldn't tell you if her life depended on it. She knew that something big was going on and Si would routinely check in with his brothers, but he assured her that he wasn't needed. So, they'd taken their time to explore this amazingly blissful new facet of their relationship. He'd taken her three more times that first night—the second time being so slow and gentle and sweet that she nearly wept from the tenderness he showed her—until she'd gone comatose from pleasure and the most profound sense of contentment and connection she'd ever experienced.

They'd had sex in his massive tub and shower, he'd taken her from behind, and she'd ridden him with abandon, and still, she was insatiable and...curious. Beyond curious. So curious about so many things it was nearly driving her insane.

She was straddling his waist, tracing shapes over his heart with her fingertips when she said, "Si, I want..." She bit her lip and looked down at his chest. He reached up to pinch her chin between his thumb and forefinger in that way that sent a shiver of desire through her for unknown reasons. She met his eyes again.

"What, Beck? What do you want?"

She met his gaze. "Everything. I want you to show me *everything*." His eyes had blazed at that, knowing exactly what she meant. He pulled her down for a deep kiss, slowly thrusting his tongue against hers, stoking her fire and making her ready to combust.

"Well, how about we start now?" he rumbled against her lips. Her stomach quivered in anticipation. "Move your hips up for me. Grab the headboard."

"Up...?"

He jutted his chin, telling her where to move and her mouth formed a small "O" in response. This was new...and exciting. She shifted to do what he'd asked, a bit unsure. She maneuvered so that her knees were on either side of his head and she looked down at him, heart racing.

"Now what?"

"Grab. The. Headboard," he growled as he moved his hands to grip her ass firmly. She reached out to wrap her fingers around two of the thick slats. He massaged her ass for a moment more, giving her the tiniest smack that made her yelp...and grow wet. *Ohhh, inter-*

esting. He pulled her downward, making her widen her knees as he settled her directly over his mouth.

"Holy fuck," she gasped as she rode his tongue and he clamped his strong hands on her hips, holding her to his mouth as she writhed. It was so new, so hot.

And it was just the beginning.

Afte that, he began to show her everything, just as she asked. Slowly, he introduced her to a whole new world full of mind numbing pleasures that she hadn't even known were possible. She didn't love everything, of course, and he was completely fine with that. They explored everything together, discovering what they each disliked, what they liked, what they loved *together*. He'd shown her toys and positions and tricks that made her mind spin.

Beck cast her mind back to that first day she'd seen him naked, to the things she'd heard from outside his door...

"I used to want to watch you, you know. With others. Fantasized about it."

"Really?" he said, that sexy smirk spreading across his face.

"Yes, really. Thought about it as I dipped my fingers into my panties..." He groaned and pulled her harder against his side. She grinned. She'd discovered that not only did she like hearing dirty talk, she liked to do a bit of it herself—and it drove Si *wild*. "But now, I don't think I could. I think I would scratch anyone else's eyes out if they touched you," she said truthfully. She still liked to *think* about it, but knew that she wouldn't be able to stomach seeing it.

He pulled her on top of him and she straddled his waist.

"Now *that* I might want to see," he said with a grin. She batted his chest playfully and then swooped down for a kiss. "I'm serious. You're getting pretty damn good at fighting, thanks to yours truly. Seeing you in action would be pretty sexy."

She scrunched her nose at him but she had to agree that she actually felt pretty badass these days. She rarely got knocked to her ass anymore and she was getting better with her power, though she still felt like she was holding back. Problem was, she couldn't figure out how to fix it because, for once in her life, she wasn't doing it consciously. It was like she had a mental block that she couldn't get around no matter how much she tried. Maybe it had been there for so long it was just a part of her now, like she'd somehow handicapped her own power along the way. She stroked the medallion and Si tracked the movement, reaching out the trace his finger over hers.

"You never take this off," he observed. "It must be very important to you."

A flare of guilt. She still hadn't divulged all of her secrets to him and that felt...wrong. She wanted to share everything with him. And she would. Soon. For now, she gave him a version of the truth.

"It is. My mother had protective wards placed on it by an enchantress when I was young. She was worried that someone might learn about Zeus being my—supposed—father and come after me. The medallion keeps me safe."

"Well, then it is now my favorite piece of jewelry," he said with an easy smile. She stared down at him. He smiled up at her she couldn't stop the words from tumbling out.

"I love you."

She held her breath, torn between incredulity that she'd actually said the words out loud, fear of his response, and relief. It felt *good* saying it. But...*what if he doesn't say it back?* She braced herself, telling herself that she'd known all along that this might be a possibility when this day came. He'd told her that he couldn't promise how much more he could offer, how much he could feel after not feeling anything for so long. She knew he cared about her, could tell it in every touch, every kiss. In the way he held her as they slept. But could he care *enough*?

So, she held her breath...and he seemed to stop breathing all together. His eyes darkened and his heart beat wildly beneath her palm where she rested her hand gently on his chest. He stared at her, looking at her in such a longing way that it made her chest ache. He *wanted* to love her, she could tell that without a doubt. He looked pained as he reached up to brush her hair back and cradle her cheek. She gave him a smile and she did her best to not let it be a sad one.

"It's ok," she whispered. He winced, as if she'd physically hurt him.

"Beck, I need you to understand. I...I won't just say the words if I don't feel them, and I do feel for you, so gods damned much. I...I want to love you. I think I love you as much as I'm capable of loving anyone. I must be truly broken inside to not be able to feel for you as much as I know I should, as much as I long to." He scrubbed a hand down his face. "I can't explain this right. I wish you could understand, wish I could make you see." He looked on the verge of a breakdown so she quickly leaned down to press her lips to his.

"Hey, Si, it's ok. I understand. It's ok. I love you no matter what and I know that you care for me as much as you're able. That's enough for me."

"I just—" He cut off, tilting his head to the side. "Gods I do *not* need this right now," he grated, his body shooting through with tension and annoyance radiating off of him.

"What's wrong?" she asked as he gently moved her off of his lap and stood from the bed.

He stabbed his legs into his pants and yanked them up irritably.

"Calypso has apparently demanded a meeting," he rolled his eyes but then gave Beck a little smirk. "Turns out she's not too happy with her all-access pass to Aqueous being revoked." Beck wasn't too big of a person to admit that this news made her happy. She wanted Callie to be irritated, wanted her to be pissed and upset and a hell of a lot more than that actually. Not solely because of jealousy, though she could admit that was a bit of it, but Callie had *hurt* Si. Badly. Beck's instincts were demanding that she hurt the bitch back on his behalf. *Protect what's yours*, that voice whispered. Her chest heated as her power surged. *Just give me five minutes with her.*

Si leaned in to kiss Beck and pulled back, searching her gaze.

"Do you want to come?"

"What?" Beck asked, confused.

"I told Cyril to let her into the throne room so we can have it out and be done with it. Do you want to come with me? I may not be able to give you everything I want to, may not be able to feel things right, but I'm in this with you, Beck, one thousand percent. I don't want to have any secrets from you and don't want anything to ever make you question my motives or intentions with you. Callie and I have... history, to be sure. So, if you'd feel more comfortable being there with me, I'm happy to have you there. In fact," he kissed her again and purred against her lips, "it would make me extremely happy if you'd come with me."

She was shocked but she couldn't deny that his words hit her in just the right spot. She had admittedly felt a twinge of unease about him being alone with Callie. Not because she didn't trust him—she did, completely—but she didn't trust that perfectly proportioned bitch one tiny bit.

Beck nodded and his smile made her toes curl. She entered her closet—because they had already begun sharing his rooms, and a second closet had magically appeared for her alone—and thought about what she should wear. Her typical jeans and t-shirt called to her as always, but something had her changing directions. That same instinct that was telling her that Si was hers, was telling her to...dress to impress. *Dress as his queen*, it whispered. The thought was tantalizing. Being his wife, his queen. Well, she wanted it so badly that she nearly staggered from the force of it.

Not one to go against her instincts, she smirked as she donned a very Grecian-inspired dress in midnight that subtly faded into an icy blue that matched the color of her eyes almost exactly. Two rows of jewels in the same ice blue wrapped around her waist, just beneath her breasts. The V dipped low and slits on either side of the wispy material rose high on each of her thighs. She quickly tamed her mane and let it fall in soft waterfall curls over one shoulder, pinning it there with midnight blue jeweled combs. She opted for no shoes because Chucks would ruin the effect, and she didn't trust herself to walk in heels without face-planting.

She turned this way and that in the mirror, wondering if it was too much. Si entered then and as she watched in the mirror, he stutter-stepped. Actually *stutter-stepped* at the sight of her. She grinned before pulling her lips in to hide it. He rubbed his hands over his mouth and strode forward in two long strides, turning her and kissing her so forcefully she had to grip his arms to steady herself. She was panting by the time he broke away.

"You are the most stunning creature I have ever seen, Beck. My *gods.*" He kissed her again and she knew that he was seriously contemplating saying fuck this meeting and just tossing her back in their bed. She smiled and pulled away—reluctantly.

"Let's go get this over with. I have *plans* for you afterwards," she promised with a nip at his lip. He groaned but nodded, straightening to take her hand and phase them to his throne room.

TWENTY-EIGHT

Talking to Callie was just about the last thing on Si's Want To Do List at the moment. The way Beck looked in that dress. *Fucking. Hell.* She was…He truly didn't have words to describe it properly. She was perfect. *So why the fuck can't I honestly tell her I love her?* He wanted to claw out his own heart in frustration. He felt as strongly for her as he could, stronger than he'd felt for anyone in so long he could hardly remember, but it wasn't enough. Why wasn't it fucking enough? She was everything he wanted, everything he needed. She made him laugh, made him feel so whole and content. She soothed him like a balm, made him burn like an inferno. When he needed it, she built him up, and when he deserved it, she knocked him down. She was…gods damn it, she was *everything*.

He truly must be damaged. He was broken and now he was convinced that he could never be fixed. If he couldn't feel more for Beck, he'd never feel more for anyone. He sighed inwardly as he grabbed Beck's hand to phase them to the throne room.

He didn't want to deal with this, but he knew Callie well enough to know she wouldn't go quietly or let this go without a confrontation, so it was better to get it out of the way now. They landed and he was glad that Beck didn't try to step away from him immediately.

Callie paced in front of the throne, whirling when she felt them appear behind her. They stood on the dais and Callie's eyes went wide as she took in Beck standing beside him there. *Where my queen should stand*, he thought. Callie seemed torn, not knowing what to scream about first: her eviction from his kingdom or Beck being there, Poseidon's arm wrapped possessively around her. She chose the first after casting Beck a killing look. To his surprise and immense pleasure, Beck simply stared at her coldly, as if she were bored. *That's my fucking girl.*

"You revoked my invitation into the kingdom? What the fuck??" Callie demanded, storming forward but stopping at the foot of the dais.

Si moved to sit on his throne, noting with a slight raise of his brow that the seat expanded without his command, making room for Beck to sit beside him. *Interesting...*The palace had a mind of its own at times, as did the kingdom itself. And apparently, it wanted Beck by his side. He had to agree. He pulled her down with him and he tried to ignore how right it felt to have her here with him, sharing his throne. He placed one large hand over Beck's exposed thigh, deciding all over again that this was now his most favorite dress in existence. Calypso's eyes flared with anger but she didn't comment, just eyed him, waiting for an answer as she ground her teeth.

"Yes, I did. You are not welcome here any longer without my express permission." *Which won't be forthcoming anytime soon after today.*

"What? How dare you!?"

His own anger spiked now. "How dare *I*?" The water outside the wall just behind the throne turned dark and ominous, matching his mood. "How dare *I*, Callie? You can't be serious. After everything you did to me before, you came back to my kingdom those months ago, after *years* without a single word, only to use me for my power, to coax a favor out of me." *And you somehow ruined me*, he thought bitterly "And," he added with a sneer, "you hunt what is *mine*."

Beck inhaled beside him, so quietly he knew that only he could hear it, and Callie's mouth dropped open. She stared at him like she couldn't possibly comprehend the words he was saying. She quickly glanced to Beck who was taking in everything in an even, unaffected manner, though he could hear her heart beat fluttering wildly in her chest. He traced soothing circles on her thigh with his thumb and fought a grin when her breath hitched quietly.

"Not fair," Beck said out of the corner of her mouth, barely moving her lips, and Si almost laughed.

"You can't possibly mean...*her*? *She's* the bounty?" Callie demanded, pointing a scarlet-tipped finger at Beck. She squinted at Beck, as if trying to see if she truly was the "mortal" the demons had been hunting, but before she could come to a conclusion, she froze.

"Wait...did you say *yours*?"

"I did," he said simply. Beck's lips tilted upward at the corners, a cold smile pulling on her lips.

"Since when do you claim any of your little...playmates as your own?" Si could see the wheels beginning to turn, everything she'd seen so far beginning to add up. Beck being here with him at all, his arms around her, his possessive grip on her thigh.

"Since now," he said with a glance at Beck. He could tell she was forcing herself not to grin, but that slight blush he loved so much crept across her delicate cheekbones. Whatever Callie saw in the look sent her into a seething rage.

"And what? You think you *love* her?" Callie sneered.

"And what if I do?" Si said, refusing to admit to Callie of all people his shortcomings in that department.

"That isn't possible," she said with quiet calculation in her eyes.

"Why? Because no one could ever *possibly* get over you?" He rolled his eyes. "Gods you are so fucking conceited..." Si trailed off, tilting his head. She hadn't said it in a flippant, jealous way. She'd said it with *conviction*. As if...

He stood so abruptly that Beck gasped in surprise. He stared down at Calypso.

"What the fuck did you do?" he demanded in a scarily calm, cold voice, his power surging around them.

Callie took a small step backwards when she felt it, eyeing him and then the water behind him warily. She swallowed hard, eyes darting, pulse racing. Si quickly warded the room so that she couldn't phase away.

"What. The fuck. Did you do, Calypso?" he asked again, punctuating every word with a step down the dais. He snatched his trident on the way, the familiar weight grounding him slightly. Leviathans appeared in the waters just outside, called by their master's rage. They swam back and forth, snapping their jaws, fire in their eyes. Callie paled, chest rising and falling faster as she took another step backwards, looking like she wanted to flee this place. Si could see it the moment that she realized she couldn't phase away, panic and fear shining in her eyes.

"Answer me," Si said again. Her shoulders slumped.

"I-I needed you to want me, Si. You were the only one who didn't and I couldn't stand it," she confessed, sounding like a petulant child. "I needed you to love me and no one else."

"What does that mean?"

Calypso stared at him for long moments, trying to figure out how serious he was. He was dead fucking serious. If his suspicions were right...Rage welled, hot and angry in his chest, scorching him.

"I...I had an enchantment placed on you," she finally admitted. He heard Beck gasp quietly behind him. The rage exploded in his chest, unlike anything he'd ever experienced. It was burning him to ash, disintegrating any lingering nagging feelings that were trying to demand even now that he care for Calypso, want her, love her.

No. Never again.

"You did what?!" Poseidon roared. A heartbeat later, two leviathans were *inside* the room, water dripping off of their massive, scaled bodies. Beck inhaled sharply from behind him, but he didn't sense fear from her. He sensed…awe. Callie on the other hand screamed and turned to run. He stopped her easily with his power and turned her back to face him, like a puppet on invisible strings. She stood, stuck in place and looking terrified as he stalked closer, the leviathans flanking him. Low growls emanated from their chests and their lips curled back from fangs the size of short swords. Calypso was trembling when he finally reached her. He towered above her, glaring downward like the powerful god he was, like the vengeful god Beck thought him to be all those months ago.

"Explain. Now," he commanded in that cold, lethal voice. The male leviathan, the larger of the two, slowly moved from Poseidon's side to circle Calypso. She flinched when he huffed a hot breath against her back, ruffling her pale hair. She whimpered when it snapped its jaws, the sound echoing through the room.

"Si, come on," she pleaded nervously, giving him one of her sultry smiles, the ones that brought most men to heel with ease. The ones that used to turn him to putty in her hands. *Because of a gods damned enchantment!*

"Do not call me that," he growled. "You have a very small window of time to explain everything to me before I lose my patience."

She paled when he released another surge of power. The male leviathan growled loudly and the other bared her fangs again.

"Alright, alright. Just…" He felt a stirring in the air behind him, a surge of heat, but he barely registered it, could barely register much of anything beyond the absolute disgust and fury boiling within him. Callie's eyes widened in terror as she glanced over his shoulder and he felt her struggling against her invisible bonds once more, trying desperately to flee.

"Ok! Ok! I'll talk, just s-stop it!" she screamed. Stop what? He hadn't ordered the leviathans to do anything other than look menacing—for now. He stared at her, waiting. She seemed to relax slightly, though she was still obviously shaken, and finally began to spill her secrets.

"Look, you never used to pay me much attention. All the times we crossed paths, you'd give me a cursory glance and nod, but then you'd move on. My allure is *legendary* but you weren't snared by it. I was...intrigued by that. At first," she added, annoyance flaring for a moment. "It became a bit of a game to me, to try to catch you. A challenge that I rarely got to pursue. But no matter what I did, you just wouldn't budge. Eventually, it stopped being a game. I *had* to have you, Si—" At his glare, she quickly amended, "Poseidon. I couldn't stand not having you. But...it became even more. I had to be the *only* one you wanted, the only one you worshiped, the only one you loved. I found someone to put an enchantment on you, an extremely powerful one. I needed you to only want me but...I couldn't deny my nature for long. I couldn't be tied down forever."

It all began to click into place: the fuzzy memories of how they'd gotten together and why; the lack of conviction that they'd even liked each other, let alone loved each other; the—Si inhaled sharply as realization hit him like a one of Zeus' lightning bolts: the reason he couldn't feel anything for anyone all this time. *She fucking cursed me not to!*

That bitch. That absolute fucking bitch!

He slammed the end of his trident on the floor so hard it nearly cracked the marble. Bolts of blue electricity flew from the prongs. His power began to build and build, becoming too much. He'd never known rage like this in all his long life. The blue bolts began to dance over his skin and the water outside began swirling like a tempest. More creatures from the darkest depths of the sea appeared, swimming among the tumultuous waters. Fangs and barbed tails, serrated fins and glowing eyes, circling, circling, circling.

Callie paled further, her body beginning to tremble violently.

"Poseidon, please. I'm sorry. I didn't mean for it to go this far. I didn't know the enchantment would be this strong or go on for this long."

"Liar!" he shouted, a tendril of power slipping his rein. It struck just beside her, close enough to make her scream as it singed her skin. She cradled her arm to her chest, clenching her teeth in pain. Her fear momentarily fell to the wayside, indignation and anger taking over as she lashed out.

"You know what, you're right, that was a lie. I did know! I knew and I *wanted* it that way," she sneered through bared teeth. "I wanted you to burn for me for eternity! Me and only me!!"

She had cursed him, had used him for years and discarded him when she grew bored, only to damn him to a half existence for centuries. He'd been a shell, desperate for any kind of connection for so long...and now, he couldn't even have the connection that he wanted with Beck.

Because of her.

The rage boiled over and he felt himself losing control. The leviathans both roared, the male scraping the floor with his front feet, digging deep grooves into the stone, the female rearing up onto her hind legs, tail whipping around her in a fury. Callie's eyes filled with terror, all her indignant bravado gone as tears built, but just before all was lost, he felt Beck at his side.

She gently placed her hand on his back, hissing in quietly as she made contact with the electricity.

"Calm down, Si," she whispered. "It's alright. *Calm.*"

He closed his eyes, struggling to do as she asked. His rage ebbed ever so slightly, her presence taking the raw edge off. He took several ragged breaths as he got his power under control. A thought hit him then, so forcefully it made him snap his eyes open, his entire body going rigid. He turned to Beck, half expecting her to be staring at him in revulsion or fear, but all he saw there was concern and...love.

"You're mine," he said in wonder. She *was* his. His one true match. It had to be the reason that he was able to feel something for her. The power of their bond was strong enough to push through the enchantment, but only *just* enough. It was why he kept feeling like he *should* be feeling more! It had to be. Her brows knit together but he snapped his head back to Calypso, excitement thrumming through his veins.

"Take it off. Now, Calypso."

"I-I can't," she whimpered, still eyeing the leviathans with concern, then eyeing Beck with...fear? And rubbing her arm where she'd been burned.

"Damn it, Calypso, this isn't a game! Take it off!" he yelled.

"I can't, I swear it! I would if I could, but I can't," she finished, beginning to cry. Her tears filled him with rage, his power burning again. He was about to lose his mind all over again. He was so close. He finally understood, finally was within reach of having everything he wanted. He couldn't lose it now! He was ready to release the leviathans to attack when several people phased into the room, just inside the towering doors. He'd only barred Callie from phasing *out*, not other people from phasing *in*.

"I have someone who can help with that," Emmie called with a self-satisfied grin. Skylar's immortal friend Lucas stood beside a fiery redhead and another large male who looked vaguely familiar. As they neared, Si's eyes shot wide, his rage forgotten for a moment.

"Conan? Er, I mean, Dean??"

His old friend shot him a grin that used to charm the pants off of anyone within striking distance. His blonde hair was a disheveled mess, as it always had been, though it desperately needed a trim now, and his gray eyes were sparkling with mischief.

And oh yeah—he was no longer a fucking cat. *Holy shit.*

"How..."

"Absolute bonkers story, mate. First we—"

"We'll have story time later, I promise," Emmie interrupted. "But for now, I come bearing gifts. Ta-da!" she sang as she gestured grandly to the redhead like she was showing off a prize on a mortal gameshow. The woman was beautiful, to be sure, but she looked a bit...ragged. Her pale skin seemed to be pulled too taut over her high cheekbones, as if she'd been starved, and she had dark shadows beneath startling turquoise eyes. Her dark gray dress was torn in several places and it looked like it may have actually been white once upon a time.

"Um, who is this, Emmie?" Beck asked from beside him. He clasped her hand and brought it to his lips, kissing her knuckles softly, thanking her silently for pulling him back from the brink.

"This is Sabina, the Enchantress Queen. She got herself locked up good and tight by some very not so pleasant folks for the last five hundred years or so, but we sprung her! Now she owes us super big time forever and ever."

Sabina cleared her throat delicately. "I can remove the enchantment for you. Emmie's right, I owe them much and will be repaying my debt for quite a while." She cast a glance at Emmie, narrowing her eyes. "Though for *forever and ever* seems a bit excessive." Emmie winked at her and mouthed *for-ev-errrrrrrrr*.

Si gave the enchantress a hard nod, trying not to let hope rise too swiftly, and Sabina strode forward. Lucas and Dean both stepped closer to Emmie, standing behind her shoulder to shoulder. The Seer reached back and gripped each of their wrists gently. *Interesting*, Si thought.

Sabina studied him for a moment, letting her gaze rove all over him. Her pupils expanded and changed to a shimmering gold and Si could feel her magic working.

"Where are you?" she muttered to herself, raising her hands in front of her and moving them through the air over Si's body. "Gods that feels good," she said as he felt the soft heat of her power pour over him. Poseidon imagined that wherever she had been held, she'd had her powers blocked somehow, at least to an extent, and now having it back must be like having a lost limb returned to you.

Si squeezed Beck's hand and she gave an answering one in return, telling him that whatever was happening, she was there. *Gods, please let this work.* He needed to feel this connection with Beck, truly feel it. It was his destiny. They were literally made for each other and he'd been searching his entire existence to find her. He wouldn't be complete until he felt the bond snap into place.

"There!" Sabina said with a triumphant grin. "Sneaky little

bastard, that enchantment." She turned to Calypso. "Who did this work?"

"Yvonna," Calypso said quietly, still being held in place and eyeing the room with fear. Beck noted that Emmie had wandered over to scratch one of the leviathans under the chin, as if he were a puppy. Dean grinned and Luke's eyes were wide as he studied the creatures with interest, fear, and awe.

Sabina nodded. "I knew her. She was good." She turned back to Si with a cocky smirk. "Before I killed her."

Si's brows rose in surprise. Well, he supposed you didn't stay queen of a faction like the enchantresses for very long without taking out the competition. It wasn't a title earned through family lines, it was earned through power and might.

"If you will be so kind as to remove your shirt."

He quickly unbuttoned his shirt and tossed it to the ground. Both Emmie and Dean began catcalling him. Lucas pressed his lips into a thin line, looking torn between amusement and jealousy.

"Oh baby! Take it off!"

"Ow owwww!"

"Luke, do you have any singles by chance?"

Beck snorted and Si's lips curled upwards.

"Wow," Sabina sighed as she took him in. She turned to Beck. "You are one lucky lady. And I'm not just saying that because I've been chained to a wall with nothing to look at but disgusting goblins for the last five hundred years." Turning back to Si, she said, "This is probably going to hurt like hell. This little devil is in there *deep*."

"Just do it."

Beck squeezed his hand again and he gave her a quick smile before Sabina began. She placed her hands over the center of his chest. She didn't touch his skin, but her hands hovered in the air just above it. Gold light began to glow in her palms and he felt the magic seeping into his chest, deep into his soul. He got the feeling that it was... searching, trying to grasp the enchantment to rip it free. It wasn't exactly pleasant, like someone digging into an open wound to find the broken tip of the spear that was still buried somewhere inside, but he'd had far worse pain. He gritted his teeth as she continued to dig, the sensation becoming more uncomfortable by the second.

Si felt it the moment she locked onto it, a strange tightening sensation around his heart. When she began to pull, pain laced through him and clenched his jaw. He locked his muscles in place as she pulled and pulled. He tried not to squeeze Beck's hand too hard, but the pain was skyrocketing. Sweat broke out over his entire body and his muscles quaked as he fought not to move. He could barely breathe, felt as if his heart were being crushed and torn apart and set on fire all at once.

"Come on you little bastard," Sabina grated. She was sweating too, her hair blowing wildly about her face in an unnatural wind that swirled just around her.

The pain doubled, tripled. When it shifted from pain to agony, he finally cried out and fell to his knees.

"Si!" Beck screamed, dropping to her knees beside him. He could feel the leviathans pacing around them, worry for their master pulsing clearly from their minds. Their loyalty meant much to him, their friendship even more so. This pair had been with him a long time and he loved them dearly. Other than Cyril, they were his must trusted soldiers and comrades in arms.

-I'm...O...K...- he managed to tell them telepathically.

"Should I stop?" Sabina asked between panting breaths.

"No!" Si bit out gritted teeth. "Finish this!" He clawed at the stone floor as the pain spread through him like wildfire. He dug into the marble, chunks of it coming loose beneath his hands.

"Let go," Sabina demanded. "Let go, you little bitch!" He felt another surge of magic pulse from her hands, an extremely strong one, a searing heat, and then he finally felt something yank from deep within him. It was pure agony as it pulled and pulled, tearing him apart as it went. A scream tore free from his lips.

"Yes! Almost...almost there now..." With one final surge of power, he felt it tear free of him completely.

He doubled over, gasping for breath. The pain was still there, but other feelings assailed him. Longing, yearning, admiration, and, above all, love. It hit him like a physical blow, knocking what little air he had from his lungs. *Beck. Oh gods, Beck.*

Everything came crashing down on him at once. All of the love that he felt for her, the connection, their bond. Everything. It kept hitting him, wave after wave, and he relished it, begged for more. It was the most intense pain, but he'd gladly take it because it meant he could finally experience what he'd been meant to with his woman. He could finally love her the way he needed to, the way she deserved for him to.

"Umm, we're all going to want to skedaddle like...right now," he heard Emmie tell everyone. "They are about to have *a moment.* Bonnie, Clyde, he's going to be ok, I promise. You both go on back out to the sea now." He wanted to grin at the names Emmie had given the pair of leviathans millennia ago, but the pain was still too intense for him to do much other than clench his jaw and keep from blacking out. Emmie's voice turned terrifyingly cold as she said, "Dean, be a dear and grab that trash on your way out."

"I'm sorry...I didn't mean to...I'm sorry," Calypso whimpered as she was assumedly dragged out of the room by Dean. Si fought to breathe, fought to make room for all of the feeling in his chest.

"Si? Si are you alright? Gods. Please say something, you're scaring me. Please."

Hearing her voice somehow helped the pain to ebb.

Beck.

Mine.

Forever.

TWENTY-NINE

Beck wasn't sure how to process anything that she'd seen and heard here today. When Calypso had admitted to cursing Si—*because enchantment my fucking ass, this was a* curse—her own rage had boiled. Her power had risen in her chest so hot and swift that it shocked her, and dark shadows of swirling smoke had appeared beside her as she'd stood in front of the throne. They were different than the illusions she'd cast before. They were like something from a nightmare that she'd brought to life. Whatever they were, they'd terrified Calypso, much to Beck's pleasure, and the bitch had finally confessed all.

Beck had no clue that the leviathans could come out of the sea and though they were absolutely terrifying, they were also beautiful and mesmerizing. *Deadly beauties.* She probably should have been more afraid of them, but she'd only felt an odd kinship with them, had just stopped herself from strolling forward to run her hand down the smaller one's glittering black scales.

Another thing Beck hadn't known? The incredible power Si truly possessed. The entire room had rocked as his power had built and built, threatening to be released at any moment. What looked like blue lightning or electricity sparked all over his skin and shot from his trident, scorching the floor. The sea had turned into a deadly looking black cyclone, all manner of nightmarish sea creatures swimming within it. Responding to his darkening mood, she assumed. She'd been reminded all over again just how terrifying the sea could be...just how terrifying Poseidon's wrath could be.

Then Emmie's well-timed arrival with the Enchantress Queen and Dean—who was no longer a cat, but a devilishly handsome demigod who looked at both Emmie and Lucas in a way that made Beck's cheeks heat. It was a look that people who'd been through something harrowing together shared, an experience that bonded them in ways others couldn't understand, a look that spoke of such an intense connection, it couldn't even be described. It was a sexy look. She was dying to know the story behind it, to know where Emmie had been these last few weeks—especially since the oracle knew that Skylar and the others had been trying to track her down.

Then the enchantress had begun working her magic on Si and it had taken every bit of Beck's self-control not to rip the woman's beautiful red hair from her scalp. She was *hurting* Si, she was hurting Beck's man. Her instincts were demanding that she protect him, but she knew that Sabina wasn't trying to hurt him. She was trying to help him, trying to fix the epic clusterfuck that Calypso had brought down upon Poseidon with her ridiculous, petulant jealousy. Just thinking of it now, rage burned through Beck. She longed to have a few minutes alone with Calypso, to teach her a lesson about screwing with people's lives. *She had been afraid of those shadows? I'll give her something to truly be afraid of.*

But that would come later. Right now, her entire world had been shrunk down to only encompass this room, this man before her. Nothing else mattered.

"Si? Are you ok?" Beck asked again, reaching out hesitantly to place her hand on his back. He seemed to be past the worst of the pain now, but he was still doubled over, his entire body heaving and shuddering with the force of his breaths. He'd dug deep grooves into the stone floor as he fought through the agony and Beck couldn't even imagine what he must have felt. His scream of agony would haunt her dreams for eternity. She never, ever wanted to hear it again. She wished so badly that she could have taken the pain from him somehow, because she would rather hurt than see him suffer.

He finally began to breathe normally and he pushed himself upward. His eyes were bright, burning, wild.

"Si?" she asked cautiously.

"Beck," he breathed the word like a prayer. He swooped in and kissed her fiercely though his hands were so gentle as they cradled her face, thumbs rubbing softly against her cheekbones. She melted into him, feeling like this kiss was different, like it was their first one somehow. They finally pulled apart and he stared at her in awe, eyes glassy. With tears?

"Beck, I love you. I love you so gods damned much. I can feel it now. I can feel *everything*." Her heart stuttered before speeding back up into overdrive. He loved her. "Beck, you're *mine*."

"Well, I thought we already established that," she said with a small smile.

"No, I mean, you're *mine*. Do you know about gods and their one true match?" She furrowed her brows. What the heck was he talking about?

"Uhh, no?"

"It's like soulmates. It's believed that a part of one's soul will reside in their one true match, the one being in all the worlds made for them and them alone, and vice versa. The missing parts of the souls will search for eternity to be brought back together. You are mine, Beck. I feel it so strongly, understand it so completely now. It's why I was able to feel anything for you all these months, even though the enchantment tried to prevent it. You're mine," he said again with a breathtaking smile, searching her eyes intently. Her heart swelled so much she thought it might burst right through her chest. *She was his.* She wanted to cry. She'd wanted to feel loved? Well, now, she was, and it was almost too much for her to accept.

"I...I think you're mine too," she whispered. "There's been this strange whisper in the back of my mind since the day I met you, telling me that I'm meant to be here, to be with you. Demanding it actually, like magnets being pulled together. I ignored it for a long time and fought against the pull, was even unbelievably angry at it there for a while, but now—" Si cut her off with another deep kiss, making her laugh against his lips.

"I'm sorry," he said, grinning. "I couldn't help myself."

He kissed her again and again, like he couldn't get enough, like it was all new and he couldn't quite believe it was real. Beck wrapped her arms around his neck as he pulled her into his lap. The kiss was scorching, rendering her to ash.

"My gods, this feeling is...it's so *strong*. It's almost overwhelming but in the best way." He brushed hair from her face, staring at her like he'd never seen her before this day. It was a look of pure adoration and it made her chest ache. "Marry me," he rasped. Beck's eyes shot wide.

"W-what?" She couldn't have heard him correctly.

"Well, it's only two words, I figured you could comprehend such a simple sentence..." He grinned that sexy, smart-ass grin that she loved to hate and she punched him in the shoulder. He laughed and rubbed the spot. "Much better. That one actually hurt," he said with approval. "I mean it, Beck. Marry me. Be my wife. Be my queen. Be *mine*. Forever."

She couldn't breathe. Was this real? She...should be freaking out, right? Should be having an existential crisis and worried about losing her freedom and being tied down and all of the other things she'd seen in mortal romance movies. But she wasn't feeling any of that. She'd never been sure of much in her life, but she was *so* sure about Poseidon. Why fight it? *Why not lean into the bliss and let myself be truly happy for the first time?*

She smiled at him and he inhaled sharply, still so affected by it in a way that made her love him even more.

"Well," she murmured as she leaned in to kiss him softly. "I *did* look pretty good up on that throne…" He smiled and she pulled away to meet his gaze.

"Is that a yes?"

"No," she said easily. He frowned and she grinned. "That's a *hell* yes."

"Ahem." They both whirled to find Emmie standing behind them once more. "So, not to eavesdrop or anything…except that's a lie because we all know I *live* to eavesdrop, probably in my top five favorite activities to be honest, but I believe I heard something about a wedding?" A mischievous glint flashed in her purple eyes. Si stood and pulled Beck up, immediately wrapping an arm around her shoulder and pulling her snugly into his side, kissing the top of her head.

He gave an exasperated sigh but he was smiling, a new smile that Beck had never seen before.

"Out with it, Seer. We all know you've already seen whatever you're about to say or do, so just tell us what's going on."

Emmie jumped up and down, clapping.

"I love when you guys completely submit to me and all of my infinite knowledge and glory."

"And modesty. Don't forget modesty," Beck said with a laugh, wrapping an arm around Si's stomach.

"Please. Modesty is for lower beings than I," Emmie scoffed as she fluffed her hair…hair that was now curled in long, elegant waves. Beck tilted her head, only now realizing that Emmie had changed since departing the room only minutes ago, completely cleaned up from whatever adventure they'd been on. She was now in a floor-length satin gown of silver, looking like liquid metal as it flowed along her slim body. Wheels started to turn in Beck's mind.

She didn't…

Emmie winked at her, as if knowing exactly where Beck's thoughts were slowly going.

"Now, Si, as much as it is crime against nature to cover you up, you can't very well get married in front of all of your friends and family shirtless." She snapped her fingers and a black button-down shirt appeared in his hand. He looked down at the shirt, and then at Emmie with wide eyes.

"Did you say *get married*?"

"Good to know that your hearing has not been lost in your extremely old age. Beck, you look absolutely perfect. I based all of the décor on your dress—excellent choice by the way." Another wink. Beck's head was spinning. They were...about to have a wedding? Seriously? Emmie clapped her hands several times, reminding Beck of a teacher she'd had just before her mother had pulled her out of school completely. Or she pulled herself out, really, if she were being honest.

"Now, come, come. It's poor form to keep your guests waiting."

Si pulled on his shirt but ignored Emmie, turning Beck to meet his eyes.

"If you don't want this, you say the word, Beck. I'll have us out of here in a heartbeat."

"I...do want it actually," she said, scrunching her nose. "I want to marry you more than just about anything else in the world, Si. And I've never planned so much as a birthday party, so, if I don't have to plan a wedding..." She shrugged and grinned. His lips curled into the most devastatingly handsome smile. He pinched her chin between his thumb and forefinger in that way that drove her crazy, and held her gaze for a long moment before drawing her lips to his. He finally pulled away and she swayed a bit at the new intensity of their kisses. *What else would be more intense now?* she wondered, toes curling in anticipation.

"Well, let's go get hitched then," he said, offering his arm.

Everything *was* more intense now that their bond had clicked into place fully for Si. Beck lay now on his chest after three days—or was it five?—of nothing but exploring this new connection, learning each other all over again as husband and wife. He raised her hand and traced his finger along the place where she'd sliced her palm during their wedding ceremony. For the hundredth time, she thought back to the day and smiled.

"Wait," Beck stopped just outside the doors of the ballroom where they'd had the Christmas celebration, suddenly nervous. Not to be marrying Poseidon, but about lots and lots of eyes staring at her. "What am I walking into here, Em?"

"Only four or five…hundred guests. Tops." Beck paled and Emmie cackled. "It's just a handful of your nearest and dearest, I swear."

Beck exhaled, thinking she could handle that much. Another thought made her pause: should she care that her mother wasn't here? It was her wedding after all. Isn't one supposed to share precious moments with her mother on a day like today? She tossed the thought around her mind and found that no, she didn't care that her mother wasn't there. A few months ago, Beck might have wondered what that said about her, if it made her a terrible daughter or person in general, but now, she found she simply didn't give a shit. Her mother had been anything but a mother to her all her life, had filled her head with needless hatred based on lies. She didn't deserve to be here for Beck's wedding, to witness Beck finding true happiness for the first time.

Beck looked to Si and nodded with a smile. Emmie pulled open the doors and Beck lost her breath. The room looked amazing, so achingly beautiful she could barely stand it. Tears filled her eyes as she took in the delicate ice blue flowers tied with midnight blue ribbons draped along the walls and hanging from the ceiling. Twinkling lights were hidden among them, casting a beautiful, soft silver glow over the room. A small aisle ran between two rows of simple but elegant wooden chairs. The ceiling had been changed to one massive domed skylight, crystal blue water shimmering above them. Sea creatures had gathered outside and Beck would have sworn that the leviathans inclined their heads to her and…grinned?

Everyone stood and turned to watch them as they made their way down the aisle, arm in arm. Skylar, Nerina, Medusa, Lily, and Zahara all beamed at her. Skylar wiped tears from her eyes and then flipped off Z when she apparently whispered something mocking about her crying. Hades, Zeus, Dean, and Lucas all smiled at them, seemingly giving Poseidon mental high fives, though Zeus kept shifting his gaze from the two of them to Z, and she kept stealing glances at him as well.

When she and Poseidon reached the front, they turned to face each other.

"Uh...what happens now? I don't know anything about godly wedding ceremonies," Beck whispered.

Emmie strolled forward and extended a knife towards Si, hilt first. It was forged of a glowing gold metal and was etched with black runes. Beck could feel the power coming from the weapon as Si gripped the blade.

"It'll only sting for a second, promise," Emmie whispered with a wink before going to sit between Lucas and Dean. Dean wrapped an arm around her shoulders while Lucas placed a hand on her thigh. The two men shared a look over Emmie's head. A...heated look, but Lucas quickly looked away. Ooo, interesting...

Beck wasn't sure what was about to happen, but she shifted her shoulders back, ready to do whatever had to be done to marry Poseidon. He unbuttoned the top few buttons of his shirt before making a quick slice across his chest with the dagger, just over his heart. She gasped quietly, but he gave her a reassuring smile as he cut his palm as well. She stared in wonder as the wounds didn't immediately heal. A blade that could truly harm a god? She eyed it warily and gripped it with the respect it was due when Si held it to her.

"Cut your hand and your chest as I did." She swallowed once but nodded, quickly copying his movements. The blade burned as it cut, but she ground her teeth against the pain.

Si stared at her like she was the most precious thing in his life. He had to clear his throat twice before he quietly said, "Blood by blood, heart by heart, soul by soul, I am bound to you. I am yours as you are mine. We are one, now and always. My power is yours. My kingdom is yours. My heart is yours. Protect them forevermore, as I will protect yours."

Beck's eyes pricked with tears. That was possibly the most beautiful thing she'd ever heard. It put every single mortal romance movie she'd ever watched to shame. She felt something begin to stir in the air around them, something powerful. He gave her an encouraging look and she understood it was her turn. She took a deep breath. She repeated his words, voice trembling slightly as emotion threatened to choke her.

"Blood by blood, heart by heart, soul by soul, I am bound to you. I am yours as you are mine. We are one, now and always. My power is yours. My kingdom is yours. My heart is yours. Protect them forevermore, as I will protect yours."

He extended his hand and placed his cut palm on the gash over her heart. She did the same and gasped as the power in the air flared like fire. She felt the bond growing stronger, snapping between them like a steel cable, felt their souls melding together. A blue-white light flared where their hands covered each other's chests. A ring of water rose up from the floor and circled around them, blue light flashing within it as it churned.

Poseidon's eyes turned black, the gold striations burning brighter than ever before and she felt his power surge before flowing into her. She sucked in a surprised breath as it filled her, becoming a part of her. She felt her own power strengthen as his fed it, felt it when it merged with his. My power is yours. *They would share each other's power now, become stronger. She'd be able to protect him and everyone else she loved so much better now.*

She could feel Aqueous itself calling out to her, beckoning her. Can that possibly be right? But it was. It was opening up to her, becoming a part of her just as Poseidon's power had. My kingdom is yours. *She could feel every inch of the kingdom, every bit of life within it, was connected to it all. Her mind seemed to expand to make room for all the new knowledge and the connections to everything all around her.*

"Whoa," she breathed. Si smiled wider than she'd ever seen before he swooped down to kiss her softly but deeply. The cyclone around them faded and the room immediately erupted in cheers.

Beck smiled against his lips and reluctantly pulled away to face their audience. Everyone quickly converged on them, pulling them apart to give hugs and slaps on the back. Beck had never felt so much love, she was nearly drunk with it.

"I didn't even bother to plan a reception because I know you wouldn't have stayed for it anyway. So, go on, go bless that marriage bed, my loves." Emmie shooed them away and they threw out quick goodbyes to everyone before Si phased them back to their room.

They undressed, kissing and exploring slowly, but there was an intense, desperate urgency behind every touch of their skin, every lap of their tongues. He held her gaze as he slid inside her, so slowly it made her quake with pleasure, and continued to hold it as he worked his hips back and forth, moving in and out in a sensual, mind-numbing rhythm. He gripped both of her hands in his, sliding them up to rest above her head as he continued to pump. It was unlike any of their other times together, so intense, so powerful. The connection between them so strong it was staggering.

"I love you," he whispered as he continued to thrust, driving her closer and closer to the brink. "I love you, I love you, I love you," he said over and over, punctuating each sentence with a kiss. With tears in her eyes and so much joy in her heart she thought she could die, Beck shattered into a million pieces, Si following soon after.

"I love you, Si. I love you, I love you, I love you," she whispered against his neck when he collapsed on top of her. She lost track of time all together after that. They couldn't seem to slow, both of them insatiable to the point of madness. They only stopped to eat, shower (though usually they ended up doing far more than bathing), and pass out from utter exhaustion.

Si roused her from her memories as he brought her palm to his lips, kissing it softly. They'd finally slowed a tiny bit, enough that she could finally really process everything that had happened—the fact that they were *married*. Which meant...*Oh my god*. She snorted with laughter.

"I only just now really realized: I'm a *queen*." She felt him chuckle, his chest rumbling beneath her cheek. "My mother will be thrilled," she said sarcastically, rolling her eyes. Then she frowned. "Actually, I take that back, she'll probably be blinded by jealousy."

"Truly?" Si asked. Beck twisted and propped her chin up on her upturned hands.

"Unfortunately, yes," she sighed. "I guess it's time for me to tell you the whole story, now that she's your mother-in-law and everything." He smiled at that. "Though, I'm sure she is one you'd refer to as a "monster-in-law" instead. She's..." Beck cast about for a semi-nice term. She finally landed on, "A lot."

"I feel like maybe I need popcorn," he said with a smirk.

"You aren't far off." She exhaled roughly. It was time. The fears and doubts she'd had when she first arrived no longer existed. There was no reason not to tell him everything. She *wanted* to tell him everything, the good, the bad, and the crazy. To finally share her complete self with him. With her husband. *Gods, I'll never get tired of saying that!*

"You know how I told you before that my mother fled to the Mortal Plane when she found out she pregnant with me? Well, she didn't so much flee, as she was...*banished* from the godly planes by Zeus." Si's brows drew together. "I know it didn't turn out to be true, but when my mother told him she was pregnant, he banished her." The V in between his furrowed brows became more pronounced. "Or well...that's what she said happened, but now...what?"

"That absolutely can't be what happened, I guarantee you, but..."

Beck wanted to scream in frustration. She had been ninety-nine percent sure that her mother had lied about that as well, but she had no doubts that Poseidon was right. That wasn't what happened. But he still looked like something was bothering him.

"But...?"

"How old are you?"

She frowned. She hadn't known where he was going, but that was definitely not what she'd expected him to say.

"You know, etiquette dictates that you don't ask a lady that sort of thing." When he gave her a dry look she told him, "Twenty-seven. Why?"

"Zeus hasn't banished anyone in *hundreds* of years. And he would never banish someone for thinking they were pregnant with his child, not a chance."

"I really didn't think so—wait. Did you say *hundreds* of years?" He nodded and she shook her head in denial. "No, that doesn't make sense. She was pregnant with me when she was banished." *Wasn't she?*

"Not possible. The last time banishment was used was almost three hundred years I think—it's a serious punishment and doesn't get handed out lightly or often. The last one was..." He trailed off before getting a strange look on his face. With eyes wide, he said with an incredulous edge to his voice, "Tell me your mother isn't *Adamantia*..." At her look he barked out a strangled laugh. "Oh gods..." He rubbed his face with both hands, making a half groan-half laughing sound.

"What?" Beck demanded.

"I'm sorry to be the one to tell you this, Beck, but your mother is certified bat shit *crazy*."

Beck was well aware of that already, but to hear Poseidon be so damned convinced of it, to hear that her mother had been banished *hundreds* of years ago? Her mother had lied to her about literally *everything*. It was too much. It was all just too damn much. Beck grabbed a pillow and shoved her face into it, screaming until her throat was raw.

"Beck, it's alright."

"No, it really, *really* isn't! She's a...and she lied...and...argg!" Beck slammed the pillow back into the bed and proceeded to use it as a punching bag. She screamed unintelligible frustrations as she pummeled the innocent pillow. She knew Poseidon was trying his best not to laugh and she loved him for it, but she was fuming. Beyond fuming. She knew without a doubt how ridiculous she looked right now, but her anger was very real, the rage burning in her chest like a living, breathing thing, snarling and clawing. Beck honestly couldn't be sure that if her mother was there, that she wouldn't be getting the same treatment as the pillow.

She leapt off the bed and quickly summoned clothing—a handy

new skill she'd received from the shared power from Si—and he watched intently.

"Get up and get Hermes here now." She glanced at him as she shoved her legs angrily into her jeans. "Please," she added, knowing that any frustrations she was feeling really shouldn't be taken out on him. He held his hands up in surrender and did as she asked. She knew Si would tell her as much as he knew, but Hermes knew all. He was the keeper of all of the histories of the gods. If anyone knew all of the dirty details about her mother, it would be him.

They phased to the throne room. Beck actually had that ability as well, she'd learned, though she was still learning how to use it with little success so far.

She paced as they waited. Si lounged on his throne and she was momentarily distracted from her ire by how damned sexy he looked there. He was such a delicious mix of casual and powerful. Her eyes shifted to her own throne beside his and her lips quirked. She'd never get used to the fact that it belonged to her. She was a freaking queen. *And right now, this queen is in the mood to smite someone down.*

"You rang?" Hermes drawled when he appeared just behind Beck. She whirled to find the Messenger God smiling at her. She had forgotten just how handsome he was with his golden curls and mischievous eyes. Poseidon merely waved towards Beck in a *this is her show* gesture. Hermes arched a brow but gave Beck a small bow. "*You* rang, my queen? The title fits you like a glove, by the way," he added with a wink.

Beck gave him a tight smile and then, after a deep breath, said, "I want to know everything about Adamantia and her banishment."

"Adamantia? Oh *gods*," Hermes laughed and shook his head. "There's a name I haven't heard in a while. She was...something, that's for sure." He chuckled a bit more, obviously recalling amusing memories, but then he became serious. "Why do you want to know about her?"

"It's personal," she hedged. "Can you just tell me, please?" she asked in a softer tone.

"Well, she was always a bit...off. She had this *really* intense desire for power, past any normal ambition or aspiration of greatness. I think it made her a bit, uh, unhinged, a tad delusional even." Well, that sure as hell tracked.

"What exactly was she banished for?"

"Attempted murder, among other things."

"What?!" Beck knew her mother had issues, but *murder*? Thankfully the *attempted* part meant she hadn't succeeded, but still. She pinched the bridge of her nose in frustration, trying to remain as calm as possible with anger and confusion roiling through her chest.

"I can show you her trial if you'd like?"

"Really? Yes, please."

Hermes nodded and closed his eyes for a few moments, sifting through the unimaginable amount of archival knowledge he possessed. When he opened them, they were a dark molten gray, swirling like quicksilver pools. From them, beams of light shot forward, forming a projection just before them. Beck's eyes widened as she took in the scene. It was as if she were standing in the room, everything and everyone looking so real that she nearly reached out to touch her mother—or maybe strangle her.

Adamantia stood on a small platform, golden shackles around her wrists. She looked much as she did now—same dark hair, same blue eyes—but there was a lightness about her in the memory that Beck had never seen before. Even manacled and standing trial for trying to kill someone, she had a strange ease in her that she'd lost long before Beck had known her.

Zeus stood before her, a small crowd of other gods and goddesses standing off to the side.

"Adamantia, minor goddess of illusions and persuasion, you stand before the King of the Gods and these witnesses to be punished for your crimes."

Adamantia's eyes blazed with anger and her hands flew forward to clench the small bar before her on the platform, the shackles clanking together loudly.

"Do not call me that!" she screeched. Beck flinched at the intensity of her mother's outburst. Now *this* part of her mother was all too familiar to Beck. Her mother seethed for a few moments before pressing her lips into a thin line and closing her eyes. When she opened them, her anger had disappeared and she smiled at Zeus. "My *crimes?* I was merely trying to take my rightful place. That isn't a crime," she scoffed, a flirtatious edge to her words.

Several in the crowd exchanged glances. Glances that said *she's insane* loud and clear. Beck couldn't blame them. She reminded Beck a bit of characters she'd seen in mortal crime shows who were delusional, committing terrible atrocities but fully believing they weren't doing anything wrong. *But we're in love, of course I had to kidnap him!* one might yell as she was dragged away in cuffs, smiling at the man she'd abducted who had never even spoken to her a day in his life.

Zeus eyed her, not with anger and scorn as Beck would have expected, but with...pity and concern.

"Do you deny that you tried to have Hera murdered?" Beck raised a hand to her mouth, not quite believing what she was hearing. Si came to stand beside her, a reassuring hand resting on her lower back. She leaned into his side, silently thanking him for being there. She chewed her lip and rubbed her medallion as they watched the scene continue to unfold.

Zeus continued, "Do you deny that you used your illusions to make my Elite believe Hera was an assassin sent to kill me in order for them to attack her?" Trying to kill Hera herself was one thing, but having the *Elite* do it? Beck honestly wasn't sure how Hera was still standing if Dante and the others had set their sights on her.

"Oh my gods," Beck whispered.

"It was close," Si muttered at her ear. "If Hera wasn't such a fierce warrior, she wouldn't have survived long enough for Zeus to intervene. When he arrived, she'd already lost an arm and had been nearly sliced in half. Dante had a sword of fire at the ready..."

Beck shuddered. She couldn't quite believe that her mother had caused that kind of violence to be done. As terrible as she'd been towards Beck and as crazy as she'd always seemed, Beck had always considered her mother to be fairly harmless. Now, she knew that wasn't the case.

"Do you deny," Zeus continued, "that you then proceeded to sneak into my private chambers—after being forbidden to enter them after being caught there *numerous* times uninvited—and attempted to use your illusions and persuasion to get me to wed you?" Zeus's voice had gotten louder and more forceful with each statement. Now, Beck could feel the power thrumming from it even through the projection. "Do you deny, that when your powers were not enough to enthrall me, you attempted to kill me yourself with a godsblade in order to take my throne?"

Holy shit. Beck understood now how dangerous a godsblade was. *And my mother tried to kill Zeus with one?!* No wonder she'd been banished! Gods, Zeus probably should have just killed her outright.

Adamantia listened to her crimes, her shoulders back and her nose in the air, acting like the queen she truly thought she was. She didn't appear contrite in the slightest—because she wasn't.

"I don't deny these things, but once again, I only did them to obtain what *belongs* to me. I should be queen. I was born to be. All you need to do is marry me, Zeus. We will rule together for eons to come." Her eyes went dreamy and she leaned towards him, voice sultry and entreating. "We'll be the greatest deities and monarchs in the history of all the worlds. We'll be worshipped for eternity." *My gods. She really is bat shit crazy.*

Zeus shook his head, looking disappointed, as if he were hoping she'd see reason. Beck knew that hope too well, had held it in her heart far too many times to count before she'd wised up. And she also knew the disappointment. Gods, did she know the disappointment.

"Adamantia, I do not wish for your death, but I cannot allow you to stay here and continue these games. You are unwell but your power is great and dangerous." He clenched his jaw several times, his eyes darkening and lightning flashing just behind him, a low rumble of thunder following. "You are hereby banished to the Mortal Plane to live out the rest of your days. Your power and immortality will slowly fade over time, and you will eventually grow old and die as a mortal."

"Banished?" her mother whispered, unbelieving. "But...but this is my kingdom. This is my rightful place. I should be a queen." Her voice rose as her sentencing really sank in. "I deserve to be a queen!" she screamed, looking beseechingly to the crowd. When no one came to her aid, many even turning away almost embarrassed by her behavior, she turned back to Zeus. "No! I will not go! I will not live among the lower beings! I am your queen!!" she bellowed, looking and sounding completely fucking crazed.

"I'm sorry, Adamantia. I truly am, but I cannot continue to let these indiscretions slide and I do not wish to lock you in the dungeons for all eternity." He nodded to Dante who began to drag Adamantia away. She continued to scream as she went and Beck had to look away. She was both disgusted and sad.

The scene faded and Hermes shook himself, his eyes returning to their mesmerizing mix of purple and blue.

"There you have it, your majesty," he said with an inclination of his head. "See. A bit unhinged."

Beck nodded absently. "And, um, when did this take place?"

"Three hundred seventeen years, four months, two days, and about six hours ago."

Beck shook her head in disbelief. "So, she lied about literally *everything*. What the fuck!?" She started pacing again and noticed Hermes giving Si a questioning glance.

"I'll explain later," Si said, waving Hermes away. Beck's chest began to burn, with power, with rage, with...hurt. She understood after seeing the trial that her mother was truly disturbed, but she had lied to Beck about so many things, had treated her horribly for apparently no reason at all. How could she have done this to her own daughter?

"Beck," Si said gently, letting her pace. He glanced around as illusions sprang from her at random, arching his dark brows but saying nothing.

"I can't believe this," she seethed. "I mean, it's one thing to lie to me about who my father was, but to lie about why she was banished? And when? What the fuck was she doing for two-hundred-some-odd years before she got pregnant with me then?!" And if she *hadn't* been pregnant when she'd been banished, all of that anger and resentment towards Beck, making it seem as if it were Beck's fault for their situation, was completely and totally unfounded. *What. The. Fuck.*

"Beck, it's alright." He caught her wrist as she made yet another pass by him and she allowed him to stop her. He pulled her into him and she buried her face in his chest, letting his warmth and his scent calm her. She wrapped her arms around him and squeezed as he rubbed her back.

"It isn't though," she mumbled against his chest. "It is so far from alright. It's not even on the same plane as alright. How could she do this to me?" The anger was still there, but the hurt was starting to overtake it. Her chest ached and her eyes watered. "All this time she...she *hated* me because she blamed me for her banishment. If that wasn't true then...then..." She choked back a sob. "Then she hated me just because of *me*."

Poseidon shifted back, and she tilted her head upwards until she met his gaze. Tears streaked down her cheeks and he gently wiped them away with his thumb.

"I'm not going to pretend that this isn't terrible or that it makes sense or that I don't want to throttle your mother." He held her gaze and wiped another tear away. "But you have got to know that how she treated you, that was all on *her*. It has nothing to do with you. You are the most amazing person I've ever met and if she couldn't see that, if she wasted all of that precious time with you," he stroked her cheek, staring at her with such adoration, such unrelenting, unconditional love, "then fuck her."

His lips curled up into a smile and she let out a half sob-half laugh, going up on her toes to kiss him with a quiet desperation. She let herself be lost in the kiss for long moments, lost in the sensation of his soft lips pressing against hers, of his tongue thrusting gently against her own. Feeling better, and surprisingly calm and resolved, she pulled away with a sigh.

"Thank you," she whispered.

"No thanks necessary, love. From what I understand, this is what husbands do for their wives." He grinned at her.

"I don't think I'll ever get tired of being called your wife." She patted his chest and gave him a small smile. "And now, I need to go have a chat with my mother."

Emmie appeared wearing a striking black suit and a chauffer's hat, and holding a cardboard sign with *Beckalicious* scrawled across the front.

"I hear you need a ride," she said with a wry smile. She tossed the sign and hat away and fluffed out her hair, and her suit disappeared, replaced by cut offs and a Blink 182 tanktop. Beck smiled but Si glared at the oracle.

"Don't suppose you've changed your mind about letting us into your realm?" he grated.

"Have I ever steered you wrong? Seriously, cut me some slack here, Si," Emmie said, glaring back. Beck knew there had been a… disagreement over Emmie giving up details on someone who might know about the key's whereabouts. All of the gods were pissed at her but she wasn't budging, assuring them that she had her reasons for making them wait. Beck trusted her and knew everything she did was for a reason, but she couldn't help but feel just as frustrated by her refusal as the others: the literal fate of the world could rest on this.

"This isn't a game, Emmie," Si said, crossing his arms over his chest.

Emmie's eyes darkened, anger flashing, and a strange wind blew around her, tussling her hair.

"You think I don't know that? You think I haven't seen thousands of possible futures, almost all of them ending in total decimation? This is beyond precarious, this house of cards can topple at any moment, Poseidon! One wrong move and everything crumbles, and by everything I mean literally *everything*. I am steering this as best as I can and the assholes upstairs are fighting me every step of the way!" she added in a louder voice, glaring upward. *The assholes upstairs?* "You have *got* to trust me."

Si exhaled roughly but he softened, giving her a reluctant nod of acceptance. Emmie's eyes faded back to her beautiful violet, the lavender ring burning brightly.

"Now, Beck, I think it's time you have a serious heart to heart with your mother."

"Do you need me to go with you?" Si asked as Beck leaned in to give him another kiss.

"No, I need to do this alone. I'll be alright, I promise." He nodded and kissed her forehead before she made her way to Emmie. A heartbeat later they appeared in a tropical paradise that took Beck's breath away.

"Whoa," Beck whispered as she glanced around. Silvery white beach leading to crystal clear water, vibrant tropical flowers and palms swaying in the cool breeze, the scent like heaven.

"I do know how to make a realm, don't I?" Emmie said, huffing a breath on her nails and then buffing them on her shirt. "This way." She nodded her head and Beck followed her along the beach towards a path between the trees.

"What did you mean before? About the assholes upstairs?"

"The Fates don't like when I meddle too much, when I try to steer the future to particular outcomes," Emmie replied, rolling her eyes. "They're pushing back against me at every turn."

"Why?"

"They don't think I should intervene, that the chips should just fall as they may, so to speak. But more importantly, I think that they don't like that I'm still more powerful than they are, even after stepping down."

Beck stutter stepped. "Stepping down?"

"Oh. Yeah, I kind of used to be one of them." She waved a hand in front of her, shooing Beck's next question away. "I'll give you the whole story another time. Right now, you have more important things to deal with."

Emmie pulled back a curtain of hanging vines to reveal a breath-taking oasis: an open-air temple sat in a deep green meadow just beside a sparkling waterfall. Wildflowers and leafy vines grew over the top of the temple like a living roof. In the middle of it was a large chaise lounge.

And on that?

Her mother.

Beck sucked in a breath. She felt like she hadn't seen her mother in a lifetime, but also like maybe she'd never really seen her before at all. Everything was so different now. Maybe Beck didn't know the real Adamantia, but Adamantia didn't know the real Beck either, she never had.

Beck's entire life had been nothing but stacks upon stacks of lies and she was about to knock the entire thing down. Was she ready for that? She shoved her shoulders back. *Fuck yes I am.*

"I'll be back in a bit. The cabin we passed on the way here? Go there if you want to get away from her—she's barred from entering. A little gift I left for the last guest. No offense, but everyone needs a little sanctuary from your mother. She is best taken in small doses... miniscule, even." Didn't Beck know it. She vaguely wondered who that guest might have been, but Emmie interrupted her thoughts.

"Ok, are you ready? Deep breath. Good job, in and out. Now, go be the queen you are and get your answers, lovie dovie. Good luck!" With that, Emmie stepped back to let the curtain of vines fall back in place between them. Beck took a fortifying breath and stalked towards the temple.

Adamantia glanced towards her when she got closer, but then seemed to do a double take. She shot upwards from her lounge, wobbling noticeably as she fought for balance. Beck narrowed her eyes as she spied the carafe of wine on the table—empty of course, as was the goblet beside it.

"Beckham?" her mother asked incredulously. "What are you doing here, dear?" A serene smile on her face, seeming more relaxed and happier than Beck had ever seen her before. She realized with a start that *this* must be where her mother had always come when she disappeared. *Ok Emmie owes me some answers as well.* Every time her mother came back, she was always better for a bit, acting more motherly, calling Beck "dear" and "dove," and making her think that she was actually cared for, if only for a few days.

Adamantia began walking forward, arms outstretched as if for a hug.

"Don't you dare," Beck spit through gritted teeth, halting her mother in her tracks. She tilted her head, studying Beck. She let her arms drop as she seemed to realize that Beck wasn't there for a joyful reunion.

"I'm here for the truth," Beck said in a cold voice. Seeing her mother had her fury rising once more. Everything this woman had put her through, all of the lies, all of the blame, it was all crashing together into a violent storm of wrath inside of Beck's chest. She knew she needed to calm, but it was easier said than done.

"The truth?" Adamantia asked, sounding confused, but Beck could see the wheels turning, see the fear in her mother's eyes as she put the pieces together. Changing the subject all together and continuing to feign ignorance of why Beck was truly there, she said, "I was coming back to you soon, dear. I just needed a quick re-charge is all."

"Seriously? A quick re-charge? I was being hunted by demons, mother. *Demons!* And it has been *months*, by the way. I'm sure all the wine and all around fucking paradise of this place made you lose track of time."

"Demons?" her mother breathed, eyes going wide. She paled and swallowed hard, but it wasn't shock in her eyes. Beck narrowed her eyes. Why wasn't her mother more surprised that it had been demons after her instead of gods or bounty hunters or hell, even Zeus himself? Something was off, but Beck wasn't sure what. All she knew was that a ball of unease began to unfurl in her belly. She ignored it, pushing on.

"Yes, fucking demons. I almost died trying to escape them. Innocent people *did* die," she grated, that stab of guilt and pain flaring once more when she thought of the team. *My fault, my fault, my fault.*

"H-how did you get away?" Adamantia glanced around wildly, as if she expected the demons to be hiding in the bushes around them. "Did Emmie save you and bring you here?"

Beck raised her chin in defiance before saying, "Poseidon saved me."

Her mother sucked in a sharp breath, looking horrified.

"You didn't! You didn't call out for him!!"

"I almost didn't because you'd filled my head with lies of how awful he was, how terrible all of the gods were! I almost died *because of you*! But yes, I did, I called out to him and he came to me. He saved my life, mother. More than fucking once."

"No..." she whispered. "Y-you've been there? With him? With... the others?" Was she worried that Beck knew the truth? She paled even further. Oh yes, she was worried.

"Yes, I have. I've met them all. Including my *father*," Beck spit, sneering as the lie rolled off of her tongue, making it plain that she knew it was complete bullshit.

"I...I..." Beck held up a hand to halt her mother's stammering.

"I want the truth. I want the entire story and so help me if you even think of lying to me again..."

She let her power flare, letting the shadowed beast illusions burst forth beside her. Her mother tumbled backwards, nearly toppling over her lounge. She gripped the edge and slowly lowered herself down.

"Oh gods," her mother whispered raising a shaking hand to her mouth. Her eyes were wide with real fear and Beck couldn't deny she got a shot of satisfaction from that fact. She let the illusions fall away and crossed her arms.

"I already know the real reason that you were banished and I know that you weren't even close to pregnant with me at the time. I want to know why you lied. I want to know why you blamed me and seemed to hate me. I want to know who my real father is. I want...I just want the truth about everything, mother. Finally. For once. I need the truth."

Adamantia wrung her hands in her lap and bit her lip.

"Now," Beck grated, trying desperately to keep her temper in check. She knew her mother was troubled, and she tried to keep that in mind, but it was hard. Really fucking hard. This woman had lied to her for her entire life, had treated her like garbage, made her grow up too fast, grow up terrified, grow up without an ounce of love. Troubled or not, it was fucking *wrong*.

Adamantia summoned more wine and drained an entire glass before wiping her mouth and taking a deep breath.

"I lied because I wanted you to hate them as much as I did. I might not have been banished for the reasons I told you, but it was still a grave mistake and I needed you to feel the same hatred I did for them. I...I am sorry I was never a good mother to you, Beckham. I intended to be at first, and I truly did try but...it was too much. I knew that I had to stay with you though, I had to protect you as much as I could because I knew he would find out one day, that he would come for you."

A cold foreboding crept up Beck's spine.

"Who?"

Adamantia gave her a bleak look.

"Your father, just like I always said. Your...your *real* father," Adamantia said softly.

"Who is he?"

Her mother swallowed hard and closed her eyes. Beck barely heard the whispered name, her blood freezing in her veins as the words floated across the space between them:

"Balthazar. The God of Nightmares."

THIRTY-ONE

Poseidon was uneasy as he waited for Beck to return. He couldn't pinpoint exactly why. He wasn't worried about Adamantia trying to hurt Beck, and though he knew this wouldn't be easy for her, he wasn't worried about how Beck would handle learning the truth. She was strong, both mentally and physically, so he had every faith in his wife being alright, but something was putting him on edge. His instincts were firing, telling him that something was coming. Was Beck in danger? Emmie assured him that wherever Beck's mother had been hiding was completely safe, but what if the demons found her?

What if...Balthazar did? Gods, did he really believe the God of Nightmares was alive and well? And that he was searching for Beck? Poseidon thought back to his interrogation with the halfling and shuddered. He might believe it.

He groaned and paced in the throne room, unable to quell the feeling. He was just about to demand that Emmie take him to Beck when Cyril entered the room. He hastened forward, urgency and tension clear in every step.

"Sir, we have news. Some of our sentinels on the Mortal Plane have found the leader of the group supposedly serving Balthazar. He's the one who put the bounty out on Beck." Rage spiked through Poseidon. Rage and purpose. He *needed* to act, to protect what was his, the bond between him and Beck absolutely demanding it.

"Where?"

Power began to build within his chest, ready to explode.

Cyril rattled off a location as Si strapped on leather gauntlets and slid numerous weapons into holsters and hidden pockets.

"Notify me the moment Beck returns," Si said and Cyril nodded.

"And where are you running off to looking like you're expecting a hell of a brawl?" Dean asked as he casually strolled into the room. Poseidon glanced his way and smiled despite the unease and battle-cold starting to seep into his bones. It was nice having his friend back, his brother in arms and by choice, if not by blood.

"It's still so weird seeing you as a man," Si said as he slid his trident into the sheath across his back. "I kind of miss your fuzzy wittle ears though."

"Well, they aren't fuzzy, but you can still scratch behind these if you'd like," he responded with a grin and a wink. Si snorted and tilted his head as he studied the man. He seemed both blissfully content and utterly distraught at the same time, though he was trying his best to hide the latter. Was it just the transition back to his normal life? That had to be quite a bit to process, but...no, it seemed like more. Poseidon would delve into that over some drinks soon.

"So?" Dean drawled, gesturing to the trident and weaponry adorning Si's body.

Si let out a long breath.

"I'm going to tangle with a demon who has been hunting my wife and may or may not be working for the God of Nightmares who may or may not be alive after all and who may or may not be the one responsible for the downfall of Pandora's Box."

"Bloody hell," Dean breathed, eyes wide. "Well, sounds like a party. I'm in."

"No, you just got back, you shouldn't—"

"Save your protests. I've been stuck on the sidelines for centuries while my friends fought battle after battle without me. Now, I can finally get back in the game. *Let me.*"

He walked over and started swiping weapons from Si's stash on the table. Poseidon shook his head but smiled, slapping Dean on the shoulder and giving it a grateful squeeze. He did feel better with Dean there to have his back in this. He knew he could handle a demon or twelve without much trouble, but it was tricky when fighting in the Mortal Plane and, as much as he hated it, he had to be prepared for the possibility that Balthazar really was there and could show his face. Even weakened, the Dark One would be a hell of an opponent.

Should I call my brothers? Poseidon didn't want to bring them all into the fray when it wasn't necessary, so he decided against it. If Balthazar showed or things got dicey, he would call them and they could be there in seconds.

"You sure you remember how to fight? Without scratching and biting I mean?"

"Don't knock scratching and biting, my friend. But—" Dean lifted a dagger and without taking his eyes off of Si, tossed it with an effortless flick of his wrist. It flew across the room with blinding speed, hitting in the dead center of the eyeball of a mermaid statue fifty yards away. "I think I still got it." His lips curled into a cocky smirk and he waggled his eyebrows.

"Alright, alright," Si said, holding his palms up in surrender. "I'd love to have you by my side again, brother."

"Then let's go kick ass and take names as Lucas says." He smiled but a bit of sadness flashed in his gray eyes. It was gone a moment later. *Ok, we definitely need to have a chat.*

They phased to the location that Cyril had provided, and Poseidon kept them cloaked in shadow as they surveyed the area. It was a small clearing surrounded on three sides by thick, towering trees, and a jagged rockface closing in the far end. Si craned his head upward and realized the rockface was actually the side of a mountain. Small paths ran up the sides, several caves dotting the stone here and there.

From behind a large boulder, a towering Rathos demon appeared. It was a different one than Si had seen in the parking lot that first day with Beck and he wondered if the first one had been... demoted when Beck hadn't turned up. *Demoted to a headless pile of limbs most likely.*

This one was every bit of seven feet tall with black horns flaring out from temples. His skin was a deep crimson and black spikes protruded from his shoulders, elbows, and Poseidon would assume down his spine. He didn't have wings, like Jeff, Hades' most trusted guard, but Si didn't think he would be any less lethal. The demon strolled forward until he reached the center of the clearing.

"Poseidon, we've been waiting for you!" he said in a booming voice, extending his arms to the side in greeting. He smiled, revealing red, glinting fangs. Si stiffened, not liking that the demon was aware of his presence even while cloaked, that sense of unease tripling in his gut. *How could they have sensed my arrival?* Even so, he let the shadows fall away and strolled forward, Dean at his side.

"Well, I'm sorry to have kept you waiting, but I am in fairly high demand," Si said with a smirk. He let his power rise, crackling in the air around them. The demon narrowed his eyes as he felt it but didn't react otherwise.

"How handy, you've brought your own messenger."

Dean arched a blonde brow and rested his hand on the hilt of the sword at his hip.

"And what message am I supposed to be delivering? If it's a message to your mom letting her know how well-endowed I am, trust me, she already knows." He threw the demon a wink and it growled in response.

Si's lips curled upwards but a moment later, darkness descended all around them. Something slammed into him so forcefully he flew across the clearing and hit the rock hard enough to send splinters cracking through the stone. Bones snapped and the air was torn from his lungs.

"Si!" Dean yelled, but he was tossed backwards into a tree. He slumped to the ground in a heap and Si strained against the dark spots in his vision to see if his friend was alright. He pushed himself to his feet, gritting his teeth as bones mended and wounds began to knit themselves back together. He quickly grabbed his trident and prepared to fight. He knew without a doubt that the demon didn't have power like this. As much as he'd denied it, he could do so no longer: Balthazar lived.

"Show yourself, Balthazar!" Si bellowed, his skin beginning to spark with blue electricity as his power surged.

"Since you asked so nicely," a deep, gravelly voice echoed around the clearing. The darkness began to swirl like a cyclone and out of the middle of it, the god emerged. He stood almost seven feet tall and though his build looked a bit rangy at the moment, Si knew just how large and muscled he would be when he was back to his full power. His skin was pale, his eyes and hair both black as pitch, and he wore thick, gray metal bands on both of his biceps. Darkness pulsed from him, making Si's skin crawl.

"You're making this far too easy. I thought I'd have to hunt..." Si trailed off when the Dark One waived his hand to part the swirling darkness once more and reveal...Beck.

No. Gods no.

She was on her knees, blood coating her chest and splattered in her hair.

"Beck!" Poseidon roared, phasing towards her, but he was thrown back as if he'd hit an invisible wall.

"Poseidon!" she whimpered. "Please..." she begged before she threw her head back and screamed in agony. Fresh blood spilled as her chest was torn open once more by an invisible weapon.

"Beck! Stop this, Balthazar!" He sprinted forward, desperate to reach his bride, his reason for living. Again, he was stopped by an invisible barrier and tossed backwards, skidding through the dirt. He dimly heard Dean yelling his name but he couldn't focus on anything but the anguish in Beck's eyes, the blood-curdling screams tearing free from her throat again and again as fresh wounds appeared and her precious blood flowed like a river.

"I knew I shouldn't have wasted my love on you," she sobbed. His heart lurched. She thought her love was wasted on him? "This is your fault. All of it. You did this to me. You let this happen!"

Si flung his power at Balthazar, over and over, but every time he tried, it...failed him. *What the fuck?* Had the bastard somehow found a way to negate Poseidon's powers? His chest seemed to splinter as Beck screamed again and he could do nothing to stop it. He fell to his knees as he watched her back bow in agony with every new wound, watched the tears stream down her face. Blood bubbled over her lips and dripped down her chin. She was healing, but not quickly enough. A distant part of his mind reminded him that she was only a demigoddess. Her healing wouldn't be like his own. She could even potentially *die* from these wounds, depending on what was making them. Dread filled him and tears burned his eyes.

"Si!" Dean cried again from what seemed like far, far away. "Poseidon, snap the fuck out of it! Fight, gods damn it!"

He was trying to fight! How could Dean not see that? He was trying to kill the bastard that was torturing his wife but he was failing. He was failing her over and over. *Deep down, you knew you would. You knew you couldn't give her what she needed, be who she deserved.* The thoughts floated through his mind and he clutched his head in his hands. He dug his fingers in, wanting to rip the whispers away. Because they were right.

She's going to die because of you. Watch the life leave her eyes...

"No!!" Si roared again, so loudly that the trees shook around him and his throat burned with impotent rage. She met his gaze and her eyes were filled with red. The vessels had burst and even her tears were now tinged crimson, making it look like she was crying blood.

"Poseidon?..." she whispered, more blood pouring over her chin. Before he could say a word, a sickening crack echoed around him, filling the darkness, followed by a tearing sound, as her head was wrenched free from her body. Both thumped to the ground and blood began to flow like the tide, soaking the ground.

He couldn't move, couldn't breathe, couldn't process what he'd just seen. No. No, this couldn't be real. He stared at the scene before him, confused.

Her...head.

Her...blood.

Gods, it can't be real.

Finally, his stupor broke and he threw his head back, bellowing as agony infused every cell in his body. He screamed her name over and over. He heard a deep, gruff chuckle seeming to come from all around him, but he didn't care. Rage and despair warred within him, but he could do nothing about either.

He stayed on his knees and stared at his dead wife, knowing that his life was over.

DEAN WATCHED Poseidon scream in utter agony while he battled a horde of demons on his own. He didn't know what the God of the Sea was seeing, but he could guess. Only one thing could make him look that destroyed, could make him scream like that. He had to be seeing Beck. Dean's chest ached for Poseidon, trying to imagine what he would think or feel if he were seeing either of the people he loved tortured before him. Real or otherwise, he'd lose his mind.

Dean knew that the God of Nightmares had tried to use his power on the brothers in the past but they'd been too strong to stay under his thrall for long. So, why wasn't Si throwing him off now? Balthazar was obviously weakened, so why...?

Realization struck Dean like a blade, sharp and cold: the difference was that now Si *truly* feared something enough that Balthazar held the power. He feared losing Beck.

Dean clenched his teeth and pried his gaze away from Si just as two more Lackey Demons charged him. He parried and spun, grabbing one's neck and using him as a shield, driving his sword into the other's gut. He took the shield's head a moment later, muttering a quick "thanks, mate," and prepared for the next attack. He had slayed fourteen already, but they kept coming.

"Fuck me, did you get these guys on clearance or what?" he yelled at Balthazar before gritting his teeth in pain as a ball of fire grazed his arm. Not all Lackies could shoot fire, but a handful could and those bastards were harder to take out. He tossed a dagger and it hit the fire-shooter straight in the eye. It screamed and fell, another immediately taking his place. Another agonized bellow filled the air.

"Gods damn it, Si! Snap the fuck out of it!! It's a nightmare! It isn't real!!"

Dean continued to fight, trying to make his way through the fray. He was technically winning—numerous demons lay dead on the ground on him and he was still standing—but he wasn't coming out of it unscathed. He had too many injuries to count, blood running down his right arm in thick rivulets and his shirt soaked with it. None of the wounds were fatal, but the pain was starting to make its way through the adrenaline and eventually the blood loss would make him pass out. His vision wavered but he forced the spots away.

Have to fight. Keep going.

He ran another demon through with his sword but the blade stuck in the bone. He yanked and yanked, raising a booted foot to the thing's shoulder to push him off.

"Oh bloody hell..." he cursed as he spied another demon approaching, hell bent on taking advantage. It slashed Dean across the chest with his claws before he could duck away. "Fuck!" Blinding pain laced through him and his vision waved for a quick moment before he shook himself. Anger flared and he managed to yank his blade free at last. He beheaded both demons and swayed on his feet. He wiped blood, sweat, and dirt off of his face with his forearm.

"Si! Come on!" Dean pleaded, eyeing the next wave of Lackies headed his way. He'd wanted off the bench, but this was ridiculous.

He'd always loved battle, relished the thrill of it, the way his blood sang as he fought. He'd always fought with absolute abandon, ready and willing to fall on the battlefield like the warrior he was.

But now...well, he was by no means ready, and he sure as fuck wasn't willing. He had good reasons to make it back alive now. *Can't leave them. Not yet.* He engaged three more demons with a renewed strength. He had things to sort out and once he made it through this, he had conversations to have. *Big fucking conversations.*

Dean tore through the demons, fighting like a man on a mission. He was a man on a fucking mission. He pictured Emmie and Dean in his mind, and they gave him all the strength he needed. He would make it back to them. There was no question. He would not entertain any other possibility. He tried again to reach Si.

"Come on, Si. You've got to fight back! She's not here. She's safe!"

"You'll never reach him," Balthazar said from across the clearing. The god wasn't engaging Dean directly. Instead he was just standing on a small rock formation observing everything. *Why* isn't *he fighting me?* Dean wondered as he felled two more demons, using their bodies to knock others back. *He could easily take me out...*

In his moments of reprieve, he narrowed his eyes at the god. His already pale skin had turned almost pallid, and sweat beaded his brow and upper lip. He was struggling to maintain his hold on Poseidon, to keep his power flowing. Dean looked around and realized that even the darkness that had descended upon the clearing was fading, the light slowly returning. The bastard was weakening more by the second. It was obvious he wasn't at his full strength to begin with, but he must have used all the juice he had on his little stunt with Poseidon. Sure, Si's pain would strengthen him, but it would take time.

"I know your secret, Sandman," Dean said with a sinister grin. "You're running out of mojo. He'll throw off your nightmare soon enough, and then you're in big, *big* trouble." The god glared at him, his black eyes shifting to blood red in his anger, but his jaw ticked and Dean knew he had him. *He knows I'm right.*

"Tell the girl I want what she has. Tell her to stop running. That is the only way to save her precious Poseidon now." *Stop running? What the hell he is talking about?* But before Dean could ask any follow up questions, he was suddenly back in the throne room in Aqueous, tumbling across the stone floor. He rolled over and over before finally stopping with a thud. He groaned as pain flared, his numerous injuries all roaring to the forefront at once. He lay there, panting for long moments before he found the strength to push himself up to his knees. Half a heartbeat later he thought better of that and landed firmly on his ass.

Emmie appeared with a towels, water, and a flask. She looked drawn, lines of strain bracketing her mouth, worry clear in her beautiful eyes.

"Are you alright?" she asked quietly.

"I'm fine. I'm assuming you already know what happened?" She pressed her lips into a thin line but nodded. He knew that certain things *had* to happen in order for the right future to come to pass, but it didn't mean he had to like it. He hissed in a sharp breath as she wiped blood away from a large gash in his side. "Will he be alright?"

"I...hope so. I'm seeing too many versions. It all depends on her."

Dean exhaled roughly and pushed himself to his feet, swaying slightly before Emmie reached out to steady him. The doors flew open and Lucas stormed in. His eyes went wide as he took in Dean's appearance and then fury flared.

"What the fuck happened?" he demanded.

"Big fight. Lots of stabby stabby. I won—mostly." Dean attempted a smile but it turned into a grimace as another wave of pain hit him. Luke rushed forward and he and Emmie steadied Dean long enough for her to phase them to Emmie's room. Dean sighed. Being within its walls made some of the tension in his chest fade.

They maneuvered him onto the bed and he collapsed with as much grace as a chimera on ice skates, crying out as pain flared once more, the poison burning through his veins. Hot blood gushed from the gaping hole in his side and he gnashed his teeth.

"Need to...find Beck..." His vision was wavering, dark spots starting to appear. He'd lost far too much blood and he was going to pass out soon, but Si was still in the grip of that prick. Dean needed to give Beck the strange message. He didn't understand it, but he knew without a doubt that the bastard had spoken true: Beck was Si's only hope. She was full on Obiwan here.

"You need to rest and heal, you stupid fuck," Lucas grated as he sat on the edge of the bed beside Dean's legs. He clenched his jaw and settled a hand on Dean's ankle, squeezing gently.

"Has anyone...ever told you...how cute you are when you're...worried, pup?" Dead huffed out between labored breaths. Lucas looked torn between wanting to laugh and wanting to punch his lights out.

"I thought I was cute all the time?" Lucas said with a half smile.

"You got me there," Dean said before a coughing fit seized him, blood spewing from his mouth.

"Gods, Emmie do something!" Luke yelled, leaping to his feet and frantically trying to help somehow. The coughing fit subsided and Dean collapsed back onto the pillows.

"Bloody hell, been a while since I've had proper battle wounds. Fuck this hurts," he laughed before wincing.

"I'll deliver the message," Emmie said in a soft voice, gently stroking Dean's cheek. "Rest now."

He looked between her and Lucas, fighting off the darkness trying to pull him down.

"When I wake up, we're having a long fucking chat." He gave them what he hoped was a stern look, but he wasn't sure if he quite pulled it off or not. A heartbeat later, he was passed out cold.

THIRTY-TWO

Beck couldn't breathe. This couldn't be real. It couldn't be true. *Anyone but him.*

"What did you say?"

"It's true," her mother said quietly. "I'm...I'm sorry."

"But...how the fuck did that even happen?" Beck fell heavily into the chair beside the lounge. She was numb but she had to know every detail, she had to understand how this was possible. Something in her chest gave a strong lurch and she rubbed the heel of her hand against her sternum. Something felt...wrong. *Probably just the absolute mindfuck my mom just threw at me.* She pushed the feeling away and waited.

Her mother took a deep breath and then, to Beck's surprise, she began speaking.

"I've always had the gift of seeking out power. I can sense it, it speaks to me, it...*calls* to me," she said, that dreamy look in her eyes again. "When I was sent to the Mortal Plane, I wandered a bit aimlessly for nearly three centuries, trying to adjust to life among those lowly creatures. Then finally, one day, I felt it. Power pulsing like a beacon in the night. It was faint at first, but I could tell the power was great...perhaps a little dark, but it had been so long since I'd felt anything like it. I *craved* it. I was a slave to it, had no choice but to follow its call. It led me deep into a mountain range near the ocean. He had guards outside, but they were no match for my illusions. It was before my power began to wane, you see," she sniffed.

"The power pulled me further into the caves, through a labyrinth of tunnels. Eventually, I came to a huge cavern with soaring stone ceilings, a large opening in the middle letting starlight filter inside. He was there, leaning against a hearth carved into the wall. He was staring at the fire and though I could tell that he was weakened, his body was still...impressive." Her eyes flickered for a brief moment, darkening with...desire? *Oh ew.* Beck waved her hand in front of her in a circular motion, begging her mother silently to move on.

"His power was still so strong, so alluring. It was like a drug to me. I ignored the darkness I felt, only focusing on how much the power sang to me. Without even turning, he said, 'why have you come here, goddess? You are one of theirs...' He turned to face me, studying me with unsettling pitch-black eyes. 'But you have darkness in you,' he added. And he *smiled* at me, as if my darkness brought him joy. He was the first—the only—to see my...flaws," Beck arched a brow at that, but let it go, "as something *positive*. He offered me wine and that was that. I stayed with him for a time, basking in the power that I'd been missing so badly. I felt like a queen again, a powerful, dark god at my side. He asked me questions about myself and about the rest of the gods, always wanting to talk. I was flattered, thinking at the time that he was simply enthralled with me, as most men were."

Beck clenched her jaw in an effort not to respond or, frankly, laugh out loud. Her mother was beautiful, to be sure, but any man would be able to smell her crazy from a mile away.

Her mother took another long drink of wine, turning a bit more somber. "He began to lose interest right around the time I found out that I was pregnant. I was desperate to hold onto him, to keep him and his power in my grasp. I...I confessed to something that I'd done, something that I knew he would be very, *very* interested in. But the second the words had left my mouth, I realized the mistake that I'd made. It was clear to me then that he'd only ever been interested in information to help him regain his power and destroy the gods. And I understood then if he regained power, he would destroy everything. Believe it or not, I was worried for you, for my unborn child. I think… I think it was the only thing that made it possible for me to see past the power and be able to leave."

"What did you confess?"

"Well, you see…" She swallowed hard, clearly uncomfortable with what she was about to say. "Before I was banished, I stumbled upon something very powerful. Again, it *called* to me, the power reaching out to me and practically begging for me to take it."

"What did you take, mother?" Beck barked, tired of the bullshit. She needed to know and she needed to know now. That feeling from before had doubled, unease turning to dread. It settled deep in her bones, her instincts flaring and that voice screaming *wrong, wrong, wrong* inside her mind. Something was happening and she needed to find Si, but she needed to know the answers to all of her questions first. She'd waited too long for this, had to know the truth about everything.

"I took…I took a key," Adamantia whispered.

"Key?" Beck repeated, confused.

"*The* key. The key to the prison where the rest of the Dark Ones are held."

Beck sprung to her feet. "Oh my gods! You gave him the key?!"

"No! No, of course not! He wanted it and I promised him that I'd retrieve it from where I'd hidden it away and return to him, but instead I fled. I know that I'm not quite…right, Beckham, but I'm not evil and I'm not stupid. I know what it would mean for him to have that key, what it would mean if they were released. I don't love the Mortal Plane by any stretch of the imagination, but I don't want it destroyed."

"Then where is it? The walls are failing at the Box. The key will soon be the only thing standing between them and the end of the world as we know it, *all* the worlds."

"Failing?" Her mother paled, shaking her head back and forth rapidly. "No, that isn't possible. Pandora—"

"Is dying," Beck interrupted, temper flaring and alarm bells going off left and right inside her mind. Something was very, *very* wrong and her need to go to Si was nearly overwhelming. *But I need to know.* "Where is the fucking key, mother?"

"It's...it's your medallion. An enchantress hid the key in the necklace and bound it to you and your power."

Beck's hand flew to the medallion as it had thousands of times over her life. It had always been a calming gesture to her. She'd always felt comforted and safe because of it. And now her mother was telling her that it was actually quite possibly the most powerful item in the universe?

"But you said this was a *protective* charm. You said it would keep me *safe*. That's why I couldn't ever take it off or give it to anyone."

"Well, that's somewhat true. The key cannot be taken from you by any means, physical or mystical. It can only be given willingly. It was the only way to ensure that it was never parted from you, and so I had to make sure you didn't take those terms lightly."

"What the fuck is wrong with you?!" Beck screamed, running her hands through her hair. "You used me as a living safety deposit box. Did you not think that it would put a giant bullseye on my back? Did you think he would just *forget* that you had the key? That he would just let it go?! Gods, mother!"

"I'm sorry. Truly, I am. But at the time, it was the best idea I could come up with. My power was waning more with each year, but in order for it to remain hidden, the key had to be tied to someone whose power was strong. I knew yours would be with...with him as your father."

Beck felt like she might be sick. A Dark One was her father. The God of fucking Nightmares. She sucked in a sharp breath. *Nightmares.* The dark dreams that had plagued her almost all of her life.

The shadowed figure always chasing her. Was that...*him*? Her mother had managed to keep them hidden from him in the physical world, but had he somehow found Beck in the dream one?

"Did he know about me?" Beck asked. Her mother pressed her lips together and that was all the answer she needed. "Oh my gods," Beck whispered as she began to pace again, rubbing her chest. Something was screaming inside her and sweat was beading on her forehead and neck. *Have to go. Have to stay. Need answers.* She squeezed her eyes shut.

"How did he never find us?"

"There was a bit of protection woven into the medallion with the key, so I didn't *completely* lie about that. It helped cloak the power from him—the key's and your own. And this realm provided additional protection." Beck frowned at her mother. She gestured around and explained, "Emmie put a protection on me and every time she brought me here, it...recharged the wards so to speak. It's why I constantly made the trips here." Beck gave her a stern look and her mother held up her hands. "Ok, ok, so it was only part of the reason. This place allowed me to feel like a goddess again. I needed that. You can't understand what it was like, to go from being who I was to... what I became. I needed to feel like I was important again. As the years went on, I needed it more and more. I'm...I'm sorry that I left you alone so much, that I treated you so badly."

"Why did you? I used to think it was because you blamed me for the banishment, but that had nothing to do with me."

Her mother let out a long exhale, suddenly looking tired.

"Part of it was because you were a constant reminder. Of him, of how stupid I'd been, of how...hurt I was when I realized that he never actually cared about me at all. I fancied myself in love with him after all, despite his darkness, and he just wanted to use me. It's not something someone like me likes to remember. And another part—a part I'm not proud of—was that I knew how powerful you'd be one day. I was...jealous of it. My power had been taken, my home, my immortality. *Everything.*"

"You brought that upon yourself," Beck spit.

"I...know," she finally said, quietly. "I don't know why I am the way I am. Sometimes, I can almost step out of myself and see how crazy I seem, how ridiculous and wrong, but I can't stay there. I always get pulled back in and suddenly everything makes sense again, my conviction of the fact that I should be a queen, the fact that I was destined for greatness and power." She shook her head, clearly frustrated with herself and her thoughts. "I can't explain it properly. Just know that I don't mean to be this way. I didn't mean to be such a terrible mother. I...did the best I could."

Beck knew she should feel sympathy for her mother, should maybe feel somewhat content that she finally had answers and that her mother at least realized how fucked up she was. That should be something, right? But she couldn't find it inside her. At least not today. Today she was filled with fury and unease and tension.

She reached for the medallion but yanked her hand away before she touched it. She wanted nothing to do with it anymore. She needed to get it back to Zeus immediately and let him be in charge of the damned thing from now on. Maybe if she no longer had the key, then Balthazar would stop searching for her. He couldn't have any interest in her merely because she was his daughter...could he? No, surely dark gods didn't have those kinds of feelings.

"I just always knew that I was meant to be a queen, don't you understand, Beck? It was my destiny."

Beck shook her head at Adamantia, irritation flaring once more. She'd been so preoccupied with this delusional destiny to be a queen, that she'd all but damned her only daughter. *Fuck her. Hit her where it hurts most.*

"You'll never be a queen, mother," Beck said coldly. "You were never destined to be...but *I* was."

Her mother stilled. "What did you say?"

Beck pulled herself to her full height and thrust her shoulders back. "I am the queen of Aqueous."

Just as she'd suspected, Adamantia's eyes flared with a jealousy so intense it almost made Beck flinch.

"You…you *married Poseidon*? How…but…"

She turned and lashed out with a screech, sending the goblet and carafe flying across the temple. She stood and began to pace, pulling at her hair. "This isn't fair! It should be me!"

Beck watched in horror and pity as her mother began to unravel before her eyes. She continued to pace and rant, muttering nonsense. Beck realized then that her mother was truly unwell, and despite everything, she felt…at peace. She was still pissed as hell of course, and she would unpack all of this metric ton of shit her mother had just dumped on her, but Beck no longer felt that gnawing pain inside, the one she'd had all her life. The pain that came from not understanding what she'd done to make her mother hate her so much, the pain that had made her feel so undeserving for so much of her life. It was gone now. She felt no more need to look back. She only wanted to look forward, to face whatever future may come for her with Poseidon beside her. Always.

Her mother stopped pacing and turned to Beck in a flash, eyes going alight with excitement.

"You could remove my banishment then! At least from Aqueous. I can come live there with you, I can be back among my own people, where I belong!"

Beck took a step backward, shaking her head. "No, mother, I don't think—"

Emmie appeared, looking tired and strained, her face pinched with worry. Dread settled more firmly in Beck's stomach. "What's wrong?" she demanded.

"Beckham, please…"

"Shut the fuck up, Adamantia!" A streak of ice blue lighting soared from Beck's hand, striking just beside her mother. She shrieked and looked at Beck with wide, terror-filled eyes. *Whoa.* Si's power? She'd never tried to harness it or unleash it before. *Think about it later.* Beck turned back to Emmie. "Tell me."

"It's Si, he's...he's been taken."

"What!?" Beck whispered, her breath getting caught in her throat. Her heart began to beat wildly and her ears began to ring.

"Balthazar. He has him." Adamantia sucked in a startled breath and Beck froze in place, unable to move or think or breathe. "He says the only way to save Poseidon is for you to stop running." Beck's brow furrowed, her thoughts spinning out of control. Stop running?

"The God of *Nightmares* told you to stop running," Emmie pressed, urging Beck to put the pieces together and seeming pained as she did, but Beck's mind was whirling too quickly. Nothing made sense. All she could think about was Si. That feeling of unease this whole time had been because he'd been in danger and she'd ignored it. All because she had to get to the bottom of the endless pile of lies her mother had spouted. *My fault, my fault, my fault.* She cast her mother a killing look and felt Si's shared power rise in her again, blue sparks dancing along her finger tips. She ground her teeth, keeping the power from unleashing and turned away from her mother. She needed to focus.

"Think, Beck, think," she muttered to herself as she paced. Stop running. The God of Nightmares. Nightmares. She gasped and stopped in her tracks. *Her* nightmares. The shadowy figure she'd always fled from, it really had been her father all this time, trying to get to her. *Stop running.* Beck swallowed hard as realization settled heavy on her shoulders: she'd always fled, but now, she had to let him catch her.

Could she do that? Flashes of Si bombarded her. His smile, his laugh, the way he touched her and kissed her and *cherished* her; the way she felt whole and wanted and loved for the first time in her life with him; the way he'd saved her, in more ways than one; the way she couldn't even put into words how much she loved him, more than anything, more than her own life.

So, yes, she could. For him, she would do anything.

"You," she spit at her mother, shaking her head. "I'll deal with you later. Stay here." She turned back to the oracle and fear made it hard for her to speak. She swallowed hard. Swallowed again. Finally, she managed to say, "Emmie, I-I need you to make me sleep."

Emmie nodded and stepped forward. In a soft voice she said, "He wants the key." Beck's eyes flared wide. She couldn't possibly give that monster the key. But...she couldn't let Si die either. It was an utter impossibility. If Beck could save him, she would, no questions asked. Even if it damned the entire world. *Because he's* my *entire world...*

"What...what do I do?" she asked in small voice, her eyes filling with tears.

Emmie took a deep breath and her eyes went distant for a moment. *Seeing the future?* She winced and Beck wondered what she was seeing. She eventually focused back on Beck's face and told her sternly, "You do *whatever it takes* to bring him back."

Before Beck could say anything else, Emmie booped her on the nose and she immediately fell into a deep sleep.

THIRTY-THREE

Beck's eyes flew open to reveal an all too familiar corridor. She knew she was dreaming and yet she felt cold sweat beading on her forehead. Understanding that this was all real, on some level at least, sent icy fear skittering along her spine, making it nearly impossible for her to think or move. She took a few deep, settling breaths, and somehow, she stood on shaking legs. She began to walk the eerie hallway, waiting for that dark, prickling feeling that always heralded his arrival.

She trailed her fingers down the stone wall and over the dark, wooden doors. Knowing what she did now, she was able to see and feel new details. At each door, she could see things if she opened her mind, get flashes of the nightmare within without actually entering it and she got the strange feeling that she could harness them somehow, to...bring them to life? She thought back to when Calypso had seen the hydraspider, and Skylar had seen the clown. Maybe she truly could bring someone's nightmares, and therefore fears, into reality. *Whoa.* Though this power was dark and tainted, she had to admit that it was...impressive.

She closed her eyes and swallowed hard when she felt him. Her every instinct was demanding that she run, her dream body tensing to do just that, but she gritted her teeth and forced herself to remain in place. After a heartbeat, she turned to face him.

As always, the tall, shadowy figure stood just down the hallway. He paused this time, tilting his cloaked head.

"You've come," he rasped. His voice was deep and gravelly and made the hairs on the back of her neck stand on end.

"Where is he?" she demanded, trying to keep her voice from shaking. She failed miserably.

"He's alive. For now," Balthazar added, and even in the shadows she could see his lips curling back to reveal a cruel smile. He moved forward and Beck fought every instinct yelling at her to run. She always had in the past, had fled from him every time as he pursued, hiding in the terrifying rooms along the hallway. Now, she had to stay. *Stop running.* Her chest rose and fell in quick bursts as he came closer and closer. She locked her muscles into place and she shook, from the effort to stay still or from fear, she wasn't sure.

As he neared, she craned her head up...and up. He was every bit of six and half feet tall, maybe more. He wasn't as large and muscular as any of the brothers, but Beck got the feeling he *could* be. He looked as if he had the build for it, but like he was sick or something. He was just outside the ring of low light. *I'm about to see my father for the first time.* She held her breath as he took that last small step.

He pushed the hood back to reveal jet black hair that brushed his shoulders, straight as a pin and standing stark against his pale skin. His eyes were pitch black, his jaw square, his nose broad. He wore a thick metal band on each of his biceps and dark runes covered his arms.

"How did you find me?" she asked, begging her voice to sound stronger. *He needs to think I'm strong. I need to be strong.*

"You're my blood," he said, as if that explained everything. "Your mother may have hidden you in the physical world, but there is no hiding you here." He gestured to the walls around them. "You share my power, my ability to walk through dreams. We're connected through this world."

She frowned. Walk through dreams? As in...*other people's* dreams? Suddenly everything made perfect sense, like a spotlight illuminating the answer she'd been searching for all her life. All the rooms in this hallway, all the strange nightmares that she couldn't understand or explain, terrors that she herself didn't recall having but had dreamed about. She had been in the middle of *others people's* nightmares, not her own. *Holy shit.*

He tilted his head as he studied her again, making her feel like she was an insect beneath a microscope.

"I wonder what other gifts of mine you share." What else could he do? What else could *she* do? She pushed the thought away. She had far more important things to focus on right now. Reminded of why she was here, fury clawed within her chest.

"I want my husband back, you prick," she spit.

"Ah, yes. Your *husband*. Felicitations and all that," he said, amusement in his tone. "I'll take you to him."

He reached out a hand and she eyed it like a viper, expecting it to strike out at any moment. He left it there in the air between them, waiting for her to accept his invitation. She knew she had no choice, so she forced herself to reach out and grasp his hand. His black eyes glinted with triumph and his lips curled upward.

"At last," he rasped before a blistering cold speared her heart and spread through her entire body. She gasped in shock and pain, and an intense pressure began to push in from all around her. A few heartbeats later, she was in some kind of cave, the pressure and cold gone. Balthazar released her and strolled to a free-standing bar across the space as she doubled over and sucked in ragged breaths.

"Bringing the physical body through the dream world is a bit... jarring at first. You'll get used to it."

She forced herself upward and looked around. It was in fact a cave, but it was absolutely massive and oddly...homey. The floor was packed earth and the walls were jagged stone, but it was furnished with plush leather couches and rich wooden furniture. Large rugs lay in various spots around the area, many of them looking to be made of animal hides or furs. It was all a bit too far on the rugged side of style for her liking, but she could see the appeal. It was very masculine-hunting-lodge-esque. A flash of understanding: this is where her mother had met him. *And ew, where I was...conceived.* She nearly vomited.

"Where is Poseidon?" she demanded, righting herself and pooling power within her. She had little hope that she could take him on, even in his weakened state, but she would sure as hell try if she had to.

Her father—*Gods, I will never be ok saying that*—peered at her over the rim of his glass before waving a hand. One of the walls began to move, the stone groaning as it slid to the side to reveal another chamber. Si was there, slumped on the floor and covered in blood.

"Si!" she screamed, rushing forward. She slid on her knees in the dirt beside him, trying not to cry. Dried blood covered his hands, chest, and cheeks. Her heart clenched when she realized there were tracks cutting through blood on his cheeks where tears had fallen. She tried to be gentle as she ran her hands over his face, his shoulders, his chest, but she was frantic.

"Si? Si, baby, look at me." Not even a hint of a response, no recognition save the tiniest flinch as if pain had laced through him. He stared at nothing, his beautiful golden eyes vacant. He was awake, but he wouldn't respond to her. She looked up and scowled at the dark god smirking a few feet away.

"What did you do to him?" she barked. Her power stirred and dark shadows sprang to life around her as that ice blue lightning sparked in her hands. Balthazar winged a dark brow upwards, studying the shadows.

"Interesting..." he murmured.

"Answer me!" she screeched.

"He used to be able to shrug off my influence somewhat easily.

Now, he's stuck inside his worst nightmare, reliving it over and over. And the strength it's giving me is *glorious*," he said, nearly moaning. Beck wanted to puke. "Fear and misery feed me, you see. Nourish me. The God of the Sea is presenting me with a certified feast of the choicest meats right now."

Beck glanced back down at Poseidon. What was he seeing? Eerily answering her unasked question, Balthazar said, "He's seeing you being tortured and killed before him, completely powerless to stop it. He's stuck in a loop, a never-ending nightmare. You cannot reach him."

Like hell I can't. This was her husband, the love of her immortal life, the best thing that had ever happened to her. She would save him. She *had* to. Her fear and panic began to fade to the background. Absolute rage burned in their place, unlike anything she'd ever known, could even possibly have imagined. This bastard—her *father*—had done this to Poseidon. Her proud, charismatic, brilliant, loving, Poseidon. Balthazar was using her to hurt the man she loved and that wouldn't fucking stand.

Beck let the rage build and build, let it overtake her. A strange wind began to blow around the cavern, making the torches and candles sputter. Darkness settled around them and Balthazar narrowed his eyes at her. The shadows began to swirl faster and faster, the wind picking up around them. She wasn't exactly sure what she was doing, but she let her power take control, doing as it wished. The shadows surged forward, blue lightning flashing within them.

They hit Balthazar in the chest and sent him stumbling backward a few steps. They'd somehow become solid enough to touch him, though they dissipated quickly. He gave her a look that was a cross between annoyance, intrigue, and surprise. He looked down to find several burn marks across the front of his sleeveless cloak from the lightning. More shadows flared to life, but he flicked his hand and they disappeared. Beck gritted her teeth, wanting to scream in frustration. Her power still seemed to be just out of her reach, though it was pulsing within her, seemingly begging to be used.

Just then she sensed something else calling to her: the sea. It was nearby, perhaps on the other side of this mountain. One of the many tunnels here probably led to a seaside cliff. The sea itself was calling to her, seeking to help her in some way. Before she could try to figure that new weirdness out, Balthazar sent her flying backwards into the wall.

She screamed out as her back slammed into the stone, bones splintering. She sucked in ragged breaths, tears welling from the pain. Invisible arms pinned against the wall, and she tried feebly to pull away to no avail. Suddenly, her father was before her.

"You have something I want, *daughter*," he sneered, eyes dropping to her medallion. "I'll admit that your mother was quite clever hiding it as she did, using your power and the enchantment to hide its call. But now that I am so close, I can see it all too well." His eyes slid closed as if in ecstasy. "I do believe I'll take this off your hands now."

He reached forward and snatched the medallion, but as he pulled, white hot pain laced through her and a scream tore free from her throat. He narrowed his eyes and pulled harder, making her shriek in agony, feeling as if her body were being sliced apart from the inside. Through it all, the necklace wouldn't give way. The back of her neck burned where the chain clung mystically to her skin and she felt blood running down her spine, but still, it wouldn't budge an inch, wouldn't snap.

"What is this!?" he roared in frustration, finally releasing it for a moment. Beck's head lulled as she tried to breathe. She'd never felt pain like this, didn't know she *could* feel pain like this. Tears streamed down her cheeks and she didn't know if she could take any more. She understood now that her mother had spoken true: the key could not be parted from her by any means until she offered it.

"I...have to...willingly give it to you...asshole," she bit out through sawing breaths.

"What kind of enchantment—" Balthazar cut off as Si bellowed in pure torment. Balthazar's lips curled as he watched. He gripped her cheeks roughly and forced her head upwards to stare at her husband.

Si rose to his knees, staring at something in front of him that only he could see.

"Beck! Beck, gods, please. Please! Don't leave me, baby. *Please.* I'm sorry, I'm so sorry," he said, voice hoarse and tears flowing.

"Si, I'm here. I'm right here!" she yelled, straining against Balthazar's hold. Hot tears streamed down her own cheeks from a whole different kid of pain now as she stood there helpless to save the man she loved.

"NO!" he suddenly bellowed. "BECK!!" His anguished cry reverberated against the stone, assaulting her ears and making her chest ache. She'd never seen anyone in so much pain, didn't know someone could feel so much sorrow.

"He's watching you die for the hundredth time, his heart being utterly pulverized yet again," Balthazar rasped into her ear. Having him so close made her skin crawl and she tried yet again to jerk her head away, but he merely dug his fingers into her skin harder, his nails leaving deep punctures. Blood tracked down her face, joining her tears.

"Oh, oh, here comes my favorite part!" he added with a delighted grin, vile glee clear in his voice.

As she watched in horror, Poseidon began to claw at his chest. *Oh gods.* With his incredible strength, he tore through the skin and muscle with ease, shattered his bones like they were egg shells, until he...

Beck retched as Si dug out his own heart, blood pouring over his fingers and down his chest. He screamed in agony, though she didn't think it was from the physical pain he was inflicting upon himself. When the detested organ was finally removed and destroyed in his hand, he slumped to the floor, motionless.

"Si!" she screamed again, panic rising. He couldn't die from this...

could he? No, no he couldn't! Gods could only be killed by a gods-blade or mystical fire...but the thought of him somehow surviving without a *heart* just didn't work in her mind.

"He'll heal and regain consciousness in a few minutes, not to worry. Sometimes it's the heart, sometimes it's the eyes. The best times are when it's the eyes and *then* the heart," Balthazar chuckled wickedly. "My power can't stop his healing, but it hinders it enough that we get a show each time."

Beck wanted to vomit. She wanted to murder her father. She wanted to save her husband. And yet, she could do nothing but watch.

"Every time, the strength he infuses me with is like the finest wine," Balthazar crooned. Again, he closed his eyes in bliss.

"Stop this," she sobbed. She'd given up on the idea that she could fight her father. Her power was too unreliable and he was a Dark One for fuck's sake. Even the rest of the gods couldn't take them down alone. She'd made him stumble for two whole seconds before he'd tossed her like a rag doll. She was nothing compared to him.

Emmie's words echoed in her mind: *You do* whatever *it takes to bring him back.*

Beck swallowed hard, preparing to say the words that she knew were so wrong, but the only way to save Si.

"I'll give you the key," she croaked. "Just stop this. Release him."

Balthazar studied her, those disconcerting black eyes boring into her until he finally released his hold. He stepped away and she tumbled to the ground like a sack of potatoes. Her wrist snapped like a twig beneath her as she landed hard on the earth and she bit her lip trying to keep from crying out from the pain. She spit blood and clenched her teeth. She'd heal soon enough. She needed to get to Si, he was all that mattered now. She half crawled-half stumbled to Poseidon's side, and to her surprise, Balthazar let her.

She eased Si's head into her lap, gently wiping away the tears and blood from his cheeks. She leaned down and kissed him.

"It'll be alright. I'm going to get us out of here," she whispered.

"I'll have my key now, daughter," Balthazar said in a cold voice from across the room.

"Don't call me that," she spit, jerking her head up to sneer at him. He merely smirked in return, as if amused. She rubbed her fingers over the medallion around her neck like she'd done a million times before. She took a deep breath and then made the decision to remove it, to willingly give it to the monster before her. The second she had the thought, her back bowed as searing hot power and pain surged through her chest. She threw her head back and screamed as she felt the key's power being torn free from her own. Blinding white light erupted from the medallion, making her squint.

A heartbeat later the pain was gone and an ornate skeleton key hovered in the air before her. She was still gasping for breath when Balthazar summoned the key to fly into his open palm, the brute lurching forward several steps as if he couldn't wait a moment more to hold it.

His eyes slid shut as he closed his fingers around it. To her horror, he began to strengthen before her eyes. Color returned to his skin and though he was still pale, it now reminded her more of her own creamy complexion, not the sickly pallor he'd had before. His muscles bulged and his cheeks filled out, not looking so gaunt. He was taking strength and power from the key somehow, using it to recharge his own.

As the changes continued in her father, changes were happening within her as well. Her own power soared, singing through her veins. She felt like she was on fire—in a good way. Like she could move a mountain or take on an entire army single handedly. She barely felt it when her wrist bone finally snapped back into place.

The power surged through her every cell, changing her... completing her. She didn't have to search for it now, didn't have to call and call only to have it refuse to answer. It was simply *there,* as much a part of her as her own heart. She closed her eyes as it continued to flow, continued to build and build, filling every nook and cranny within her being. She realized then that the key's power had been dampening her own, too much energy being spent trying to keep it bound and hidden.

Now that energy was free within her and she nearly moaned at the feeling. It was glorious. Delicious. Heady. She felt almost intoxicated by it. Between her parentage and her shared power with Si from their marriage ceremony...Well, she may have just become a goddess with which one should not fuck, as Skylar would say.

Beck snapped her eyes open and gently settled Si's head back on the ground before rising. She took a brief moment to check Poseidon's chest and was relieved to see that his wound had already closed, his heart already regenerated and beating once more.

Her father's eyes were still closed, the key's power still strengthening him. She stalked closer, silent as death. She caught sight of herself in a mirror over the bar and arched a brow. Her eyes were a deep cobalt blue, but forks of black lashed out from her pupils, flashing like lightning. The ice blue electricity so like Poseidon's danced faintly down her arms. *That's new...*

"Yoo hoo," she quipped.

Her father's eyes flashed open and they were no longer black. Bright crimson irises stared back at her first in triumph, then in confusion...and maybe even a little trepidation added in. *That's right dad, be afraid. Be very, very afraid.* Before he could even breathe, she sent a flare of power soaring directly into his chest. It flung him across the cavern this time and he slammed into the stone fifty yards away—and fifty yards off the ground. Rocks rained down as he fell, crumpling to the ground with a groan and a satisfying thud.

Beck reached out with her mind and latched on to her father's fears, as if she'd done it a million times. The fears...called to her now. Among the usual death, inadequacy, and other intangible things, she found some terrifying snake-like creature with two bulbous heads topped with two rows of dark horns, mouths full of serrated fangs, and barbed tails that dripped with some kind of poisonous goo. *Ew. What the fuck are these things?* She had no idea, but she did know that her father feared them.

Moments later, three of the monstrous creatures appeared to surround Balthazar.

"Skalabra," he whispered, his eyes flaring wide. He scuttled back until he could move no further, eyeing the creatures wearily as they bobbed their heads and bared their fangs. He rose to his feet and seemed to shake himself, casting her a killing look.

"Your illusions are strong, I'll give you that, but they are just that." He strolled forward, head high and casting disdainful looks at the skalabra. They hissed and flicked their tails back and forth in irritation. She titled her head and one of them struck, sinking its fangs into Balthazar's thigh.

He bellowed in pain and kicked the creature away. Blood welled from two large punctures and streamed down his leg. Beck smirked. They *weren't* mere illusions. She could actually create physical manifestations—and control them. She waved her hand and another creature struck.

"What the fuck!?" Balthazar roared, fighting off the skalabra and sending her a look of pure shock. The places where their fangs pierced his skin grew red and swollen, black puss oozing from the wounds. Whatever poison these creatures had, it affected even gods. *Good to know.*

The sea called out to her again then, seemingly roaring in her ears, desperate to help its queen. She connected with it, sensed creatures out in the depths waiting for her. Moments later, two leviathans appeared, flanking her and roaring in anger, tearing at the earth with claws as long as her forearm. She gave a small nod of her head and they attacked, springing at Balthazar with a terrifying ferocity.

If he hadn't gotten some of his strength back from the key, they would have destroyed him easily, but a bloody and vicious battle ensued. Beck cast shadows and bolts of lightning or electricity or whatever the hell it was at her father as the leviathans clawed and bit. The remaining skalabra continued to strike, though they looked fearful of the leviathans and soon began to retreat from the fray. She waved them away and they vanished, returning to the nothingness from which they came.

Balthazar managed to summon a longsword that was so large Beck wasn't sure how he could even lift the damn thing. Her heart clenched in terror as he shoved it directly into one of the leviathan's chests. The smaller female. *Bonnie. That's what Emmie had named this one.* Clyde roared in fury and knocked Balthazar across the room before moving to nuzzle his fallen mate. Beck sprinted to put herself between the sea dragons and her father.

-Get out of here- she told them

-We will not leave our queen- Bonnie said, but Beck could hear the pain in her mental voice.

-You will if she commands it! I don't want you hurt. Please- she added. With reluctance, the two obeyed her command and disappeared from the cave, returning to the sea. She'd check on them later. *If there is a later.*

She faced Balthazar and jutted her chin up. He was breathing hard but he smiled as he wiped blood from his lip. The next moment, Si's agonized screams pierced the air once more. She whipped her head to her husband, guilt and pain spearing her heart. In her moment of distraction, Balthazar tried to phase away, but he wasn't quick enough, the poison making him sluggish.

"Oh no you fucking don't." Quicker than lightning, she lashed out with a tendril of shadow and lightning, and clamped onto his ankle. It was enough to keep him in place, her power commanding him to stay stronger than his power attempting to leave. "You're not going anywhere," she gritted out.

He looked annoyed but then his lips curled into that cruel smile once more. He closed his eyes and stretched his arms out to his sides, and a second later, ten dark creatures flanked him, five on each side. They seemed to be made of black swirling smoke, but blood red eyes stared at her from within it. She'd seen them before, both in her nightmares and... in Si's study. *That's the king of the Wraiths in there,* Emmie had said.

Wraiths. *Fuck.*

They were dark, sinister creatures who served the God of Nightmares. They could become fully intangible, just cyclones of smoke that couldn't be killed or harmed, but in their corporal form, they were terrifyingly strong and fast, with nails tipped with the same toxin that was mixed into the metal when godsblades were forged. So, these bastards could truly kill her if enough of them attacked at once without giving her time to heal. *Double fuck.*

"Ah, my children. I've missed you." Children? Beck's brow furrowed and then her stomach dipped uncomfortably. Did he mean that...literally? Had they been *created* by him? *Does that make them like...my siblings?* She shook herself, not having the mental capacity to touch that at the moment.

"Deal with that, will you?" Balthazar said in a bored tone. The wraiths shot forward with unfathomable speed, becoming black blurs as they sped across the cave towards her. Beck wasn't sure how to fight something that would only become tangible the instant before it stabbed her through the heart. And with ten of them coming at her? She didn't stand a chance. Fear shot through her, but she braced herself, refusing to go down easily.

She kept a tight hold on Balthazar's ankle as he tried to shake her off, slashing at her shadow and lightning with his sword, but it couldn't cut through. She could *feel* it though, felt every blow as if he were cutting her flesh, her power an extension of her body, just as Hades had told her during their training sessions. She didn't think he'd meant it quite so literally at the time, but, here she was.

As the wraiths drew closer, she fought not to scream from pain and fear. Beck held out her hands ready to fight as best she could, but just before they reached her, the wraiths...*stopped.* They froze, hovering in the air mere feet from her, confusion in their red eyes. She'd wanted them to stop...and they had. She could control them too? She glanced over their shoulders to her father who was frozen in shock, but vibrating with fury. She tentatively reached out with her power, dipping into the wraiths' minds as she did with the leviathans, connecting with them.

-We are yours. Command us- one said inside her mind, inclining its head.

"Holy fuck," she whispered.

-That isn't exactly a command...-

Was a wraith...cracking jokes? She almost laughed. She almost cried. She thought she was very close to a mental breakdown, but she shoved all of that aside.

"Go," she whispered, showing them telepathically what she wanted them to do. The one who she thought had joked nodded and then the wraiths turned in unison and sped back towards Balthazar. They attacked as one and though he fought, they sliced at him again and again with their claws. He roared as he battled his former soldiers with a viciousness she'd never seen, never thought possible. She sent her own power at him, burning his chest and legs and across one cheek.

He met her gaze as he ripped a wraith's head from its body, tossing it at the others, and she swallowed hard. He released a pulse of power strong enough to force the wraiths back for a few moments. He was breathing heavily, covered in blood, and looking weakened once more. *Good*, she thought, lips curling upward.

Though he was definitely injured badly, she knew better than to hope it was enough to kill him. It would slow him down though, and gods knew they needed him slowed down, since she'd given him the key that would unleash pure evil into the world and possibly end it all together. *Fuck.*

His red eyes flared with rage before he seemed to use all his remaining strength to send another surge of power straight for her. She screamed as it careened into her chest, knocking her backwards and sending her rolling across the floor. She lost grip of him as she slammed into a stone table, pain erupting across her back. She met his gaze as he gave her a cold smile that sent fear skittering up her spine.

"See you soon, daughter." With that, he disappeared.

She lowered her forehead to the ground, breathing hard and trying to even begin wrapping her mind around anything that had just happened. It was all just too much...and it was far from over. She pushed herself upward as the wraiths returned, surrounding her. She eyed them warily, unsure what to do with them now.

One of them took his corporeal form and knelt down beside her. She tensed when he extended his hand towards her, but he didn't attack. He was...offering her a hand up? She eyed it nervously and, to her surprise, the deadly tips disappeared, sliding backwards into his claws. Her eyes widened but she cautiously placed her hand in his. He helped ease her upright and the remaining wraiths became corporeal as well. They looked very human, minus the red eyes. Their features were sharp and chiseled, but oddly striking.

"Umm, thanks?" The one who'd helped her inclined his head. "Can you, uh, talk?"

"Yes," he said, and she thought he might be trying to hide his amusement.

"Oh, that's...that's cool," she said a bit dazed. The power and adrenaline spike that had hit her during the fight was fading. Now she was just...confused. "Are you like...mine now?" She scrunched her nose. "No, wait, that doesn't sound right. I mean are you mine to command? Are you my, um, soldiers now?"

"Yes to all of those things," he said easily. "Your power is greater than your father's. It is your right to command us now." *Greater* than her father's?? *No fucking way.*

"I..." She trailed off, not sure what to say to that, but then a pained moan sounded from behind them. *Poseidon.* Her heart thudded in her chest as she sprinted for him.

"Si? Si, I'm here. You're alright. I'm alright." She stroked his cheek but his eyes were still vacant, unseeing. How was he still under Balthazar's thrall? *Oh gods.* Was there a point where one could never escape it? Was he stuck in this nightmare...forever? No. She refused to accept that. Tears pooled but she wiped them away angrily.

"No, damnit! You are not staying in there forever. I may have just started the actual apocalypse and I'm going to need you by my side when that goes down, Si. No way in hell I'm dealing with that mess alone. So, we're going home and I'm going to fix this," she said, trying to sound confident.

Beck looked over her shoulder at the wraiths who had moved to stand behind her in a loose semi-circle.

"Umm I guess you can come with us? Is that...is that alright?" They nodded and turned to smoke once more. She didn't ask how they would follow or know where to go, and at the moment, she didn't care.

She cradled Si's body to her and closed her eyes, phasing them home.

THIRTY-FOUR

"Beck!" Poseidon screamed, throat raw and aching. Blood bubbled over her lips and dripped down her chin as he watched helplessly. "Baby, please. Please stay with me!" he strained forward but he couldn't reach her. *Gods, no. Please no.* Balthazar was torturing her but every time Si tried to lash out with his power, it failed him. Useless. He could only sit there and watch his wife, the reason for his entire existence, scream in agony.

"Stop this!" he yelled, begging the Dark One. "Please! I'll give you anything, do anything!"

The bastard merely smirked. Beck met his gaze and her eyes were filled with red. The vessels had burst and even her tears were now tinged crimson, making it look like she was crying blood.

"Poseidon?..." she whispered, more blood pouring over her chin. Before he could say a word, a sickening crack echoed around him, filling the darkness, followed by a tearing sound that made bile rise in his throat. A second later, her head was wrenched free from her body. Both thumped to the ground and blood began to flow like the tide, soaking the ground.

"No!" he roared so loudly the ground shook. His heart splintered and he tore at his chest, needing to rip the damned thing from him. He barely felt the pain as his fingers clawed through skin and muscle easily, ripped his chest cavity open and yanked. Blissful darkness came for him swiftly.

~

"Beck!" Poseidon screamed, throat raw and aching. Blood bubbled over her lips and dripped down her chin as he watched helplessly. "Baby, please. Please stay with me!"...

~

"I don't know how to get to him," Beck whispered, broken. She'd tried, but she hadn't figured out that aspect of her power yet. She'd entered the dream world over and over again, and to her relief, her father wasn't there. She wasn't sure if he was merely too weak to find her in the dream world now, or if she'd managed to block him, but she found that without him, the corridor looked...different. It wasn't dark and terrifying anymore, and she didn't feel fear as she walked down it. Now, she understood what this place truly was.

The corridor was now lit with soft, glowing light, and she discovered that there were different types of doors: some light, some dark. Upon investigation, she'd found that the dark doors were nightmares, as they'd always been, but the lighter doors were simply dreams. Nothing terrifying to be found. She yearned to explore everything more, to understand her connection to it and her power over it, but that was for later. Now, all she wanted to do was find Si, but she didn't know *how*.

She'd spent hours upon hours opening every single door, just hoping to find him, but the hallway was never-ending. It could take her centuries to find his door just by randomly guessing. There *had* to be a better way, but she hadn't been able to figure it out. Now would have been a grand time to have an actual non-evil psycho-pathic parent to teach her the ropes.

"Beckalicious, I have known you for a very long time and I have complete faith in you," Emmie said.

Beck frowned. "We haven't really known each other very long at all...?"

"Silly child, I brought you into the world." At Beck's incredulous look, Emmie scoffed. "Do you really think Adamantia could have navigated a mortal hospital alone, or kept a newborn alive on her own? When she fled your father, who do you think was the one to intercept her and whisk her away to safety? I'll give you a hint: she's a stunningly beautiful oracle with a heart of gold." Beck rolled her eyes but smiled. "I helped her secure housing and false documentation for the both of you to survive properly in the mortal world, helped her through those first few months of motherhood, found the enchantress to help bind the key. I even suggested the last name— *McQueen*?" She giggled. "Man, I really am exceedingly clever. I even popped in to play the mother role for those pesky parent-teacher conferences before I floated the brilliant suggestion of home-schooling her way."

"You..." Beck pursed her lips, finding that it did make perfect sense. "Really?"

Emmie briefly transformed into Adamantia, wiggled her eyebrows, and returned to her true form. She nodded and tapped her temple.

"Seer, remember? I knew that you'd be the one for our Poseidon and how important you'd be in everything that will soon transpire. We all needed you safe. So, I took care of you. I visited often when you were a child—your first word was *mi-mi* which I still maintain was you trying to say "Emmie"— and watched over you from afar once I could no longer be such a staple in your life. Though I *am* sorry that I couldn't make everything a bit...better for you. I can't control everything, unfortunately, and I was already pushing things as it were. So, I had to leave Adamantia to her own devices in the mother-hood department as the years went on."

Beck thought back over her life and though she agreed that it was mostly wretched, there *had* been a few good spots and every-thing that she'd suffered had made her the person she was, the person that Si loved. If not for her experiences, she never would have met him. If she hadn't been so adamant about hating him in the beginning, maybe he wouldn't have seen the novelty of it, the bit of challenge in pursuing her. Maybe he wouldn't have even bothered trying for more. Without him having to earn her trust and slowly chip away at her walls, maybe she wouldn't have fallen so deeply for him because she knew just how much he loved and wanted her, to go through all of that and show her all the patience in the world.

"I'm not," she finally said. "I'm not sorry. My life was exactly what it needed to be to get me here. To him. To all of you." She sighed and glanced to Poseidon, twisting and straining deep in his nightmare on the bed. She reached up to stroke her medallion only to remember it was gone and let her hand fall heavily. "Now if only I could get him back."

She knew he'd be screaming in a few minutes, the same cycle repeating itself over and over as he watched her be tortured and then die. They'd swapped out his usual sexy-time restraints attached to the bed for mystically reinforced chains that could hold even a god. They'd strapped him down to keep him from clawing out his eyes and heart again. Seeing that happen once had been enough to last her a thousand lifetimes. Seeing it over and over? Well, it wasn't something she'd ever be able to forget.

"You will."

She turned to Emmie. "Are you saying that as a fact stated by a powerful Seer, or as a hopeful statement for a friend?"

"Hmm...both? The future keeps flickering but I'm...eighty-seven percent sure you reach him."

"And if I don't?" she asked quietly.

Emmie's eyes grew dark and she shuddered. "Let's just stick with you finding him, yes?" She leaned down to kiss Beck on the top of her head. "Go get our boy," she whispered before phasing away.

Beck stared down at the love of her life, wincing and squeezing her eyes shut as he screamed her name in utter anguish. *I have to stop this. I have to reach him.* She opened her eyes and wiped the sweat from his brow, the tears from his cheeks.

"Beck," he sobbed, voice broken. She felt the bond between them flare white hot every time he'd thought that she'd died, his soul rebelling against the idea that his match was gone, but then it would right itself, realizing that it was just a dream. If only it could tell his mind that. She braced herself for it now and as it flared within her, her eyes flew wide. The fire faded but an idea had sprung. Her heart beat wildly and despite everything, a smile curled her lips.

"Alright, baby, I just need you to go through this one last time for me."

"Beck!" Poseidon screamed, throat raw and aching. Blood bubbled over her lips and dripped down her chin as he watched helplessly. "Baby, please. Please stay with me!" he strained forward but he couldn't reach her. *Gods, no. Please no.* Balthazar was torturing her but every time Si tried to lash out with his power, it failed him. Useless. He could only sit here and watch his wife, the reason for his entire existence, scream in agony.

"Si," a soft voice whispered from behind him. His brows drew together in confusion. He knew that voice but...Beck was in front of him, screaming. "Si, look at me."

"I-I *am*," he choked out, confused.

"No, you aren't, love. That isn't me. This is a nightmare. Balthazar has you trapped inside it, but I'm here to drag you out." He closed his eyes, refusing to let the hope sparking in his chest take root. It would be too much to hope only to realize it was a lie. He squeezed them tight, pressing his lips into a hard line.

"Si, listen to me."

He shook his head at the voice.

"No, not real. I'm…I'm losing my mind. I—"

A mule kick to his back sent him sprawling forward.

"Listen you stubborn ass, I'm flattered that your worst nightmare is losing me because losing you is mine too, but this has gone on long enough. This isn't *real*. I'm real and you're going to snap the fuck out of it right now. I have tons to tell you and we might have one hell of a battle ahead of us, but mostly, I need you to get it together because I love you and I refuse to let you continue to suffer here." Another kick to the ribs sent him tumbling a few more feet away. He landed on his back and blinked up into the darkness surrounding them, still hearing Beck screaming and sobbing in the background, as…*Beck* appeared above him. Her lips were titled up in that sweet, almost smile of hers. *What is happening? Don't understand. What's real?*

Another kick to the ribs and he groaned.

"Unless me kicking your ass is also part of your worst nightmare, I think you can believe me now."

Her lips parted as she smiled, a real, perfect, dimple-revealing smile and his heart skipped a beat. *Now* that's *my wife.*

Poseidon shot upright in bed, gasping for air.

"Si? Si, it's alright," Beck said, sounding frantic.

What the hell? What was happening? What the fuck was that?? He didn't understand anything.

"Beck?" he rasped, throat raw.

She threw herself at him, wrapping her arms around his neck and squeezing him so tightly he was glad he was a god. It would have felled a mortal. *Has she always been this strong?* He moved to return her embrace but frowned when he met resistance. He was… chained to their bed?

"If you wanted me tied up again, all you had to do was ask, love," Si said, trying to smile past too many emotions making it hard to breathe.

She pulled back and smiled at him through tears.

"Oh my gods, I thought I'd lost you."

She peppered his face with kisses.

"What...what the hell happened?" He thought back to what he'd just seen. The screams. The blood. "Wait...is this real?" he asked wearily. He couldn't be sure. Was this a dream? A hallucination his mind had conjured to protect him from the devastation of losing his wife? He slid back a few inches, his back hitting the headboard.

"This is real," she assured him, cradling his face between her hands, holding his gaze. "*This* is real. When you went to that clearing with Dean, Balthazar managed to get you under his thrall. You couldn't shake it off."

Si's brows furrowed as he tried to recall what had happened. They'd approached the demon leading Balthazar's forces and then the bastard himself had appeared and...

"I watched you die," he said on a broken whisper. It had been so *real*. He'd heard her screams, smelled her fear and blood.

"It wasn't real. It was just a nightmare."

"How...how did you—the real you, I mean I guess—just appear in the nightmare with me then?"

She glanced away briefly, biting her lip.

"Well, I've got a lot to tell you, but bottom line is that I share his ability to walk through dreams. I followed the line of our bond to find you trapped within it. It promise it was just a nightmare," she assured him again.

"But..."

He didn't know what to believe, couldn't shake the confusion. Before he could say more, her lips slammed into his in a bruising kiss. His eyes flew wide but then slid shut, the feeling of her kissing him enough to erase everything else, at least for a time. She kissed him fiercely, forcing his lips to open for her and thrusting her tongue against his, demanding that he accept her, that he feel her and understand.

"I'm real," she whispered as she kissed him. "This is real." She continued to kiss him, running her hands along the back of his neck and clutching at his shoulders as she settled her knees lower on either side of his waist. He hadn't even realized she was straddling him until he felt her heat against his cock, already hard and aching. He hissed in a breath as she rocked against him. This couldn't be a dream. Even in his sweetest ones, he could never duplicate the feel of her, the scent of her.

He groaned against her mouth and she seemed to sag with relief, as if she knew the moment that he accepted that it was real. He moved to stroke her face but again those chains held him. He pulled away and arched a brow in question, rattling the manacle around his wrist and the chain connecting it to the headboard.

"You...um, kept tearing out your heart and eyes," she said quietly, looking down at his chest and lightly grazing her finger down it. "We thought it best to restrain you." He'd truly done that? She quickly leaned over to the table, grabbing the key, and unlocked both shackles.

He wasted no time, one hand flying to cradle her cheek and bring her to him for another scorching kiss, the other gripping her hip. She gasped and her shirt...*disappeared*. He pulled back, brow quirked.

"Oh, I've got all kinds of new tricks now. I'll explain it all later. Right now..." She gave him a mischievously sultry look and his lounge pants were gone in an instant.

"That's quite handy," he said with a grin against her lips. The kiss became desperate and frenzied as the enormity of everything that had happened, or could have happened, settled over them.

"I need you, Beck. I need to know you're really here."

He couldn't explain it more than that but she seemed to understand completely. Seconds later, there was nothing between them and she was gripping his shaft, positioning it just beneath her. He hissed in a harsh breath when the swollen head kissed the wet heat of her as she sank down on him.

"Oh *gods*," she moaned when he was seated so deeply within her that he couldn't tell where her body ended and his began. Their gazes collided and they both understood the need in each other's eyes. She gripped his shoulders and he gripped her hips. She rose upward and then he wrenched her downward, thrusting up as he did. She cried out and he grunted in primal need and pleasure. Over and over, he impaled her and she rode him. Her nails dug into his shoulders and her breasts bounced with each forceful thrust. They were both slick with sweat and panting when she moaned his name in the way that let him know she was close.

She met his gaze and he was shocked to see that strands of black now forked through the cobalt, flashing like lightning.

"Fuck," he grated as she screamed out in pleasure, her orgasm rocking through her, her pussy walls clenching him so gods damned tight. It was almost too much, but he wasn't ready to be done. He still needed her, needed to be inside her all night to prove to himself that she was here, that she was whole and safe and his. He moved quickly, tossing her to her back and covering her body with his own. She was still shuddering as he continued to plunge inside her.

He kissed her hard, and then buried his face in her neck as he thrust over and over, her hot, wet, sheath gripping him like a fist. He bit her neck and shoulder and she scratched down his back, leaving deep grooves in his ass as she dug her nails in, urging him to go faster, harder. He pushed back to his knees and yanked her hips upward, holding her there as he continued to pound into her.

"Yes, Si, just like that! Oh gods!" She came again and he growled in satisfaction. *So hot. So tight. So wet.* It was too much. He bellowed her name and came harder than he ever had in his long life. It went on and on but eventually, he collapsed on top of her. Eventually, he shifted so they were lying on their sides, facing each other.

"I love you, Beck," he whispered, tucking her hair behind her ear and gently stroking her face. "Gods, I thought..."

"Shhh," she said, kissing him softly. "I know. But I'm here and I'm fine. I'm not going anywhere. I love you too much."

He kissed her again and she began to roll her hips subtly. He was already getting hard again and they both grinned.

"My bride is an insatiable little harlot, isn't she?"

"Oh you have no idea…" She cut off in a gasp as he moved his hand between them, rubbing her clit as he slowly rocked his hips forward. "Mmmm," she groaned. He kissed her neck, continuing to rub and drive her mad. A rush of wetness made him lick his lips in pleasure and wanting. *Want to taste her*…but a glint of metal caught his eye. He smirked as an idea rose. A second later, she was on her back, those manacles clasped around her wrists.

"Oh!" she gasped in surprise before her eyes went heavy lidded and she bit her lip in anticipation. The black in her eyes flashed brighter. *Damn that is sexy.*

"I hope you weren't planning on sleeping anytime in the next few days…"

THIRTY-FIVE

"So, he has the key," Zeus said, scrubbing a hand over his face.

"Correct," Beck confirmed.

"But the key used to be hidden in your necklace and tied to your power."

"Also correct."

"And he's—"

"Yes, he's my father," Beck interrupted, pinching the bridge of her nose. "I know the story is batshit crazy, but we've already gone through it all three times."

"It's just, well, like you said: batshit crazy," Skylar added from her perch on Hades' lap. They had gathered in Zeus' palace on Mount Olympus to discuss everything that had happened, everything that Beck had learned, and what was to come. Well, after a couple of days in bed with her man that is.

Her and Si had both had a strange, primal need to prove to themselves that everything was alright, that they were both alive and safe, and that the nightmare was behind them. After too many bouts of mind-numbing sex for her to count, they'd both gone nearly comatose for a full day.

"And the wraiths are...good guys now?" Z asked, twirling a strand of her sleek black hair around one finger. She kept glancing sidelong at Zeus and he was shooting her surreptitious looks when he thought no one was looking too. Looks that clearly said *I really want to see you naked and do depraved things with you.* Apparently, Zeus had called in his days-owed, probably due to the whole impending doom thing, and the sexual tension radiating out of both of them was palpable. Z gave him another long look and Beck quirked a brow.

Hmm, maybe the look is more like I've already *seen you naked and want to do* more *depraved things with you.*

Beck shook herself. Z and Zeus' possible sexcapades weren't important right now. *Impending doom, remember?*

"Oh, um, yeah, they are. Turns out the species isn't actually inherently evil even though they were created using Balthazar' blood."

She'd been more surprised than anyone by that turn of events. The wraiths from the cave had followed them back to Aqueous and Emmie had let Cyril and the rest of the army know that they were alright to hang around. Nerina had even gotten them all settled in the guest wing and they'd patiently waited for Beck and Si to come up for air so that they could have a meeting.

Balen, the second in command and de facto leader while their king was imprisoned in the crystal ball in Si's study, had explained that they'd never wanted to serve the God of Nightmares, but had been bound to him. He had, in fact, created them with dark power and his own blood, and so they were a part of him, his to command. But he was a cruel master, not caring whether they lived or died.

He'd...experimented on them, forcing them to breed with other immortal species to find new, possibly stronger combinations, which had explained the halfling that had entered Aqueous. Only a handful of full-blooded wraiths remained with him among the half-breeds in the Mortal Plane. The rest had been cursed to remain in their incorporeal forms and hidden in a pocket realm while Balthazar tried to regain enough strength to bring them back. Remaining in their smoke form for too long was painful, but they'd welcomed the pain in exchange for a reprieve from serving him. They were all too happy to have found another with his blood who had enough juice to overpower his command.

Beck had managed to summon the rest of the wraiths from the pocket realm and now they were all staying in Aqueous with them. *One big happy family.* They were bound to her now and she didn't exactly *love* that idea. It wasn't that she didn't appreciate their unwavering loyalty and she did feel a certain protectiveness for them, but she didn't think anyone should be *forced* to serve another. She thought back to Si's story of the leviathans, of how he'd given them a reason to respect and revere him, made them *want* to follow him not out of obligation but out of love. She decided she would do the same for the wraiths.

Her first step? Freeing their king.

Emmie had been right: Lyander was pissed as hell at being locked away all those years, but thankfully his concern for his people outweighed the anger. He calmed surprisingly quickly once he realized his allegiance had shifted from Balthazar. He'd sensed the lack of depravity and darkness within Beck and had immediately sighed in relief, muttering a soft *thank you* as his eyes slid closed.

"You've freed me and my coven. For that, I owe you my life," Lyander had said when he opened them again, inclining his head.

"You owe me nothing," Beck had responded. "I won't force you to serve me. You are free to do whatever you would like with your freedom, all of you." She'd bitten her lip. "But...a war *is* coming. A big one. And you and your coven would be great assets to our forces."

"We would be honored to fight with you. We do not want the Dark Ones to rise."

Pulling herself back to the conversation at hand, she continued, "So, yeah, we've got them on our side this time around."

"And you're crazy strong now, right?" Skylar said with a grin and a waggle of her blonde brows.

Beck blushed. "Umm...kind of?"

"Psh," Skylar scoffed. "I've got it on good authority that you are a certified badass! Bringing nightmares to life—if you put a real life clown near me though, I will not hesitate to go full phoenix on your ass—the cool blue lightning like Si, walking through dreams, controlling the wraiths. Girl, own it." Beck couldn't help but smile back at her friend.

"Ok, so, I'm a little badass..." she said sheepishly.

"Hell to the yeah! You went toe to toe with a fucking *Dark One* and lived to tell the tale. Using your full power for the first time to boot!" Skylar punched Hades in the arm and he smiled, inclining his head at Beck in acknowledgement.

Flashing a proud, panty-melting smile, Si said, "My girl is not to be fucked with."

"Can I have your autograph?" Z grinned.

"Alright, alright. We all agree: Beck is super awesome and scary now, but we need to focus. Emmie, can you give us any clues on timeline?" Zeus asked, stroking his chin.

Everyone turned to the Seer who was sitting between Dean and Lucas. She looked even more strained than the last time Beck had seen her and now she understood why. A possible apocalypse was on its way and Emmie was seeing all the possible futures tied to it, most of them no doubt bleak beyond reason. How many of them had she seen fall in battle? How many of their deaths had she witnessed?

"Beck and the wraiths bought us some time. He's weakened once more and won't risk trying to make his way through the wasteland to free the rest of them, not yet." Sadness filled her eyes. "Dora is going to perish soon and when she does the Box will fall. The rest of the prisoners are going to remain there, use the prison as a fortress of sorts while they prepare for war. They know that the key will be coming and they'll wait for the Dark Ones to be released. Most of them anyway. A few hundred will escape and make their way to the Mortal Plane to wreak havoc."

Skylar's face pinched at that. She'd grown up there, just as Beck had, but unlike Beck, she had actual friends there, people she cared about that she didn't want to see harmed.

"So, we gather our own forces, strengthen our numbers and prepare our armies. We'll make our stand there, in the wasteland," Ares said, matter of factly. "I've already contacted the Titans. Most of them have agreed to fight with us again."

The Titans mostly lived on their own plane and kept themselves completely separate from the gods. They weren't enemies exactly, but they kept their distance. When too much power and god-sized egos all mixed for too long, the results could be catastrophic. But apparently, the end of the world was one of the few things that brought the gang back together.

"I'll gather as many immortals from the Mortal Plane as I can. We aren't gods but we're strong and vicious fighters," Dalton said and Lucas nodded in agreement. Dean clenched his jaw, looking like he wanted to protest, but Emmie laid a hand on his arm and he exhaled roughly, pressing his lips into a hard line but remaining silent. He didn't want Lucas fighting in this war? Beck didn't know exactly what had happened with them on their quest to rid Dean of his feline form, but it was obvious that the three of them had become a unit and that there were feelings there—*strong* ones—going all directions.

It made Beck's heart swell and made her lips curl upward in a smile. She was happy for her friend. A few months ago, she never would have been able to have a thought like that, because she had no friends to speak of, not really. Now, she had a plethora, a full-on squad as the mortals said. *Gods, what did I do to ever deserve this life I have?*

Ares inclined his head. "I've watched many immortals in battle. They will be assets to our cause."

"The two harpy factions will call a truce long enough to fight side by side with us as well," Emmie added, eyes going vacant for a moment, seeing into the future. She shook herself and they focused once more. "Lily is shitting bricks over it, but she's going to Amara tomorrow." She rubbed her temples and Lucas rubbed her back soothingly, sharing a worried look with Dean. "A month, maybe less," she added, answering the original question.

Hades blew out a long exhale and Si tensed beside her, squeezing her hand tighter. They all exchanged glances, knowing what this meant. It was war, *real* war, with an enemy unlike anything many of them had ever seen or even imagined. It was coming now, no stopping it. *Because of me.* She couldn't stop the guilt from flaring, but she also wasn't sorry. She would have done anything to save Si.

And now, she would do just about anything to keep him safe, to keep all of them safe. She was growing her power more and more every day, learning all the facets of it, strengthening them. She had tricks her father couldn't even fathom and a part of her she hadn't known existed until now longed to show them off, longed to battle for the ones she loved. The Dark Ones had no idea what was coming for them.

Beck looked at Si. One month. That was potentially all the time she had left with him. She didn't want to waste a single second of it. The meeting dissolved not long after that, and smaller conversations broke out here and there. Zeus was asking Beck more about the wraiths, still a bit uneasy about their involvement, when she spied a beautiful goddess waltz into the room. Beck had never seen her before, but she tilted her head as she watched the woman. There was something...off about her. Nothing bad, just something seeming to surround her, slightly fuzzy around the edges. Skylar and Emmie joined her, a strange excitement thrumming through them both, but Skylar was practically vibrating with it.

"This is it," she muttered, gripping Emmie's wrist.

"What's happening?" Beck asked, but Emmie immediately shushed her and pointed to the trio across the room.

Dalton was speaking animatedly with Ares about battle strategies, his back to the newcomer. She laid a hand on Dalton's shoulder and he went rigid, every muscle tensing beneath her touch.

"Excuse me, I'm sorry to interrupt," she said in a melodic voice.

Dalton turned and glanced down at the hand, then slowly up to the goddess. His eyes flew wide and his jaw went slack as he took her in. He blinked several times and actually staggered back a step as he rubbed the heel of his hand against the center of his chest.

"And *that's* what it looks like when a lupin finds his mate, kiddos," Emmie whispered happily.

Beck whirled. "His mate?" Skylar's eyes were glassy as she watched, her smile so wide her cheeks had to be hurting. Emmie smiled widely, the strain momentarily hidden.

"Yep. Been waiting a long time for this one but tell me that's not worth it." Beck returned her gaze to Dalton and her lips curled. He looked completely lost and utterly found all at once. "That's Aphrodite by the way. I'll introduce you later. Oh and the weirdness you're picking up on is a glamour. She's very shy and her legendary beauty draws too much attention. It makes her uncomfortable."

"*That's* what she looks like when she's trying to hide her beauty?" Beck asked incredulously. She was gorgeous. Beyond gorgeous. Beck couldn't imagine what she would look like in her true form, but she thought it might be a little like looking at the sun, almost painful.

"I...I..." Dalton stammered. Aphrodite's eyes had shifted from green to deep gray as her gaze collided with Dalton's. Had she found her match too then?

"Ditey, this is Dalton, Skylar's father. Her other father." Ares frowned. "The man who raised her I mean. This is confusing," he mused. "Dalton, this is Aphrodite."

"Hello," she breathed with a shy smile. *Gods, she's not only gorgeous, she's freaking adorable.*

Ares tilted his head as he glanced between the two of them, a small smile curling his lips, lightening his normally stoic face and turning it downright handsome.

"See, lots of good is coming out of this mess," Emmie said as she rubbed her temple. "You and Si, Dalton and Ditey," she shifted her gaze to Z and then flitted it to Zeus, "...maybe a few others. Bonds are being made that will only strengthen our forces. Everything will be ok…" she added quietly to herself, but it didn't sound like a fact, it was more like something she was willing to be true.

Si finished talking with Hades and sidled up behind Beck, wrapping his arms around her middle and murmuring in her ear, "ready to go home?" She nodded, already breathless thinking about everything those four words could promise.

They phased to their chambers and Si immediately pulled her hard against him. She wrapped her arms around his neck.

"You know, I don't think I ever thanked you," he said brushing hair from her face.

"For what?"

"For saving me. Not just from the nightmare. You saved me well before that, Beck." Her heart swelled and her eyes watered.

"Ditto," she croaked, leaning up to kiss him. "But technically you saved me first when I called out for you in the water that day. So, I owed you." She shrugged and he swung her up into his arms. He kissed her again and she giggled against his lips.

"What are you doing?" she squealed. He got that wicked gleam in his eye, the sexy one that promised pure bliss and made her ache with wanting.

"Well, speaking of that day in the water. I don't think I ever received proper recourse for all the hurtful things you said to me. How did you phrase it again? My *ilk*?" She scrunched her nose, hating to remember how terrible she'd been to him at the beginning, but loving that they could both laugh about it now. "Perhaps a good spanking is in order…" Her toes curled and her pulse sped up.

"Well," she said, breathless, "it's only right that I accept whatever punishment the great King of Aqueous decrees."

"Have I told you today how much I love you?" he asked as he eased her down on the bed.

"Only twenty or so times," she responded with a smile, pulling him down with her.

"Well, that just won't do." He leaned down to kiss her, whispering over and over, "I love you, I love you, I love you."

As he slowly undressed her, Beck lost herself in the moment, in the feel of him and his *I love yous* surrounding her like a warm embrace. She knew dark times were coming, but she wasn't afraid. She knew that they would face it together, and together, they could do anything. Before that fateful day on the ship, she'd had no one she could count on in her life, had always had to take on the world on her own.

Never again. Forevermore, she had a partner, a soul mate.

She had Poseidon.

And she'd never let him go.

Acknowledgments

As usual, this book wouldn't have been possible without a whole host of people, so I need to thank:

- My husband, for always supporting me in this crazy hobby.
- Lexie, Kayleigh, and Kala (never not funny) for being my nonstop cheerleaders and bullies. Jeff Beans. Get the pudding. Love you.
- My amazing PA, Nancy, who I couldn't survive without!
- Every single reader who decided to give a little indie author a chance by picking up this book.

ALSO BY K. D. MILLER

Adult Contemporary Romance

- Carpe F*cking Diem
- Wrong Place. Wrong Time. Right Viscount.
- Puck the Holidays (Vipers Sin Bin - Book 1)
- Puck of the Irish (Vipers Sin Bin - Book 2)
- The Pieces You Kept

Adult Paranormal Romance

- Red
- Dark Burning (Veracity of the Gods - Book 1)
- Sweet Tempest (Veracity of the Gods - Book 2)
- Untamed Fate (Veracity of the Gods - Book 2.5)
- Vows Forged in Blood

Young Adult Sci-Fi/Fantasy

- Titan Rising (Outliers Series - Book 1)
- Titan Unleashed (Outliers Series - Book 2)
- Titan Reckoning (Outliers Series - Book 3)
- Evansfire